DEF.

GREGG DUNNETT

Gregg Dunnett.

no 3 of 60

:)

Storm
PUBLISHING

This is a work of fiction. Names, characters, businesses, places, events and incidents are either the products of the author's imagination or used in a fictitious manner. Any resemblance to actual persons, living or dead, or actual events is purely coincidental.

Copyright © Gregg Dunnett, 2025

The moral right of the author has been asserted.

All rights reserved. No part of this book may be reproduced or used in any manner without the prior written permission of the copyright owner. This prohibition includes, but is not limited to, any reproduction or use for the purpose of training artificial intelligence technologies or systems.

To request permissions, contact the publisher at rights@stormpublishing.co

Ebook ISBN:978-1-83700-207-8
Paperback ISBN: 978-1-83700-209-2

Cover design: Henry Steadman
Cover images: Shutterstock

Published by Storm Publishing.
For further information, visit:
www.stormpublishing.co

ALSO BY GREGG DUNNETT

Detective Erica Sands Series

The Cove
The Trap
The Hunt

Standalone Thrillers

Little Ghosts
The Lake House Children
The Wave at Hanging Rock
The Glass Tower
The Girl on the Burning Boat
The Desert Run

The Rockpools Series

The Things You Find in Rockpools
The Lornea Island Detective Agency
The Appearance of Mystery
The Island of Dragons

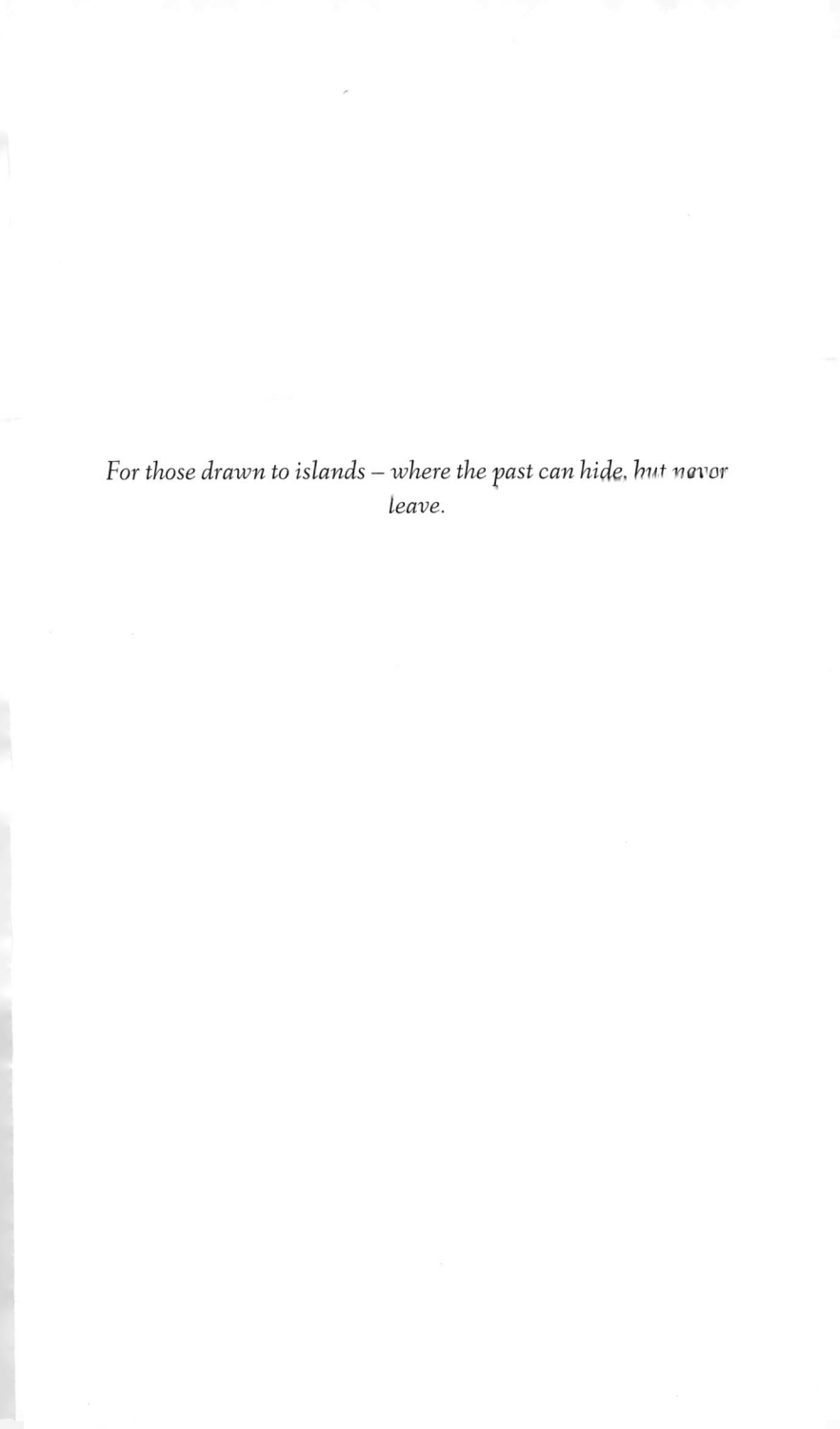

For those drawn to islands – where the past can hide, but never leave.

WELCOME TO
ALYTHOS
AEGEAN SEA
HELIO
MT. APTOS
FERRY TO
PANACHORIA
KASTRIA
KYFRO
CAVE
MALLIOS
ALYTHOS STRAIT
APTEOS
BAY
AEGEAN
DREAM
RESORT
SKALIO
TRIKREMNOS
COVES
SKALIOS BAY
Wish You Were Here...
N
W
E
S

PROLOGUE

Twenty-Two Years Ago

The sun was yet to rise behind the hills that formed the spine of the island, mottling the sky with pinks and pastel blues. The sea was still, the bay a flawless mirror to the colours above, broken only by the wakes of two small fishing boats returning to harbour after working through the night.

She parked the van in the hotel's parking area and swung open the double doors.

There were two boxes to deliver that morning – peppers, green and red, glossy aubergines, tomatoes and a paper-wrapped slab of feta cheese. She stacked them one on top of the other and lifted the load into her arms. The van she left open. Theft was a problem for the mainland, not here.

The kitchen door was propped open to let the heat from the ovens escape. Inside, four white-jacketed chefs moved with brisk, early-morning purpose.

"Thanks – efharistó," said one. She didn't know him, but smiled at the attempt at the local language. The resort had a steady flow of foreign workers. Most stayed a season. Some didn't last the week.

"Parakaló," she replied – you're welcome. Then: "Is Jason here?"

"The boss man? Haven't seen him yet." The chef switched to English and turned to the room. "Yo! Anyone seen Jase?" The other workers looked up, but no one had.

"What you need him for?" the man asked.

She hesitated. "Just an issue with the payment. I'm sure it's nothing."

"He should be here later," the man replied, then frowned. "He should be here now."

"Yes," she agreed. "He normally is."

They shared a glance. Jason lived for this place. Never took a day off. He usually worked from before dawn until long after dark. It sometimes seemed the resort couldn't function without him.

"You could try his room," the man offered.

The thought of him needing sleep surprised her. "Where is it?"

"You know the staff block?"

"I think so."

"Just past that. Nothing else there, you can't miss it."

She took the van out through the manicured gardens, past the low row of basic rooms where the off-island staff were housed. A few minutes further, she pulled up outside a small, single-storey building and alongside Jason's battered Land Rover.

She got out, looked around, and then approached the porch. She saw then that the door was slightly ajar.

"Hello? Jason?"

The woman considered turning back. But there was nothing to fear here. And the resort had missed a payment. She had to speak with Jason. It would be a simple mistake, nothing to be worried about, she was sure.

"Jason? Are you here?"

She reached the doorway. Through the gap she could make out something of the shapes inside: a double bed. A thing on the floor. What was that?

She knocked, her fingers inadvertently pushing the door a little further open, revealing more of that thing. She waited. No reply.

She had no right to enter. But something in her was now afraid. The hairs on her bare arms lifted. She felt a chill despite the warmth of the day.

She pushed the door wider open.

The smell hit her now. Something cloying and metallic, undercut with the sulphur note that reminded her of fireworks.

"Jason? *Mandy?*"

She pushed the door again, and took a step forward.

The curtains were drawn, so it took a moment to adjust to the dark. Then her eyes went back to the thing on the floor. Deck shoes, socks, a pair of legs, tanned but twisted. Then his pastel-blue shirt, the staff uniform Jason always wore. His arms – one over his body, the other wedged underneath. Then she saw his head.

Her eyes took in the small, neat hole beneath his chin first, connected it with the way his head was driven back, exposing his throat. But when she looked for his face it was gone. Just a ruin remained – a gory mess of blood dripping off white bone, the pale grey jelly of brain. One eye stared back at her. The other was missing. The wall behind him, once whitewashed, was now painted in a fan of red.

She blinked, gasped, inhaling the thick, coppery air which now made her gag. No scream came. She couldn't. Her breath came in jagged bursts. Her mind reeled.

She took a step back, her hand over her mouth. But then her

eyes widened further. She couldn't just leave, she had to check, on *her*. The woman swallowed, from somewhere found the courage, then moved forward further into the room.

Oh no. *Oh no.*

Mandy's body lay half-hidden behind the double bed. Only her torso and head were visible, cheek pressed to the tiles, eyes wide open. Her blonde hair, once so pretty, was tangled and matted with blood, a pool of it lay on the ground around her.

The woman tried to look away, but her eyes fell back on Jason's empty half-head. Then she screamed.

A moment later her breath came back, in panicked gasps. She noticed the bed. In the centre lay a single sheet of folded paper. A note.

Her eyes fixed on it. She nearly reached out. But her senses returned. Whatever it said, she had to leave it for the police. She had to get out, call for help.

She began to turn, her mind urging escape from this place of sudden, awful death... and that's when she heard it. Unmistakable.

The sound of breathing.

There was someone else in the room.

ONE

Present Day

"Hey babe, we meeting for lunch today?" Kevin rolls out of bed as he speaks, stretching his arms towards the ceiling, throwing an admiring glance at his biceps.

"What do you mean?" I reply. Surely he hasn't forgotten?

"Lunch. You know, that meal that people have at..." He sees my face and abandons the sarcasm. "Shit. You've got that meeting?"

"Yeah."

That meeting is with the university's Academic Review Board, so they can decide whether I take resits in the summer, or if they're gonna kick me out right now.

"They're not going to expel you," Kevin says, his confidence flowing back. "So you failed a few exams? You're gonna be an awesome doctor, I know it."

"Yeah, but did you also know that people who fail their exams don't get to be doctors?" I tell him. "It's this weird idea they have about knowing what's wrong with people and keeping them alive."

Kevin doesn't answer this. He's doing Economics and Business Studies, while I'm in my fourth year of a medical degree. And quite possibly my last.

"You'll be alright." Kevin pulls on his jeans, but leaves his T-shirt off. He likes to stroll around my house like this, with his abs on display, so my housemates can see them. When we first got together I quite liked this habit, he does have a good six-pack. Now though, it kind of irks me.

"So... lunch?" he asks again.

"I don't know," I snap back. "Maybe I'll see how I feel?"

He raises his hands, like I should calm down, then breaks into a bored smile.

"Cool. I'm gonna take a shower. If you're making coffee, babe..." He pauses. "Unless you wanna come in?"

I shake my head, and he pads off barefoot down the hallway to the bathroom.

I do make coffee, for Kevin too, but I shower when he's drinking it. Then afterwards I walk down the hill onto campus. It's early May, but up here on the northeast coast it's still cold. It's always cold. That's what I associate most about my time at the University of Sunderland. Being cold.

The Medical School is a six-storey building, and my meeting's on the top floor. I take the stairs, mostly because now I'm here, I want to delay things as much as possible. But that's never going to be a long-term strategy.

Miss Whitaker, thank you for attending...

There are three people seated in front of me. My tutor Dr Samson is on the left, he likes us to call him Gavin. There's Dr Evans, who is the academic representative. I don't think he has a first name anymore. Then there's an older woman – I don't catch her name, but she's introduced as a Student Support Officer, except she looks about as supportive as a wasp at a picnic. I try to give each of them a bright smile, to show how much I want this to go well, but then I wait, watching them shuffle their papers.

"The panel has reviewed your performance in the April exams," – it's Dr Evans who leads the meeting. – "pathology, anatomy and physiology, and while your grades have improved a little, they still fall below what is required for you to move onto year four of your degree."

"I know," I say, biting my lip and launching into my defence. "The trouble was I ran out of money. I was working all through Christmas, and it just didn't give me the time I needed to study. But I won't work over the summer. I've saved enough, so I'll do better with the resits." I've prepared this defence in my mind: sympathy, a hard-work ethic. Owning my mistakes. Even if it's not necessarily true.

Dr Evans and my tutor share a glance, then he turns back to me. "But you'd still need to be studying your fourth-year material, alongside the resits for year three?"

That *is* true, and it's been stressing me quite a bit.

"Yeah, but I can do it. I just need to really focus."

There's a silence. Then from the papers in front of him, Dr Evans pulls out something else.

"This wouldn't be the first time your performance here has raised concerns, would it Miss Whitaker?" He holds up the paper to show me.

"You were emailed a warning in October, and then again in February. Both explicitly stated that a failure to achieve the progression requirements in the April exams would result in your place being at risk. You understand that?"

"Yes."

Dr Evans furrows his brow, and hums under his breath. I've only had him for a few classes but he's weirdly humourless. I remember one class where I came in late, because it was the morning after Kevin's birthday. I wonder if he's remembering it now too.

"Miss Whitaker." He smiles suddenly, sickly false. "Medical school is highly demanding, and a certain percentage of students simply find they're not up to the challenge." He pauses, looking me right in the eyes. "There's no shame in that. Many people go on to find fulfilling careers outside of medicine."

We stare at each other as my brain fills in the implications. Others don't. Then Gavin breaks in.

"An alternative possibility, Ava, is that you take a break from your studies now, and possibly re-apply at some point in the future." I turn to him, and see what I guess is supposed to be a helpful smile.

"What do you mean?" I still feel Dr Evans's eyes burning into me.

"A year, perhaps two? Take some time, find out who you are and what you really want from life." He smiles like he's just given me the gift of wisdom. But his face falls when he sees I don't want it.

"I want to be a doctor," I tell him.

Gavin's face crumples. "Look, Ava. We all understand how hard you've worked to get here, we really do. But Dr Evans is quite correct. This is a very challenging environment, and perhaps you're just not quite ready? You said you had some money saved? Perhaps you could use that to gain some life experience? Afterwards you might come back, when you're more able to dedicate yourself to your studies."

I don't reply.

"You could travel," Gavin goes on, warming to his theme now. "A lot of young people take gap years, and they can be hugely beneficial. Do the backpacker route in Thailand, go island-hopping in Greece..." He smiles at the idea, but it jolts with me – does he know I'm half-Greek? I told some people here, but not him...

He's still talking though, and I tell myself to concentrate. "Of course we can't *guarantee* you'll be re-admitted, but you've passed years one and two, so the admission panel may look favourably on you, particularly if it seems you've... matured in the intervening time."

I look back at Dr Evans, who seems bored now with the proceedings. He even glances at his watch, like I'm keeping him from lunch.

"I'm sorry, I don't really understand exactly what's happening here," I say, even though I think I do. It's Gavin who replies, hesitantly.

"Ava. The panel is strongly recommending that you voluntarily step back from the course. I think that's where we're at." He smiles again, as if he's offering me a holiday. All expenses paid.

"Miss Whitaker," Dr Evans cuts in. "What Dr Samson is saying is that the panel is prepared to frame this as you deciding to step away. But if you choose not to, we *will* fail you. And that will be the end of your career in medicine. Is that clear enough for you?"

Maybe I was wrong about the expenses.

I swallow. I think somehow I didn't really believe it was going to come to this. Even though I've seen others leave, because they didn't get through the exams, or couldn't find the money. I thought somehow I'd be different. But apparently not.

"My mum's gonna kill me," I mutter, not meaning anyone to hear me, but Dr Evans does.

"Excuse me?"

"Nothing." I shake my head. Trying to think. "Do I have to... decide this right now?"

Again Gavin and Dr Evans glance at each other. The Student Support Officer gives me a sympathetic smile, apparently the full extent of the support I'm getting.

"It would certainly be helpful if you could give an answer now." Again it's Gavin who answers, still playing good cop. Dr Evans tuts and checks his watch again. Gavin explains. "The panel is only meeting this morning, and it's only your case that we're considering. I suppose we could..." – he looks to Dr Evans hopefully – "An hour?" Then he turns back to me, his smile brighter now that he's won me this victory.

"If you could let me know within the hour, we can get this wrapped up?"

I try to think, to make sense of things. Is this really happening? My mum is going to go crazy. She's helped me so much to get here. She's supported me, she's been so proud that I'm going to be a doctor... and now I've totally let her down. I start to feel a hollowness inside me, that I know is going to get so much worse.

"Well, I think we're done here." Dr Evans claps his hands together, happy with his morning's work. The Student Support Officer offers another supportive look.

After I leave, I see the noticeboard where the exams results get pinned. My embarrassing failure still on display for all to see. I don't look and go back to the stairwell, hoping I won't run into anyone I know.

My steps ring out as I work my way down. I'm not really thinking yet, just aware of the light from the windows, bright and cold. The clouds outside scudding by on a stiff north breeze, just like they were before I went in. Yet everything else has changed.

That's when it really hits me. That this is actually over. I've worked so hard, for so long to get here, and now it's done. I'm not going to be a doctor. I failed.

As I push my way outside my mobile buzzes in my pocket. It's a message from Kevin.

> Lunch, Babe?

I stare at the screen a second before stepping out into the cold.

TWO

I meet Kevin at The Hub cafe. Or rather, Kevin and two of his mates, Sam and a guy called Fraz, who regularly reminds me that people call him The Frazster.

"Hey Ava." Kev gives me his smile, and just the slightest raise of his eyebrows, so I assume he's been wondering how it went.

"Hi Ava," Fraz says. He's on the same course as Kevin. "Hey, d'you know that Elon Musk once bought a McLaren F1 car for one million dollars, and then deliberately drove it without any insurance. And do you know why?"

I stare at him, blinking a little. "No. Hey Kev, can we... maybe have a word?"

"It's because he knew it would put this pressure on himself," Fraz goes on. "You know? Because of the consequences if he crashed it. You manufacture your own pressure, so it pushes you harder to succeed." I flash a look in his direction, willing him to shut up.

"Kev?"

"Sure." Kev studies my face, then nods. "There's some tables over there."

The Hub is in a big hall, only about a third full, so there's space for a private talk. Kev carries his tray with sandwiches. His usual bottle of Prime.

"You want anything to eat?" he says, as we sit down. Since we're now the opposite end from the serving area, it's awkward for me to say yes. But I'm not hungry.

"No."

We're both silent.

"So? What's this about?"

"What? You haven't forgotten *again*? My meeting?"

"No," – he screws up his face, wounded – "of course not, I just didn't know if you wanted to talk about it."

I don't know whether to believe him, but maybe I'm being unfair.

"How'd it go?" he asks.

I can't answer at once, I feel the pressure of tears behind my eyes, but I don't want to cry now. I glance back to see that Sam and Fraz are both looking over at us. Curious about what's up. Under the table I tap at the floor with my foot.

"Not great," I say in the end.

Kev makes a noise, halfway between supportive and dismissive. "They always make it sound worse than it is," he tells me. "*Not great*'s probably a good outcome. They just want to scare you into doing more studying." I sense him warming to the theme, so I shake my head.

"No." I swallow. "They said I either leave, or they'll kick me out. They gave me an hour to decide."

Kevin puts a half grin on his face. He thinks I'm joking. "An hour? As in—"

"As in sixty minutes, that's right." I realise I didn't even take note of the time when Gavin gave me his ultimatum.

"Damn." He pauses. "How long you got left?"

"*I don't fucking know, Kevin.*" I look away. "It doesn't matter either way. It's just so they can spin it that they haven't expelled me. Make it my decision to leave. I dunno. It's better that way for their records or something."

Kevin stares at me. It's like I've suddenly become this exotic creature. Different from him, and everyone else here. An actual *ex*-student.

"Can't you, like – appeal it?"

I screw up my face, I hadn't actually thought of this. I'm slightly annoyed that Kevin did before me.

"I don't think so." I think back. It didn't exactly sound like it.

We're both silent a while. Kevin looks at his sandwich, pink ham drooping out the side. He doesn't pick it up.

"So what are you gonna do?"

After a few moments I shrug my shoulders. "I guess I'm gonna email my tutor and tell him I've decided to leave."

"No I mean, what are you gonna *do*? Are you gonna stay here?"

Sunderland is seven hundred miles from where I live, south of London. Kevin lives in the city though. He's a local boy. I try to think how this is going to work.

"I don't really have a choice. My mum isn't going to support me to stay here, she's hardly supporting me anyway." I feel that familiar creep of financial anxiety, but every student gets it. Most, at least.

"What about us?" Kevin eyes me nervously, and I can't meet his gaze.

I shrug. "There's the holidays. Summer and that." I force myself to look at his handsome face. "Maybe you could come down south? Get a job for the summer?"

"Sure. Right." He nods, as he considers this idea. "Where would I stay though? Like, with your family?"

The way he says this grates on me. It's the word *family*. I've told Kevin about a thousand times that it's just Mum and me. But he's the middle of three brothers, and he seems unable to conceive of a life without a big, boisterous family around him.

"Yeah. Maybe." Not even I believe this. I tip my head back, staring at the ceiling. Taking stock of my life falling to pieces around me.

"It's just..." Kevin goes on, "I've got that internship lined up here with the football club. Sports is like, really booming now, such a good area to get into."

At that moment a girl walks past, carrying a tray towards another table, where two other girls are sitting deep in conversation. As she passes she smiles, waggling her fingers at Kevin. It seems to send a jolt of electricity into him, and he breaks into a sudden, wide-mouthed grin.

"Hey! How's it going?" he says. It's like I'm not here, that this conversation isn't happening.

I almost say nothing, but I can't stop myself.

"Who's that?"

"Oh it's no one," – his voice is quiet now that she's out of hearing – "just Anna." He frowns as he thinks. "She's in some of my lectures, and then I see her in the gym. But she's no one." He glances over to watch her slide her narrow backside into a chair. No question she knows he's watching.

"Fuck, Kevin! You're moving on already? We haven't even broken up yet."

"Is that what we're doing here? Breaking up?" He fires back at me so quickly it leaves me breathless. I feel outflanked, unable for a moment to find any words.

"*I don't know*," I say. "I don't want to."

We're both silent for a while, while the buzz of happier conversations around the room washes over us.

"Well, how else is it going to work?" Kevin says after a while. "If you're not here, and I can't..." He glances back towards the table with his mates. "You know, maybe this isn't the best place to have this conversation?"

"Oh? You think?" But I'm pissed off, because he's less worried about breaking up with me than whether or not The Frazster is watching while it happens.

"Look, Ava. I'm sorry, alright? But both of us knew this thing was never that serious? And if you really wanted it to work, then maybe you could have put more effort into studying?" He shrugs again, like it was obvious all along.

And that hurts. I think for a few moments, about how I've helped him with his studies, reading over what he's written, testing him before his exams. Making sure he runs his essays through the anti-plagiarism checker before he submits them, because he always uses AI to write them. I think about telling him this, I hear the snark in the voice in my head. But what's the point? Really, why bother? Instead I reach over and pick up his bottle of Prime. I crack the seal and take a deep swig. Then I stare at him.

"Why do you even drink this crap? You're not twelve years old."

I put the bottle down too hard, so the liquid fizzes up and out onto his sandwich. Then I get up, shake my head, and walk away.

THREE

I think about phoning Mum, to ask if she'll come and get me, but that's hardly fair. Besides I can't face a six-hour journey of her disappointed silence. So instead I book a ticket on the next day's Megabus to London. It's eight hours of misery, but a bargain at only £17.99. Then I pack up my room. I manage to fit my whole life into one backpack and two plastic carrier bags. I email my landlord, thinking I might get some of my deposit back, but he replies with the contract, explaining how I have to give notice, so technically I owe him, but he won't charge me if the room isn't damaged. How do you even damage a room?

I have a few drinks with my housemates that evening. They tell me how much they'll miss me, that we'll keep in touch, but I know we won't. I'm not the first to drop out of medical school. There's so much work, and everyone's under so much pressure. There's just no time to remember the people that fall by the wayside. People like me.

The next day, I watch the side of the road slide by, the garbage, the weeds. I wonder what I'm going to do next.

But already I sort of know.

The Megabus drops me in London Victoria, and it costs me twice as much for the last leg down to Guildford. I walk the final mile, from the train station to the house where I grew up. We live on a new-build estate, with views of the sports field from my old secondary school. I could actually see my house from my old biology classroom. I used to sit in there and think about one day being a doctor. In the perfect future I imagined would just happen, all on its own. I guess I was wrong about that.

Our house is bigger than we need for just the two of us. Mum's done well for herself, and she's always on about how I need to do the same, which isn't going to make this moment any less awkward. But as I get to the gate there's something else. Mum's car is on the driveway, her white Audi SUV, but there's another car here too, a black Tesla that I don't recognise. I stop and think about turning around, but where else am I gonna go? This is my home. At least, it sort of is.

Damn. I open the gate.

At the door I think about ringing the bell, but I still have my key, so I slide it in before I can change my mind. I turn it, and push open the door.

There's a man's voice. I hear him a fraction of a second before I see him.

"I'm just taking out the recycling..." He's tall, a receding hairline shaved into a buzz cut that doesn't look too bad for a guy his age. He's carrying the plastic tub we use for plastics. He stops, freezing as he sees me. But he recovers first.

"Hello?"

"Hi," I say.

"I was just... you must be..."

"Yeah. I'm Ava." This is already going badly, but I step inside all the same. "Karen's daughter."

"Of course. She's..." He smiles like he was about to say she's talked a lot about me, but maybe she hasn't? "I was just..." He holds up the recycling bucket as if this explains his presence in my house. *Just popped over to help with the housework.*

"Sure."

I struggle out of the straps of my backpack. I might not have much in this world, but I've still carried it a mile from the station. Now the man holds out his hand.

"Matthew." He tries to smile, a cool smile. "Call me Matt. I'm a... friend of your mother." He doesn't get the chance to say anything more, because then Mum sticks her head around the door.

"Ava?"

"Hi, Mum."

"What the hell are you doing here?" Her voice is cold. I hear the anger already.

I glance again at the man – Matt. Why does she have to have some guy here? That only makes this a thousand times worse. But also, why on earth didn't I tell her I was coming? Obviously I should have done that. I can be such an idiot. I take a deep breath, try to look her in the eye.

"I'm really sorry Mum. I got kicked out."

FOUR

The whole trip back I've been wondering what her reaction was going to be, whether she'd scream and shout, how I'd defend myself. But she just repeats the words, like they don't make sense, the way I've put them.

"You got kicked out?" She stares at me, like she's never heard of this happening before, like she didn't even know it was possible. It's pretty hypocritical of her.

"Maybe I should leave you two to talk?" Matt says, giving up on the recycling by gently putting the bucket down on the floor.

"Yes, perhaps that's a good idea." Mum replies, without taking her eyes off me, then she does turn to him with an actual smile. "I'm sorry, Matthew, I wasn't expecting to be interrupted like this." When she looks back at me the smile has gone. But I just wait, still standing by the front door, while Matt gets his things together.

"Do you want to know what happened?" I ask Mum, a full minute later.

"Of course I do," she snaps back at once. But her eyes tell me to wait.

Matt's ready at last, and he gives my mother a meaningful look, before sliding a "good luck" glance my way and slipping out the door. Then it's just the two of us left, Mum and me.

We go to the kitchen where Mum tops up her glass of white wine, and puts Matt's glass into the sink to wash. After a moment's thought she fetches a second glass for me.

"So... this is final? There's nothing I can do?"

"I don't think so."

"Well, that's a bloody shame."

"Yeah," I say. "I'm sorry about Matt," I say.

She waves a hand, as if she couldn't care less about that, but she stays quiet.

"How long have you been seeing him?" I ask. "He seems cool."

Mum's love life is complicated – has always been complicated. First of all, I don't know who my biological father is – so there's that. But there were men down the years. Shawn, the South African I used to call Dad – he left when I was eight. Then Jeremy, who gave me the creeps. John was a drinker. There were others too. When I was a teenager I think Mum gave up, and concentrated instead on getting me into medical school. I didn't really even know she was dating again. She definitely deserves some good luck with guys.

"I don't think how long I've been seeing Matthew is the issue here, do you?" Her voice is ice.

I swallow. OK, this is how we're doing this. Can't say I'm surprised.

"It's not entirely my fault," I hit back. "The university were kinda unfair. They could have let me do resits."

"If you hadn't failed your exams you wouldn't have needed to do resits."

"I had to work," I blurt out, then immediately wish I hadn't. "I ran out of money. I had to get a job. It didn't give me enough time to study."

She's silent in response to this, but takes a sip of the wine through thin lips.

"Well, that's disappointing to hear," she says in the end. I wait, not sure how to reply. "Extremely disappointing. We worked through a budget that was quite sufficient for you to live off," she says. "In fact it was more than generous. And had you told me you were having financial problems, I could have helped. *Jesus Christ Ava.* Do you know how much I've invested in you? Do you think I couldn't have thrown you a couple thousand more?"

I don't know how to answer this. "I didn't want to ask you again. I wanted to do it on my terms." I'm quiet a moment. "I thought that's what you wanted?"

She looks away, blinking her clear blue eyes a few times, before turning back.

"Your terms," she repeats. She inspects the wine in her glass. Eventually she looks up at me.

"I really don't believe this, Ava. I don't believe you could have done this to me."

I can't take this anymore. It was always clear where this argument was going to go. I think we both knew it, the moment I walked in the door. We might as well get on with it.

"To you? That's rich. When all I've done is exactly the same thing that you did, when you were my age."

She opens her mouth, pretending to be shocked.

"You went to medical school, got kicked out, and then buggered off to Greece. Only you went a lot further, because then you got pregnant with me. But it turned out OK. You're always saying how well you did, going into pharmacy, starting the business..."

"I'm well aware of what happened in my own life, Ava. It's a very big factor in why I wanted a better life for you." She takes a meaningful sigh, mutters under her breath: *"Jesus Christ.* You had it all going for you, Ava. You had it all handed to you, and now..." She shakes her head.

"Maybe I did..." I try and foster some energy to my argument. "But did you ever think about whether I wanted it? Whether I wanted to be a doctor, or whether you were just pushing me into it, all because you failed—"

"I didn't *fail*, Ava. I..." She stops, calms herself, and takes another sip from her glass, so that she's icy-cool again.

"I understand. You're framing this as *my* fault? Because I wanted the best for you?"

We're both silent for a long time. I don't know what to say.

"Ava, you *told* me you wanted to be a doctor. When you were five years old."

I look down at the floor, trying to control myself, the way she does, but it's hard. I've heard this *so* many times, and maybe I *did* say that. But I also wanted to be a primary-school teacher, and a zoo keeper. They were just the jobs I knew about.

"It's a good career, being a doctor," Mum goes on. "You have a good salary, you're respected..."

"It's a bit late for that, Mum." My anger bursts through. "It's over. They've kicked me out."

My outburst seems to shock her. She runs her hand through her hair. It's quite short, very blonde. With my dark hair, people often don't realise we're mother and daughter.

"What did you want to be then? What dream did you have that I prevented you from chasing? For God's sake, Ava..." She doesn't want an answer, but I don't have one to give anyway. Truth is, I don't know. Maybe I wanted to be a doctor. Maybe I still do. But it was never this big life-ambition, this dream I was chasing the way she told people. That was always her more than me.

"Why did *you* leave medical school?" I ask. But she shakes her head.

"I don't think this is the time to discuss that."

"Yeah, but it never is, is it? You never talk about that. You never talk about Greece. You never speak about what happened when you were there. I don't know why we left. I've never understood why it's all such a big secret."

"It's not a secret, Ava. It's never been a secret." She tightens her brow, considering. I think she knows this time it's different. This time she's going to have to give me something.

She takes a deep breath. "It's just a period of my life that I'm not particularly proud of. A time where I made some mistakes that I sincerely hoped you wouldn't repeat." She fixes me a look, but I don't care right now. I ask her again.

"I still want to know. You've still never told me. Like, literally never told me. I know I was born in Greece, but I don't know the circumstances. It's just weird why you've never said anything."

"That's not true, Ava. That's nonsense." She pulls herself up straight in her seat, she's a little taller than me. "I don't find it necessary to dwell on the past, but you're well aware of the basic facts. I took a summer job on the island of Alythos, when I was in my fourth year at university. And then..." – she looks away – "I found myself pregnant. It wasn't practical to continue my studies with a baby, but I'd done enough by then to transfer onto a pharmacy course. So that's what I did. That enabled me to bring you up while making the best use of my skills. And I didn't think I did too bad a job. At least not until today."

It's hardly the full story though, is it? Like, why didn't she come back to England when she found out she was pregnant? When did we come back? How old was I? And most important of all, who the hell was my dad, and why has she never – not one single time – talked about him?

But something stops me saying this. Something always has. It's just the way we are as a family. She's always made it clear this isn't a subject I'm allowed to know about. Don't ask. Never tell.

And yet here's the really weird thing: I *know* she was happy there. Happier than I've ever seen her, my whole life. I know because she keeps this photo in her office, at the back of a filing cabinet where she thinks I've never thought to look. In it, she's standing with this other girl, Imogen Grant. Both of them are about the same age I am now, and behind them is a sign for a place called the Aegean Dream Resort. There's these rocky mountains in the background, and beautiful, lush, green gardens, and this hint of sparkling blue sea. But it's the look on their faces that has always drawn me back to this photo, which I've stared at when I know Mum's out of the house. They both look so happy, Mum and her friend. So excited, so content, so filled with life. I've literally never seen Mum look like that in real life. Not one time.

"What will you do now?" Mum's thin voice cuts me back to reality.

I shrug. "I guess maybe I'll look for a job?"

"Where do you intend to live?" That shocks me a little.

"Um... I was thinking here," I say awkwardly. "At least for a while. Maybe I'll get my own place, when I can."

She scoffs suddenly. "Your own place? Do you know how much your own place would cost around here?"

"I don't mean to buy, I'm talking about renting."

"*I'm* talking about renting. And the wages you can expect to get without a degree, without any qualifications... what kind of job?"

"I don't know. I'll do some temping I suppose."

"Stacking shelves in the local supermarket?" She shakes her head. "Oh, Ava, what have you done?"

Not as much as you, I want to shout at her. *At least I didn't get myself pregnant.*

"My tutor talked about reapplying," I tell her instead, after a moment. "He suggested I go to Thailand. Find myself. That maybe in a year or two I could apply again. He said maybe they'd let me back in." I didn't really believe him, but I figure I'll offer Mum some hope to cling onto. She doesn't go for it.

"Thailand," she repeats. "The Buddhism hippy trail. Get stoned and rack up an enormous debt for no good purpose. That sounds a *terrific* idea, Ava."

I'm quiet a moment.

Fuck it.

"Well actually I did have one other idea," I say. I don't look at her. I can't while I say this.

"I thought I might go to Greece. To Alythos."

Mum's face is frozen. It's not the reaction I'd hoped for, but then I don't know what I expected. Very carefully she shakes her head.

"I think that's a very bad idea, Ava. An extremely bad—"

"Why?" I challenge her. "It's where I come from, but I don't know *anything* about it. I was born there, but you've never told me how, isn't that weird?"

"I told you, Ava. I associate that place with a difficult period of my life. A dark period."

"Having me was dark?"

"No. *Goodness*, no." She sinks down into her chair, and finally I've broken through to something motherly. "No, I don't mean that. Ava, I really don't. You were the light at the end of the tunnel, the candle *in* the darkness. What I suppose I'm saying is, I don't want to face up to who *I* was, when I was there. And I never have. And I'm so sorry."

But I don't understand. I've never understood this. She looks so happy in that photo.

"Well, you don't have to come with me. I looked at it online. There's jobs there. I could work in a bar, isn't that what you did?" I've pieced together a few snippets over the years, times when Mum's let slip tiny details.

"I just want to see the place. Find out about where I come from."

Mum frowns, then shakes her head again. "No. That's a very bad idea, Ava." She holds a hand to her forehead, like she's getting one of her migraines. "This is very hard. You come home unannounced, telling me how you've wrecked your future, and now suddenly this? No." She takes a sip from her wine, then a second. Finally a third.

"Look, I don't know very much about Thailand, but if travel is what you want to do, then fine. I'll help you, financially. But not Greece. Do you understand me? That's off the table. Not going to happen. Is that clear?"

I stare at Mum for a long time, trying to read her, trying to understand. Then I drop my head and study the floor. There's a chip in one of the tiles, it happened when John – that's the one who drank – threw a wrench down on the floor. He hadn't known I was home, because it was during school hours, but I was sick that day. I crept down the stairs because of the shouting, and I saw him there, like he was threatening her with it. My mum's definitely known some dark times, and she's stood up against them. So maybe she's right? Maybe I should leave Greece well alone? But at the same time, this is my life, and I want to know about it. It's my right.

"I want to go to Greece, Mum," I tell her. "I want to go to Alythos."

She stares back at me. Her eyes are bright blue, and just for a moment I sense there's panic behind them. She's been able to shut this down my whole life. But I've grown up and things have changed now. She can't stop me.

"Why?" she says in the end. For the first time I realise I've defeated her. "Why do you want to go so much?"

I blink at the moment, and finally just shrug, because I don't have an answer to give her. At least not one that I can say out loud. Because the truth is stupid, it's impossible and there's no logic behind it. Just something else, a kind of itch that I have to scratch. Even though I know it's stupid.

I want to go to Alythos to search for my dad.

FIVE

I'm not stupid. I don't mean it literally. I said Mum's never talked about my father, but that's not quite true, a couple of times she's said something, when she'd had too much to drink. Once she told me he was a waiter – a Greek waiter. A proper cliché, as she put it. But she wouldn't tell me his name. I couldn't even understand if she knows it. Maybe that's what she means by not being proud of that time of her life? I don't know. But what I mean is, I understand there's no chance of me *actually* finding my father. But what I do know is that there's this island in Greece, a place where I was literally born, and it's real. So I want to see it. I want to know what it's like. I want to meet the people who live there. And yeah, maybe I'll get lucky, and bump into an older guy who looks just like me – but I'm not kidding myself. I just don't know why it's such a big deal for me to find out more about where I'm from.

Our "discussion" peters out, like it always does, and Mum tells me she's going out – she and Matt already have a restaurant booked. But she tells me there's leftover take-away in the fridge. So I eat that and when she's gone I pull out my laptop. You've got to act decisively if you want to achieve anything, that's one of her favourite phrases. So I run a search for flights to Alythos Island. It doesn't actually have an airport, but there's one nearby, in a place called Panachoria. Only, this time of year there's just one flight a week and I've just missed it. But when I look at flights to Athens instead, there's a discounted flight tomorrow. The website tells me there's only one seat left at that price. I leave it flashing at me, for a long while. You've got to act decisively if you want to achieve anything.

I pull out my bank card and book it.

I feel sick when it's done. Physically sick, like I've set something in motion that I'm not in control of. Then I go into the utility room and empty my bag. I dump almost everything into the washing machine and then go upstairs and raid my drawers for all my lighter clothes – I never needed them in Sunderland. I start packing. And then I stop, and do something I probably shouldn't. I make my way into Mum's office, which is in one of the spare rooms. I pull open the filing cabinet where she stores the accounts. At the back, there's an envelope and I pick it up. I open it and slide out the photo. There's Mum and her friend Imogen, both about my age, looking so bright, so sun-kissed, so *happy*. I know I shouldn't, but I slide the drawer shut and carry the photo back to my room, where I stash it in my laptop bag.

That was yesterday. Now I'm here. Waiting at the gate at London Heathrow airport. For the plane that's going to take me home.

I left Mum a note. That was probably cowardly, not telling her to her face, but she had to go to work this morning and I did tell her yesterday, when we argued, so it's not like she doesn't know. And it's not really her business. I'm paying for the flight. And it's my life. Even so, I didn't feel I could relax at all until I'd got to the airport and through security. All the time I was looking behind me, like she was going to physically drag me away. But now she can't. Now she can't get me back.

I open my laptop bag and pull out the photo. In the harsh light I look at it more carefully than I ever have before. It's the first time I've been able to do it without worrying about her coming home and catching me.

I guess Mum is actually a couple of years older than I am now, maybe twenty-four? Her hair is loose, much longer than she wears it now and lighter too. Her face is golden and she's got freckles I don't usually see. She's beautiful. Really she is. I don't want to sing my own praises but I'm OK looking. I have more olive skin than Mum – presumably from whoever my dad was – but I don't look as good as Mum does here. Maybe after I've had a summer of sun? My eyes shift over to Imogen. It hasn't really registered before, because I've always known her as this weird, messed-up, middle-aged lady, but she was pretty then too. Her hair is dark and tied back in a loose ponytail, and there's a light in her eyes that the camera has caught, like she's sharing a secret.

I should say something about Imogen, because it's a strange relationship that Mum has with her. It's like they're friends, but not because they like each other. Only because they once used to be friends, and each of them feels they ought to keep it going in some way? I don't know. I've always felt that Imogen relies on Mum for some sort of mental-health support, like maybe she's bipolar or something, and Mum feels obliged to help, even though she normally doesn't like people who are weak, which is what Mum says sometimes after Imogen has come around to visit. Like I said, it's kind of weird. And I haven't seen her in a few years. We used to see her more when I was younger.

I turn the photo over. There on the back is something I'd never noticed before. It's a date: *August* 2000. The year before I was born. I calculate... actually, it's exactly nine months before I was born. Which means – if my high-school biology classes and three-and-a-half years at medical school has taught me anything – that this is the exact time my mum was busy having me with my dad, whoever he is.

There's a bong on the intercom as my flight is called. Most of the people at the gate stand up at once, and begin waiting to board the plane. I wait though, joining the line when it's reduced to nearly nothing, and the flight attendant checks my passport and ticket. I half expect her to tell me there's some problem, that Mum's phoned through and explained I can't go, but she won't have seen my note yet. And the woman just gives me a vacant smile, and hands my passport back, so I walk down the tunnel towards the plane. I step inside, and squeeze into my seat near the back and by the window.

There's a long delay, while a queue of planes take off before us. Finally it's our time and we spin around onto the start of the runway. We don't even stop, and the engines roar. I'm pressed back into my seat, then I feel twice my weight as we climb up into the air. We bump and roll, up towards the clouds, and then the damp outskirts of London vanish into a blanket of grey and we rattle our way up, higher and higher until suddenly we break through the top of the clouds. Here the sun beats down on a secret landscape, soft and endless, like you could step out and float forever.

I try to read on the flight, but my mind's working too much, so instead I study the people around me. I'd say the plane is half full of people on holiday, but the other half look different, like they're on business, or have some other reason to be going to Athens. I wonder if any have a mission quite like mine.

The landing in Athens is kind of scary. It seems they built the airport right in the city, or maybe the city just grew around the airport? Either way, as the plane comes in it drops lower and lower over what seems to be endless apartment buildings, and by the time we're nearly down, some of the tops of the buildings, right beside us, are actually higher than the plane. You can look inside the apartments, seeing snatches of people's lives as we thunder past, in this tube of aluminium weighing hundreds of tons. Then we're down, and some of the tourists try to give a cheer, but most of the passengers are already snapping their phones on and reconnecting to their lives. I look out of the window. It's sunny here. Not a cloud in sight.

I take a bus from Athens to Panachoria. It's the closest city to the island of Alythos, and it takes four hours. I'm pretty used to buses what with riding the Megabus so many times. But this one is more interesting, because everything out of the windows is Greek, and this is where I was born. Or at least the correct country.

It's a bit confusing in Panachoria bus station, partly because a lot of the signs aren't written in English but the Greek alphabet, and I don't understand a word of it. But an older guy helps me find a connecting bus to Kastria, which is the main town on Alythos. I'm not sure how it's actually going to get there, what with Alythos being an island and everything, but I just have to trust. And after twenty minutes we pull up to a tiny little port just as a small ferry is boarding a dozen or more cars. It's really cute. The bus drives right to the front and then bumps onto the ferry. The other passengers around me – locals definitely now – barely even pay it any attention, not even getting off the bus. But then one couple do, so I follow them and climb up into the passenger area. Here I stare out at the sea around me, drinking it in. Ahead of us I can see what must be Alythos, not far away. There's other islands around and beyond it. I hear a blast from a whistle as the ferry starts to move. I stare down at the clear water below its steel sides.

It's only fifteen minutes, and I'm called to get back on the bus. We dock, and again we're first to drive off. Then it's a ten-minute drive to the town of Kastria. When I disembark here, there's one more bus to take, down to the town of Skalio, which is down in the south-east of the island. It's easier to find this time, because Alythos is quite small. There aren't many other places you can go.

I'm the only person who gets off the bus at Skalio, and the driver pulls away at once, leaving me in a cloud of diesel fumes. When that fades I get a whiff of garbage. It seems the bus stop here is also by the town's bin store. There's only one way to go: behind me are olive groves, leading up the side of a mountain, with pine forests higher up. In front of me, a few low apartment buildings, and up ahead a glimpse of the sea. I shoulder my bag and walk towards it, trying to quell the feeling that I've made a terrible mistake. But as I get a bit of distance away from the bins there's another smell. It's warm but fresh, from the sea I suppose, but something else too. Something earthy and sharp. It takes me a second to place it, because it's quite rare that Mum likes to cook with it, but sometimes she does. It's thyme. I look around and I see it's growing wild everywhere in the scrubby land around me, filling the air with this low, herbal hum. It's nice.

I follow the directions on my phone – and also my nose – down to the seafront, passing a little supermarket with baskets of fruit outside that looks like something from Instagram. A cat slinks past, stretching lazily, and from somewhere I hear voices, low and relaxed. I suppose it's Greek that I'm hearing. Words I don't understand but which sound like waves rolling in.

When I get to the waterfront the sun is just touching the horizon, sinking into the water like it's dissolving and turning the whole sky above me pink and orange. There's a row of fishing boats rocking in a little harbour, ropes creaking softly as they pull against the dock. Around them various tavernas have set out tables, and there's maybe a dozen people dining, with many more tables. It smells amazing, grilled seafood. The relaxed murmur of conversation. I'm ignored, able to look around unobserved.

That's when it really hits me.

This is it. Skalios Bay – *Alythos*. The place where I was born. Where I was conceived, at least as far as I know. But also the place I know nothing about, because my mum has never spoken about it. Never answered my questions, and there's only so much you can know about a place from searching it online. But now I'm here to find out for myself. Already it's not quite what I expected. More three-dimensional. Sights I recognise from photographs not connecting in the way I'd imaged they would.

I don't know what I expected to feel though. Some kind of instant connection? A weird sense of recognition? But there's nothing like that. Instead it's just this sort of... anxiety, uneasiness. Like I'm not supposed to be here. Like I've done something wrong in coming here, and I should have told Mum, let her find a way of stopping me. But I didn't.

A waiter notices me now – far too young to be my dad – and half-heartedly he tries to interest me in a table. I back away. I bought plastic-wrapped sandwiches at the bus station in Panachoria, but even so I'm hungry enough that the restaurants are setting my mouth watering. But there's no way I'm eating out here alone. I feel watched suddenly, like someone's about to notice that I'm here and shouldn't be. I can see on my phone that my hotel is only a few minutes away. So I take one last glance at the water, the sky now shifting into purples and deep blues as the night takes over. I turn back down another narrow street, following the comforting blue line on my phone, and I can't wait to check in to my room.

I'm here. But something about it makes me want to hide myself away. Like I don't want the island to know I'm back.

SIX

I make the most of breakfast the next morning, eating as much as I can, then buttering a couple of extra bread rolls and slipping them into my bag. I only booked two nights, because it's all I can afford. Afterward, I pull on some shorts and take a walk. It's time to see my new home.

Skalio, population about 1,500 – I'm guessing – sits at one end of a long sandy bay. There isn't much to it, maybe a half-dozen restaurants, some now closed but others with tables outside, and people sipping coffee in the sunshine. The little supermarket I saw last night is open again, and I think I spot the same cat, but there are fewer boats in the harbour, I guess they've gone out to fish. Beyond the little port I spot a couple of beach bars and what looks like a diving centre. It's all quite relaxed, but it has a peaceful energy. Like it's a real place, where real people live, and not just somewhere tourists come. But when I look further around the bay, out towards where the Aegean Dream Resort should be, I get my first surprise.

It's not there.

I mean, the building is still there. But clearly it's not still operating. I can see that from here, and it looks like it hasn't done so in a very long time. I suppose I could have checked on Google, if I'd thought to do so. It just didn't occur to me. The old hotel is about a mile around the bay, and maybe because I feel a little conspicuous wandering through town, I walk along the beach to get there. At first, I follow the shoreline, but the sand is soft, and trudging through it under the heat of the sun is exhausting, so I move up to a narrow path that runs along the scrubland behind the beach. The air is thick here with the rich scent of wild thyme.

As I get closer, it's obvious the Aegean Dream Resort isn't just closed – it's completely abandoned. There's a two-storey building that would have been the guest rooms, laid out so the ones on the lower floor have wide verandas with views down to the beach, with the upper floor getting balconies. But now the entrances are boarded up, wood nailed across the openings. Except some of them have been smashed open, the jagged edges of glass still clinging to the window frame behind the broken, time-worn wood. I step close to one, standing on what would have been a beautiful terrace, years ago. There's nothing stopping me going further, so cautiously, I push my way inside the room.

The smell hits me first – a sharp mix of urine and damp – even in this heat. The walls are scrawled with graffiti. I switch on the light on my phone and shine it at the wall. A lot of it's in Greek, but there's names of couples too. I read that James was here, 2015. And then somewhere else, a bit unsettling, someone's scrawled *The Killing Zone* in red letters. I feel relieved when I step back out into the sun.

I keep going, past the rooms towards the main building. There's a low, crumbling structure that must have been a restaurant, and beside it, the pool, or what's left of it. It's big, with elegant, curved edges, but its once-bright tiles are cracked and dirty, and it's littered with debris. There's no water, obviously. But there is a rusting fridge tipped onto its back, lying in the deep end, and bizarrely, an old office chair tangled with what's left of the metal steps. Someone's made a fire down there too, charred black stains turning the blue tiles black.

The pool bar is still here. This is where I think Mum worked. At least, it's what she said, on one of those few occasions when she said anything. She was drinking a cocktail and she said she used to make them, by the pool here. That gives me a weird feeling. To actually be here where Mum worked. There's quite a lot of the bar left. It was made of concrete, which I guess is why it's still standing. Maybe once it was covered with tiles, I don't know. The roof has partially collapsed though, so that the years of sun have weathered everything, and the iron rods reinforcing the structure are poking out through the crumbling ruins.

Something makes me step behind the bar, standing where Mum must have stood, all those years ago. I try to picture it as it must have been. The pool bright and clean, the music playing. I can almost see her here, how beautiful she was, flirting with the guests, as the heat of the day slips away. But I can't picture it. What's actually here is too powerful, this empty shell left to rot. The smell of decay, and suddenly I get a bad feeling. I didn't see any signs, but probably I'm not supposed to be in here. Places like this are dangerous, and now I get the sense that I'm being watched. That someone's going to shout at me to get out, so I look around quickly and then walk back through what was presumably once beautiful gardens towards the beach.

It's odd though. Why is it like this? A place like this, right on the beach, must be worth a fortune. Why abandon it? And why hasn't it been redeveloped? Why's it just been left here?

I'm getting hungry, so I sit down to eat my rolls. I look out over the sea, which is blue and flat and beautiful, but after a while I realise I still feel a little uncomfortable with the Aegean Dream

Resort ruins so close behind me. Anyone could be hiding in there. Anyone could be watching me. So I get up again. I move a little way back down the beach towards Skalio, where at once I feel better.

When I finish my lunch I try to think. If I'm here to find out about my past, I'm going to need to ask people. But the thought of that scares me a little. I'm not quite ready yet. So instead I strip down to the bikini I put on this morning, and step down the sand towards the calm blue water. It's cooler than I expect, but not actually cold. Nothing like the wind-whipped grey North Sea I'm used to seeing. Not that I ever went in.

I stand for a while, letting the gentle waves lap around my ankles, feeling the sand shift beneath my feet. Then all at once I wade in, pulling at the water with my arms until I fall forwards, letting the water envelop me, feeling the taste of the salt on my lips. It's lush. I open my eyes underwater, and wish I had goggles, because I can see how clear and blue it is, even though it's murky to my eyes. I find a warm patch, the water heated by the sun, and I float instead, just lying on my back, letting the rays of sunlight soothe my body. Feeling it restore me, welcome me. The temperature is perfect, I could stay here all day. Except, of course, I can't. I didn't come here on holiday. There's something I have to do.

I get out and wait while the sun dries me, before getting dressed. I feel the stress trickling back into me, as I try to work out what to do next.

Eventually, I head back into town. I pluck up the courage to sit down at a table outside one of the restaurants I saw earlier, and after a few minutes, a waiter comes out to take my order. I could ask him. I could start right now. But I don't. I just ask for a coffee, in English, and I'm not sure if he'll even understand me. But he just nods and goes back inside.

I make a mental plan as I sip my coffee. I need to find somewhere cheaper to stay, that's the first task. And after that, I'll need a job. After that, I can start investigating. But it makes sense to take this one step at a time.

The waiter doesn't reappear, so after a while I step inside the restaurant to pay at the bar. It's cool inside, and I can smell garlic from whatever they're cooking for later. I see a different waiter sitting at a table, absorbed in his phone. He spots me and gets to his feet, clearing his throat like I've caught him doing something wrong. I smile, and use my best phrasebook Greek to ask how much, but he replies in English. That slightly disappoints me. I thought I looked Greek enough to pass for a local. But I guess that's just silly.

I think about asking him now if he needs staff, but the transaction is over before I find the words. Before I know it, I'm back outside. I head up and down the seafront strip a couple of times, taking stock of my options. And then I remember the supermarket. Maybe they have a noticeboard there? It kind of felt like that sort of place.

The supermarket has three aisles, tightly packed together, but somehow it contains everything you could possibly buy, from food to small household goods like dustpans, brushes and toasters. There's even wool, and computer keyboards. But even though I scan carefully, there's no noticeboard. An older woman waits patiently by the old-style till. I sense her awareness that there's something I'm searching for.

"Can I help you?" she asks, in lightly accented English.

"Oh, no." I'm startled. "I was just wondering if there was a noticeboard or something like that."

She frowns slightly, a hint of a smile on her lips. "No noticeboard. What was it you were looking for?"

I almost repeat that I was looking for a noticeboard, but I see what she means.

"Actually, I was hoping to see if there were any jobs."

"Jobs?" Her eyebrows lift slightly, and she looks me over. I think she's going to say no, but she doesn't. "It's a little early in the season. There'll be plenty in a month or so." She smiles like she realises that's not much help. "What kind of work are you after?"

"Oh, um." I pause, thinking. "Bar work, I suppose."

"Have you tried the ones on the beachfront?"

I feel stupid again, having to confess that I haven't. But she shrugs. "I think I heard Hans was looking for someone. He usually is."

"Hans?"

"Bar Sunset. It's the last one on the beachfront. You'll know it from the techno music."

SEVEN

I was going to head back to the hotel, but I can't afford to hide forever, so instead I go back down towards the beach. The woman in the supermarket is right, Bar Sunset isn't hard to spot. It's a kind of large wooden shack, with tables that spill out onto the beach. Already a few of them are occupied, mostly with guys on their own with large glasses of beer. Behind the bar is a tall man with light-brown hair tied in a ponytail. Below that is a linen shirt, open at the neck. He watches me as I go up to him, his head nodding gently to the beat.

I perch on a stool, and for a moment he ignores me, then he strolls over, drying a glass as he goes.

"Hey there."

"Hello." I pause, I could just launch into this, but maybe it's better if I order a drink first? Try and figure something out about the place. I glance at what they have, a shelf full of spirits, a couple of fridges with glass fronts. Heineken, some German-sounding beers, then others that look more Greek.

I point towards one. "Um, can I have a bottle of Mythos please?"

"You most certainly can." He spins around and pulls the

bottle from the fridge. With a practised flourish he prises off the cap and puts it down in front of me. I don't seem to be getting a glass, so I take a swig.

"Thanks."

He nods once by way of acknowledgement, but doesn't move away.

"English?" he says, a moment later.

"Um, yeah. How did you know?"

"I saw you earlier. Walking past. You looked English."

"Oh." I'm not sure what to make of that.

"Are you Hans?" I ask instead.

He seems surprised by this, like somehow I've beaten him at some game by guessing his name.

"That's right." His eyes narrow a little.

"I'm Ava," I say, holding out my hand, then I go on. "The woman in the supermarket gave me your name." Then, under the bar where he can't see my hands, I cross my fingers. "I was asking if there was anywhere that might have any work?"

He doesn't react at once to this, but after a while he says: "You spoke to Maria?" I've no idea who I spoke to, but I nod. Probably it was Maria.

"And Maria said I was looking for someone?"

"Yeah. She said she thought you might be."

He steps away, places the glass he's dried on a shelf, and takes another. He dries it carefully for a few moments, then glances around the very-much-not-busy bar.

"You have a work permit?"

"A work...?"

"That's right. You're English. You voted for Brexit. So now you need a work permit. Can't employ you without one."

I didn't actually vote for Brexit. I was thirteen years old when the vote happened. But it doesn't feel helpful to point this out. Either way, I do have a solution.

"I have dual nationality," I tell him. "I was born here. I've got a UK passport and a Greek one."

"OK." His head nods to the beat a little more, as if this was the answer he was expecting.

"So you speak Greek?" he checks, after a moment.

"Um." This is more of a problem. "I know a bit," I say, exaggerating slightly. And immediately I wish I hadn't, because he goes on, saying something in Greek, and I have no idea what it is.

"You don't speak that much Greek." He switches back to English, showing his teeth with a grin. I open my mouth to reply, but there's little to say.

"You worked in a bar before?" he asks next, and I'm happier about this one.

"Yeah. Plenty of times," I lie.

He tips his head on one side, like he's actually considering this, which I take as a good sign.

"How long you here for? You're no good to me if you're moving on in five minutes."

"I want to stay the whole summer," I say. "But obviously I need a job first."

He seems happy with this answer and I start to feel more confident. It would be a great start to my time here if I can get a job right away. It would certainly help with my money issues. But if I thought this was going well, I might have misread it.

"A lot of the customers we get here are German. I really need someone who can understand them." He pauses. "You gonna pretend you speak German too?"

I don't have an answer for this one.

"Um... probably not."

He begins to shake his head, but before he can say anything he's interrupted by a customer along the bar. He clears his throat loudly to get Hans's attention, and I look too. It's a large guy – huge even – with an enormous gut and shorts that reveal horribly white hairy legs. Hans gives me a "hold on" look, as he spins around to serve him. I take a dejected swig of my Mythos. Clearly I'm not getting a job, so I might as well enjoy the beer.

But then, as the fat man waits for Hans to fetch his drink, I feel his eyes sliding over to me, not even bothering to hide it. I have a look I use on these occasions, every woman does, a "fuck-off stare", and I'm just about to deploy it when I change my mind. Instead of giving the guy an evil look, I offer him a warm and friendly smile. His eyes widen in surprise.

"Hi there," I say. There's a few strands of hair falling over my face, and I brush them behind my ear, feeling the guy following my every move. "How's your day going?"

"Hallo," he says, when his brain realises I actually spoke to him. I smile again, then when it's clear he doesn't even have a response, I turn back to Hans, who's watching the both of us, the litre of golden beer he's just poured frozen in his hands. The fat guy pays, then finally he takes his drink back to a table, where he changes his seat, to give a better view of my rear sitting on my stool. Hans wanders back to me, a thoughtful expression on his face.

"OK," he says. "No German. But most of the guys like to order in English. I guess I can give you a couple of shifts."

And just like that, I have a job.

EIGHT

There's still time to finish my Mythos though, and there's still one obvious problem to solve: I only have one more night booked in the hotel, and even with a job I can't afford to stay there much longer. So since I'm on a roll, I ask Hans again.

"You don't happen to know of any rooms to rent do you? Here in Skalio?"

He fixes me a look, like somehow the fact I don't even have somewhere to stay yet means I've tricked him.

"Not much about, this time of year."

"OK." I try not to feel disappointed. It had already occurred to me that I might need to find somewhere in Kastria, the island's main town, and get a bus down here.

"I have a friend though. He lets out some apartments. In the back of town."

I feel a surge of hope. "In Skalio?"

"Of course in Skalio, where else?" I don't know what this means exactly, but I don't get time to consider it.

"He's a good guy. Klaus. He comes from Germany, like me."

"OK." I wait, again, while Hans seems to consider a little longer, like maybe he's made a mistake.

"You have a handy? A mobile phone?" He pulls out his and reads out a number, then adds me to his contacts.

"I'll give him a message, tell him you're looking," Hans says. We agree too that I'll do my first shift the next afternoon, so I can get used to the bar before it gets too busy at the weekend.

I head back to the hotel feeling pretty pleased with how things have gone. I'm hungry though, so soon I head out again. All the restaurants are open now, some with waiters outside trying to draw the wandering tourists in. I feel a bit self-conscious, being here on my own, but the smells are incredible. In the end I pick the cheapest-looking place, and I order a moussaka, with a salad and a glass of wine. Sometimes, when Mum is in a good mood, she cooks moussaka at home, and I've always loved the richness and the soft aubergines, but this one is way better than anything I've tasted before. It's a bit more expensive than I can really afford, but it's been a good day, and I don't care.

It is weird though, eating alone. I realise at one point that I've never done this before. And I do feel eyes on me. A couple sat a few tables away, a man and a woman. I sense her judging me, somehow disapproving, like it's my fault her husband is glancing over at me when he thinks she's not looking.

Klaus texts me at eight the next morning, just before I head down to breakfast again in the hotel. I arrange to meet him at eleven, in front of what turns out to be one of the less-than-attractive apartment blocks where the bus dropped me off. I had to check out of the hotel by ten-thirty, so I have my backpack with me, and already my T-shirt is wet with sweat.

At ten past eleven there's still no sign of Klaus, and I check several times that I have the right place, but he sent a location on WhatsApp, so if it's wrong, it's not my fault. At twenty past eleven he finally turns up, a wiry, skinny guy who doesn't stop sniffing. Like he's got a cold. Or he's half-fox. He doesn't say anything about being late.

"You're Ava," he tells me, like I wasn't sure. His eyes run me up and down, and he gives a visible shrug, like I've passed some test.

"Apartment's just here." He pulls a huge set of keys from the pockets of his camouflage combat trousers, still sniffing, while he tries to find the right one. I get the sense that, if Hans says he's a good guy, that might mean my new employer isn't the most reliable judge of character.

The apartment is on the ground floor. I hoped it might be higher, perhaps with a view of the sea, or at least a glimpse. But when we go inside, I see this apartment only faces the bins and scrubland at the back of town.

"You're lucky Hans called me," Klaus tells me, as we pause in the main room. It's small, dingy, the walls stained yellow rather than painted. "Very little accommodation in Skalio this time of year. Apart from this, nothing." There's a smell too, old fried food. I try to look for the positives. It's dark because the windows are small, but also because they're covered with semi-translucent netting, I suppose to keep the heat of the summer out. I could always take it down.

"One bedroom, comes furnished," Klaus shows me. "And you have your own toilet." He says this like I ought to consider it a major perk. "Super good location too. Close to the bus station."

"How much is it?" I ask, trying to see if I can stomach living here. It's not exactly nice. But after three years in Sunderland student digs, I've definitely seen worse.

He sucks air through his teeth. "High season coming up..." This seems to pain him, and he shakes his head. "I could fill this place with tourists. Easy."

"Really?" I seriously doubt this, but I back off as a look of annoyance crosses his face. "What's the price?" I ask again instead.

He sniffs. "Because you come from Hans..." He seems to calculate in his mind. "Five hundred a month."

I actually have no idea if this is a good deal or not. But I have my bag on my back, nowhere else to go, and no other leads to follow. Plus I have to work in the bar, starting almost now.

"Can you do it for four hundred?"

It's the first time I've seen him smile.

"You're kidding, right? For a place in Skalio? With a view of the mountains?" He lifts the net curtain, then has to rub at the pane of glass to see through the grime. Politely I move closer to see the view. You *can* see the mountains, if you look beyond the bins.

"Four fifty?"

"Uh huh. Five hundred, and I need an answer now. Got someone else coming to look this afternoon."

Like hell he has.

Klaus looks at his watch, and sniffs again, and I have to make a decision. It's a pretty shitty place, but I can always find somewhere better, once I get myself more established.

"Can I pay weekly? I only have enough to do that right now, but I have a job." After a moment I add: "with Hans."

He shrugs, like this isn't an issue for him.

"No problem."

"OK." I nod, expecting to feel a buzz of success, but it doesn't come. Instead I get a sense that this might be another mistake. But I push it back down, refusing to listen.

"Alright great. I'll take it."

NINE

I don't have time to do much more than drop off my bag before I'm due for my first shift at the Bar Sunset. It's a good thing it isn't busy yet, though. I wasn't entirely honest with Hans that I've worked in bars before. But I've *been* in a lot of bars. It can't be that hard.

Hans shows me around. We stock a couple of international beers, in bottles. There's Heineken and Carlsberg, and then local beers, Mythos and Zeos. Then there's two taps on the bar, which run to barrels in the storeroom at the back.

"You know how to change a line?" he asks, and when I hesitate he shakes his head. "Don't worry. Just keep an eye on them, give me a shout when they're low." I'm not quite sure what this means, but I reason I'll know it when I see it.

He runs quickly through the spirits. We have whisky, brandy, white and dark rum, and then local spirits Metaxa and ouzo.

"There's Raki too, the locals sometimes ask for it."

He watches as I serve the first customers, and it is easy enough. They both ask for beers from the fridge, and all I have to do is pop off the tops. I'm feeling pretty pleased with myself, until another German comes in and orders a Palisberg. At first I don't know what this is, but he helps me by pointing to the tap right in front. The labels face the customers, not me – and I've already forgotten what Hans said was on which. I then make a right mess of pouring it. I watched Hans earlier, and it looked easy, but while his beer was mostly golden liquid, with a smooth head of foam, mine is more foam than beer.

"What the hell is that?" Hans mutters from beside me. "You pouring a beer or a bubble bath?"

He edges me out of the way with his shoulder.

"Hold the glass at an angle. Like this." He shows me, and the beer is perfect. Just a dribble of foam running down the side. The customer raises his eyebrows at Hans, as he takes it from him.

"Try again," Hans passes me another glass. I pour it, and it's not great but better.

"Slower. Control the flow with the pressure."

I do, and this time I'm pleased with my effort.

"So where was this bar you worked in before?" is all Hans says.

After that I try to be proactive. I study the cocktail menu, surreptitiously googling to learn how to make the drinks we offer. I think that Hans hasn't noticed, but when another customer asks for a mojito, he strides across.

"That's white rum, lime juice—"

"Sugar and mint leaves." I brush him out of the way and get on with it. I didn't completely waste my time at university.

The first few hours fly by, but then there's a lull in the customers. Hans sidles over.

"What exactly is a pretty girl like you doing all alone on Alythos?"

The question takes me by surprise, and actually I've almost forgotten, at least for the moment. I've been so focussed on learning the job. I'm cautious though, not sure of how much it's sensible to tell a guy with friends like Klaus.

"I was at university in England," I tell him. "It didn't go too well. So I thought I'd travel for a while, work out what to do next."

"I get that. I only came for one summer. Still here five years later." I think his curiosity is satisfied, but I'm wrong. "The Greek passport? Where'd that come from?"

I might as well say. "My mum. I was actually born on the island."

"Yeah?" He picks at a tooth with a fingernail. "She a local?"

"No... she worked here." I pause. You can see the remains of the resort from here. An empty dark shell a way down the beach. "In the Aegean Dream Resort."

"Seriously?" He seems interested by this, then he gives a gruff laugh. "The Aegean Nightmare Resort, I call it."

I have no idea what he means by this. When he doesn't explain, I ask.

"Why do you call it that?"

"You don't know?" His blond eyebrows rise up his face.

"Know what?"

"What happened at the ADR?"

"No. What happened?" Something about the look on his face unsettles me.

Hans leans against the counter, wiping it down with slow, deliberate strokes, like he's enjoying drawing this out.

"It was before my time. Probably for the best, you know?" I don't but he goes on quickly this time.

"I think it was one of the guests, or maybe one of the staff, I'm not so sure. But he went crazy. Killed like half a dozen people. Cut one woman's head clean off, threw it in the swimming pool when people were still in it."

For a second I think he must be joking, but I can see from his face that he isn't.

"Oh my God."

"You didn't know? I thought you said your mum worked there?"

"She did, but..." I stop. Oh shit. Is *this* why she doesn't talk about it? The idea flares in my mind, that I've had this all wrong, totally misjudged her. But not for long.

"When was she here? Maybe she knew the guy? I think he was English, like you."

"I was born here. So twenty two... years ago?"

Hans shrugs. "Probably not then. This was more recent I think. Ten years or so."

Even so, I'm pretty shocked.

"Is that why it's empty now?"

"Sure. The locals won't work there, not after what happened." He shakes his head. "And it's no good for tourists. You wanna go on holiday to a place where people get decapitated?" He laughs at the thought.

TEN

I finish my shift at ten, and I'm exhausted by the end. I grab a take-away *souvlaki* on the way back, it's this hot spiced meat with salad in a soft, warm pita bread, and it's totally, amazingly delicious, if not the heathiest choice. The arrival at my new home is less wonderful though. It wasn't lovely in the warm midday sun, and now it's dark it's even worse. Even though Klaus told me how hard it is to find anywhere to stay at this time of year, all of the other buildings around mine seem empty and dark.

Inside the apartment I throw all the lights on, to try and cheer it up, but the bulbs are the cheapest, low-watt versions you could possibly get. Probably this is good though, because the place really is filthy. The bed has sheets, that's the good news. The bad news is I don't think they've been washed since last summer. But it's late, and I'm too tired to care too much.

The next morning I head straight down to the harbour for a coffee and breakfast. Then on the way back, I stop by at the supermarket. I'm not working today, so I'm going to clean my house.

The same woman who gave me the tip about the job is

serving again. I remember now that Hans called her Maria. She gives me a friendly smile as I come in, and I smile back. I still don't see how this shop does it, but even though it's tiny, it seems to have everything I need, and somehow it's all arranged exactly where I expect to find it. I buy bathroom cleaner, bleach, rubber gloves and a scrubber, and I even find sheets and lightbulbs. I gather it all and head up to the tills, where Maria is serving an old man. Serving and chatting, I should say. To my slight surprise, they're both speaking English. The man takes a copy from a stack of newspapers.

"So, the old ADR is coming down then?" the man says, glancing at the front page.

"That's what they say," Maria replies. "About time, if it's true."

I'm only half listening, but then I remember Hans used the term ADR for what he called the Aegean Nightmare Resort. The ADR must be what the locals call it.

"No doubt the Mayor will get his piece," the man goes on, and I glance up at him, seeing how this seems to annoy him. Maria simply gives him an indulgent smile.

"No doubt." She seems to be aware of how I have my arms full of products, while the old man looks happy to stand there talking, leaving me waiting with nowhere to put them. "He always does."

Finally the old guy pays, and Maria starts to scan my shopping. The place does have a real old-fashioned feel, but at least she does have a scanner.

"I hear you were successful with Hans," she says, looking up suddenly.

"Oh, yes," I say, then I add, "thank you."

"A pleasure to help. But do watch out with that one."

I'm not sure what she means by that. Or maybe I do. Either way, I hold out my hand. She seems kind.

"I'm Ava."

She stops what she's doing and takes my hand. "Hello, Ava. I'm Maria."

"I know," I say, smiling at the momentary confusion on her face. "Hans told me."

"Ah." She continues to scan my shopping. My eye falls on the newspaper. I hadn't noticed, but there's a picture of the derelict Aegean Dream Resort on the cover. There's not much point me buying a copy though: it's written in the Greek alphabet.

"He told me the story of the old resort," I say, slightly blurting the words out. "It's really shocking."

Her reaction isn't quite what I expect. She nods, but it's like she doesn't fully agree with me.

"Well. It was a long time ago."

"Yeah," I reply. I feel like I've slightly insulted her, which wasn't my intention. I'm curious what the newspaper article is about though.

"What's happening to it now?" I indicate the newspaper.

"Oh." She brightens at this. "There was a planning meeting, last week. They finally agreed to knock it down and replace it with apartments. I expect they'll be too small, and too expensive for local people..." She shrugs. "But you know. It's been a long time," she repeats.

I stand for a moment, wondering about the horrible thing that happened there.

"Hans said the man there was English." I'm not sure why I say this, and Maria looks confused too, which makes me try to clarify. "The man who killed those people? And threw the head in the swimming pool."

"The head in the swimming pool?"

Now I'm confused. "The man killed all those people, and then cut the woman's head off?"

Maria stops now, looking at me closely. "This is what Hans

told you?" She shakes her head. "No, no. Nobody got their head cut off."

I want to know more, but she does too.

"What exactly did he tell you?"

I reply, giving her the story of the man who rampaged around the resort, killing guests and decapitating one woman. Now I have to repeat it, here in the shop, I feel foolish. Even more so as a disapproving frown rises on Maria's face.

"No. That's not what happened. Not what happened at all." She shakes her head again. "It was long before Hans was here, but he clearly has an appetite for a story." I think she's not going to continue, but it seems she's just organising her thoughts.

"It had nothing to do with the swimming pool. And only two people died. Although that's more than enough to qualify as a tragedy, don't you think?"

I don't know. I wait for her to go on.

"The man who died was English, that part is true. And I suppose he must have gone crazy, in some way. Because he was a nice man. A very nice man. Up until he did what he did."

I wait again.

"What exactly did he do?"

She watches me a moment, and I'm not sure if she's going to tell me. But then she shrugs, almost lightly.

"He was the manager of the resort, and one night he killed his girlfriend, apparently. She was a lovely girl who also worked there. She was also the mother of his baby." She shakes her head now. "Then I suppose he couldn't live with the shame of it, so he took his own life right afterwards. Such a horrible thing. A horrible, horrible thing." She falls silent, seemingly lost in thought.

"Apparently?" I ask, because the word snags in my mind. She hesitates still.

"That's what they said. And I suppose they'd know. But

there have been rumours over the years, and it never quite seemed to add up to me. That's forty-four euros please."

My hand jerks to my bag, I'd nearly forgotten where I was. I find my purse and hand over the notes. While she gets my change I find myself asking another question.

"What was it that didn't add up?"

She stops what she's doing and looks at me. I shouldn't have asked. I was just in a good mood this morning, because I'm going to tackle my apartment. I'm about to apologise for prying, when she starts to reply.

"I suppose it's the baby. Normally when you read about these things – these murder-suicides that happen from time to time – the man kills the wife *and* the children. But this time he left the baby alive. I always thought that was strange."

I don't reply to this, and she seems lost in thought again, her hands still holding my change, but doing nothing to hand it over. I see her eyes go to the newspaper, the headline in Greek about how they're finally knocking it down.

"The actual owner of the resort was an Englishman too." Maria seems to come back to life. "He was a nice man as well. He had a house on the island, but his wife refused to stay, after the murder. Then she got ill, back in England, and he wasn't able to reopen the ADR. He was too busy looking after her. We all thought it was going to reopen, at some point. But it never did. Then when he died a few years back, I think there were issues with the will, and it's taken that long to get permission to knock it down and start again." She pulls in a deep breath and finally hands me my change.

"About time. It's been empty more than twenty years." She smiles.

I'm about to say something else, when this catches in my mind.

"Twenty years?"

"Mmmm."

I want to correct her, to tell her that Hans told me it was only ten years since the tragedy, but everything else Hans told me is bullshit. So that makes me pause.

"Are you sure of the date?" I ask instead.

"Oh yes." She looks at me like I'm the crazy one. "It happened the year my daughter was born. And she'll be twenty-three next month."

I open my mouth to reply.

Then I close it again.

My skin prickles. Twenty-three years ago, the manager of the resort murdered his girlfriend and killed himself, leaving their baby behind.

Twenty-two years ago is when my mother was here. Working in the same resort.

And I'm going to be twenty-three next month too.

ELEVEN

When I get back I want to hit Google right away, but the smell of the apartment changes my mind. Instead, I dump my bags in the kitchen and get going with the cleaning.

I start with the bathroom. The sink is stained yellow all over, and there's more alarming yellow splattered around the toilet. I spray everything with bleach and scrub, trying not to think too much about what it is, nor breathe too deeply. The showerhead is crusted with limescale, and when I test it, the water comes out at a weird angle, mostly onto the floor. There's no shower curtain either, just a rail where one used to be. I make a mental note to grab one next time I pass Maria's shop.

Next, the kitchenette. It's not exactly well-equipped. I have three plates, none of which match, and just one mug, although I supplement this with four glasses I "borrowed" from the bar. I have a frying pan, probably older than I am, and which wasn't washed up properly by whoever used it last, so I can almost tell what they cooked. I dump everything in the sink, fill it with hot water and leave it to soak while I clean the insides of the cupboards. Next I tackle the oven, filling a plastic bag with unidentified burnt objects and restoring a degree of clarity to the glass window. One good thing about having the bins so near is I can easily get rid of the waste I'm producing. I wash the crockery now, dry it and put it away, and then wipe the surfaces down.

Then I pull the stupid net curtains off the windows. It occurs to me that maybe Klaus will insist I put them back when I move out, so I stick them in another plastic bag and stick it in a cupboard. Then I clean the windows, inside and out.

By the time I get to the floor, I've given up on being disgusted and just want to get it over with. The first pass with the mop turns the water black, but by the third go, some of the suds remain, and I even see that the floor tiles are terracotta red, or at least used to be. By early afternoon I have the place looking and feeling better. At least I can finally walk around without my feet sticking to the floor.

I save the bed for last. I strip off the questionable sheets Klaus' last tenant left behind and replace them with the ones I bought earlier. The mattress underneath is thin and lumpy, but at least it's not too-obviously stained, which feels like a win at this point.

Finally, I collapse onto the tired two-seater sofa that takes up most of the lounge, exhausted.

Only then do I reach for my phone.

Now I can Google.

Pretty quickly I discover that Maria's version of events is the true one. There isn't a huge amount I can find about the murders, but an old *Guardian* article has most of the details:

British Couple in Apparent Murder-Suicide at Greek Resort

Guardian, 5th August 2001

A British couple working on the Greek island of Alythos were found dead in what local police have described as an apparent murder-suicide.

The bodies of Jason Wright, 34, and Mandy Paul, 27, were discovered early on Sunday morning at the Aegean Dream Resort, where both had been employed. Authorities state that Wright is believed to have fatally attacked Ms. Paul before taking his own life.

The couple's infant child was found unharmed in the residence they shared, and is now in the care of Greek social services.

Local police were alerted after a staff member failed to reach either Wright or Paul on Sunday morning. Upon entering their accommodation, officers discovered Ms. Paul had suffered a blow to the head, and Mr. Wright a self-inflicted gunshot wound.

Greek police are treating the case as a domestic incident that turned violent, but the investigation is ongoing.

The Aegean Dream Resort, popular with British holidaymakers, has announced it will close temporarily following the tragedy. The British Embassy in Athens confirmed it is providing consular support to the guests and remaining staff at the hotel, many of whom have British or American nationality.

Authorities have not disclosed any further details about the circumstances of the deaths, and post-mortem examinations are due to take place later this week.

The dates interest me. The murder happened on 25 June 2001, and I was born six weeks before that, on 6 May. So I suppose that Mum wouldn't have been working then – I mean, I guess she'd have been on maternity leave, or whatever it's called here. But even so, maybe she'd have known the people who died? That would have been horrible. But at the same time, is it really enough to explain why she's never told me anything about this? It still strikes me as odd.

I keep searching around, trying to find more information, but it was a long time ago, and maybe murder-suicides are quite common, or at least common enough that it's not big news. Either way, I don't find anything else, except this one strange blog post, which is much more recent, but at least refers to the murders:

Posted by: IslandTruths | 14 April 2024

Well, it's finally happening.

After two decades of crumbling concrete and broken promises, they're knocking down the ADR – the Aegean Dream Resort. And what's going up in its place? Affordable housing for islanders? A school? A clinic?

Don't make me laugh.

It's luxury apartments. Which, if you know Alythos, means overpriced ghost homes for rich Athenians and foreign investors. Built quick and sold quicker, empty nine months of the year.

But let's talk about what no one else will: why the ADR really closed in the first place.

The official story is the tragic murder-suicide in 2001. Resort manager Jason Wright killed his girlfriend, Mandy Paul, then turned his gun on himself, leaving their little baby alive. Case closed.

Except, as almost everyone who was there back then knows, it probably isn't the whole story.

Because – what about the drugs flooding the island at the time? Were they connected? Where did Jason get the gun? And what about all the ADR staff, flown home right after the deaths, instead of giving their stories to the police?

The investigation was never done properly, and now we'll never get the truth because the whole place is about to be bulldozed into silence.

I don't really know what this means, or at least, there's a lot of it I don't understand. But I am starting to understand one point. Whatever happened all those years ago to the resort manager – whether he went crazy and killed his girlfriend, or even if someone set it up to look like that but really he was murdered too – it's nothing to do with why *I'm* here. I'm just here to find out where I came from. Who I am. Maybe even who my dad is. So whatever happened back then at the ADR – it doesn't matter now. It has nothing to do with me.

And I feel a lot better when I work that out. Like I can concentrate on my issues. And not worry about other people's problems buried in the past.

TWELVE

The next day I head out for breakfast, armed with the photograph I stole of Mum and Imogen standing by the sign for the old Aegean Dream Resort. I pick a cafe with a terrace and sun umbrellas giving just enough shade, order a croissant and coffee, and try to get my head in the right place.

I still feel confident. But I'm nervous too – not about what I might find, but about actually doing it. Walking up to strangers and asking about something that happened twenty years ago. It's the sort of thing that looks easy on TV, but the thought of actually doing it feels weird. What if they ask why I'm asking? What do I say to that?

There's something else too. A deeper feeling. I think it's because I've spent my whole life being told – or just understanding – that I'm not supposed to know about this part of Mum's past. That it's off-limits. Not my business. Even though it's literally all about me.

But this is what I came here to do. So I skip the idea of a second coffee and make myself stand up. I walk to the bar to pay, and the waiter who served me follows. When I tap my phone on the reader and the payment goes through, he smiles politely – like we're done.

But we're not.

"Um, excuse me," I say. "Can I ask you something?"

His eyebrows go up. I realise I have no idea if he speaks any English beyond "coffee" and "croissant".

"Yes?"

I slide the photograph onto the bar, holding my breath. It looks strange sitting there, on the old chestnut wood.

"This is a picture of my mum. She worked here, twenty-two years ago. I wondered if you might remember her? Or know anything about her?"

He looks at me like I'm stupid, and immediately I feel like I must be. This guy's only about ten years older than I am. He'd be, what, ten years old when Mum was here? Of course he's not going to remember her. But even so he leans in for a better look. And he looks for a long time. After a moment I can sense what he's thinking. Like I said before, both Mum and Imogen look stunning in the picture. I wait, growing impatient as the waiter continues to peer down at the photograph, but eventually he looks up.

"No, sorry, I don't know."

I nod and thank him, moving to pick the photograph up, but he stops me.

"This one is your mother, no?" he says, stabbing a finger at the photograph.

"Yes." I smile awkwardly, then correct myself when I see where he's pointing. "No, the other one. This one." I point at Mum.

"Very beautiful," the waiter says. "Very beautiful girl."

"Thank you," I say, picking the photo up this time, and feeling my cheeks flush as I do so.

So, that was a good start then.

. . .

But I don't give up. Holding the photograph facing towards me, I walk hesitantly along the seafront area, looking for more targets. There's a few people around, some who look like tourists, and others who I take for locals – or at least people who are living and working here on the island. I try to find some older people, because at least they will have been old enough to remember Mum when she was here. I spot an older man, maybe in his sixties? He's walking towards me with a tracksuit on, fast walking, like he's training for something. Again I tell myself to be brave and just do this.

"Excuse me." I hold out the photograph in front of him, forcing him to slow and stop. "I was wondering if you might recognise the people in this photograph?"

He frowns, clearly annoyed, and then he puts his hand to his ear, and I realise too late that he has earbuds in, and hasn't heard a word of my question. So I try it again.

"I'm sorry to interrupt you, but do you know either of the people in this photograph?"

His response this time is a rapid flow of Greek, none of which I understand.

"These people..." I point at Mum in the photo. "Do you know them?"

More Greek, he sounds more annoyed this time. I step back.

"Sorry." The man puts his earbud back in and goes on his way, shaking his fist now.

Damn it. This is kind of hard.

Even though there's very few people around, it feels like everyone is watching me now, and either laughing, or judgemental of how I'm spoiling everyone's day. But I've come this far, so I try again, with a woman who clearly noticed what happened with the exercising man. She turns out to be Dutch, and takes a good look at the photograph, but tells me she's only been on the island for seven years, and doesn't know my mum. I stop another older man, carrying a fishing rod and bucket – but at least he doesn't have earbuds. His English isn't very good, but he does look at the photo, and at least appears to consider whether he recognises Mum. But in the end he too shakes his head. He tells me, in broken English, that many people come to work on the island, but they usually don't stay long. I thank him, and glance into the bucket. There's an octopus in there, its arms and suckers still moving. He notices me looking and holds it up, as if he expects I'll want a better look, but I don't. I smile and step back instead.

By now I've moved well away from the harbour, and along the seafront, down towards where the town stops. It's basically a long line of restaurants, Aetos Diving, the water sports centre I saw the other day, and then a few bars, with my one at the end. I can see Hans is there already, getting ready to open later on, but I know there's no point asking him. But then I think about the lady in the shop – Maria. She knew the truth about what happened at the Aegean Dream Resort, so she's probably a good person to ask about this too. Although I'm not exactly sure what I think she might be able to tell me.

I cram this doubt back in its box and set off at a much faster pace, back along the seafront and then inland, towards the supermarket. On the way I wonder if it will be open still, but it is, and I'm relieved to see that Maria is there again. Half-relieved and half anxious all over again.

"Hello." She smiles a welcome. I remember my need for a shower curtain, and use that as an excuse to start a conversation.

"Over there." She points to a couple hanging from hooks by the stationery section. I take one and bring it to the till.

"How did the cleaning go?"

"Oh, good thank you." Before I lose my nerve I pull the photograph out and hold it up to her. "This is a really strange question, but I wonder if you happen to remember the woman in this photograph? I'm trying to find out more about her."

Maria looks at me first, then picks up a pair of spectacles and fixes them carefully in place. Then she takes my hand, pulling it and the photograph closer. She looks for a long time.

"May I ask why you're interested?" she says, after a few moments.

"Oh. Yes, of course." How do I say this? There's only one way really.

"She's my mother. I'm trying to find out more about her."

Maria looks at me a long time after that, without speaking. She has big brown eyes, and they blink slowly, like she's assessing me carefully.

"I'm sorry, has she passed away?"

"Oh! No..." I stop. This is hard to explain, and maybe it's easier not to. "Not exactly. It's just, complicated. I was born here on the island and I'm trying to find out more about it. About me." I try to smile, but feel my cheeks heating up again, and I'm frustrated. If I want to find out about Mum, why don't I just ask her? Because it's not that easy. I don't know. But Maria doesn't seem to pass judgement. Instead she looks again at the photograph, drawing in a deep sigh.

"There are many people who come to the island, every summer," she tells me, like the other guy did, down at the beach. Maria shakes her head. "It's very hard to remember every face – and I have a good memory for faces."

She looks at me again, and I think about the story she told me about the Aegean Dream Resort. Does she think that's what I'm really interested in? That I'm some kind of weird horror-story enthusiast? If so she doesn't say that.

"I'm afraid I don't remember either girl, I'm sorry." I'm about to nod and think who else I could ask, when she goes on.

"But the man here..." She points to the gardens in the background of the image. There's a figure there. I'd noticed him before, because he looks kind of hot, even though you can't see his face. "I think this is Kostas. When he was younger he worked as a gardener for the ADR, before it closed." She smiles, like she expects I'll recognise the name.

"Kostas?"

"Kostas Aetos. Aetos Diving? Down on the seafront. You can't miss it."

THIRTEEN

Aetos Diving is a cool-looking place, clean and ordered, and obviously busy. Out in front it has a jetty, with two large rigid-inflatable boats moored on it. Each of them has two shiny black engines fitted to the back. Some of the people walking around have a purposeful air, and they're wearing T-shirts with the word TEAM on the back, which kind of gives away that they work here. Others, looking slightly awkward in wetsuits, I guess are customers. There's no one that looks like an older version of the man in my photo.

I step inside the centre. It feels modern, with a big Mac computer on the reception desk. The girl working behind it glances up as I come in and gives me a friendly smile, but she's on the phone, so I wait, looking around some more. There's a rack of stand-up paddleboards leaning against one wall. Another has dozens of metallic air tanks, and tubes that I suppose are there to fill them up. On a rack high up – out of easy reach, I suppose – there's a few spear guns, which look kind of frightening. There's a noticeboard too, where hundreds of photographs have been pinned up. I move closer to take a look while the girl's on the phone. Some are underwater: divers, fish, a wreck of some sort, and some ruins. Others are on the water, but it's all to do with the sea. In a lot of the photos I see a man with a thick dark beard and a stern expression. I look at every photo, and there's not a single one where he's doing anything other than scowling. Unfortunately, it's pretty obvious he's Kostas.

"Hi there, can I help?" I turn to see the reception girl has finished with the phone. She's about my age. Her short black hair is streaked with green – unusual, but it suits her. She's pretty.

I step closer, and I can see over the counter now, at her desk strewn with paperwork.

"I was..." – how to put this? – "Is Kostas here?"

"Kostas...?" She looks momentarily uncertain. "He is, but..." She glances behind me, at a closed door I hadn't noticed. "He's a little busy this morning, we have to register everything with the safety board." Her voice has an American lilt to it. "What's it about, can I help?"

"Um." I feel the same anxiety as before. Why is this so difficult?

She smiles curiously as I hesitate, the corners of her eyes crinkling in a way that's engaging. I smile, like it's nothing really.

"I wanted to ask him about someone who came to the island, about twenty years ago. I was told he might know them."

"Oh, right." She considers this for a few moments. "OK, well that's... odd." She thinks for a moment, then brightens. "I could go see if he's OK to talk? He might like a break." She gives me a grin. "He gets so pissed off with how slow the website is. Like, we have a super-fast connection here, but it's a government website and they're *so* slow. You know what I mean?"

I nod, and she looks towards the office, but doesn't walk over there yet.

"You're Ava, right?"

"Um. Yeah. How did you know?"

"You started working at Hans's place. It's kind of a small island." She gives an apologetic shrug. "You're from England?"

"Yeah." I hesitate now, then something about her manner, how friendly she is, makes me go on. "Actually I was born on the island. That's what I want to ask Kostas about. Whether he maybe knew my mother? Whether he can tell me anything about her time here." I don't mention my father, somehow that feels a step too far.

"Oh wow," the girl says. "Well I don't know. He's been here for years, so it's possible." Then she holds out her hand.

"I'm Sophia, by the way. Nice to meet you."

I shake her hand, her skin is soft, supple. She smiles at me for a moment, then it disappears.

"That sounds pretty heavy," she goes on. "Is she dead? Your mum? I'm sorry—"

"No." I shake my head quickly, then smile. "You're actually the second person to ask me." I pull in a breath. "She's not dead, it's just I can't ask her about this."

"Oh." Sophia looks at me strangely for a moment, but doesn't push it. "But that's why you've come out here? To find out about her?"

"Yeah." I bite my lip. "That, and because it's just a really nice place."

She smiles at this. "Yeah. It is." She glances towards the office again, but still doesn't move.

"So where are you from?" I ask. "Are you American?"

She laughs at this and screws up her nose. "No. I just grew up watching a lot of American TV. No, I'm from here."

I feel a bit – I don't know, foolish, when she says this. Because even if I was born here, really I'm just a foreigner while she's properly from the island. I sense she picks up on it too, and she's back to business.

"Let me go and see if he's in a mood to talk." She raises her eyebrows and starts to move from behind the desk, and I change my mind at once. My gaze goes to the noticeboard, the stern-looking man in the photos.

"No, it's alright, if it's not a good time—"

"No." Sophia holds up her hand to stop me. And she seems to read my mind. "Kostas looks scarier than he really is. Believe me." She touches me lightly on the shoulder as she moves past to the office door. Before I can do anything to stop her, she knocks and pushes the door open at the same time. She disappears inside. I hear classical music, and then voices – Sophia and Kostas presumably – but they're speaking in Greek. A few moments later Sophia comes back out, leaving the door open this time.

"Yeah, he's got a moment." She offers me a supportive smile. "You can go in."

The music drifts from the open door. Soft, soothing, somehow at odds with the man in the photographs.

I press my fingers against the photograph in my pocket, which captured Kostas all those years ago.

"Yeah. OK – thanks."

I take a breath and step inside.

FOURTEEN

I slip into the office and see Kostas at once, seated behind another Mac computer, his eyes tight with frustration as he stares at the screen. Something about him makes me shut the door behind me. It's like visiting the headmaster.

"Yes?" He doesn't offer a seat.

I step forward, already feeling my words tumble out too fast. "I'm um... I'm sorry to bother you. I have a photograph of my mother, here on the island, before I was born. I'm trying to find out about her time here. I was told you might be in it too." I pause, I hope he speaks English, I should have asked Sophia. "In the photograph?"

His eyes narrow further. But he holds out a hand, silently indicating the chair in front of him. I sit in it, but his hand doesn't move, and I suddenly realise he was actually asking for the photo.

Shit. "Sorry," I mutter, as I get back to my feet, reaching into my pocket for the photograph. His hand doesn't move, he just waits impatiently, his black eyes not leaving my face. I find it and hand it over.

Now Kostas looks carefully at the image. His expression

doesn't change, but he scratches absently at his beard. Then he looks up at me, a questioning look on his face.

"Um, I was told that this might be you?" I lean forward and point at the figure in the background, the gardener. "Could it be?"

He studies me for a long moment before his eyes return to the image. Finally he meets my eyes again.

"Why do you ask this?"

I launch again into my now familiar speech. "I've come to the island to try and find out more about my mother."

"Your mother? Which one?"

I realise his English is just fine. More of a local accent than Sophia, but he understands me at least.

"The blonde girl. Obviously she's much older now," I say with a stupid laugh and then I get myself under control. "Her name is Karen Whitaker." Then I add, because he's still sitting there in silence, staring at me. "Do you maybe remember her? Do you know anything about her?"

He stays silent a while longer. It's odd. His beard is so thick and dark that there's a blackness to his face. It changes when he opens his mouth, showing ruby-red lips.

"When was this taken?"

"Um. I think it was the summer of 2000."

He absorbs this without reaction, but after a while he responds.

"This is out by the old Aegean Dream Resort. It closed in 2001," he says.

"Yes. I know."

His eyes narrow a little now, perhaps with curiosity. "You know what happened there?"

"Yes. The murder?"

Now he really stares, his eyes narrow and searching my face. They then flick to the door, like he's checking it's shut. When he speaks again his voice is a growl.

"Who said this was me?"

I don't know what it is, but I don't want to tell him about Maria. It's silly, I know, but at the same time it would make sense that I don't know the names of the people I've been speaking too.

"I'm not sure of their name."

Please don't ask me to describe them, I think.

He doesn't, thank God. Instead he just offers a half-shrug.

"This is me. I worked there for some years. I was part of the gardening team." He watches me closely. He seems very confused, almost suspicious. "What is it you want to know?"

But it's the first success I've had, and it thrills me. Finally I'm getting somewhere. "I wondered if you might remember my mother. She's the blonde one," I say again, trying to keep my hopes low but feeling them soar. But he doesn't react again, he just examines the photograph, scowling at it some more.

"Do you... do you remember her?"

It looks as though he's trying hard to remember something, or work something out. I'm not sure which.

"She came back the year after as well, in 2001, and she was pregnant then, and obviously..." I smile, because maybe it's only obvious to me. "She would have given birth, in May. To me. That's why I'm trying to find out about it. I don't know much about that time. I don't know if she was still working at the resort."

I don't notice exactly when he does it – because I'm gabbling now – but at some point he must have looked up at me, because when I've finished he's still staring at me.

"You said *pregnant?*"

"Yes."

He stares at the photograph again, seemingly lost in thought.

"Has she... passed away, this woman? Your mother?"

"No it's..." I stop. "It's complicated, but I can't ask her about it."

I feel him examining me. Eventually he nods, as if he understands. Or it's not his problem. Again I'm not sure which.

"So... do you remember her at all? Like I said, her name is Karen Whitaker, I think she worked in the pool bar at the resort, and the other woman is an American, Imogen—"

"No." Just with one word he completely cuts me off. My mouth hangs open a moment, until I quietly shut it.

"I am very busy this morning. Safety registration. Everything has to be put into this... very irritating website, no?" He takes a deep breath into his broad chest. I wait, not sure how this is relevant to me. "But I cannot help you. I do not know these people." He stops again, and he studies me a while longer, like there's something about me he's trying to understand. But whatever he's thinking, he doesn't tell me. He holds the photograph out for me to take, dismissive now.

I hesitate though. Something makes me want to push, yet there's no way to do so. Instead I take the photo, thank him and find my feet taking me outside, pulling the door shut behind me. As I do so I glance across, and see him scowling at me again. I take a moment, staring at the closed door. I feel somehow humiliated. I've never done diving, but this feels a bit like walking out of a pressure chamber.

Sophia is back behind her desk but watching with interest.

"How'd it go?"

I think a second, then shrug. "Not so good. He didn't know anything."

Her face falls, as if she's somehow become personally invested in my quest.

"Well, who are you trying next?"

It's a good question, and I hold out my arms in a shrug. "I don't know. Kostas was like, my only good lead."

She smiles again, like this is her idea of fun. "Why did you think Kostas might know your mother anyway?"

I tell her about the photograph, and because she looks so intrigued, I show it to her too, even though she'd be way too young to know anyone from that time.

"The ADR?" she says at once, seeing the sign that Mum and Imogen are standing under.

"That's right. She used to work there."

Sophia replies at once. "OK, well I know who you should speak to next then."

"Who?"

"There's a writer guy, he lives up on the mountain. He's kind of a creep, but he used to work at the ADR, right up until it closed. So he'll definitely know something."

FIFTEEN

"A writer guy?" I ask.

"Yeah. Duncan. Gregory Duncan?"

Sophia waits to see if I know him, but the name means nothing.

"I've never heard of him."

"Don't worry," she laughs again. The contrast between her easy manner and Kostas' stern reserve is striking, I can feel myself relax into her presence.

"He's not like a famous author or anything, though he thinks he is." She grins. "He lives up in the hills. So that he can look down on everyone. Like, literally and metaphorically. Come." She takes my arm and leads me to the open front of the dive centre. I'm surprised at how easily she's assumed it's OK to touch me, but also, I don't really mind.

"Up there." She points up towards the mountainous interior of the island. I can't see what I'm supposed to be looking at to begin with, but then I see a house. Maybe less impressive looking than I was expecting.

"That's him."

"OK." I try to think. *I'm not working today.*

"You think he might be there now?"

Sophia shrugs. "I dunno. Probably. Sometimes he comes into town and sits in the restaurant, writing on his laptop. Over there." She points again, towards the place opposite. It's one of the more expensive restaurants, where I didn't eat the other night.

"But he's not there now, so maybe he's home?" She looks hopeful on my behalf.

"OK," I say again, and glance back at the house. It's a long way away. Up a pretty big hill.

"Is there – like a bus or something?"

She grins again. "Up there? What do you think?" She bites her lip teasingly.

"How about taxis?" I ask. I don't much like the thought of this as it'll be expensive. And even with my job I'm burning through cash faster than I'm earning it.

"No... I mean there are, but they'd have to come from Kastria, and then take you up there, it'd cost a bomb." Sophia glances at me again, looking thoughtful. "But if you like, you can borrow my moped? I'm stuck here helping Kostas the whole day, with this stupid website."

"Wow. Are you sure?" The offer seems absurdly generous, but she lifts a hand to dismiss it.

"Sure I'm sure."

"That's amazing."

"Actually, have you ridden one before?"

"Oh. Shit." I didn't think of this. "No, I haven't."

She frowns, but just for a second. "OK, well don't worry, it's super easy. You can ride a bike, right?"

"Yeah." I haven't though, not in a long while.

"It's basically the same. Just... faster." She roots in the pocket of her jeans shorts, and pulls out a little silver key. The keyring has a green plastic alien. She holds it out to me.

"Come on, take it. I trust you." There's a strange expression on her lips as she waits for my decision. Then I take the keys.

"Thanks. Thanks a lot."

"You're welcome," she says, in her American Greek English. "And good luck with Duncan. You'll need it."

SIXTEEN

There's a helmet dangling from the handlebar of the little moped, and I pull it on, fastening the strap under my chin. Then I feel the weight of the bike as I rock it backwards off its stand. It's heavier than I expected. I glance back at Sophia, who is now stood in the doorway, arms folded and grinning.

"Don't worry, you'll get the hang of it," she calls out. "Oh, and it pulls to the left when you brake hard, so don't brake hard."

Great. Now she tells me. But she seems to sense my nervousness, and walks over to give me a thirty-second lesson on how to ride the thing. It has no gears thankfully, so you just twist the handlebar grip to go and squeeze the brake to stop. Just not too hard.

"Go on, you'll be fine," she says.

I climb on and press the starter. It roars into life and after a moment I twist the throttle. The moped lurches forward, throwing me backwards so that I overcorrect, squeezing the brakes too hard. I shudder to a stop, and I plant my feet on the ground, my heart racing.

Sophia calls out again. "Try a little less throttle," she says thoughtfully.

The next time I'm too easy on the throttle, and I roll forward so slow I have to use my legs to keep me upright. So I twist a little more, and then finally I find a balance. It's not so hard. I pull onto the road that runs along the seafront and do a little test one way, then slow and come back the other.

"See, I told you!" Sophia says, and I turn again, so I'm pointing the right way. I go to reply to her, but I see Kostas behind her, and she simply raises a hand and goes back inside the centre. So instead I just set off, down the street this time. And all at once it's glorious. I've walked this route so many times now, and it's difficult in the heat. But on the moped the buildings zip by, the air feels wonderful on my bare arms, fresh but warm. I have to resist the urge to call out, like an excited child on a fairground ride.

Sophia told me the route up to the villa where Gregory lives, but it would be easy to guess anyway. There's really only one road, and I can see it snaking out in front of me.

I clear the town and the road opens up a little, and so do I. The moped's motor hums beneath me, the sun is warm on my arms, and the scent of pine, olive and thyme floods past. I could get so used to this.

About a mile further on, I reach the beginning of the hill, and ahead of me I see a tractor that's taking up most of the road. I start to slow, but then I don't need to as the driver, an old guy, turns around and sees me, then indicates with his arm that he'll putt across to the right to let me pass. I move to the left side of the road to maximise the space, but then suddenly the tractor does the same, so the road is blocked. I have no choice then but to brake hard, and just as Sophia said, the moped pulls violently to one side, nearly throwing me off before I come to a shuddering halt.

For a second I can almost feel the damage I would have

done to myself had my bare skin scraped across the rough road surface, but I didn't, and now the tractor moves aside again. This time the driver raises his hand in apology, and I see what the problem was: a cat lying asleep in the road. It gets up now, and lazily walks away, like it played no part in the little drama. The tractor driver shouts something at me now, in Greek so I don't understand. He might be apologising, he might be telling me off for driving too fast. Either way, I carefully pass him and carry on up the hill.

I need a moment though before I get to this guy's house, and I stop at a little layby where the road widens. It's kind of a viewpoint, and I stop the moped here, pull it back on its stand and walk to the edge. Here I see the whole of Skalios Bay laid out beneath me. I can see the dozen or so streets of the town, even make out my apartment building, the little supermarket and Hans's bar – but from up here they're all tiny, like models, and dwarfed by the dazzling blue sea. From up here the distant islands look closer too, though they're still shrouded in a haze which gives them an almost ghostly appearance. But despite the almost absurd beauty of the place, there's one thing that seems wrong. It's the remains of the Aegean Dream Resort. I can clearly make out the dirty blue of its empty pool, and from up here I see that some of the old accommodation block no longer has its roof. It's like an ugly scar on an otherwise beautiful face. I stare out for a while, then hear the noise of the tractor, following me up the road. I don't want to have to overtake again, so I get going, and then around the next corner I'm at Duncan's house.

Up close, it's kind of an odd place. Even less impressive than I'd assumed from a distance. Maybe it was once some sort of agricultural building, like a place for goats or sheep, but it's been rebuilt as a home, except not quite finished. And then maybe not maintained very well either. The guy's car is here though, another white Fiat that everyone here seems to drive. At least I assume it's Duncan's. There's something about the place that tells me he lives alone. I draw in a deep breath, filling my lungs with the scent of mountain pine. I still don't really know what I'm going to ask this guy, but I have to try.

There's quite a long wait between when I knock on the door and when it opens, and I hear him inside. It sounds like he's grumbling, but I'm not sure because he's speaking in Greek. Finally it opens and he stares at me. No smile, just a stare, his eyes magnified by thick glasses.

"*Neh?*"

I frown for a second, till I remember that's Greek for "yes".

"Hello, erm... Mr Duncan?" Sophia did tell me he was English, or has he gone full local?

His face is guarded, suspicious. "Who are you? What do you want?"

"I'm sorry to bother you," I begin, trying to slow down my speech so I don't gabble like I did with Kostas. "I was told you used to work at the Aegean Dream Resort, just before it closed, and I wanted to ask some questions about it."

"You're a journalist?" he asks, his eyes narrow behind the lenses.

"No, I'm..." There's no putting this off. "My mother used to work at the resort. In 2001, when it closed. I'm trying to find out more about that time."

He frowns deeply now, pulling the door open a little more, but only so he can see me better. He seems to take a long time processing what I've just said.

"Your mother?"

"Yes."

He cocks his head on one side. He's very tall, and I'm reminded of a heron, stalking through a river trying to catch fish.

"Why? And why would I have known her?"

"Um." I decide to answer the second question. "You used to work there? That's what I was told."

Unlike Kostas he doesn't ask who told me, so I push the point.

"I was told you'd be a good person to speak to."

He accepts this with a grunt, like he agrees with the theory. But he doesn't answer, and we just stand there for a while, me on the doorstep and him still inside, until I speak again.

"I'm sorry if I've disturbed you. If you were writing?"

"Well, yes," he replies at once. "Yes, I was, and you are rather..." He looks out past me, a vexed expression on his face. "I'm sorry, what did you say your name was?"

"Ava," I swallow. "Ava Whitaker."

At this he seems to freeze. Behind the lens of his glasses his eyes blink several times. Then one of the eyes twitches, pulling his whole face into a strange spasm.

"Whitaker?"

"Yes."

He blinks again, then breaks into a nervous-looking smile.

"I'm sorry, that means nothing to me. Good day to you."

He goes to shut the door on me, but there's something about his manner that made me expect this, and I throw myself forward, my hand stopping him from doing so.

"Wait! Please."

He stops again, eyeing me now with clear anxiety. I'm not sure why, and I have no idea what to say next.

"Please help me, I have no one else to ask." I give him my best pleading look, trying to make myself seem as vulnerable and appealing as possible. "Please could you just take a look at this photograph? See if she looks familiar?"

He seems to take an age considering. Then behind me I hear a juddering noise. I don't even really notice it at first, but I see his eyes focus on something behind me. It's the tractor, the one I overtook on the way up. It's finally got here, and now it seems to be stopping. The driver kills the engine and the noise stops. There's a fence opposite Duncan's house, and the driver ambles over to it, yanking at the wooden structure and finding a bit that's broken. Then he whistles as he goes back to the tractor for some tools. As he does he seems to notice me – or maybe Duncan – it's hard to see, but he raises a hand in greeting either way. I turn back to the writer,

"Please Mr Duncan?"

Slowly his eyes come back to me and my hand, still preventing him from closing the door. There's a look on his face that's odd, he looks scared.

"I'll look. But not here. It's better if we go inside. Quickly."

Without waiting for an answer he pulls the door open and stands back so that I can walk past him. The change is startling, and there's a moment when I consider whether this might be a bad idea. But I can't exactly say no now. I take a deep breath.

"Thank you," I say, and step inside.

SEVENTEEN

I try to look around, but the place is pretty dark.

"Would you like a drink? Some tap water perhaps?"

I don't, but I say yes anyway and follow Duncan into his kitchen. It's quite small, and he obviously hasn't cleaned up from breakfast, nor last night's dinner. This seems to embarrass him, and he tidies away a half empty bottle of wine, a plate that goes into the sink. This seems to give him second thoughts about the tap water and he goes to the fridge instead. His hand hesitates by a bottle of Diet Coke, but it's mineral water he takes out.

"The water here's fine to drink," – he gives a nervous laugh – "but it comes out warm, so I fill this from the tap."

"That's fine, thank you," I say, as he looks for a clean glass. As he pours I look around some more. There's an open door leading off to some sort of study where I can see his computer screen, sat on a wooden desk. I can see the cursor blinking at the bottom of a page of text. I guess I really did interrupt his writing. On the walls are framed pictures of what I suppose are the covers of his books. And pencil sketches too. Views of the island maybe – landscapes anyway, and a pencil sketch of a girl, just inside the door. They're all quite good, the portrait especially, but maybe not *quite* good enough to justify hanging on the wall?

"The problem is island infrastructure is very poor," he goes on, not making eye contact with me. "And with the heat... unbearable. Especially in the summer. It's essential to keep hydrated." I realise he's still talking about the water, so I take a sip. I feel a strange need to put him at ease, not for my sake exactly but... I notice on the table there are five pencils, a sharpener and a pile of shavings. He's made them all the exact same length.

He laughs again, the same anxious sound.

"I apologise if I seemed rude – or awkward – outside." He speaks cautiously, one hand fiddling with the button on his shirt. "I was... writing, you see. When you knocked? It can be challenging to be pulled so suddenly out of one world and into another. So to speak."

"Sure. Of course. I'm really sorry to disturb you." I'm kind of regretting coming in here, and it feels rude not to ask, so I do. "What were you writing?

For a moment he looks at me like this might be a trick question, and then he gives his laugh again.

"Haha!" He tries a smile, but one side of his face doesn't move. "I was..." – his tongue comes out of his mouth and licks all the way around his lips – "defusing a bomb in a bank vault in Geneva. Well, *I* wasn't," he clarifies, relaxing a little now. "My *protagonist* was. We were literally seconds away from it detonating, when you appeared. Perhaps if I look a little startled, that will explain it?"

"Of course." The way he talks about "we" is totally weird. But I make myself smile encouragingly.

I pause, and now I notice on the kitchen table a stack of three identical paperbacks. I sense he's not going to tell me anything until he relaxes, and this seems the way to make it happen. "Is that yours?" I pick one up, turn it around to see the cover: *The Shadow of Theseus*.

I may have got that wrong, he looks like I've just pulled a gun on him. But he gives his nervous laugh again. "Yes, my latest."

"It looks..." I think what to say. I've started down this path so I might as well continue. "Amazing."

He laughs again, but then waits, like I'm holding some valuable treasure and he expects me to study it some more. So I do. I turn it over and scan the blurb:

When British historian Daniel Mercer is sent a mysterious letter, written in an ancient language that nobody on earth still speaks, he travels to Greece to try and find the key to unlock the mystery. But as he journeys through the ancient landscapes, his personal history begins to unravel around him. What if the woman who left him could now be trying to hunt him down?

"That actually sounds really good," I say again. I kind of mean it too.

"Yes, well. Thank you." His eyes dart onto mine, and then away again. He watches the book, until I put it back down.

"But you didn't come here for books?" It's half a question but he doesn't give me a chance to answer it. "How exactly do you think I can help?"

I pull out my photograph, then hand it over to him.

"I'm trying to find out more about my mother's time on the island," I explain. "I know I was born here, but I don't know much else. I was wondering if you might have known them. If you could tell me anything."

He doesn't say anything but studies the photograph for a while. A couple of times he looks up at me, then back down at the image. He turns the photograph over, examining the back, and then coughs when he sees the date written there.

"Your mother..." he begins, speaking carefully. "What was her name? May I ask?"

"Karen." I smile hopefully. "Karen Whitaker."

It's not exactly a look of recognition, but the name seems to do something to him. He gives his nervous laugh again. Then he walks to his office door and casually pulls it shut.

"Well, I did work at the resort." He speaks slowly as he crosses the room back towards me. "I suppose anybody here will tell you that. I'm rather well known on the island..." He hesitates, and goes on when he sees I don't really understand that.

"The books. There are not many authors on Alythos," he says, "much less published ones, so people tend to know me."

"And do you know her? Karen Whitaker?" I ask. He peers at me now through his glasses, but after a moment he shakes his head.

"I don't recall. I'm sorry."

"The other woman is called Imogen Grant. Maybe you remember her?"

There's something weird about his reaction again, but I don't know what. It's like he's thinking I'm somehow testing him, and he doesn't know why.

"Imogen?"

"Yes."

"*Imogen?*" He repeats the name to himself, half under his breath, staring now at the wall.

I watch him, as various emotions undulate across his face. This guy would either be hopeless or amazing at poker, because I can see he's thinking something, but I don't know what. He goes back to studying the photo again. When he looks up he seems defeated. He shakes his head sadly.

"No, I'm sorry..." He screws his eyes shut, stays that way a moment, then opens them again and looks at me. "It's *possible* I remember that name, but... barely. You know?" He stares at me, like he's hoping I'll accept that.

"Are you sure?" I ask, disappointed. At one point today it felt like I might actually get somewhere with the search. Now it seems every lead has gone nowhere.

"Yes. I do apologise. There's nothing I can say that will help you." He hands me the photograph. "And now if you will excuse me, we do have to get back to our story. I cannot leave myself in the bank vault for ever, the police are on their way."

I don't want to take the photo, but I can't not. And I can't think of anything else to ask him, if he won't tell me. But even so, I'm certain that he knows something. More than he's saying. I'm just not sure quite why, or what.

EIGHTEEN

When I get back to the dive centre it's bustling, busier than before. I spot Sophia, but she's deep in conversation with a group of customers, occasionally pausing to haul one of the air tanks onto a trolley, which I suppose will go down to the boats. She catches my eye for a second, offers a quick nod, but doesn't have time for more.

I set the key down behind her desk, suddenly unsure of what to do with myself.

I don't want to go back to my apartment. Instead, I just walk.

I follow the shoreline, past Bar Sunset and out towards the old Aegean Dream Resort. But I don't stop there this time. I know what it is now – an empty, gutted shell of a place, that shouldn't still be here but is. Instead, I just keep going, following the curve of the beach.

I keep on, right until the end of Skalios Bay, where the soft sand gives way to a rocky cliff where a path has been worn upwards by untold numbers of feet. I take it, wishing I'd put on better footwear, but not really caring because the rocks have mostly been polished smooth. I come up onto the clifftop, the water below me a thousand shades of turquoise and in some places emerald green.

But I'm not really looking at the views. Instead, I'm thinking. About what I'm doing here, and if I'm ever going to find anything out. Why did Kostas seem so... suspicious of me? And Gregory Duncan was clearly nervous about something, but what? Or is he just a nervous guy? Someone who's not used to visitors, who lives alone and writes his books and people like Sophia think of as a creep? I don't know. Most of all, why is it that Mum has always been so secretive about her time here? Or have I got that wrong too? Have I always had it wrong? Perhaps there's no secret, I'm just something that happened a long time ago when she was young and careless, and she wants to put it behind her – put it behind *us*, and move forward with our lives? Would that be so bad? After all, she did get pregnant from some random Greek waiter, and it's not exactly something to be proud of.

But doesn't that also mean she's not proud of *me*?

My head hurts now. Stupidly I didn't bring any water, and this part of the island is wild, with no building in sight, except for a lighthouse up ahead. I was sort of aiming towards it, thinking I could turn around there, but now I think I should probably turn back, because the sun is slipping down quickly and the path will be difficult in the dark. I go on a little further, then I give up and turn back along the cliff path and down towards the sand.

Maybe I do have *some* connection to the murder – or the murders – at the Aegean Dream Resort? My mind keeps coming back to this. What I mean is, it seems almost certain that my mother would have known the couple who died. She worked for them, after all – even if she wasn't working when it happened, because she'd have been with me. So it seems plausible at least that their deaths are connected to her reluctance to tell me about her time here. And why not? This would have come on top of whatever shame she felt about getting knocked up by the waiter. On top of that her boss goes crazy and murders his girlfriend, or someone murders both of them – and it's a small island, as everyone keeps telling me, so probably she'd have known the people who were suspects at the time, if there were suspects...

It's easy to see why I've got this in my mind now. I'm nearly level with the old resort again, and with the sun so low over the sea, the ruins have a really brooding, intimidating presence on the beach. They're illuminated only from the front, and it gives the impression that anything, or anyone, could be hiding in the shadows. I wonder which of the rooms the deaths happened in, and I stop to take in the twin accommodation blocks, one in a reasonable state of repair, the other's roof partially collapsed into it.

I stop, suddenly aware of something. It's a light, flashing at me from behind the closer accommodation block, the one with the tumble-down roof.

No. Not a light, but a flash of light, like a reflection off something. I suddenly feel very exposed. There's no one on the beach around me – I haven't seen anyone at all since I left Skalio two hours ago, and the town is still a good mile ahead of me. I stand still, just watching the resort, trying to see if the flash comes again. I almost convince myself that it's nothing, that I'm just tired and paranoid, or that even if I did see something it would have just been the sun glinting off a piece of broken glass. But then it comes again, clearer this time. The reflection of something, right beside the wall of the second accommodation block. I start to get this crazy feeling that someone there's watching me, and this is the glint of sunglasses, or even binoculars – which is stupid because there's obviously no one there. But then I find myself moving forward, towards where the light flashed from, in an effort to prove to myself I'm mistaken.

It's amazing how easy it is to get onto the old resort grounds.

If this was in the UK there'd be fences everywhere, covered in signs warning of the danger and telling you to keep out. Here there obviously was a fence once, but only the posts remain, and I can just pass between them. So I step off the beach, into the old gardens, and carry on right up to the ruined, broken-tiled pool.

I can feel my heart fluttering in my chest as I get there. I don't know why, and I'm not sure why I'm doing this, except I need to prove to myself that I'm not scared, even though I am, actually. A little bit. I pause at the pool – taking another look at Mum's old haunt, but then turn left towards the accommodation block where I saw the light. It's only fifty feet away now, and I'm sure it would have been beautiful back then, but now it's overgrown in places and bare in others. And there's a nasty roll of tangled barbed wire that was presumably once a fence. I make it to the front of the accommodation block, the rooms in front of me have been broken into so there are holes in the wooden boards blocking the entrances, but they're so small that very little light from the sinking sun illuminates the interiors. The deaths could have happened in any of these rooms, I realise. Or a different one. I don't even know why I'm thinking it.

I'm nearly at the corner now, and I stop again, wondering if I'm actually being foolish, if this is actually dangerous. This place could be used for all sorts of things, drugs... I try to list in my mind what else could happen here, and I can't think of anything – burying stolen treasure? I almost laugh out loud at how silly this is, when another thought cuts through. It's just the sort of place you'd come to if you were a psycho, needing somewhere quiet to torture or murder your victim.

God, Ava. Give it a rest, I tell myself. This is Alythos, there's no crime here, and all I'm doing is proving that. I keep going, pausing just before the wall runs out and I turn the corner to where I thought I saw the light. And then I hear something. Or maybe I don't. I hesitate though, scared now to take the last few steps. But this is silly. I do it. I turn the corner.

There's nothing there. I knew there wouldn't be. It must have been the sun hitting some glass, just as I thought. It's not just broken bottles, there's other bits of garbage strewn around on the ground, and some of the window frames have shards left in them, sharp and jagged. I force myself to speak out loud, thinking it might settle my nerves a bit.

"See? Nothing," I say. But it is creepy. On the side of the building there's a doorway, the actual door long gone so that I can see inside. Or I could if it wasn't pitch black in there. But then I hear it again, clearer this time. A noise, a cough? But then something else, a kind of shuffling sound. I'm certain this time. Something – or someone – is inside the building, right next to me.

I look around, there's no one else here. No one who could help me. *Why did I have to come here? Why did I have to prove how brave I am?*

The shuffling noise comes again, and now I think that maybe whoever's in the room is moving closer to the doorway. Closer like they're readying themselves to rush out and grab me. It's crazy, but it feels real. I take a step back, keeping my eye on the door, and right away I stumble on something half-buried in the ground, and then I feel a hand on my shoulder, grabbing me, pulling me down to the ground. But it's not, it's just a branch from an overgrown bush. And I see I tripped on a broken, twisted piece of paving slab. My heart is racing now. The sound of it thudding inside my head. For a few seconds I just sit there, staring at the dark opening, waiting for whoever it is to come out.

Another sound. Soft, but there. A breath? A whisper? The barest scuff of movement.

My body takes over. I scramble to my feet and start to move. I don't want to run, I don't know why. Perhaps because that would confirm that this is actually real, and the thought terrifies me. So I walk. Fast. Feeling eyes on my back as I cross through the ruined gardens and back towards the fence line, where the few posts stand like sentinels.

As I get there the pressure is too much and I turn, fully expecting to see someone there, running towards me. But there's nothing. No one. Just the empty, black windows of the old accommodation block, as if the broken building itself was watching me.

I hurry along the beach, and only really start to relax as I get close to Skalio. But already I'm revising in my mind what just happened. If there was someone there, it was probably just kids. Maybe it's a place they come to play? If so, maybe I scared them just as much as they scared me? Or, worst-case, it was just the local Skalio peeping-tom, a little weird and creepy maybe – but not dangerous. Either way I overreacted, and I was stupid to go up there in the first place.

With the drama in my head I almost don't notice, but the bay around me has transformed into something absolutely spectacular. Lights are coming on in the white-painted town up ahead, as the restaurants open up around the harbour. The distant mountains are ghostly shadows rising up from the sea, but most of all it's the sunset. Above me, all around, there's a screaming cacophony of colour, as the last of the glowing red sun slides away. It's hard to stay scared when surrounded by such an absurdity of beauty.

I stop at the supermarket on the way to grab a few things for an easy pasta dinner. Maria's not serving now, but another woman, who's not unfriendly, but not as friendly either. I pay, stuff everything into my bag and keep walking, trying to get my mind back to my mission here, and what, if anything, I learnt today. Something snags in my memory about Gregory Duncan's office wall, before he closed the door on it. Why did he do that? Why did I notice it? I try to think my way into the question, but whatever it is, it's not going to come.

Back in my apartment, I pull a beautiful pepper from the bag and find a knife to chop it up. But the thought I had earlier hasn't completely gone away. I try to see back inside that office. The flashing cursor on his computer screen, the pencil portraits of the harbour, and the people. They weren't very good, but they weren't *that* bad. And then, just like that, I realise what's bugging me. It's the girl, the portrait on the wall of Gregory Duncan's office.

I only saw it from an angle, but it looked a hell of a lot like a young Imogen Grant.

NINETEEN

I'm working again the next afternoon, so there's not time to do much. Even if there was, I'm not sure exactly what I can do. I don't feel like I'm making killer progress out here. But at least I'm earning money, while living on an actual Greek island. Maybe it's like my old tutor at university said: just being here is enough for me to grow up and find myself?

I have that thought in mind as I head down to the bar for my shift, a little early. There's no particular reason for that, except maybe there's only so long I can take in the view of the garbage bins from my apartment. Maybe I should have asked Gregory Duncan for a copy of his new book.

I don't walk along the road though, but along the shoreline. There isn't much tide here, I've noticed, not like in Sunderland, but there is still a small difference between low and high tides. And now – with the tide out – there's a narrow strip of firm sand that's nice to walk along. And so, with my sandals dangling from my hand, I step barefoot on the sand, occasionally detouring into the shallow sun-warmed water.

There's something that's been worrying me a bit since I've got here. It's whether I should say anything to Mum, like update her on my progress. Until now I've not spoken to her, not even sent her a text. I did see some postcards in the little supermarket, and I thought about that. *Wish you were here* – but I really don't. Anyway. I pull out my phone and tap out a message before I can change my mind. I just say I got here safe, and I've found a job, and everything's fine. I think for a second, but then hit send and wait, like there's any chance she might answer straight back. But of course she doesn't. After a few moments I slip the phone away and keep walking.

But now I see my path is blocked ahead by one of the RIBs from the dive centre. I'm about to turn up the beach when I notice it's actually Kostas himself on the boat. He seems to be doing something with the engine – he has the cowling off. He stops, suddenly wiping his hands on a rag. It's obvious he's seen me too.

It's awkward, but I figure I can just walk by and maybe nod politely or something, but he surprises me by stepping forward. He still has that super stern look on his face, which I find unnerving.

"Hello again," I say, because the silence is stifling.

He just nods, then glances around at the Bar Sunset, further along the beach.

"I hear you're working with Hans," he says, with little indication of whether he thinks this is a good thing or a bad thing.

"Yeah," I say, because I am, and I have nothing to hide.

"And you went to see Duncan yesterday? The writer?" His dark eyes seem to burn into mine as he speaks. And again I nod. I don't know how he knows this, but then I have an idea – the farmer, on the tractor. Sophia did tell me news travels fast on this island.

"Um... yes."

"He tell you anything?"

"No." I feel my brow furrowing. Why does he care, all of a sudden?

"He didn't remember them," I find myself saying. I don't understand why I'm telling him this, but maybe it's to fill the silence. "Except maybe he seemed to recognise the woman my mum was with, but he didn't say." I don't tell Kostas how I think Duncan had a sketch of her on his office wall.

"Imogen," Kostas says, then nods to himself, as if he's not surprised by this. But I certainly am.

"You know her?"

"Knew. Not anymore." Kostas looks up and down the beach. There are a few other people around, but no one close by. "Duncan was obsessed with Imogen." Kostas fixes me again with his look, then glances up at a couple coming down the beach. They're walking to the other boat, where another guy wearing one of the dive centre's TEAM T-shirts is getting it ready.

"Um," I say again, trying to make sense of this. So Gregory Duncan did recognise Imogen. But why did he lie?

"I'm just fixing this," Kostas tells me suddenly, picking up the engine cowling and expertly lifting it back into place. "I've just fixed this," he corrects himself. "But I have to give it a run out. A spin around the bay. Do you want to come with me?"

The suddenness of the offer throws me. And the strangeness. What's he offering exactly, a pleasure cruise? Why? For a second I imagine really weird scenarios, like he wants to attack me, or even drown me – but that's crazy. It's broad daylight. And there's no reason... Then I notice the way he's looking at me, and I sense something else. There's something he wants to tell me.

"What... right now?"

"Yes."

I try to calculate. I don't start my shift for forty-five minutes. So I've got time. Part of me wants to ask why he wants me to go, why we can't speak here. But I sense something else too, that maybe if I don't go he'll change his mind. And he simply won't say whatever it is he knows. I take a deep breath, and nod.

"OK."

He doesn't seem thrilled by this, but he nods back. And then jumps out of the boat and walks up to the front, which is resting on the shore, so that the stern and the engine are hanging into the water. He's surprisingly agile for such a large guy.

"There's a buoyancy aid on the seat. Put it on."

I do what he says, slipping my arms into a blue vest-type lifejacket that smells faintly of oil. Kostas pulls one on too, putting it over his shirt. Then he looks around, up and down the beach, before nodding again, apparently satisfied by something.

Then he pushes the boat hard from the front – the bow, I suppose it's called – so that it slides backwards out into the water. When it's fully afloat he vaults expertly over the rubber side and steps past me back to the engine. I don't know what he does there, but then he comes and sits, one powerful thigh either side of the central seat, and turns a key on the instrument panel. The engine strums into life. It's much quieter than Sophia's moped, you can barely hear it, until he puts it into reverse gear and very slowly edges us backwards. Then it purrs, but more like a lion than a cat. He turns us carefully around. When that's done he slips it into neutral, looks around carefully, then into forward gear.

"Hold on," he instructs, waiting until I do. Then he pushes the throttle again and we accelerate smoothly, an ever-growing tail of creamy, bubbly wake stretching out behind us as he keeps adding more power. I grip on tightly to the rubber handle sewn into the side of the boat as the engine's growl rises to a full roar.

And then we're flying along, skimming so fast I can barely keep my eyes on the flashing water ahead, and even though my hair is whipping out behind me, getting in my eyes, I need both hands to hold on and stop me falling from the boat.

TWENTY

We're like that, me holding on as tight as I can and Kostas driving, one hand on the throttle, the other on the wheel, for a couple of minutes. It's long enough to put us a good distance offshore and away from the beach. Then he turns the boat in a long smooth arc, so that we're facing back towards Skalio, but too far to make out any of the buildings now. He pulls the throttle right back so that we slow, falling off the plane, and finally rolling slightly as the waves we've just created catch us up and rock into the side of the boat. Kostas lets the engine idle a few moments, watching it carefully, then he cuts it. There's near silence, just the sound of the last few waves slapping against the rubber side of the boat.

"Seems OK," Kostas says.

"The engine?"

"Yes."

He's not looking at me, his eyes are fixed on the horizon, out to sea, not back at Alythos. Finally he goes on, still not looking in my direction.

"When you came to me the other day, I said I didn't recognise either of the women in your photograph," he begins, then stops again. He looks gravely serious. "That was not the truth."

He falls quiet.

"OK," I say after a while. Because I don't know what else to say.

"This is not easy for me to say. I do not like to be caught in a lie. But I had not thought about Imogen in a long time." Finally he turns to me, as if wanting to know how this line lands. I don't know what to say.

"OK," I say again.

"A very long time."

"Uh huh." I nod. I glance over the side. The water must be deep here, the colour is almost black – like Kostas' hair, and his eyes. I get the thought that he's taken me out here into his element. It's a bit weird. Unsettling.

"The truth is I do remember Imogen. I remember her very well. We became... close. When we worked at the resort. Friends." His eyes flick away, glancing towards the derelict remains of the hotel far away on the shore as he says this. "We were still close when the murder happened. But it tore us apart."

I stare at him, sort of stunned.

"Why? Why didn't you tell me?"

He takes his time again, like he's thinking how to put it.

"The man who died – Jason Wright. He was the resort manager, in charge of everything. The woman he killed was both his girlfriend and the resort's deputy manager. With both of them gone, there was no one left to run the hotel. It was closed down. Everyone who wasn't from the island – the guests of course, but the staff too – were sent home. I don't remember how they did it, maybe the owner in Britain hired a jet to get everyone away – I do not know."

He's quiet for a moment, he seems to be thinking. I just

wait, perched on the side of this little rubber boat over an abyss of water.

"What I am trying to say, it happened just like *that*." He snaps his fingers suddenly as he speaks, catching me by surprise. "*Gone*." His face twists, I see anger in it. Regret, something else too. He falls silent again.

"I remember your mother too. Karen Whitaker," He looks at me sharply, watching. I just wait.

"She and Imogen shared a room. In the staff quarters." I think I knew this, I think she told me once – or maybe Imogen did, I can't remember.

"OK."

"She did not have a baby."

That takes me by surprise for a moment. "I know she didn't. Not that first summer. I was born the year after, the second year she was here—"

"No. You weren't." His words cut me into silence. For a few moments neither of us speaks.

"I'm sorry, I don't understand," I say in the end.

"There was no child."

I don't know how to answer this. Obviously he's making a mistake, or he's just mixing her up with someone else.

"Um..." My voice fades away. I stare at the water. There's just the tiniest sheen of oil on the surface now, I think from the engine's cooling system. A tiny swirl of rainbow. It's easier to focus on this than what I'm suddenly being told.

"Perhaps Karen was pregnant when she left the island? Perhaps you were born after, back in England. Or somewhere else, another island." Kostas' words keep coming. *Insane. Completely wrong.* I shrug, shaking my head at the same time.

"No. It was definitely... Alythos." I have my passport in my bag. Hans needs to see it for my work permit. It lists my place of birth. And the date. But I don't pull it out, I don't show it to him. I'm not here to prove myself.

He turns away, as if me not believing him is insulting. But he's just wrong.

"I will take you back now. Hold on."

And then he fires up the engine again. Moments later the boat has climbed back onto the mountain of white water that its engine produces, as we power back towards the beach. For a minute or so there's no possibility of talking, with the noise and the movement of it. It could be thrilling, but my head is spinning. I don't understand what he's just told me, why he'd say it.

But we don't quite get to the beach. Instead he kills the engine, spinning the boat around again when we're maybe a quarter of a mile from the sand. The water here is bluer, but still dark and deep. It makes me want to get closer still. To where I could definitely swim ashore if I needed to. If he tried to throw me off.

"I do not know if I should tell you this." His words cut into me again. "I do not understand this."

I let go of the handles to lift my hands into a shrug. "I don't think I do either."

"You are the daughter of Karen Whitaker?" His dark eyes bore into me. "The woman in your photograph – Imogen. We are talking about the same Karen Whitaker who was friends with Imogen Grant?"

"Yes. Yeah, I think so."

He draws in a deep breath, then shakes his big head again, like this cannot be the case. Then he half-unzips his buoyancy aid, and reaches a hand inside. He stops. Seems to consider again.

"Imogen and I... our relationship was casual. Typical of its time. I mean by this, we did not know so much about each other, outside of the island. This was a time before mobile telephones, the internet. This you understand?" He waits until I nod, before he goes on.

"I did not know where she lived. Of course I knew America,

but I could not contact her, when she left the island, after the murders."

Now he turns to face me properly, looking me square in the face. "This was hard for me. I believed myself to be in love with her at this time. And her with me. Yet I had no way to reach her."

I can't see where this is going, but it must have been hard. I can sort of understand what he's telling me.

"So did you find her? Afterwards?"

"No." He shakes his head. Like a powerful but tragic bear. "I have never seen Imogen Grant again. Not after the deaths."

"Oh." I nod, for what must be the fourth or fifth time. I mean, this is super interesting and stuff. But I'm not sure why it's that relevant to me. I still don't really know what I'm doing out here. But it turns out Kostas isn't finished.

"At first the police sealed off the resort. Everything was off limits. But after a few days, it was clear they did not have enough men to keep it locked down. They put police tape. Keep out." He glances at me, then looks away, so that I see the whites of his eyes. I just wait. Whatever this is, it seems it's difficult for him to tell me.

"So one night. I went down there. To the hotel. I broke into Imogen's room. Imogen and Karen's room. You understand?"

"Um, not exactly—"

"I wanted to find an address – something to help me get in touch with Imogen. Maybe I did not think the relationship could last forever, but it should not have ended the way it did."

I wait, then reply.

"But you didn't find anything? Otherwise, you'd have contacted her?"

He nods, his eyes absent again.

"Nothing from Imogen. No." His frown deepens, his brow knotting like he's pulling something up from the past. "I should not have done what I did next. It was shameful. I have felt a guilt over this for many years. Perhaps if I hand this over to you, it will remove this guilt? I do not know..."

He stops again, and I have to press.

"I'm sorry, I don't understand. Hand what over?"

"Your mother, Karen. She kept a diary of her time on the island. I found it when I searched their room. I am sorry to say I took it. Ever since, I have kept it, I cannot say why, I do not know..." He fixes me with his dark look again, and then his hand disappears further into the buoyancy aid. Underneath, tucked into his shirt, is a clear plastic bag, and inside that, I see the corner of a book.

"I wasn't sure I still had it, but after we spoke I looked and..." He shakes his head. "You tell me you were born here, on Alythos? To Karen Whitaker?"

"Yes."

He shakes his head.

"Then you must read this. I do not understand, but it will tell you the truth."

He pulls the book now from his shirt, looks at it a moment longer, then holds it out to me. For a moment I'm unsure what to do. I just stare at it, in total shock. This is something real. Mum's actual diary. I just blink at it for a few moments, and then I take it from him. I tuck it in the waistband of my shorts, because I can't even look at it yet. He nods – I think at this – but then I see it's at the rubber handle, telling me to hold on again. And moments later we're flying again, as he powers the boat full-speed back towards the shore.

But I don't feel I'm going forward anymore. I feel like I'm already falling backwards. Back into the past I'm so desperate to understand.

TWENTY-ONE

I'm still in shock as Kostas noses the boat back onto the beach and waits while I jump off. We don't speak, except I tell him my shift is about to start, and then I hurry along to the bar. And then it's the first really busy shift I've done. The season is just getting going, Hans tells me, and a hotel nearby has just opened up for the summer, with mostly German guests. It seems half of them have come down to the Sunset Bar to kick off their holidays, and they mean to start it drunk. So I spend the next six hours pulling pints and clearing glasses, and delivering plates of fries and burgers. And I almost forget about the diary I now have tucked away in my bag, and what it might tell me about my mother.

Almost.

Hans finally lets me go just before midnight, and I decide I'll read it when I get home. On the way I grab another takeaway *souvlaki*, because I didn't get time to eat at work. I'm dead on my feet when I get back to my apartment block. But right away something feels off.

I don't know what it is. I suppose it might just be that it's dark, and the lighting around the entrance isn't very bright.

Half the places around here are rentals, and whoever is going to live here for the summer hasn't arrived yet, so it has a creepy feel anyway. But it's more than that, I have a real sense I'm being watched. I resist the urge to run, but slip my key between my fingers, so it's a kind of weapon. But it won't be much good, the way my hand is shaking. There's nothing else I can do but walk fast, and at the entrance to my building I concentrate hard to slip the key into the lock first time and not fumble. I do it, and push open the door, pulling it locked behind me. Then I finally breathe again. It's nothing, I'm just freaked out, by what Kostas said, by what I'm doing here.

The lobby is pretty dark and dingy, illuminated only by a single dim bulb. And I'll feel properly better when I get into my apartment. As I fit the key into the lock there, a thought suddenly comes into focus. I'm using the same key I just used. I don't know how that works, but Klaus only gave me one, which operates both my door and the main door to the building. Does that mean anyone who lives in this block could get into my apartment too? Had someone already? I don't really know, I'm not an expert on locks, but it seems odd. I try to forget it though as I put the key in again. I think about something nicer, the warmth I can feel from the food, which smells amazing. But I don't have long to think about that either.

The moment I open the door, I know what's happened. All my clothes were in the chest of drawers. Now they're strewn all over the floor. The kitchen cupboards are open, two of my three plates smashed on the kitchen floor. And on the table, where I left my trusty MacBook Air, there's nothing but an empty charging cable.

TWENTY-TWO

My first thought is whoever did this might still be in here.

I flicked the light on when I came in, so if there is, they'll know *I'm* here. I think about turning it off again, but I don't want to be in darkness. It's a small apartment, but there's still lots of places I can't see from where I'm standing, lots of places where someone could hide.

Shit.

I go to shut the front door, but then change my mind. If whoever did this *is* still here, then I want to give them some way of escape. If I trap them, they're more likely to hurt me.

I step forward cautiously into the bedroom. Look around, nothing. Another step and I'm in front of the wardrobe, it's like the most obvious place. I reach out, hesitating on the handle, then pull it wide open. Nothing again. I turn, bend down and look under the bed. Nothing but dust. The room – apart from my clothes all over the floor – looks just how I left it. I check the bathroom next, I still haven't put the shower curtain up, so at least no one can redo in reverse the whole *Psycho* shower scene on me. It's obviously empty. I go back into the kitchen/living room part of the space, and there's not really anywhere left to hide. I look behind the sofa, open the rest of the cupboards, which are too small to hide in anyway, and then take a huge sigh of relief.

So then I go back to the door to my flat, and this time I shut it, I lock it, and I pull the kitchen table in front of it, so that no one can push it open again from the outside. At least not easily. Only then do I really stop to think.

I didn't see any signs of forced entry. I mean, I'm not a detective or anything, and I'm not sure I'd know for sure. But the lock didn't look any worse than it normally did – which is pretty shaky if I'm honest, like it was the cheapest option when it was fitted, and that was twenty or thirty years ago. Could someone have opened it with a pick? I don't know. Or what about how the key opens the front door and this apartment, is that how they opened it? I look around the room again. What about the windows? I'm on the ground floor, but I'm certain the windows were closed when I left, and they still are now. But just like the door, they're not the most secure-looking I've ever seen. Far from it. Yet the little levers that hold them shut are still in place.

Another thought hits me. Perhaps it's someone who stayed here before and kept a key? Or even Klaus, my landlord? I wouldn't put it past him. Maybe this is how he makes extra money on the side?

And then I wonder, I'm assuming this was someone just breaking in to rob me – but what if *that's* wrong? Maybe there's some other reason? But as soon as I think that it seems ridiculous. What other reason?

I don't know. I think I'm just freaked out. Freaking out. Here all alone, and feeling super vulnerable. But what do I do now? Should I call the police?

This probably sounds stupid, but I actually have no idea how to do that, here in Greece. Obviously back home I'd call

999, but it isn't 999 everywhere, right? In America it's 911. So what is it in Greece? I have literally no idea.

I could Google it. But even if I do call them, what am I actually going to say?

It was pretty dumb, the way I left my computer on the table. I didn't think, but anyone passing by in the street could look in and notice it. I removed the net curtains, I cleaned the windows, none of that helped. I guess I was just distracted, what with this being a beautiful Greek island and everything, I assumed there wouldn't be any crime here. But of course there is. There's crime everywhere, and a MacBook is going to be easy to sell, obviously valuable. I start to feel less freaked out, and a bit more... embarrassed.

It's pretty obvious, now I think about it, that this was just a burglary. And I begin to count myself lucky that there wasn't anything else to steal. I had my money and bank card on me, plus my phone, and my passport too, luckily, because I needed to show it to Hans. So the only thing of value was the computer.

And anyway, even though it was an expensive laptop – back when Mum bought it for me – that was a few years ago now, and it's been well used since then. I've been thinking for a while I need to get a new one. So maybe there's no need to tell the police? Maybe I just chalk this one up to experience?

And if I don't have to call the police, I don't have to tell them that some part of my brain is telling me to link what happened here to the person I thought I saw watching me at the ruins of the Aegean Dream Resort. Because I don't want to do that at all.

And besides. Now that the adrenaline has worn off – a little – I'm still starving. So instead of calling the police, I sit down at my kitchen table and eat my *souvlaki*, unpacking it onto my final unbroken plate. Only then do I remember the diary. But I can't face it now. It's just too much.

I have the whole of tomorrow off work, I'll read it then.

TWENTY-THREE

I wake up late the next morning, the sun is already high in the sky and pouring through the kitchen window. It should be nice in the apartment – you could make it nice, with plants and redecorating – but the way Klaus has it at the moment, the sun just makes it stuffy. So I have a quick shower and get dressed, then head down to the harbour. My plan is simple. I'm going to find a table in the shade and drink fresh orange juice and coffee. And I'm going to read what my mum said about her time here twenty-two years ago.

I'm finally going to get some answers about who I am.

The little town is quiet as I walk down towards the seafront. I pick a bar with a view of the fishing boats and the little yachts nestled together in the harbour. I order the drinks, with a bowl of yogurt and fruit. The waiter is a young guy, not much older than me, and he tries to flirt, but I couldn't be less interested. He keeps on though, and I almost think about finding another place just to get the hell away from him. But eventually he gets the message. I eat quickly, and then pull the diary out of my bag.

I take a deep breath.

Mum's diary is a red exercise book, quite thin, with just the word "Diary" and the year 2000 printed on the front. I open it and I recognise her handwriting, even though it's different to how she writes now – the letters rounder, somehow obviously more youthful. I flick through the contents, not yet ready to dive in. I notice how she's written on some pages, but then left whole sections blank, sometimes three or four pages of nothing, as if she meant to go back and fill them in, but never did. I turn to the front, there's a few scrawled contacts, an email address, and then a cute little bookmark thing, made from an origami bat. I can see handwriting on the wing, and when I lift it up I see it says: *Imogen & Karen, summer* 2000. I close the book for a moment, feeling suddenly dizzy about what I've got, what I'm doing.

This really could be the answer to everything I've wondered my entire life.

But then, what was it that Kostas told me? How he didn't remember her being pregnant, and how I need to read this to learn the truth. That doesn't make any sense, what did he even mean? I take a sip of my orange juice, my hand shaking as I put the glass down. I don't know what the hell any of this means, I certainly don't understand it. But maybe I'm about to. I just hope I'm ready for it.

I open the diary again, turn to the first page, and I start to read.

TWENTY-FOUR

May 15th, 2000

Alythos

Well, I finally made it. We flew from Gatwick Airport to Athens, then got a bus to a town near here – I don't remember the name – and then we got on a little ferry to the island, and then another bus down to a place called Skalio, and then it dropped us off here – at the Aegean Dream Resort.

It's amazing. It's this huge hotel building, right on the beach, but away from the town, so it's kind of private. And there's a massive pool, all set in really nice gardens. And then behind us, you have these mountains covered with olive trees. It's so gorgeous.

On the plane, I noticed a few people who looked like they might be coming here too, but I didn't say anything. Not until we got on the bus – then we all started figuring out who was who. It seems like most of the staff are from England – there's a couple of girls who are working in the kids' club. Chloe, who was here last year, and Sarah, who's new like me. And there's one American girl called Imogen.

When we got here the deputy manager – she's called Mandy – she had a list of who was going to share with who, and I got put in a room with Imogen, so she's actually lying about ten feet away from me right now. She seems nice, but she's a bit quiet. I figure she'll open up a bit once we all get to know each other.

There's loads of boys though. On the beach part of the resort, they have all these different types of boats for the guests to use. And there's also waterskiing and windsurfing. So a lot of the boys are instructors for that. Some of them are way hot.

Then apart from that there's the catering people. Some are chefs, and then there's sous chefs. I don't know the difference. Then there's the people looking after the kids.

But my job is going to be the pool bar, and I saw it for the first time this afternoon – it's so cool! It's only open during the day, and apparently it's a super-chilled job. It doesn't really get busy, it's mostly just iced coffees and afternoon cocktails and that sort of thing, and it closes at six-thirty, which is the same time the boys at the beach stop work. That means we're all going to be free at the same time. And that's gonna be awesome.

The town – Skalio – is really close, a twenty-minute walk? Apparently there are loads of really cool bars there, so that's going to be fun. I need some fun too, after getting so close to qualifying, and then fucking it up. But that already feels a long way away. All of Dad's hassling and getting on my back. It's good to leave that behind.

I don't know how much I'll be able to write this diary. My plan is to try and write something every day, so that in the future, I'll be able to look back and remember everything that happened.

So hello, future me, if you're reading this. And if you're not future me, then what are you doing reading this? Get the hell outta here!

TWENTY-FIVE

May 16th, 2000

Sooooo. Second night here, second diary entry. So far, so good!

Another bus arrived, with a few more people who are going to work here, so that now everyone's in place. I'm not going to list everyone – there's about thirty of us staff in total. But some are locals, so they don't really count.

I probably could name them all if I wanted to, I've been pretty good about introducing myself and figuring out who's cool and who isn't. There's a guy called Neil – he's the head of the beach section. He was here last year as well, and he's super hot.

I'm not so sure about the girls, there's no one I've really bonded with yet, except – luckily – Imogen. She's actually really nice and super funny, but in a dry way. She's going to be working in reception (when we get the guests I mean, they don't arrive until Saturday). She was helping me this afternoon, getting the bar ready, making sure we've got all the drinks, and then making a menu of what I'm going to serve. So that was really fun, making up cocktails and testing them out!

Imogen's actually really pretty. I didn't notice at first, maybe because she's got a bit of puppy fat still, but she's got this long dark hair and big, round eyes. Today she said she wished she had my figure, which was sweet of her. But I think she's way prettier than she realises. I've already seen guys staring at her.

We had this weird thing happen today. The resort manager is called Jason. He's also going out with Mandy, the deputy manager. He's alright – kind of sexy – but also super tough.

Anyway, he lined us all up, the whole staff, and he gave us this lecture about how we had to follow his rules, and if we didn't, there wouldn't be any warnings – it would be bang, first plane home. And he stared at us, one by one, while he said it, like he really wants someone to mess up so he can prove it.

And the biggest rule of all is no drugs. He sounded super paranoid about them, but apparently it's because the police here are super-hot on them. Like if they catch anyone it's years in prison. They could even close down the whole resort. It all sounded a bit full-on to me, but I guess they have to be strict. Anyway, alcohol isn't such an issue, thank God. Jason did make the point that we have to get all the work done first. But when we do, he doesn't mind us letting our hair down. In fact Jason said he was looking forward to going into Skalio and dancing on the tables. I've no idea if he was serious or not, but Neil swore he was.

We actually had a bit of a session this evening. Someone brought out a bottle of Metaxa that they bought in the supermarket in town. So we just sat on the balcony of the staff block, and drank out of plastic cups that the nannies stole from the nursery. It was fun, a nice way to get to know people a little better. Metaxa and Diet Coke is super delicious!

TWENTY-SIX

May 18th, 2000

OK, so I'm writing this in the morning, because last night all the staff headed off into the town. Tomorrow is when the first guests arrive, and Jason said we'd all worked really well, and he wanted us to gel together as a team. He kept buying rounds of drinks for everyone – every time you went near the bar someone just gave you another one, so everyone got wasted. And then by midnight, Jason shouted it was time, and he pulled off his shirt, climbed up on the bar, and started dancing like a maniac. And pretty soon we were all up there, dancing away. It was so awesome.

It was actually cool, because there were people there from some of the other resorts and hotels on the island, like all the workers together. You can sort of see how we're like this big family. Or maybe like a family that all wants to hook up together.

I had to save Imogen today from this geeky guy on the beach team, his name's Gregory, and he's weird looking, a proper nerd. He came up to reception to print out the new prices for the waterskiing and wakeboarding, since they don't have a printer down on the beach. But then he just wouldn't leave. He kept wanting to change things and get her to do them, adjust the layouts and that, and all the while he was staring at her, and asking her all these questions about where in America she was from, what other places in Europe she'd visited. I sensed she wanted to get rid of him, so I asked her to remind me what position her boyfriend back home played in American football. After that Gregory went really quiet and went back down to the beach. Imogen said she felt sorry for him, but she thanked me as well.

Another thing about Imogen. Because she works in reception, she's really close with Mandy, the deputy manager, because her office is right behind the reception desk. I hadn't really noticed before, but Mandy is really dumb. Like amazingly stupid. Imogen says, when you ask Mandy a question, you get this thirty-second delay while she processes it, before she gives you an answer. Part of Mandy's job is to make sure all the guests get from the airport to the resort OK – organise the buses and taxis, that sort of thing. But Imogen says that basically Mandy can't do it, and Jason has to come in and help, and it's not like he doesn't have enough to do. So basically Imogen reckons Mandy's only here at all because Jason's shagging her. Imogen's pretty funny sometimes, like when you don't expect it.

Speaking of shagging, I probably could have hooked up last night. I sort of half-tried, with Neil. But I didn't want to overdo it and seem too easy. But it definitely counts as groundwork. At the same time, I did see some other guys that I liked too. I hadn't really considered the local guys until last night, but some of them are way hot. There's one of the gardeners from the resort. I think he's called Kostas. He's dark and handsome, kinda mysterious but with muscles. I'd totally do him.

I'm quite tired now. But I've got to go work now. More later!

TWENTY-SEVEN

I take a break. It feels so strange, reading Mum's thoughts from when she was here. Invasive and unsettling. She doesn't even sound like Mum, she's so obviously immature. But then, I didn't know her at that age... And am I so different? An image of Kevin comes into my mind: I've made my own mistakes.

Partly this is the problem though – the whole reason I'm here. I just know so little about this part of her life, even though in her case it's where *I came from*. And doesn't that change it? Doesn't it give me a right to know... something, at least.

I feel a sense of something else now, just for a moment, and I guess it's kind of shame. Like what am I doing here, reading my mum's intimate, private thoughts from years ago. She'd hate it if she knew, I know that much about her. But then, she had her chances to tell me. She had the opportunity, but instead she drove me out here.

I catch the eye of the waiter and order another coffee. He makes it with a heart shape in the froth, and sets it down carefully in front of me, then he tells me it's a beautiful drink for a beautiful girl. Maybe another time I might appreciate it –

though probably not. I'm careful not to do anything that might lead him on, and I turn my chair so it faces away from where he's sitting.

I'm just about to go back to reading when I see Sophia's moped go by on the road. But rather than drive past, she stops, gets off and walks into the cafe.

She goes right up to the bar without noticing me, and starts speaking with the waiter who just served me. I don't know what they say – it's literally all Greek to me – but both of them seem angry about something. A few moments later, he hands her a wrapped parcel of something, and she takes it and goes to walk out. And then she can't not see me, because of the route she takes.

"Hi!" I say, as she gets to my table.

I don't know, maybe I overestimated how friendly she was the other day, or whether it meant something that she lent me her moped, because now she doesn't smile. She seems irritated, like she just wants to get away.

"Oh. Hi," she says. She stands there a second, holding the parcel, which I see is some pastry thing. She looks awkward. And suddenly, I don't know what to say either.

"Thanks again, for the loan of your scooter," I go on, because I didn't get the chance to thank her properly the other day.

"Yeah. No problem." She looks uncomfortable for another moment, then flashes an unconvincing smile. "I have to go."

She turns and walks out at once. Then she gets on her moped, and drives off without looking back.

I don't know why, but this unsettles me more. It's not like we're friends or anything, but she was definitely much more friendly the other day, and I just assumed... I don't know, that she would be again? I guess I got that wrong.

I turn back to the battered diary in front of me on the table, and I know what I have to do. I pick it up. Back to hunting for clues about my identity. And this time it doesn't take long. Because when it comes to sex, it turns out my mum didn't mess around.

TWENTY-EIGHT

May 19th, 2000

I slept with Neil last night.

It was kind of awkward actually, because Neil shares a room with this guy Baz, and Neil thought he wasn't there, but he was, so we had to go to my room, and I had to beg Imogen to sleep outside. It's OK, we have these hammocks strung up on the balcony area now, they're made from old sails from the dinghies on the beach, and they're really comfortable, and it's warm enough to sleep out all night. And Imogen was really good about it, so she just came out to the hammocks, while Neil came into my room.

It was nice. I wouldn't call it exactly spectacular. And yeah, for the record, I didn't come. Actually, he only lasted a minute or so, which was sort of funny, but he's got a hot body so it doesn't matter. Afterwards, we cuddled for a bit, then I said he should go, so that Imogen could come back to her bed.

This all happened because the clients have arrived – about sixty, which isn't that many, when we get busy there'll be three times as many.

Anyway, after work, we all came back to the staff house and got drinking, and that's how it happened. We were playing cards, and Neil kept cheating, looking at my cards, and I kept pushing him away, and it was really funny. Then some of the other guys went to sleep, because we all have to get up early to get the hotel ready, and he said he was going to get a bit of air before he went to bed. And since we were already outside, I knew what he meant, so I said I'd go with him.

We didn't even make it to the beach.

There's a little shed, down by the pool, where the cushions for the sun loungers are kept, and we went in there and started kissing. It got pretty heated pretty quickly, and we could have done it there, but Neil said we shouldn't, because if Jason saw us there, or if one of the guests caught us, we'd be on the next plane home. Besides, neither of us had any condoms on us, but Neil had some in his room.

So we went back, and luckily Imogen was just cleaning her teeth before going to bed. So I asked her if she'd mind chilling out for a while in the hammocks.

And yeah. That was that.

TWENTY-NINE

I stop again, because there's something I need to face up to. It's not just that it's weird reading about your mother having sex – though it is – it's also what this means. It's like, all the while I'm reading, I'm doing the maths in my head. My birthday is May 20. My date of birth is 20/05/2001 – that's the year after Mum first went to Greece. So this Neil guy, he could *literally* be my dad. If Mum was still sleeping with him around August 13, which is when she had to conceive me.

But there's this other thing too, kind of connected to what Kostas said. And right now, it's really nagging at my mind.

It's hard to explain, like a lot of this. But I'll try my best.

You see, even though my birthday is May 20, there's this weird thing about it. Actually it's *very* weird, although I've tried not to think about it too much. I've almost got used to it, like it's just part of who I am. Even though... even though that makes no sense at all.

I was about to turn twelve when it happened, maybe it was the night before? I remember we had the fire going in the living room, this old gas type that glowed orange and red. Anyway, I know I was excited about my birthday coming up, and I was telling Mum I couldn't wait to unwrap my presents, or for my party – or something like that. But this was right when Mum's boyfriend had just left, one of them. She was pretty messed up, and she was drinking. I don't want to give the wrong idea – Mum's not an alcoholic, but sometimes she does drink when things get her down. I guess this was one of those times for her.

Anyway, there was me, saying how I was looking forward to my birthday, and Mum had emptied at least one full bottle of wine, and maybe a bit more, and she just looked at me in this really weird way, and told me that tomorrow wasn't my actual birthday, it was just the day we'd chosen to celebrate it on. And I remember I asked what she meant by that, and who "we" were – but she wouldn't answer then, and she's never said since. The few times I was ever brave enough to ask what she meant by it, she always cut me down straight away, or even denied saying it in the first place.

So then. August 13 is the date where I'm finally going to discover who Daddy is. Except maybe it isn't. And maybe I'm not?

I read on. One way or another, I have to find out.

THIRTY

May 25th, 2000

It turns out Neil is a dick. A dick who doesn't know what to do with his dick. His tiny dick. I wasn't thinking we were like a couple, or anything like that. But after we slept together the other night, he could at least acknowledge me? But... no, it turns out he's a dick. First of all he totally ignored me the other night, when we all went out in Skalio, then I heard he spent the night in Sally Nanny's room – she's one of the nannies, and she's called Sally – hence the name. But she's rancid. She has these massive tits, that she sticks in the boys' faces all the time, but they're super droopy already, like she's fifty. I felt a bit humiliated actually, but Imogen was good about it. She stayed with me all night at the bar, then we walked back together, singing songs about Neil and his super-tiny dick.

I said before how she might be one of those people who's a bit shy at first, but really fun when they get going. And she is, but there's a bit more to it. She told me this big secret, her parents are Mormons. I didn't know what it was at first, I thought she said morons! And maybe I wasn't that far off, because they have these really strict rules about alcohol, and no sex before marriage and stuff like that. She's not fully Mormon now, like she does drink a little, but her family don't know. Anyway Imogen was saying she reckons half the waiters in town have got the hots for me. She said I have the best body in the whole of Skalio. Hers isn't that bad either, to be fair, and because her faith doesn't let her wear a bikini, it's not like people see if she's a bit fat.

May 26th

I love this freaking island!!! Last night was so awesome. We went to this bar on the other side of town, and it played this cool music. And mostly it was just me and Imogen, but we had this amazing talk, and we danced for ages. It was like neither of us were worrying about boys at all. Then when we got back to the staff house we sat outside and kept talking, long after everyone else had gone to sleep. There were these bats flying around, and you'd think it would be creepy, but it wasn't. And then Imogen made this origami bat, and she told me I had to keep it forever, so I never forget this time. And I won't forget, I promised her.

June 6th

So we've been here nearly a month already – it's crazy. I've not written in a while, because we've been soooo busy. Like, working every day, obviously (except for one day we get off). And then we've been going out most nights too. I've got to know Imogen really well. It's not just because we're roomies, it's also because she works in reception, and I'm by the pool, which is just outside. So when things are quiet she comes down to the bar where I am, and we can just chat with the guests, or help out if it gets busy. And if I'm quiet I can go in there, to chat to her too and still see the pool if anyone wants to get served.

. . .

We had a really big heart-to-heart too. It turned out she was feeling a bit, like intimidated maybe, by how easy I was finding it to hook up with guys (since Neil I was seeing Harris for a few days, but then I ditched him for the waiter I talked about before, he's called Stephan). Anyway, Imogen told me she's only ever had one boyfriend, this boy from her church back home. (I wasn't wrong before, he actually was an American football player!) But here, she's really got the hots for this guy in the gardens – Kostas. I liked him too at first, but he's not really my type, he's kinda quiet and doesn't really go out. But I told Imogen I'd help her hook up with him. So I'm gonna be playing Cupid. That's a Greek thing, right? It's gonna be super fun...

THIRTY-ONE

July 1st

Wow. July already! Almost a month since I last wrote anything. I've left some gaps, so I can go back and fill it in, but I'm going to do better from now on. I'm going to write something every single day. Scouts honour.

July 4th

Oops. I'm going to do better this time.

Actually there hasn't been that much to talk about the last few days. Plus, I couldn't find my pen, which isn't the best excuse, I know. But it is hard to write a diary without a pen.

Anyway. Today I do have a pen and something to report. It seemed like it was going to be bad, but then it turned out to be good.

What happened was, Mandy messed up BIG time.

Something happened with the guest flight so that it was coming in seven hours late. I don't know what, but all the newly arriving guests, who thought they were in for a four-hour flight, actually took eleven hours to get here, which is pretty bad, obviously. And then Mandy had to make sure the bus went to pick them up at the new time. There's no point sending it early and having the driver sit there for seven hours, he'd just go off and get drunk on ouzo, knowing Greek men.

Anyway, because Mandy is the dumbest person on the whole planet, she got the new flight arrival time wrong – Imogen says she can't even read the 24-hour clock – so the plane landed with all these exhausted clients, and there was no fricking bus to meet them.

We only found out when one of them phoned the owner of the resort – he lives back in London – and he phoned Jason to ask what the hell was going on.

After that, Jason went ballistic and came in and organised it himself. At first he was going to blame it on Imogen, but he saw that it was Imogen who'd actually already phoned another driver, and sent him down there, basically saving the day. I think Jason knew it was Mandy's fault anyway. If you sleep with someone every night, you must get a pretty good idea if they're an idiot or not? And Mandy doesn't exactly hide it.

So anyway, Jason was super angry, and even though Imogen did nothing wrong, he still shouted at her, and that made her upset. But who do you think was walking through the hotel lobby at just the right moment?

You guessed it: Kostas.

He didn't say anything at the time, but afterwards, when me and Imogen were at the staff house, he came up and asked if she was alright. He said he thought Jason had been unfair and ungentlemanly. He actually used that word!

And then he asked if we were going into Skalio later on.

I said we probably would, and he asked which bar we were going to. I told him, and he said he might go too. And Kostas never comes out. So I knew what that meant.

Anyway. Imogen got all nervous, because she really likes him. She didn't even want to go out at first. But I forced her to. Got her to have a few drinks, just to take the edge off.

And we had a fun time, except it seemed like Kostas wasn't going to turn up after all. But then he did, and he was in a really funny mood. Like actually funny, not his usual weird-funny.

And when we were going home, I went the other way, because Stephan had just finished his shift at the restaurant, and he has his own room, in Skalio, so that's handy.

But apparently, on the way home, Imogen and Kostas stopped off by the lifeguard tower and spent like forty minutes snogging. When I came home this morning, to get ready before work, she was looking all dreamy and happy. She wouldn't tell me at first, but she was so excited!

Like, the only thing is... it's kind of a waste that she's not going to shag him?

THIRTY-TWO

July 10th

One of the problems of Mandy being so dim is that if we need to see someone official, like a doctor or something, we have to go through her first. And me and Stephan, like, after a while you don't want to be using condoms the whole time – you know what I mean? So it would be really helpful to go and see the doctor to get the pill. I explained all this to her, and she actually asked if I was pregnant. (Did I mention she was stupid?) So I explained to her that NOT being pregnant was kind of the whole point of the contraceptive pill. And she just blinked at me, like she had no idea what I was talking about.

She did let me go to see the doctor though, and that was humiliating. The doctor was this old guy, and he looked really disapproving the whole time, and asked all sorts of questions, like how often I was having sex, and how many partners I'd had, and even if my partners were finishing! I think he was just getting off on having me there. But I'm quite good at men like that and I just kept smiling and answering whatever he asked with a blank face, and eventually he started to look uncomfortable, and he wrote me a prescription. Ha! Can't wait to tell Stephan. It's gonna be fun.

July 14th

Me and Stephan broke up. We were out the other night and he was super off with me, and I heard someone saw him with another girl. I'm not that bothered though. We were running out of things to say anyway. Plus there's a new guy down in the beach team called Simon who I kind of like. He's come to teach people how to sail the yachts, and he's worked in Greece for a few years, so he knows lots of the laws. Like one thing he was saying was, even though the Greek police are really anti-drugs, the law doesn't apply if you're on a boat, like because you're not actually on Greek land? Plus he told me he's known Jason for ages, and he uses drugs all the time, he's just really quiet about it.

Anyway, because all the rooms at the staff house are full, Simon's living on one of the resort yachts. The clients use it in the daytime, and it's his room at night, which is cool, plus he gets to use it on his day off. He said he'd bring a few of us out next time, like a party yacht.

The only problem is, Imogen reckons that Sally Nanny is going hard for Simon too. She saw her sticking her big milky tits in his face. She's such a cow.

THIRTY-THREE

July 17th

It's been really fun this week. Jason likes to move people around, so we don't get bored in our jobs, so I've been working down on the beach for a few days. And we had some really fun clients come out too. It was this big group of teenagers, who all know each other from back home. And we had a great time teaching them wakeboarding, and we did this beach-Olympics thing. And then afterwards we saw them in town, and they were all super drunk, even though most of them are only fifteen or something.

Today we all sailed up to town, in like this flotilla of different boats. We moored up in the harbour, and we all had pizza for lunch, and then ice creams. Then we all sailed back again. I think they really liked it. I think they appreciated the sense of independence it gave them. And maybe because we let them drink alcohol too, even though we weren't supposed to.

July 19th

OH MY GOD!!! You're never going to believe what happened! Sally Nanny got sent home! She was such a slut, she had it coming, but it's still way shocking. Those teenagers I was talking about, well one of them was pretty fit, but he was super young. But Sally Nanny being Sally Nanny was all over him on client night, when we have to mingle with the guests over dinner, and I heard she got off with him afterwards down on the beach.

And then last night, we all went out to Skalio, and I wasn't drinking much cos I was tired, but Sally was, and her and this kid were at it again on the walk back, they kept stopping to have a snog, and he had his hands permanently in her top. And when we got back to the hotel, she said she was gonna go for a swim in the pool, which is a really bad idea. It's one of the things Jason said we really weren't allowed to do, because loads of the rooms overlook the pool, and the guests don't want to see us all drunk. Anyway, Helen went in, just in her knickers, but Sally Nanny stripped off totally naked – big floppy tits and her fanny out – and she wasn't even quiet about it. Then Helen came back to the staff house to dry off, but Sally stayed with the kid, and apparently he started taking her from behind, on one of the sun loungers! And then these clients, out for a nice midnight stroll, they came walking up the path by the pool, and they got to see everything – Sally Nanny at it with this fifteen-year-old kid.

Anyway, the next day, the clients came in to see Jason. Imogen was there, and she overheard everything. Apparently they were really upset, they said they hadn't come on holiday to Ancient Greece!

When they'd gone, Jason called Imogen in and got her to book the first flight home for Sally Nanny (notice how he doesn't trust

Mandy to do it!) – and then he called Sally up from the crèche and told her she was fired, and that she better stay out of sight until she leaves, or she might get thrown in prison for actual rape.

So we're down one nanny! Can't say I'm sorry though.

July 22nd

Bit of a weird day today. Because the crèche is still short staffed, Jason told me I had to help out, so I spent the whole morning in this room full of babies. I thought I was going to hate it, because I've never really wanted kids, but actually it was weirdly alright. I wasn't going to do any nappy changes, because it's not my job, but it was sort of fun playing with them. We took them for a walk around the gardens just before lunch and then down to the beach in the afternoon, and they followed us around like little ducklings. They're actually quite sweet.

July 25th

Last day in the crèche, we've got a new nanny coming out, thank God. It's not that I mind the crèche, but it does have this smell, like poo and detergent, and it gets all over your clothes. The new nanny is called Suzanne. I haven't met her yet but according to Imogen she's got really bad acne.

Aiden wants to cool it, which is fine by me. He's this guy I've been seeing, but he's pretty boring actually. All he talks about is sailing.

Everyone's going out tonight. I'm writing this at the staff house, and me and Imogen are already halfway through a bottle of

Metaxa. It feels like I haven't had a good night out in ages. I feel like I need to let off some steam.

THIRTY-FOUR

As Mum gets closer to the month of August, I'm getting this sense of – I don't know – dread? Like, is this *really* how I want to find out the name of my father? How am I gonna feel if he's just some kid, like a drunken one-night stand? And what if he's *literally* a teenage tourist? Plus, it's actually quite hard to keep up, there's so many, and sometimes the first I hear about them is when she breaks up.

I don't know, for some reason, even though Mum wouldn't ever say anything about who my dad is, I still imagined him as a proper grown up – like someone I could maybe meet one day. And like – there'd be meaning behind me. A moment of something that meant something to her. But from her diary, it's obvious how immature she was, just partying around. I mean, I guess it's fine – I'm not judging her. Not too much. Like, she's lived the life she's lived and that's fine by me, but I just want to find out where I fit into it. Is that too much to ask?

But I keep reading, and then there's a problem.

THIRTY-FIVE

August 9th, 2000

So I haven't written for a while, but that's because

THIRTY-SIX

That's it. That's all she's written. For the entire month of August. And the next entry is September 15. What does *that* mean? Why hasn't she written anything? I page backwards and forwards several times, as if that's going to somehow make more text appear. But obviously it doesn't. So – feeling... I don't know, cheated? Relieved? I'm not even sure – I keep going, but I feel pretty sick by this point.

September 15th

My bad for not writing in ages. I must get better, but it's been sooooo crazy busy what with the school holidays and all the kids we've had running around, like little vermin. It's been way fun though, all the same. I've like, had four guys on the go, too, for most of the summer, but it's all been fun, nothing serious.

There's only a few weeks left of the season, and Jason says we have to start packing things away for the winter. But he also started talking about jobs for next year. He left this sheet with Imogen, where we could all put our names down, and she made sure that hers and my name were on the top of the list. And then she sneaked into Mandy's office where they'd been discussing who they wanted to come back, and who they didn't, and they'd put a tick by both of our names. I mean I'm not surprised, because we've both been super reliable and stuff, but it's still cool to know for sure.

October 2nd

It's really different, this time of year. It actually rained today. I don't think I've really seen rain in months, but the sky was grey and full of dark clouds, and then it just started raining, and just didn't stop. I didn't have a single customer at the bar all afternoon. I just sat there staring at the raindrops splashing onto the surface of the water. It was pretty.

Then afterwards, when the rain stopped, all the staff went out into town and we had a meal in the restaurant by the harbour. It was all paid for by Jason. He gave a little speech thanking us for all our hard work, and saying how he was looking forward to seeing us come back next year too. Then he looked at me and made a joke about the bars needing the winter to restock all the booze. It was sweet though.

October 19th

Oh my God. I cannot elieve we're going home tomorrow. I don't mind – I could use a rest – but I'm sad for Imogen because of how Kostas broke up with her. I mean, you could see it coming, because how's it going to work, with her going to America for the winter, and him staying here? And with her parents and how strict they are? But even so she was pretty cut up about it. It's gonna be weird though. I'm actually gonna miss her.

THIRTY-SEVEN

The next entry is January.

I flip back and read it again, trying to see if I've missed anything. The last guy I can see that Mum was with when she conceived me – in August – was this guy *Aiden*. And then afterwards, she mentions four guys – but doesn't give their names. So any one of them could be my father. Which means that, even with the best piece of evidence I could possibly hope for – a handwritten, first-person record of who Mum slept with – I still don't know. *I don't believe it. I literally don't believe it.*

I stop and cover my face with my hands, blacking out the world. Is this all just a complete waste of time? Am I doomed to fail here? It really is beginning to feel like it. But then I think a bit more, and see I'm being hasty. After all, there's more to read, and once she realises she's pregnant, then obviously she's going to put in her diary who she thinks the father is. I mean, you would, wouldn't you?

You just would.

So with that in mind, I keep going.

THIRTY-EIGHT

January 1st, 2001

So. Several New Year's Resolutions. Number One, I'm giving up smoking. I think I can do it when I'm sober. The problem is going out, it's almost impossible to not want a fag when other people are smoking. Number Two: I'm going to learn Greek. I think it would be way useful, particularly if I'm going to do another summer on Alythos. Three. Diary. I didn't exactly succeed in writing this every day, but it's good to have a record of things, and reading this back, there's loads of nights I might remember better if I'd written about them. So this year I'm really gonna make an effort. On that note, here goes for a catch up of the last week or so:

Christmas was dull-as. I was at home the whole time, and we barely did anything. Just ate, drank, and watched TV. I went out a couple of times with my old school friends, but I feel like I've moved on from them. Like, because I've been abroad, and they haven't? Home just feels... small.

Dad's still way still pissed off about me crashing out of uni. Him and Mum want me to go back. But I keep telling them I do actually have a job, in Alythos – it just doesn't start till April. They don't seem impressed though.

I wish Imogen lived closer. I tried to get her to come and visit, but the tickets are too expensive. I miss her.

January 9th

I'm temping in an office that processes insurance claims. It's sooooo boring. I just sit there all day, typing numbers into a computer. Honestly, a monkey could do it. Actually, it couldn't – it would die of boredom.

Got an email from Imogen today. She says she's not sure she wants to go back to Alythos anymore. I phoned her straight away – even though it costs a fortune – and it turns out she's worried about being there if she's not with Kostas.

So I told her there are loads of other guys, and they'll probably get back together anyway, because they were so good together. Which is probably a lie. I thought about telling her to promise him a blowjob if they got back together, because that would probably help.

Anyway, I had to beg her, tell her I wasn't going to go if she didn't, and that would ruin my life, and in the end she said alright.

January 10th

Night out with the girls. Don't actually remember getting home. My head hurts now.

I stop reading and count on my fingers. August, September, October, November, December, January. *Shit.* Mum would have been five months pregnant at this time. Surely she'd have noticed? And if so, shouldn't she have slowed down on the drinking? I mean, a little bit? Maybe this explains some of my issues? Like why I find it hard to concentrate sometimes? Why I sometimes feel so down?

For God's sake.

I read on.

THIRTY-NINE

March 20th

I met up with the girls from school last night, since I'm off to Greece again next week. It's been nice seeing them, although they're funny about me going again. It was fun, and we all got pissed, but Sharon cried because I was leaving her again, as if I was still her best friend and everything. I didn't cry, but I did pretend.

Actually it made me think of Imogen, and like – even though I've known Sharon since we were kids – I'd definitely say Imogen is a closer friend now. I've really missed her. I guess it's just because we've been through things together. Things that Sharon and me haven't been through.

I can't wait to go now. My parents are driving me mad and I'm soooo bored at the monkey job. I'm just counting down the days.

April 1st

Back in Alythos! Yay! Not kidding either. (Check the date, future me!) It is soooo good to be back. It's weird though, because a load of people from last year haven't come back, and there's all these new people – who are fresh and over-excited about everything, and don't really know about how it all works. But other than that, it's just like last year. Jason even gave his first flight home speech.

April 4th

Wow, I'd forgotten how hard pre-season is. The new people are useless, but eventually we get the hotel looking OK, and then Jason said he'd take everyone out again, like last year. But then he cancelled it, on account of Mandy feeling "unwell". So that was... kind of shit.

Imogen says her winter was boring too, and she's way nervous about seeing Kostas. I asked her if she spoke to him over the winter, and she didn't have his number, so she couldn't. It's like, come on girl.

April 19th

Big night out last night. We started off at the staff house, then went into town, and honestly I kind of blacked out a bit, because I must have drunk too much. It was alright, but something feels different this year? Maybe it's just the mix of people isn't quite right? I don't know. It's also Imogen. Even though she's still really nice, she's back with Kostas (that took all of one week) and she spends most of her time with him. And even when she's not with him, she's always saying she feels ill or tired. I think she just doesn't want to go out. Not now she's back with Kostas, the love of her bloody life.

May 20th

Mandy's gone into hospital. It means Imogen's doing all her work, and Mandy's work too. Plus she's moaning about not feeling well again – Imogen, I mean. I think it's the kids' club. It finishes at five, when the kids get served their meal. And we started this thing where we dared the kids to steal platefuls of pizza and chicken nuggets and bring it over to Imogen at reception. And now it's like a thing, because all the guests overlap, all the new kids learn about it from the old kids. So Imogen keeps eating it. I keep telling her not too. Like, does she think Kostas is going to hang around if she really bloats out? I don't think so.

At least I still look good in a bikini.

FORTY

I put the book down. My heart is thudding in my chest. I don't know what to think. I just don't know. I re-read the entry for May 20, 2001. The day I was born. Or apparently, the day I wasn't born.

May 20, 2001. My mother reports how good she still looks in a bikini. Not that she's given birth. Not that this is – unexpected perhaps – but the happiest day of her life.

What the fuck? What the actual fuck?

My eyes suddenly start running with tears. I wipe them away, slip my sunglasses on, and turn around to the wall, so that no one can see my face. I can hardly breathe. There's no air.

But I have to keep reading. And things are about to go from weird, to fully surreal.

FORTY-ONE

May 24th

So I didn't mention, but Mandy had her baby. Did I say she was preggers? Well she is/was, because now she's had the kid. Honestly, I do not know how that woman is going to survive looking after a child. She is soooo useless. And it's not like Jason's going to help. First he now has to do all her work, because he's too much of a control freak to let anyone else have any responsibility. Like, I could do soooo much more than run the pool bar. I already am really, but he won't let me do it properly. It's soooo annoying.

Talking of... guess who I saw in town doing a little transaction with our friendly local drug dealer? You guessed it. Our ever-hypocritical manager. I couldn't see exactly what it was he was buying, but Simon said Jason's been hitting the speed really hard this summer, and you can see it in his eyes. Simon said he got some really good coke though, from the same guy, he's this Russian who's been hanging around. Simon said we should go out on his boat sometime for a party. I think I will, if he asks me again.

May 27th

Fucked Simon in his yacht last night. I was talking to him in the bar, and we were both pretty wasted, and I just said to him straight, we've known each other ages and we ought to fuck. He looked a bit shocked, but then he grinned and said alright. So we went down to the harbour, because he's still staying on the yacht. We did a bit of coke, but not much because he was nearly out. But he says he can get some more. It's funny. It's a very small boat, I kept banging my head on the roof while we did it.

FORTY-TWO

June 4th

Mandy is being a total nutcase – more than usual – now she has the baby. First of all she won't let anyone touch it, or even look at it, except me and Imogen. It's like she thinks the three of us are best friends just because we've known each other for two summers. Or maybe because Imogen works with her up in reception, and Imogen's my best friend. Anyway, she lets us look at it, and hold it, even though neither of us even wants to.

But that's not the thing. Mandy apparently decided her room was too dirty, and she told the cleaners to come in and give it a proper deep clean. I only heard this from Imogen, via Kostas, because obviously all the cleaners only speak Greek, but they came in, and it was really hard to clean, on account of all Mandy and Jason's stuff being everywhere, and all the baby stuff too, but when they were doing it they lifted the mattress and they found a gun there! Kostas reckons it's because of all the drugs Jason's been buying from that Russian dude. It's made him even more paranoid than usual. Or maybe he bought the gun from the Russian dude – I don't know. Anyway, they didn't know what to do with it, so they just put it back, cleaned the room as best they could, then left.

June 12th

It should be my day off tomorrow, but Jason came past the bar as I was closing, and told me I couldn't take tomorrow off, because he didn't have anyone else to cover the bar I was so mad. I told Jason it wasn't fair, but he got super pissed and told me he hasn't had a day off in over a month. But that's not my fault. He shouldn't have knocked up his girlfriend. Anyway. I was supposed to be going out with Simon, on the yacht, for a bit of you-know-what with our friend Charlie, but now that's not going to happen.

June 23rd

Day off tomorrow, and it's actually happening this time. God, I so need it! I don't remember last year being so tiring. Anyway, me and Simon have been making this plan, the last few days. He managed to score again, and he switched his day off with Dan and he's finally fixed the rigging on the Sigma 27 – so we're going to sail over to the mainland, and have lunch there, and have a look in the shops, and we might even stay over in the marina overnight, before coming back early the next day. It'll just be soooo nice to get away from this fucking place. I soooo need a break.

Or rather (I'm writing this later). It would have been nice. Here's the problem: stupid Mandy just grabbed me at the bar and said she really needed my help, because she has to go to Athens tomorrow, for some sort of paperwork for the baby. I told her to take it with her, but she won't because it's four hours on the bus each way. So I told her to dump it in the crèche, but she went mental and said she didn't trust them. She only trusts me. I asked why Imogen couldn't look after it, but Mandy said she'd gone back to her room feeling ill. Which is fricking typical of Imogen too.

So I don't know what I'm gonna do. Tomorrow is my first day off in fricking ages, and the last thing I want to do is spend it looking after Mandy's fricking sprog.

I've so had it with this place. And everyone in it.

I turn the page, expecting to keep reading, but there's nothing there. Quickly I thumb forward, but that's it, there's nothing more. This is the final entry. Then the date registers in the wheels of my wildly spinning mind. *June 23, 2001.* She would have written this entry the night before Jason Wright went crazy and murdered Mandy Paul. Leaving their four-week-old baby alive.

I stare at the words. Not seeing them now. Instead I see my hands, gripping the edges of the book. And suddenly they look wrong, the fingers comically twisted, sickening. Alien. Like two ugly claws. *What am I?* I feel the air, in an instant, punched out of the restaurant around me, shooting away at light speed into space. At once my chest begins scraping, in and out, grasping for oxygen. But it's gone. I can't breathe. I can't think.

There's a flutter, then a rush, as panic overwhelms me. I realise this is real. I *actually* cannot breathe. What is this? A heart attack? A heat in my chest quickly builds to a burn, a screaming terror inside me.

I *feel* the world. I feel it spinning, trying to fling me from its surface, yet wrenched back by the violence of gravity. Pinning me here, pressing me into my seat. Stuck between these epic forces, powerless and minute.

My final thought, before I'm crushed into nothing, my stopped-heart, oxygen-starved brain flickering in and out of awareness. This cannot be happening.

Not again.

FORTY-THREE

It's a panic attack. I know it now, I've had them before. Back in university, when things got too much. A waiter appears beside me, speaking words I don't hear, but I'm concentrating. Counting my breaths, like they told me. Forcing my chest to suck in for five useless seconds, then out for five more. It's like breathing through a straw, not enough, but it's not nothing either. *Relax, Ava. Let it go.* You know what this is. It feels like death but you just need to calm down.

Let it go. In for five. Out for five. Close your eyes. Step back. Step away. Just for a moment.

A glass of water has appeared on my table. I guess it must be the waiter. I pick it up and sip. It's cooling, almost magical, I feel the sensation of it trickling down inside my body. I hear the waiter's words again. *Are you OK?* I nod, not looking at him, still counting the breaths. The straw I'm breathing through widens a little, lets in a bit more air. *I'm OK. I'm going to be OK.* I sip again. *It's just a panic attack. You've done this before. You know how to get through.*

I rub a hand over my face, and it's *my* hand again, no longer the alien claw I saw before. These panic attacks, they're terrifying, like a glimpse of how the world really is, a reality normally hidden from us.

I shudder, feeling myself slipping back down into my earthly dimension. Yet one that's forever changed.

A few minutes later I'm able to leave. I don't check the bill, just drop a twenty-euro note on the table and risk walking. I'm back, yet not the same as I was. What I've just read, the implications of it – my whole world has fallen to pieces. I'm not who I thought I was. I don't know who I am.

I don't know where to go either. Not my apartment, and not the beach either, where there'll be people, staring at me, and where I'll see the derelict Aegean Dream Resort, where my mother worked. The woman who isn't my mother.

But I have to move. I have to walk. If I don't the panic will come back, and maybe it'll beat me this time. So I just begin, taking streets at random, whichever has the least number of eyes watching me. Soon I'm in a part of Skalio I haven't seen before, and then the town itself starts to thin out. I go past paddocks, a field of chickens, another with donkeys. I keep walking, buttoning up my brain, not letting myself think about what I've just read and all that it means.

Eventually the town stops all together, but I keep going, more steeply uphill now, up the side of the mountain where Gregory Duncan's house is, but long before I get there, the heat takes its toll. I only sipped at the water from the cafe, and I've walked for over an hour. And maybe I've cried a lot of liquid out too. Either way, I'm thirsty. I keep hoping that perhaps I'll come across a well, made of beautiful stone, where I can bring up bucketfuls of silvery, cool water, but of course I don't, because that's in my head, my mind still running two scripts, reality and something else.

Even a tap would do though. But there's nothing. So I stop – really stop. Try and regain some sort of control.

Somehow it's six o'clock already, the whole day gone, and even though the heat is cooling a little, my throat is still parched. I begin to make my way back down the same dusty, rocky path I've been walking up. I suppose I'll go back to my apartment. From there... I have no idea.

As I pass the first few houses on the edge of town, I become aware of the noise of a motor, and for a moment I'm confused, because I recognise it. Then I see her, on her moped that pulls to the left – Sophia. She slows down just in front of me – I think for a moment because she's seen me, but then I realise because she's about to turn into a house. But then she *does* see me. She stops, lifts the helmet off her face.

"*Ava?* What are you doing here?"

FORTY FOUR

I want to hide. I don't want to speak to her, or anyone. I'm not even sure I remember *how* to speak. But I have to try. I used to be human, after all.

"Um..."

"Hey, I wanted to apologise," a part of my brain hears her say. She doesn't catch my mumbled reply. "About before in the restaurant. I was in a bad mood." She tips her head on one side, inspecting me curiously. "I used to go out with Darius, you know, the waiter there? We broke up months ago, and he won't accept it, and he was being a dick..." She shakes her head. "It's just Kostas sent me in there to pick up some breakfast and... hey are you OK?"

I think I must be crying. I know I'm crying. But I try to mask it.

"I'm fine," I say, but clearly I'm not.

"No you're not. Hey, come here." She pulls the moped onto its stand and goes to hold me. For a moment we just stand there, her supporting me. Then she steadies me as she pulls back, looking in my face. "What is it?"

I turn my head. I still have my sunglasses on, but the tears are falling down my cheeks, impossible to hide.

"It's nothing." I step back out of her hands and wipe my cheek. Coming face to face with something real has broken the spell I've been in since I put the diary down. I face her, forcing a smile, amazed how easy it is to pretend everything's OK. "I'm fine. Just tired."

"Alright." Sophia bites her lower lip, still staring at me. "So what are you doing up here?"

It takes me a moment to answer this, I'm not sure what she means, like – is this a place for locals only?

"I was just walking."

"Why?"

Why? And like a punch to the stomach, the directness of her questions just floors me. I don't have an answer. Why am I here? Because my legs took me here. Because my mother *isn't* my mother. Because I'm so thirsty. Suddenly it registers Sophia must live here. In the house we're standing outside of. It has a pretty porch with purple flowers growing up around. They must need water. They must *have* water.

"I'm adopted," I hear myself say, out loud, before I have a chance to stop myself saying it.

"*What?*"

"I'm adopted. I just found out I'm adopted," I say again, and I stare at her now, horrified at the phrase I've just uttered. But after a few moments of looking confused, she actually smiles.

"I'm adopted too."

"*What?*"

"Yeah. I've always known – well, not always, but for as long as I remember. My mother – not my real mother, obviously – but I've always called her *mamá*, she never hid it from me though. Her and my father said it didn't matter, we were still a perfect family..." She stops talking and bites her lip again.

"Hey, I'm sorry. You've just found out, right? That must be a shock. Do you want a drink, some water or something?"

Dumbly I nod my head. I don't know how she knows, but I don't care. I think I might die if I don't drink something. I follow her like a puppy through her gate, and into a small garden, where she parks the moped properly and sits me down at a table in the shade. She pulls open a French door and disappears inside, before coming back with a tall glass of water and a pretty jug with more. I take the glass and put it down empty.

"Wow. You want more?"

I nod. She refills it, and I empty it once more.

"More?" Her voice is edged with fun. She's enjoying this. She seems able to enjoy anything.

I shake my head now. I feel so foolish, sitting here. Being like this.

"Is this where you live?"

"Yeah." Sophia glances around, as if noticing for the first time, but then her interest comes back to me. "Yeah, I grew up here." She hesitates a moment. "Well, here and the supermarket. That's where my mother works."

It takes me a moment to understand this, to make the connection. But there's something about them both. "Maria, the lady from the shop? That's...?"

Sophia laughs. "Yeah. That's her."

"What about your dad? Your adopted dad?"

"He was a programmer, computers. Stuff like that." There's a new note to her voice, a brittleness. "He died a couple years ago."

I don't say anything at first, but I blink at her.

"Oh, I'm sorry."

"Yeah," – she bites her lip – "pancreatic cancer, when I was nineteen." She rolls her shoulders, like this is how life goes, but it still sucks.

"I'm really sorry."

"It's OK. I mean yeah, me and *Mamá* too, obviously. He was English by the way. Came out here to work, met my mother and stayed. That's how I speak OK English, it's what we spoke at home. But you don't need to hear about me. Let's talk about you. I guess you found something out?"

I don't actually know if I want to tell her, or if I need to tell her. But I find I'm already speaking before I wonder if it's a good idea to share.

"I was reading my mum's diary, from when she was here, twenty-two years ago. I was hoping it might tell me who my dad was, by working back from when I was born, and seeing who she was... sleeping with."

"Well, that is how it works." She flashes a grin, which fades as she waits for me to carry on.

"Only there were... lots of men. Different men. I couldn't tell which of them was the right one."

Sophia purses her lips at this.

"Well, that's not gonna be the easiest of reads."

I shake my head in agreement. "But that's not it. The diary goes right up to when I was supposed to be born, only she doesn't seem to be pregnant, and then – on the day I actually *was* born, there's nothing, she just complains about stuff. Says she looks good in a bikini."

Sophia thinks about this. "So it doesn't *say* you're adopted? You just figured it out?"

I nod. But my mind flares, screams in protest, and I have this need now for her to understand.

"Except I still don't really know for sure, because this one time – when I was younger – she told me this thing on my birthday, that it wasn't actually my birthday, it was just the day 'they'd' chosen to celebrate it on. Like what the hell does that mean?"

Her smile has disappeared. Now she just looks confused.

"Maybe you need something stronger than water?" She

takes my empty glass and disappears inside, while I just wait. A few moments later she comes back with it refilled, heavy with ice. She sets it down, then crosses the garden to a small tree. I didn't notice, but now I see it's laden with yellow fruits, huge lemons. Around it are roses, white and red. It's really pretty. She twists off a lemon, sits back down and carves two slices with a pocket knife. She drops one into my glass, the other into hers.

"Gin and tonic," she says. "Hope that's OK, it's all we've got."

I nod, then take a sip. The fizz, the acid, the bite of the gin. It helps. A bit.

"Can you talk to your mother?" Sophia says, moments later. "Ask her what it's all about?"

I blink at her. Trying to imagine that. I tip my head back, really trying to see if that would work. What would it mean to ask her, what would she say? I know she'd be angry. Humiliated that I read her diary. Maybe justifiable. She's angry already, she never even replied to my text. I find myself shaking my head.

"We don't really have that sort of a relationship," I tell her, then give a crooked smile, as if I know how strange that sounds.

"So this was all in a diary?" Sophia says again, sipping her drink. I sense she's about to ask where I got it, but she doesn't. I reach into my shoulder bag and hand it to her. "Here."

She hesitates, like she isn't sure if she ought to look at it, but I press it towards her, and sit back while she flicks through.

I nurse the drink while she reads. I just surrender to the place, the fragrance of the roses. The buzz from the gin. I don't know how much she gets through, but she looks up.

"So, what..." Sophia looks confused still.

"I was born on 20 May. Or I thought I was. The second year that she was working at the resort. Except obviously I wasn't."

"You should speak to her," Sophia tells me again. "You have to speak to her. I mean, even if she isn't your mother, she's still your *mother*, right? She brought you up? And whatever happened, it doesn't change that. The important thing is you have someone who loves you."

I blink at her again. The words don't connect.

"The important thing is you have someone who's *honest* with you," Sophia goes on, and this time I burst out laughing. A mirthless laugh.

"OK." Sophia presses her fingers to her temples. "Wow, this is super heavy. I mean, could there be other explanations? Sometimes women don't know they're pregnant, not until super late. Could that explain it?"

"I don't see how. I never heard of someone not knowing they were pregnant until four weeks after the baby was born."

Sophia grins again at this. "No. Fair point. I guess not. Well what about this date thing? What do you think she meant by that?"

"I don't know." I've thought about it for years, and I have no idea.

We both fall silent.

"So what are you going to do?" Sophia asks next.

FORTY FIVE

"What *do* you know?" Sophia asks, a few moments later.

"What?"

I realise I must have been sitting here a while, just resting in the silence. It's a lovely peaceful place, scented by the flowers and the lemon tree, shady but still warm.

"About where you were born and everything? What do you know for certain? You said you were from the island?"

"Yeah." I nod, pulling myself up straighter. "I was born on the island. At least, that's what my passport says..." I stop, it's here with me, I put it in my bag this morning, after what happened last night in my apartment. I rummage for a second and pull it out, then hold it out to her. Sophia turns to the back.

"OK. So a British passport, but place of birth: Alythos, Greece."

I give a shrug.

"Well, that looks pretty official. And it has your date of birth. May 20, 2001." She smiles suddenly, a flash of white teeth. "You're exactly one month older than me. That's cool."

The smile lingers, then fades away. "How about a birth

certificate? You have one of those? You must have had one to get a passport?"

"Yeah." I frown. "I think so. At home. I'm sure I've seen one."

"English or Greek?"

"Greek."

"And you don't have it here?"

I shake my head. "No. Mum's always looked after that sort of thing."

"Yeah. Mothers are good for that."

We're both quiet.

"Maybe you can find out from the records here? If you were born here, it would have been recorded... although..." She makes a face.

"What?"

"It's just... Greek bureaucracy, it can be difficult." She gives a lopsided look. "That's kind of an understatement. It's a nightmare."

"Do you know anything about it?" I ask, suddenly hopeful, but she shakes her head again.

"No. *Mamá* might. I mean, she went through it all, when she adopted me, I suppose. But that was a long time ago. I'm not sure how much she'll remember. And since then it's probably all changed."

For the first time it hits me that, however hard this is for me to deal with, I'm not the only one who's gone through tough times. There's a portrait on the wall inside the house, Maria and a younger Sophia, with a man who must be her father.

"Is that your dad?" I point to it now.

"Yeah."

"He looks nice."

She looks wistful a moment. Sad, she nods. "Yeah. He was."

"I could ask my mother, about the adoption stuff," she goes

on quickly. "I don't know if she'll be able to help, but I'm sure she'll want to. She's pretty good like that."

I look around before answering. I'm not sure how I came to be here, sitting at this table, looking out over the pretty garden, the lemon tree, the ancient stone wall covered in roses. The view up to the mountainside beyond. I find myself nodding.

"Would you? Yeah, that would be cool."

Again we both fall quiet, but only for a moment.

"Do you want some olives?"

Before I can answer Sophia jumps up again. When she comes back, it's not just with a jar of giant olives, under her arm she also has a laptop. She puts it on the table and unscrews the jar. She spoons out a dozen or so olives onto the plate, and pushes it towards me.

"I was thinking you could try and find the people in the diary. Track them down. Maybe they could tell you something?"

I'm confused by this. "How would I find them?"

She pops an olive in her mouth, it's so big it makes her cheek puff out, like a hamster. She tries to answer like that, but the words come out all wrong. So she bites the meat off the olive then pops the stone out and tries again.

"At the front of the diary?"

I don't know what she means, but she shows me. Right on the front page are some contact details. There's only two there: *Imogen Grant*, with a phone number, which I think has an American code in front of it. The second one is an email address: SimonWalkerDenzil@popmail.com

"Are there any other 'Simons' in the diary?" she asks. "If not this has to be the guy your mum was with, just before the murders." She doesn't seem to be listening, so I don't even answer, but I move my chair to better see her screen.

"What are you doing?"

She still doesn't answer, but her fingers are working fast on the keyboard, typing into a black window that's appeared on her screen. I'm distracted by the background photo on her desktop. It's her riding some sort of flying surfboard thing.

"I'm pinging it to see if the email's still live. There." She sits back, waits a second, and a new line of text appears:

451 Temporary Local Problem

"What does that mean?"

"It means Popmail still exists," – Sophia turns to me, looking thoughtful – "but this Simon guy probably doesn't use this email anymore. Or he might have died." She brightens. "Let's find out."

She turns back to the computer, clicking open another browser window, and her fingers blur as she types a search for *Simon + Walker + Denzil OR Walker-Denzil*. "Funny name," she explains, as the search runs.

She's much quicker than me scanning the results. She's already clicked the fourth one down before I've finished reading the summary of the first. A new page opens, which seems to be some sort of crew-finding service for yachts. There's a photograph of a man in his late thirties, with brown hair and tanned skin. He's standing behind the wheel of a large sailing yacht, braced against the boat's heel.

"Here we go," Sophia says. "Superyacht Crew International. Simon Walker-Denzil. He's a captain, with a 'Master 3000 GT licence' – whatever that is, and full STCW training. Good for him. But this is four years ago." Already she's clicking back off the page, and hitting another link. This time a newspaper article opens. There's another picture, of an enormous boat this time, more of a ship really. The article seems to be about corruption, as much of it as can be read before Sophia has covered the text with another search box. This zooms straight to where Simon's name appears in the article. A snippet of text:

Celestial's captain is thought to be a British man, Simon Walker-Denzil. The rumours are he was hired because he keeps his mouth shut. However the yacht has been flagged for "security reasons" in multiple ports.

"This is better, it's from last year," Sophia says, though I can't see where she's seen this. "Let me see, *Celestial*..." On a new tab she runs a search for *"Yacht Celestial"*, then another for *"Yacht Celestial + location"*.

"I could try with AIS, but I doubt most of these superyachts would bother turning it on."

I wait for her to explain, but she doesn't. "What's AIS? And also, how do you know all this stuff?"

"I told you, my dad was a programmer. But he used to work on fishing boats too, so I know a bit about boats. Hence the AIS."

"I... what...?"

"It's the identification system that ships use. You can track them on sites like MarineTraffic. So it's like air traffic control, but for ships." She glances at me, a little embarrassed. "It's maybe a bit geeky, but... I'm a bit of a geek."

Another window appears on the screen. It's a map of this part of the Aegean, with little flashing orange and blue triangles, that I suppose must be ships? Sophia runs another search, typing *"Celestial"* and ticking the option for private yacht. But nothing comes up.

"Don't worry," she tells me. "We'll find it."

She runs the search again in Google, but clicks on *"News"* this time, and now she picks the first story on the list. It's dated from two days ago.

Superyacht Celestial spotted in Athens Marina

"Here we go. I've got a friend in Athens. There're always loads of these boats there, the owners hardly ever use them, so they just sit there. I bet it's still there."

I'm a bit bewildered by how fast she did all that.

"But I still can't contact him. I mean, you can't just walk onto someone's superyacht?"

For the first time, Sophia looks beaten. She bites her lip, and her fingers stay still. Then, just as she's about to answer, the black text window she first used appears again on the screen.

220 mail.popmail.com ESMTP Service Ready

250 2.1.0 Sender OK

250 2.1.5 Recipient OK

"Oh," Sophia says. "That is still his address. So maybe you could just email him?"

FORTY-SIX

It takes me ages to figure out what to write. Because what is this guy going to say? But in the end – and with Sophia sitting there telling me to just do it – I do. I tell him who I am, that I'm in Greece and I'm trying to find out about my parents. And I ask if it would be OK to speak to him. I figure there's a one percent chance he's even going to answer is, but I hit send and the email flies away.

After that, Sophia invites me to stay for dinner, but I've been here long enough, and I'm not really hungry, just shattered, emotionally but physically too. So she gives me a lift back on her moped, and when I get inside my apartment I lock the door behind me, lie down on my bed, and fall straight asleep.

I check my phone when I wake up, not expecting anything, but I can't believe it. There's a reply from Simon Walker-Denzil. As I open it I anticipate a refusal – a polite brush-off maybe, or something saying he's moved on, they're now in the Caribbean, or somewhere else where I can't get to. But instead he sounds... friendly. Cautious though. He says he doesn't know how much help he'll be. But he's still here, and happy to try.

I phone Sophia at once. She's on her way to work, but there's no doubting what she thinks I should do. I tell her I need to work too, but she scolds me. What is it I'm doing here? Working for Hans or finding out who my parents are? She tells me that Bar Sunset has survived for years without me, and it'll cope for a day or so more. So before I can think too much about it, I email Simon back, asking when he can meet. He comes back five minutes later saying that today works, if I can get to him. So then I find myself at the bus station, booking a seat on the eleven o'clock to Athens. Klaus did say the location of my place was handy.

The journey is the same one I took to get here, only in reverse. The local bus from Skalio to Kastria. Change to the busier service to Panachoria, which takes me off the island on the ferry, then change again for the main service to Athens. It's only half-full, and it has air con which helps because it's a hot day. I'm even a little cold as I look out on the dry, rocky valleys and mountain slopes of olive groves. As we get closer to Athens though it becomes more industrial. It's not so different to England, except there's a dusty griminess to the surroundings instead of the dampness of home.

As I disembark in Athens bus station I'm assaulted by the noises, smells and heat of the capital. But not for long. Simon told me to text him as I was arriving, saying he'd send a car to pick me up. I told him there was no need, but he emailed back again saying it was the only way I'd make it through security. So I look around, not knowing exactly what to expect. But then – parked in the space where a bus is supposed to go – there's a huge black BMW, a man standing outside, young and smartly dressed. He's leaning casually on the front, watching me, as if he's not yet sure if I'm who he's come to collect, but he suspects that I am. In a way I'm even more unsure. I have to force myself to approach him, and I don't know what I'm going to say, especially if I've got this wrong and he's nothing to do with me. But he speaks before I get the chance.

"Ava Whitaker?" He looks at me a little too long. Up close I notice his strength, firm muscles under his shirt and around his neck. Like he's half-chauffeur, half-bodyguard.

"Um, that's right."

He pushes himself off the car and pulls open the back door. "Take a seat." I don't know where he's from, his accent is hard to place, maybe Eastern European, maybe something completely different. I hesitate just a moment, wondering if this is a bad idea, but I don't have much choice. I climb inside, onto the cool leather seats. The man presses the door softly shut behind me.

The traffic is bad but he's skilful, sliding the big car in and out of gaps, and using its presence to force other cars out of his way. He also makes liberal use of a bus lane at one point. Athens is a shipping city. Through gaps between the buildings I catch glimpses of the stunning blue sea, but also of shipyards and long rows of gleaming white yachts. As I look about I notice the driver's eyes watching me sometimes in the rear-view mirror, but he doesn't speak again.

We pull off from the busy streets onto a motorway, and then take the next exit straight off again. This takes us to a part of the city that feels much quieter. We slow at a gate that divides a long and high security fence. Two men in uniforms, batons hanging from their belts, approach the car. As they stand there talking to the driver, I notice they both have handguns too, in leather pouches on their belts. It all seems fairly relaxed though, even when one of the guards pulls out a device that looks like a mirror on a trolley, which he wheels under the car.

"Looking for bombs," the driver's voice suddenly explains, making me jump.

The second guard raps on my window, telling me to open it,

then looks in at me and the cabin of the car but seems satisfied I'm not much of a threat. They wave us through.

I can see the yachts now, not just one but dozens, maybe thirty in all. Some look almost modest, while others are enormous, hundreds of feet long. Mostly they're moored with their sterns towards the pier, and there are cars parked up behind – all expensive, Range Rovers, Mercedes.

"*Celestial* is that one." The driver points now, watching my reaction as I see where we're going. "She's the third biggest here, which is why we have to moor alongside." I don't know what this means at first, but I figure it out, because just a few of the very largest boats are moored more like ships, side-on to the dock. We pull level with it, and I see just how huge it is, towering over the dock. The driver stops the car about midway along the ship. I wait, unsure if I'm supposed to open my own door, or what's supposed to happen next. The driver gets out, opens it for me.

"Simon's waiting for you up top." He holds out his hand, indicating a gangway that leads from the harbourside to a door in the side of the yacht.

I look around before I step onto the gangway. It's odd – although I'm surrounded by more luxury and money than I've ever seen in my whole life – this part of the marina feels somehow normal. There's an old red Fiat parked a little further on. There's a garbage bin, next to it a bench that someone has left a newspaper on along with an empty take-away coffee cup. Something makes me want to stay here a moment longer, in the real world. But the driver keeps his hand held out, ushering me onto the *Celestial*.

The gangway shifts beneath me as I put my weight on it, and my feet clang on the metal. It's mesh with holes through it, and I can see the water beneath, not quite still but moving lazily. A broad-backed fish glides past, a couple of smaller ones in its wake. I reach the end of the gangway and step into a narrow, recessed platform just inside the yacht's hull. The air feels different here – cooler, quieter, contained. The outside world, the sun, the sounds of the city – it's all instantly left behind.

An older man in a crisp white uniform is waiting for me. He nods with a polite good morning and introduces himself as John. He doesn't ask my name, and there's something in his manner that tells me he's used to dealing with the very rich. He closes the door behind me then gestures down the corridor.

"This way, Miss Whitaker."

I follow him. There are no windows here, the walls are lined with soft leather panels and discreet, recessed lighting. There's no sound except the hushed hum of air conditioning. Our feet sink into soft carpet. The passage is flawlessly clean, not a single scuff mark. There's a smell, like furniture polish.

We take a turn, then another. I start to realise just how big this yacht really is. I already couldn't easily find my way back.

John stops finally at a heavy automated door, presses a button, and it slides open without a sound. I realise it's an elevator. We get in, and the doors close. There don't appear to be any controls, but I feel my weight pushed down as we rise up.

The elevator hums to a stop. For a moment, nothing happens. I glance at John, but he's as motionless as before. Then, without a sound, the doors slide open.

"Here we are, miss. The captain is waiting for you outside."

I blink at the man, expecting to follow him, but he gestures again, a simple move of the hand that tells me he won't be getting out, so I step through alone.

The contrast is immediate and startling. Suddenly I'm in blazing sunlight, the glare bouncing off cream-coloured teak decks and gleaming chrome railings. Around me, below me, I see the squat concrete pier where we parked, and beyond it the sprawl of Athens with its hills. I squint, adjusting. Then I see him.

Simon Walker-Denzil is sitting at a table, reading some papers. He's wearing a loose cotton shirt, open at the neck, with chinos and deck shoes. No socks. He's tanned, slim, unshaven. Better looking than I expected, but somehow, also exactly as I imagined him.

He looks up and smiles, everything about him relaxed. He puts the papers down and stands.

"Ava, you made it."

"Yeah." I can't stop myself from holding out my hands in a "ta-da!" moment, which I instantly regret. He smiles at it though, and I try to cover it up.

"Thank you for seeing me. For coming to get me."

There's a flicker of something in his face, amusement I guess. I must look so naïve, so out of place.

"Let's see if you still think that by the time we're done," he says, with a smile I don't quite get.

He nods towards the lounge area, white leather sofas shaded by a sleek overhang that's more spaceship than sailing boat.

"Let's talk."

FORTY-SEVEN

"So, you want the spiel, or did Dominic already give it you?"
"Um. Who's Dominic?" I reply.
"The guy who picked you up. What'd he tell you about us?"
"Oh. Not much."

Simon laughs. "Right. Man of few words, our Dom." He lifts his eyebrows playfully, they're bleached blond from the sun. He takes a deep breath, then begins.

"She's ninety-five metres long, that's three-hundred-twelve feet, if you like it old style. Four decks above water, one below. Fifteen-and-a-half-metres beam – that's your width – with a draught of four-point-three metres, meaning we can get her in surprisingly close to the shore for such a big beast." Again the eyebrows go up.

"Cruising speed of fourteen knots, max speed twenty, and a range of six-thousand-five-hundred nautical miles, so we're transatlantic capable. We have a crew of anywhere between thirty to forty and typically won't take more than eighteen guests, since we just have the nine staterooms." Simon smiles sarcastically at this. "You could fit more in at a push." He sees me looking around. You could fit a hundred just on this deck.

"She was built in Germany, by Lürssen Yachts. Launched in 2010, but refitted a few years ago. Heated marble floors, Italian furniture, gold accenting, you name it, it's here. We have floor-to-ceiling windows, glass-bottomed jacuzzi, fully fitted gym, spa, steam room and sauna. Cinema room – one-hundred-sixty-inch screen," – the eyebrows go up again – "plus there's a whisky bar and a walk-in humidor." He pauses at this, cocking his head on one side and falling quiet suddenly. I fall right into the trap.

"What's a humidor?"

"I so hoped you'd ask. OK, picture this, because I'm sure you have this problem most days. You're sitting there smoking your thousand-dollar hand-rolled Cuban cigars, but they don't taste exactly right? You know what I mean? A little too moist, you can't quite get the notes of sweatshop-poverty? What you need is a temperature and humidity-controlled room to store them in. That's a humidor."

"And you have one?"

"Lined with the finest Spanish cedarwood. We very much do." He chuckles.

"Then we have the beach club. Tender garage has two speedboats and *all* the toys. I'm talking sea bobs, foiling boards, e-surfboards – you ever try one of those?" He pauses until I shake my head. "Then we have a retractable swim platform, jet skis – obviously – and..." – he grins again – "my favourite Bond-villain touch, the mini sub."

"You're joking."

"Uh huh. Seats four comfortably, six if you know each other well. Goes down to a thousand feet. Not that *I'm* going in it." He smiles as he watches my reaction. "I prefer to be on the water, not under it." He waves a breezy hand towards the deck behind me.

"There's a few other bits and bobs. Helipad, bulletproof glass of course, twin panic-rooms, just in case you're panicking too much to find the first one when we get attacked – if we get attacked – forgive me, you've had a long trip and I didn't offer refreshments. What can I get you, tea, coffee, glass of wine? What's your poison? We can feed you too, if you're hungry? Got a hell of a chef, let me tell you."

"Um," I glance around. "OK? A coffee would be good."

"Excellent choice." There's a walkie-talkie radio on the table, and he picks it up, pressing the button, then mouths at me, *how do you take it?*

I ask for a cappuccino and he snaps his fingers, leaving one pointing at me as he relays the request.

"Have a seat," Simon says, taking one of the sofas that face each other over a low table. I take the other.

"So you're Karen Whitaker's daughter?" he says, shaking his head a little in apparent disbelief. "You look like her." His eyes narrow, as if evaluating this after he's said it. "At least, you're pretty, like she was." He sits back and props his arms comfortably along the cushions of the sofa. Meanwhile the elevator opens and a white-uniformed steward steps out, carrying a tray with our drinks. It's not John, though he's dressed the same. The man puts the tray down on the table between us, adjusting the silver jar of sugar so that it's not touching the cups. Then he gives a subtle nod to Simon. He doesn't look at me.

"Cheers, Terry," Simon says, not looking at the man as he stirs in a spoonful of sugar and sits back again on the sofa. Terry leaves.

"So. Ava. What exactly do you think I can help with?"

As crazy as all this is, I have thought about what I'm going to say on the bus ride here. So I launch into my explanation now.

"Like I said in my email, I'm trying to learn about the circumstances around my birth, and maybe even discover who my father is. I know that you and Karen... were friends... just before the Aegean Dream Resort closed. I wondered if you could tell me anything about that time."

Simon doesn't answer at once. When he picked up his coffee he kept the spoon, and he stirs it again now, watching me.

"One thing first. You say you're looking for your father, is there any part of you that thinks that would be me?"

I feel my heart rate jump. I have sort-of considered it, but not really, the dates don't match up and... there are plenty of other candidates. But I don't get a chance to think any more, as he goes on.

"Because I'm pretty certain I'm not. We were – young and careless in some regards, but not in that one. Plus I saw Karen a year after Alythos, in London, and she didn't have a kid."

"No. I don't think that." I feel my cheeks heating up. "I don't really know what you might be able to tell me. It's just confusing."

"And Karen won't tell you? Who your dad is?"

I shake my head. "I don't know why not. It's like there's some big secret. Something she doesn't want to face."

Simon stops stirring at this, just for a moment, then he nods. "That figures. I guess."

I don't understand this, but I don't question it.

"How'd you find out about me? She tell you?"

"No. I..." I don't know if this is a good idea, but I say it anyway. "I found her diary. She kept it the whole time she was working at the Aegean Dream Resort. Right up until it closed." I don't tell him where I got it, and he doesn't ask. He's thoughtful though.

"And she mentions me?"

"A bit, yes. She says you were... together in the summer of 2001. Up until the murders. I don't know what happened after that, because the diary stops just before."

He studies me a second.

"Just before?"

"The last entry is the day before the murders."

He seems to process this.

"And when were you born?"

That question's hard to answer, in the circumstances, but I do my best. "My date of birth is May 20 2001. A month before."

Simon pulls a face, like I can't have that right. Then he turns away. He stares at the sleek, interior wall of the yacht, but he doesn't seem to see it. He's motionless for just a second too long, and I see the tension in his jaw. Then he exhales, rubbing a hand over his face.

"Alright," he says in the end. "OK. I understand why you're trying to figure that one out."

I don't know what to say to this. I feel almost foolish that I don't know these basic things about myself. But there's something about his reaction, like this surprises him, but not in the way I expected it to.

"Mum doesn't mention..." I go on. "In the diary, she doesn't say she was pregnant. She doesn't give birth on the day I was supposed to be born." It sounds so strange saying this out loud, it sounds like a secret I should be keeping. But if I don't ask these questions I'll never know. "I know this sounds crazy, but was she? Pregnant, I mean? Could she have been?"

Simon laughs out loud at this, showing teeth that look too white. When he regains his composure he leans forward, putting the cup back on the table. "No. There's no way your mum was pregnant at the ADR. Not when I was with her. You don't have to worry about that." He watches me again, his blue eyes probing into mine.

I sort of do though.

"She also mentioned," I say, picking up my cup, "this one time, when she'd been drinking." I take a sip of my coffee, trying to build up to this. "That maybe my birthday wasn't my birthday. That maybe it was really later."

Simon cocks his head at this, then gives a crooked grin. "Well, I guess that explains it. Mystery solved." I don't know if he's joking and meaning the opposite. I'm still confused.

"Except – I don't know when. Nor why she would lie about my birthday. My passport has the date of birth I know." I take a breath. "I think that's what I was hoping you might be able to help with. That you might know something about it?"

Simon shakes his head, then goes further, letting the action merge into a somewhat offhand shrug. "No. Nope. Sorry. I've no idea."

I feel frustrated, but I can't give up yet.

"You said you saw her in London, after the ADR closed. What was that about, did she say anything then that... I don't know, might help me?"

He pauses a moment, but shakes his head again. "I was just between jobs. I thought I'd look her up, see if there was still anything between us." He pauses, then shakes his head. "You know, romantically. But there wasn't. Not for either of us."

"This is a crazy question, I know," I press him. "But are you sure she didn't have a baby? Could she have had one, but not with her when you met?"

"I suppose that's possible. It seems unlikely, and I don't see why she'd hide it. But... how would I know?" He seems to have tired of the topic, and his eyes go to my cup, now empty. "How about we have that tour? Have you been on a boat like this before?" He jumps up, before I have time to answer. He takes my cup from me and puts it down.

"Don't worry about that, Terry's got it. The man lives to clean up."

FORTY-EIGHT

We start the tour at the helipad, which Simon tells me is large enough for a medium-sized helicopter, such as a Leonardo AW139, or a Eurocopter EC155. It's information I don't know what to do with.

"Is he here?" I ask, "The owner?" *Whoever that is.*

"You wouldn't be here if he was," Simon replies, his eyebrows raised again. "But don't worry. He hardly ever turns up unexpected." We come to the jacuzzi, a little smaller than I might have imagined.

"Looks small right? But press this button here, and the whole platform slides out over the sea, so you can look down and wave at the fishies." He grins at me. "We're not allowed to operate it here in port, but..." His finger lingers over the button, like he wants to break the rule. "Better not." He turns away. "Here we have an observation lounge, telescope, night-vision binoculars blah blah blah." We come to some stairs, and Simon leads the way down.

"This is the Upper Deck, which I cannot show you." He pauses, and turns so that I can glimpse in through closed glass doors. I can't see much inside, but there seems to be a grand piano. "It has a pair of VIP suites up towards the bow, but most of it is the owner's personal area. Not even I'm allowed in, not without good reason." We keep walking down.

"Who is the owner?" I ask, following on behind.

"Technically it's more of a what than a who," he says, turning to enjoy the look this brings onto my face.

"He's a Russian, named Leonid Antonov. He's in oil, shipping, defence contracts, that sort of thing. But since the war in Ukraine it hasn't been easy for the Russians. A lot of their toys have been confiscated. Assets frozen, yachts seized. Even had to give back their football clubs. But Antonov has Bulgarian roots, so he's got away with it. And *Celestial* herself is owned by a shell company based out in the Cayman Islands, which'll protect her, even if the sanctions get tougher." He stops suddenly. "But don't get the wrong idea."

"What wrong idea?"

"Russian oligarch, an actual superyacht. You're thinking he's a gangster, Putin's poodle, pushing people out of windows – that sort of thing?"

I shrug lightly. "I suppose it crossed my mind."

Simon shakes his head. "He's more complicated than that. This is more complicated." For a second he stares into my eyes. Then we step off the stairs, into an absurdly large space.

"Main Deck. We call this the Grand Salon. Can you see why?"

I look around. It's like being in a museum. Everything is marble, or gold. Or gold marble. We walk past a gigantic dining table, the largest I've ever seen.

"Up here is the main pool. Beyond that the cinema, the whisky bar."

As we walk, Simon casually points out the details. "There's another pool at the stern, with a waterfall. It's nice to sit in while you watch the sunset. Over there, the humidor, just tell me if you want a cigar."

We pass through a long internal corridor, with suites leading off on either side. Eventually we come to more stairs, but as we go down, the feel changes. It's still plush, but more utilitarian.

"OK, Lower Deck. This is the crew and operations area. We have a galley, engine room..." It's still vast, even down here.

"And then through *here*..." Simon pushes open another door. I'm getting completely lost.

"Oh my God."

"I told you," I've no idea how often he's done this, but he still sounds delighted. "What did I tell you? An *actual mini sub*." It really is. It's painted bright blue, with a semi-circular dome of thick glass on the top, and I have to reach and touch it, just to be sure this is actually happening. Beside it is a massive RIB boat, a pair of jet skis. They're painted gold.

"So how do you mean, he's more complicated?" I ask, turning to Simon. "He's not just a gangster with golden jet skis?"

Simon looks rueful. "They do like their bling, that's true, these crazy fucking billionaires... But he's not a bad guy, underneath all that." He looks wistful now. "When I was being tapped for this job – and you wouldn't believe the way that happens, by the way. The hoops you have to jump through, the background checks they do. I had to do an IQ test, I was wired up to two lie-detectors, two different teams of psychologists. They staged a mock kidnap to see how I'd react... But it works both ways. I was given the chance to look into Antonov too. To see if I was a fit for him, not just the other way around."

I wait, I'm not sure where this is going.

"Don't get me wrong, he's not a friend. I absolutely work for the guy, and there's nothing I wouldn't do..." He lets that sentence fade away unfinished.

"And the fact that most of the time he's not here to use all this – that's a bonus, for sure. But all the same, he isn't what you'd think. I'm sure there are issues with how he got his money. And plenty more with how he's holding on to it. But if you want to know where he is, right now? The answer is he's probably lobbying somewhere for the expansion of marine conservation zones. Quietly, I mean. And he's got ships, working with oceanographic institutes, tracking illegal fishing, funding coral reef restoration in the Seychelles and the South Pacific. That's what he lives for. The jet skis are just to... I don't know, just so his oligarch-buddies think he's the same as they are." He stops, looks around at the room full of expensive water-sports toys. Mostly they look brand new.

"Partly, at least."

He looks at me, like it matters to him that I don't completely dismiss this.

"Look, Ava, this is freaky as hell, you coming here, and I don't expect you to believe me straight off. But that summer in Alythos, with your mother? It changed me. It changed the whole direction of my life. I might have been the guy who would hold his nose and work for a killer – that definitely could've been me. But after what happened?" He shakes his head. "Nah-uh. Not after that."

Then he does something strange. He reaches out as if he's going to touch my face. I have no idea why, and guess the look of surprise on my face stops him, but for a moment his hand hangs there, just an inch from my face. There's a moment when I can't read his motives at all, and down here, in the bowels of this yacht, it's clear no one could hear if I had to scream. Then he drops his hand back down, puffs out his cheeks.

"Let's go back upstairs. There's something I have to tell you."

FORTY-NINE

We walk back upstairs in silence, returning to where we spoke before. But instead of sitting at the sofas, we move inside, to an area that seems less about luxury and more about where the ship is driven from. There's a table here, and Simon invites me to sit down.

"Did Karen's diary say anything about the day before the murder?" Simon asks, his eyes on his hands, clasped together in front of him.

I think back. "Something. It said she was planning on a day out, on the yacht you were living on and fixing up."

"*Sunbeam*." He pauses and smiles deeply. "She was a twenty-seven-footer." He glances around ruefully at the absurd luxury that now surrounds him. "She say anything about the baby? Mandy's baby?"

I'm anxious as he brings this up, and I'm not sure why. At least, I'm not sure I want to admit to myself why. But I nod my head. "She said Mandy had to come here, to Athens, for some sort of paperwork, and she wanted Karen to look after it."

"Yeah. That's right." He nods, looking out the window at

the ship's enormous bow, but he's not looking at anything, more buying himself time.

"She was a strange girl, Mandy." He turns back to look at me. "It was obvious what Jason saw in her, but..." – he makes a face – "I'm not saying there was *actually* anything wrong with her, just she wasn't bright. It's like..." He sticks out his jaw, then rasps the stubble with his hand. "There weren't many people there who even cared she'd had a baby, except maybe the nannies, who were cooing all over it. But she decided the only people she was gonna trust was Karen or Imogen. No one else could even look at it."

He stops and looks away, then he gets up suddenly, walks to a fridge built into one wall, and pulls open the door. He takes out a can of 7Up, then holds it out to me. "You want one?" I don't get a chance to answer before he grabs a second, closes the fridge and comes and sits back down, sliding one can over to me. He pulls the tab on the other, looks at it a moment, like he's not sure where it came from. Then he takes a sip.

"What I'm about to tell you, I've never told another soul." He doesn't look at me. He drinks again, then sets the can down on the table, leaving his hands together, like he's praying. He goes on.

"It was our day off, Karen and me. We'd only just got together, a few weeks before that. But we'd clicked. We were both into the same stuff." He shakes his head. "It's hard to explain what it was like working there, at the ADR. It's *every* day. You'd get up at six-thirty, start work at seven, and you don't stop until the evening. Then you're still on duty, socialising with clients, maybe take them out to a bar, come back at two, three in the morning, and it's expected, day after day. And mid-summer, there's no time off. And with Mandy having the kid, she wasn't working, and Jason was busy, distracted. It was even more intense." Now he does look at me. "Look, I'm not proud of this, Ava. It's not who I am now, but

I'll be blunt: I scored some cocaine. We were going to take *Sunbeam* out, get high and... take advantage of a chance to unwind. A rare moment of privacy. You know what I'm saying?"

"I think so."

"Alright. But on the day, there was a problem. Mandy had dumped the baby with Karen, saying she had to get the early bus, something like that." He looks down at the can on the table, then back at me.

"I told her, put it with the nannies – that's literally why they're there, but she refused. She knew what Mandy was like and didn't want her to freak out. I think Karen thought she could get Imogen to take care of the kid, but she was sick or something. So instead, Karen comes up with this idea. We'll just take the kid onto the yacht." He fixes me with his blue eyes.

"It's not as crazy as it sounds. This was a super quiet baby, you never heard it cry. Plus it was the calmest day ever. You've been there, you've seen what it's like? Some days in Skalios Bay the water is an actual mirror, not a breath of wind. So we thought, we'll strap the kid in its car seat, park it in the cockpit with some shade. It wouldn't get in the way."

I don't reply, just wait.

"That's what we did. We motored out of the marina, out in the bay, I put the sails up, because... I wanted to sail. Back then I hated motor yachts, called them floating caravans..." He takes a moment to shake his head at the literal ship he's sitting in. "But we didn't move, there wasn't any wind." He stops again, his eyes have a faraway look to them.

"So there we are, a half mile out, not moving, Karen gives the baby a bottle and it falls asleep. And we've got this cocaine... So we head downstairs, do a couple of lines each. One thing leads to another. We're drinking a little too. We've got a stereo playing, so we don't hear too well. And then..."

Simon's tongue is poking just slightly out of the corner of

his mouth. His blue eyes turn to me again, I sense they're pleading with me not to judge him. But I don't know what for.

"What happened next?"

"I don't know if you've seen it, but sometimes in the summer, you get those calm days, and then the wind comes in sudden. Strong?"

I shake my head, but he just waves this away.

"It happens, believe me. And that's what it was, that day. Look, picture it. I'm high as a kite, drunk too. I'm stark bollock-naked, and this yacht's got her full sails up and we go from zero knots to forty, like that." He clicks his fingers.

"She's pressed flat – one-eighty-degree capsize, until the steering pulls her into the wind and she comes up a little. It's almost impossible to even get out of the cabin to get her back under control. All the while I'm thinking, we're taking on water, we might even sink. The sails catch the water and we could lose the mast. But..." He stops again.

"What?"

He gives a sudden smile. "I'm not just a pretty face, I know my way around a boat. I did back then. I work like a madman. I release the sheets, I yell at Karen to pull in the genoa before it flogs itself to death. I dump half the main, get it tied up and – we're still naked – you know? But we get it under control. And now the wind's stabilised, still blowing force six, maybe seven, but suddenly we're *sailing*. We're flying along, glorious sunshine, and I'm thinking what a lucky escape, and what an adventure. We go below, put some clothes on. And that's when Karen remembers."

"The baby?"

Simon nods. "Yeah. The baby."

"Where was it?"

He doesn't answer. "Well I don't exactly know, but it wasn't on the boat."

I feel my eyes widen. "What do you mean?"

"I was living on *Sunbeam* at that time. She wasn't in service because it wasn't safe for the guests to use her." He waves a hand. "A few things, but one of them was the guard rails around the deck. As in, there weren't any."

Again, I just wait.

"When we went below, we weren't completely stupid. We left the baby in the bottom of the cockpit, strapped into a car seat. There's no way it could have gone anywhere. But we couldn't have anticipated a full capsize..." He shrugs. "I suppose it must have floated out."

I'm quiet a second.

"You lost the baby?"

Simon stares at me, his eyes haunted. "Yeah. We did."

"Oh my God." This is horrific. But I blink in confusion. Because I don't understand what this means.

"But the baby was *found*, the next day, when they found Mandy's and Jason's bodies. He killed her, then himself, but left the baby alive."

"I haven't finished yet." Simon's voice is quiet. But he takes a moment. "When the wind comes in, the sea gets rough quick. And we're moving six, seven knots. By the time we knew it was gone, we were already a half-mile from where it would've entered the water. There was no chance of finding it.

"We tried anyway. We tacked back and forth in that fucking bay over and over, hoping against hope. But it was obvious. I don't know, I thought maybe the car seat would have just sunk, and drowned the kid in seconds. A small mercy maybe, but it didn't feel like it at the time. Ava, you have to understand the situation, what it meant for us. We'd killed a baby. Worse, everybody there knew I was into the coke, I bragged about it. And the Greek laws on drugs, without the sort of protection that wealth gives you? Oh my God."

He takes a swig from his 7Up.

"So our lives, as we knew them. They were *over*. We were

gonna have to go ashore and say what'd happened, and we were going to prison. For sure. For a long time. On top of that, we'd still got a whole load of coke inside us... So we made this plan. We were gonna run away. On *Sunbeam*." A bleak smile comes across his face now.

"I don't know if we'd have done it. I don't think it would even have worked. A coastguard cutter would have caught up with us long before we got out of Greek waters. Even then, it wouldn't have made any difference..." He sees that I'm not following, and winds back a beat. He draws in a deep breath.

"We took *Sunbeam* back to the marina. Karen got off, she was going back to the staff house at the resort. The idea was she'd grab clothes, her passport, any money she could find, meanwhile I'd fill up with fuel, fresh water. We were desperate. We did the rest of the coke, just to try and keep our heads level." He shakes his head again. Then takes a deep, calming breath.

"So I finish victualling the boat, and then I'm sitting there waiting for Karen, shitting my pants because she's taking so long, and I think the police are gonna come before she does. But eventually I see her, walking down the dock. And she looks... I don't know. Like something's been wiped clean. Rewritten. There's no bags, no panic – just this crazy look of calm on her face."

"Why? What happened?"

"Well that's the thing. The next thing she did was give me this crazy, crazy fucking story."

FIFTY

"What did she say?" I ask.

He's silent for so long I think I'm going to have to ask him again, but then he fixes me with his eyes, gives a half laugh, and suddenly crumples the empty 7Up can. Then gets to his feet, walks over to the fridge and gets another. He doesn't open it though. He goes to the window, which looks out over the bow. Beyond the marina, you can see the city of Athens, a plane coming in low, landing gear down. He turns back to me.

"She went back to her room, she packed her bag. And she was walking back to the harbour, when she saw something on the beach. I don't know what made her go look, with all that going on. Divine intervention maybe?" He stops again but stares through me.

"What did she see?"

I hold my breath. Yet he takes his time.

"It was just sitting there. On the sand."

"What was?"

He lets out a slow breath. "The car seat. The baby was still strapped inside it. This little baby, four weeks old – whatever it was. I don't know. It was alive. It didn't have a scratch on it."

I'm silent. I feel my mouth hanging open.

"It was a miracle. Seriously, there's no other word for it, no way to explain it. It didn't just survive the capsize, it must have floated for a mile before it got washed up. But on top of that, it was *Karen* who found it, before anyone else even saw it." He shakes his head. "No one else saw. She was able to get it back to her room, clean it up, give it dry clothes and some milk or whatever it needed, and it was *fine*. When I saw her, she'd just got back from Mandy's room. She'd given it back. Happy as you like. No one saw, no one knew. Our worlds *ended*. Then just like that, we were off the hook."

I don't know what to say.

"What did you do?" I manage in the end.

He shrugs. "I mean right then? I probably did another line." He looks at me suddenly, his face breaking into a grin like he's still feeling the relief. But it fades away, and I find he's still watching me. Watching for something. And deep down I know what it is. But it's hard to let myself think it. Hard to let it in.

"Why are you telling me this?"

He stares at me for a while. I hear him sucking his teeth.

"I don't exactly know. You send me this crazy email, telling me Karen's your mother but you don't know anything about how you were born. I don't know..." His voice fades out. "I don't know why I told you. I figured you maybe deserved to know."

I want to ask: know what? And why. But I already know what he's hinting at. How can I not? My birthday, my *supposed* birthday, is exactly a month before all this happened. The same birthday as the baby in this incredible story. I close my eyes, and in a flash I can see it all – the ocean, rolling and lurching. I'm there now, in that car seat, the terror, bewilderment of seeing the yacht disappear into the distance in front of me. I feel the bite of salt in my throat.

Except of course I don't. I couldn't. *I can't.*

I snap my eyes open, my pulse hammering. I look down at

my hands on the table, they're shaking. I have to bring this back to reality. To focus on something simple.

"What about Karen? What did she do next?"

He shakes his head lightly, as if I've shifted his train of thought too. "I don't remember." He seems careless now, this isn't an important detail for him. "Went back to her room, I guess. We were tired. Emotionally wrung-out, you know? And then of course, that night..." A shadow comes over his face.

"What?" For a second I've actually forgotten.

"That was the night. When Jason lost it. He stoved Mandy's head in, blew his own head off. But this little baby." His eyes are on mine, deep, blue, unblinking. "It goes and survives *again*." He's quiet a moment. "You ask me, that says something. I don't know what exactly. But maybe something's meant to be." He keeps looking, his blue eyes piercing into mine, but I can't handle what he's implying. I don't even *know* what he's implying, not exactly. Only that it's something. Some unspoken signal that I feel him beaming into me, or trying to.

"What?" I ask in the end, looking down at the table to escape his gaze.

"Karen's never spoken about this? Never hinted at it?"

"No. Never."

There's a pause, a humourless chuckle.

"What's she like, these days?"

The sudden banality of the question knocks me sideways, I give a little laugh of my own, at the mental shift he's asking me to make.

"She's... I dunno – she's just like always." I stop. I remember her from the diary. How immature she sounded then. That isn't the woman I know as my mother. "She said once how having me made her grow up in a hurry." I risk a glance back up at his face. This seems to be what he expects to hear.

"I bet it did." He shakes his head again, with something of a grin this time.

"So what's she up to? She working?"

We're really doing this, this line of questions.

"She runs a chain of pharmacies, we have three of them."

"Nice." He absorbs this without further reaction.

"I'm not... without regret, you know?" he goes on after a moment. "I've wondered whether what happened that day contributed to what Jason did. I don't understand how exactly. Karen told me she never said anything to Mandy, but maybe she did? Or maybe Mandy guessed, found out? Told Jason? And that somehow flipped him out? I don't know. He was wound pretty tight. All of us knew that." He breathes quickly, pulling himself back in his chair.

"What I'm telling you, Ava, I carry a burden of guilt over that, and I always will. But at the same time, if Jason was the kind of dude to beat his girlfriend to death, then perhaps it was always gonna happen, just a matter of time? Either way. I've chosen to focus on the other thing. There were three people saved that day. Not just the baby, but Karen. And me."

FIFTY-ONE

After we speak, Simon asks if I'll stay and eat on the *Celestial*. He explains how they have to keep the galley stocked at all times, because at any moment Antonov can turn up demanding a literal banquet. So tonight they're eating lobsters, most of which will go in the bin. He even offers for me to stay the night in one of the guest suites and catch the bus back to Alythos the next day. But I don't want to. I just want to get off here. Get the hell away.

So in the end, Dominic runs me back to the station, just in time to catch the last bus. It's a relief to climb back on board, my knees hitting up against the cheap hard plastic of the seat in front. But I can't relax, not after what I've been told, and my mind races the whole way home. It's gone midnight though when I finally arrive back on the island, far too late for the bus to Skalio, but a taxi takes me there. It's far too late to think clearly too.

I wake up late the next day. There's a few moments when I just *am*, with the sun streaming through the cracks between the blinds, but then I remember that I don't know who I am. Nor how I fit together. My phone already shows a message from Sophia:

> I asked my mother about the adoption thing, she says you should check if you're listed at the records office. She can help if you want?

As I'm reading it a second message comes in:

> How did it go with Simon Double-barrelled-Denzil? Anything exciting?

I stare at them a long while, but don't reply. Instead I stand up and take myself to the shower. I try to let the water wash away what I'm feeling, but it can't, and eventually I give up, dry myself and find my phone again. There's another message from Sophia.

> Hi Ava, don't mean to hassle, but Mamá's going into Kastria today, if you did want to check the records office?

I stare at it a while, still wrapped in a towel. Then my thumbs press out a reply.

> Sure. Yes. Thanks.

They pick me up at midday. Sophia comes into the apartment building to get me, while Maria waits outside in the car. Before we get there, Sophia asks again how it went with Simon, but I tell her I'll explain later. When I get to the car, Maria is kind and chats lightly. I thank her but she waves it away, saying it's no big deal, and she has to go into Kastria anyway to fill in a prescription for a neighbour. She seems to understand my need for this to feel as normal as possible. A regular outing for regular people.

"So, Alythos doesn't have a main hospital," Maria starts

chatting as she drives. "But it has a clinic which does handle some births. So if you have a passport that says you were born on the island, it's likely that's where you were born, and they should have some record of it."

It's a simple but good idea. I can't believe that I didn't think of it.

"Yeah, thanks."

I'm in the front seat beside her, and she turns to smile at me. "What's less clear is whether they'll agree to release it. Greek bureaucracy can be very opaque, and sometimes who you ask, and the way you ask, is more important than what the rules say." She raises her eyebrows before turning back to the road.

"Sophia tells me it's difficult for you to ask your mother these things?" Maria goes on, not turning back. "She doesn't want you to learn about your roots?"

"That's right," I tell her.

"Well, these things can be tricky," Maria concludes. "It's always been better in my view if these things are out in the open, but I know other people don't feel the same." She gives me a sympathetic look, and turns the car into the parking area of a small medical centre on the outskirts of Kastria.

"Here we are."

We go inside, where everything happens in Greek. First we stand at a reception desk where Maria explains what we're after to a girl not much older than me. She points at me several times as she does so, and I feel the girl looking at me with interest. While they speak, Sophia explains to me in a low voice what's going on. Then we're told to wait. Ten minutes later the three of us are led to an office, where an older woman listens again to Maria explaining my situation. The woman then asks for my passport, and turns to the page at the back that lists my place of birth as Alythos, Greece. She nods at it, then focusses on the computer screen in front of her. For a few moments she ignores us while she runs a search. We can't see the screen, but her face tells us she isn't seeing what she expects.

"What's the problem?" I ask, but before anyone can translate this, Maria and the older woman begin speaking in rapid Greek again.

"What's she saying?" I ask Sophia, but it's not possible for her to listen and translate at the same time. Eventually she turns to me.

"She's saying there's no record for an Ava Whitaker being born on Alythos."

"What does that mean?"

"She doesn't know. That's what they're discussing. It could be a mistake. The records weren't put onto computer until about five years ago. So perhaps it was just missed off? Or if you were adopted, you might be entered into the system under a different name. But if we don't have the original name, she can't search for it."

"Can't we just get a list of all the names, all the children born in that year?" I ask. Sophia considers the question a moment, then interrupts the woman and her mother to translate it into Greek. Again there's a long conversation I don't understand, a bit more heated this time. Finally Maria turns to me.

"We're not allowed a list of all the children born here in 2001. Sophia's just arguing that she went to school with most of them, but I don't think we're going to get it."

"How about my date of birth? Were any other children born on that date? 20 May? Because that has to be me? Right?" Maria nods, then interrupts, putting the question to the woman behind the desk. We wait again while she enters it into the computer, then she frowns at the results on the screen.

"What? What is it?" I ask, as the conversation flares up in Greek again. It takes a while again, but eventually Maria translates.

"There is one birth registered on 20 May. But it comes up

only as 'unknown female', and the record doesn't lead anywhere."

"Why not?"

"She doesn't know. There's no name, not of the parents nor the child, and no other details attached. She says she's never seen anything like it before."

It seems we can get no further and we leave, Sophia and I then wait in the car while Maria drops by the pharmacy. She asks again about what happened with Simon, but I'm not ready to answer. Then we drive back towards Skalio. On the way I feel a sort of pressure. That this is an opportunity I have to take. Maria is less talkative now, driving in a thoughtful silence. It's kind, but also unbearable. I feel the words bottled up inside of me. If I don't say something now, I might never say it. As we pull up outside my apartment I force myself to speak.

"Something happened yesterday. I think it would help if I told you."

Sophia gives me a sharp, confused look, but Maria simply nods.

"Would you like to come around to the house, Ava? I have a few things I could offer you for lunch?"

FIFTY-TWO

At the house Maria puts some *spanakopita* in the oven to warm – filo pastry parcels filled with spinach and feta cheese. While they cook, she pulls out *taramasalata*, *tzatziki* and sliced tomatoes with fresh basil from a pot in the garden and drizzles over olive oil. She warms soft pita pockets in the oven, and Sophia cuts them into strips to dip in the mezzes. Then we carry it all outside, into the pretty garden surrounded by roses. And there I tell them what happened with Simon Denzil-Walker.

"Oh my God," Sophia says when I'm finished. "That's wild. Like really, super crazy."

"Yeah. I know."

"What does it mean though?" she asks.

I shrug my shoulders. "I don't know."

Maria doesn't say anything for a long while, then she tells us she's going to make tea. She carries the empty plates back into the kitchen and returns a few minutes later with steaming mugs of mint tea. She hands one to me, but hesitates.

"If you would rather not say, I will quite understand, but may I enquire exactly what it is that makes you believe you're adopted? I feel there are details I don't have."

For a moment I don't answer. There's an element of this that feels almost like a betrayal of Mum, and everything she's done for me. But at the same time, I know I can't move forward if I don't resolve this, and the only way to do so has to be to pull it all out into the open. And there's something about Maria that makes her easy to trust.

"My mum always told me I was born on Alythos, when she was working here at the Aegean Dream Resort. But she would never tell me the details. I found a diary she wrote when she was here, and she isn't pregnant. She doesn't give birth." I shrug, at the stupid simplicity of it. "I can't see any other explanation."

Maria listens in silence, her clear eyes watching me carefully.

"And there's no way you can ask her?"

I shake my head. "We don't speak about it. We never have. Whenever I've asked her about where I come from she..."

"She what?" Maria asks gently.

"I don't know. She shuts me down. The most she's ever done is make it a joke – but one she doesn't want to tell. She said he was a waiter – like a total cliché, an embarrassing mistake. Like maybe that's the reason she won't say, or maybe she doesn't even know his name. Or which one he is." I think of the parade of men in the diary. "It's hard to explain."

"OK." Maria looks like she understands, but she's quiet for a long while.

"When we spoke in the shop, I told you about the tragedy at the Aegean Dream Resort, the deaths of the couple managing the resort, and how their infant daughter was left alive?"

"Yes."

She purses her lips. "Alythos is not a big place..." She stares at the wall, and her words fade out. She turns to me, smiles.

"Ava, would I be correct in thinking you suspect a link between yourself and the child left alive that night?"

I don't answer for a few moments. Finally though I shrug again.

"The dates seem to fit."

It's weird, hearing the idea in the open. I glance at her, not quite looking. From the corner of my eyes, I almost hope she's going to burst out laughing at the idea, but she doesn't.

"Yes. They do. It does seem at least plausible, if not probable, that there's a connection. And the baby listed in the records, born on that date—"

"Why wouldn't they tell us about that?" Sophia asks, "at the medical centre?"

"I don't know." Maria looks at her daughter. "My guess would be the records were sealed when the baby was adopted. In Greek law this is often done to protect the child whose parents die. So they can grow up without the burden of knowing a difficult truth."

"But Ava already knows what happened, everyone does. The manager guy murdered his girlfriend then killed himself. So how does that protect her?"

"Well in this case it doesn't. *If* Ava really is this baby." She turns to me, but I hardly hear her. In my mind I'm there that night. An infant, lying where, in a crib? On the bed? While my dad beats my mother to death, and then kills himself. How long was I there, waiting to be found, their bodies growing cold beside me? *Was* I even there? Was it really me?

"There must be other records?" Sophia asks. "If Ava was that child she must be able to find out from somewhere. She has a right to know!"

Maria doesn't answer at once. "I don't know. I imagine so. I expect that, if you can prove you were the child, you might be granted access. But if you can't prove it... if the only proof is *in* the files... I imagine it might be difficult." She looks at me heavily. "It could take a long time. It will certainly be expensive."

"But that's unfair? Surely she has a right to know who her parents really were?"

Maria doesn't answer Sophia this time, but turns her eyes on me. I look down at the table.

"I'm not even sure I want to know. If my dad was a monster."

Maria doesn't say anything. Instead she gets up and begins to clear the rest of the plates. I go to help her, but she stops me, then lets me when she sees I need something to distract myself. We take a break while her and Sophia bring a dessert, something they call *galaktoboureko*. When it arrives it's a sort of creamy custard pie wrapped in layers of filo pastry. Maria cuts a generous slice and hands me a plate. I can smell the lemons and cinnamon.

"There is one way I may be able to help," Maria says quietly.

I look up.

"Perhaps two."

I wait, a forkful of the dessert quivering in front of me.

"The detective who led the investigation into the murders. He's a man named Nikos Papadakis. He's retired now, but back then he was the head of the island police. Before that..." – a quiet smile comes to her lips – "A *long time* before that – we were in school together."

I stay quiet, unsure where this is going.

"I can't say if he'll actually remember what happened to the child. But it was a big case, and I'm sure he'll know something. What's less clear is whether he'll speak to you. But I wonder if I come with you..." She looks thoughtful. "There might be something he could tell you?" She shrugs, like she barely believes in the idea herself.

I think about it. I'm not sure.

"You said there were two things?" Sophia asks.

Maria turns to her, a sharp look on her face, just for a moment. Then she looks back to me.

"Yes." She falls quiet.

"This is perhaps a more difficult thing to say. And I see how this is already a lot for you to bear, but I believe I have to say it. You come here to find your father, and you learn he might have been a murderer. I don't know if that's true. I knew Jason Wright. I'm not sure I ever believed that he was responsible."

There's a silence. Finally Sophia breaks it.

"Isn't that what the police said?" she asks.

"Yes. They did but—"

"But what? I mean, surely they'd know, they were there, the ones who—"

"Ava, there's something I need to tell you at this juncture." Maria interrupts Sophia quietly.

"OK," I say, unsure where this is going. I wait while Maria composes herself, before she goes on, keeping her eyes on me.

"If you are the child that was left alive that day, then I was the person who found you."

I see my own expression of surprise mirrored in Sophia's face, but she gives it voice too.

"What do you mean?"

"I was the person who found the bodies. I was delivering groceries to the hotel that morning, and I had to see Jason, a problem with the billing. He wasn't in the hotel, which was unusual, and I was sent to the room where he and Mandy were staying. Up past the old staff house."

I look to Sophia. I can see she knows the places that Maria's mentioning, and I think I've seen them too, when I looked over the resort.

"The door was ajar, so I knew something was wrong. When I pushed it open, I saw Jason lying there. He was clearly dead, and I knew he'd shot himself – or been shot. I'd never seen a gunshot victim before, but I knew." She waits, swallows.

"And I knew about the baby, so I went into the room, looking for her. That's when I found Mandy. She wasn't shot, she'd been hit over the head, but very hard. There was no doubt she was dead too. And as horrible as it was, that's when I heard the sound of breathing. At first I was scared, I thought that perhaps whoever had done this was still there. But they weren't, not alive at least. But the baby was. It was just lying there, in a crib by the side of the bed. I picked it up and took it out of there."

It seems as she's speaking that she's not really here, but now she's finished she comes back into herself. She offers me a smile.

"So if you're somehow connected to whatever horrible thing happened that day, in a way I am too."

FIFTY-THREE

I have another evening shift at Bar Sunset, and I walk down along the road this time. On the way, as I go past Aetos Diving, I see a figure I recognise in a restaurant, hunched over a laptop. It's Gregory Duncan, the writer who I spoke to up in the hills. He pretends not to see me – or not to recognise me – but I think he does really. I remember how Sophia told me he sits at this table sometimes to work, so there's no reason to be concerned by it, but once I walk past I look back, and sure enough I catch him watching me. He drops his head at once, as if he's just absorbed in his work, but I know what I saw. I see Kostas too, working at the back of the dive centre, lifting heavy bottles of compressed air onto a rack as if they were nothing. He notices me too, but doesn't try to hide it. I don't know what the expression on his face means, but it's not friendly. He gives me a curt nod and turns his broad back.

The bar is busy, which is good, because it allows me to just exist and serve customers and clear tables rather than stress over who I am. It's just a shame Hans is in a mood with me. He says I let him down the other day, and if I do it again I'll be easy to replace. So it's nice to know I'm valued. That punctures my mood a bit, and then I'm just unsettled further when Sophia drops by. She tells me the detective, Papadakis, has agreed to speak. It's dark when I finish work, and I glance at the restaurants as I pass by, looking to see if Duncan's there again. But if he is I don't see him.

It's two days before the meeting with Papadakis takes place, during which I stew a little in the growing heat of the island. But finally I find myself sitting beside Sophia as she drives her mother's car towards the island capital. Maria is with us too, sitting in the back. But the time passed has changed the atmosphere somewhat.

"So what's he like, this Nikos guy?" Sophia asks, turning to look at Maria.

"I'm not sure. I've not seen him in a long time."

"But you two were what? Like boyfriend and girlfriend, back in school?"

"Absolutely not. Where did you get that impression?"

"So he liked you, and you weren't interested?" Sophia grins at me, I think she senses that a big part of me doesn't want to go today, and she's lightening the mood.

"Well, would that be such a surprise?" Maria answers after a moment. "I was popular enough with the boys when I was younger."

"Oh I know that," Sophia answers. "If only I could have inherited your looks."

Maria stays silent about this until a few minutes later, when she says:

"His house is up here on the left."

The house is tucked into a narrow backstreet just far enough from Kastria's main square to escape the noise. It's somewhat hidden behind high, whitewashed walls, but an iron gate is open, and inside a cat lies asleep in a shaft of sunlight.

There's an old-fashioned knocker on the door, which Sophia raps three times.

"Hope he's here."

A second later we're assaulted by a barrage of noise, dogs barking, followed by a man's voice shouting at them in Greek. The cat wakes up, stretches and wanders away, just before the door opens.

Papadakis is a small man with round glasses, dressed in a loose shirt. He takes his time looking at each of us, his expression unreadable, until his eyes land on Maria.

Then he steps back, opening the door fully.

"Come in quickly, before they get out."

I'm not quite sure what this means, but we all go inside to a small hallway, which then opens into a bright kitchen – and then I do know, because half the floor is given over to a pen containing a dozen black-and-white puppies, standing on their hind legs, their curled tails wagging furiously. They climb on each other's backs, almost clearing the fence that keeps them in place.

"Oh my God," Sophia says at once, moving there and crouching down. "They're adorable."

"They're a terrible mistake, is what they are," Papadakis replies. Then he takes Maria's elbows and lightly kisses her on both cheeks.

"You must be Sophia?" he says to her, then to me, "And the English girl?"

"Ava." I hold out my hand. He looks at me with warm interest, then shakes my hand.

"How old are they?" Sophia asks, still crouched by the pen, and trying to stroke as many of the puppies as she can at once.

"Six weeks – no, seven," he corrects himself, watching as she continues to fuss.

"What breed?"

"*Ellinikós Pimenikós*," – he glances at me – "Greek Shepherd dogs. They used to live among flocks in the mountains, protecting them from wolves, jackals, even bears here, in the old days."

Sophia pushes her face into the pen, and a dozen pink tongues fight to lick it. The dogs are pretty cute, but I'm feeling too raw to pay much attention.

Papadakis watches for a moment, then says, "These ones will not be facing bears, though. On the mother's side they are interbred with a Poodle – their coats do not shed. People like that. It is better for families."

We watch Sophia a while longer, burying her face in their soft fur.

"I was wondering what you might be getting up to," Maria says. "Now that you're retired."

"I'm enjoying the quiet life." He lifts his eyebrows ironically. "Can I offer any of you a drink?"

We meet the father of the pups as we wait outside in the courtyard, sitting at an iron table. He's about the size of a Labrador, but sturdier and much calmer. After checking us out he seems content to let us be. He lies down and falls asleep in the same spot where the cat was. Papadakis emerges after a while, with a tray containing teapot, cups and saucers.

"In a box, on the table. One of the puppies – the runt of the litter, I think you call it. I've separated it from the others, they bully her. If you want you can fetch her," he says to Sophia, who gets up at once.

He pours the tea as she comes back, holding a floppy-eared pup, its tiny mouth yawning. She sits down with it on her lap.

"So, Maria, you wished to speak to me about the events at the old Aegean Dream Resort, correct?"

"That's right." Maria's eyes widen as she leans forward.

"I heard they're knocking it down," Papadakis replies. "Not before time."

"Quite." She smiles. "We're interested in the events that led to its closure." Maria glances at me to be sure I'm still comfortable. I nod lightly.

"You were in charge of the investigation into the murders?"

"One murder," he corrects. "One murder, one suicide. But yes. I led the case. A horrible business."

Maria nods. "Perhaps that's a place to begin. I'm interested in the rumours – I'm sure you've heard them – about whether Jason Wright really was responsible, or whether there was any doubt. Is that something you can speak about?"

Papadakis is still for a moment. "I can tell you our report concluded the former."

"But was that really the truth?"

He sits back, holding his cup and saucer and taking a sip of tea. "In just about every investigation I ever participated in, I could never be completely sure what the truth was."

Maria blinks at him, and it seems she's unsure what to say next.

"Forgive me, Maria, it's lovely to see you, but I still don't exactly understand the purpose of the visit," Papadakis continues, the smile on his face thinning very slightly. "Are you able to explain your sudden interest in the resort, and what happened there all those years ago?"

She thinks a moment longer, then turns to me.

"Ava was born on the island, just before the resort closed," Maria replies. "Her mother is English and worked at the hotel. She was sent home after the murders." She stops.

"I see."

"Maybe you'd remember her? She has a photo."

I open my bag and pull out the photograph of my mother and Imogen. I show it to Papadakis, who takes it from me and studies it closely.

"Their names?"

"Karen Whitaker. With the blonde hair. The other girl is Imogen Grant."

Papadakis studies it a while longer, then shakes his head.

"No, I'm afraid not." He hands it back to me.

"The rumours about the crime," Maria continues. "For years I've heard that drugs might have been involved? That some aspects of the crime scene didn't make sense?"

He's about to answer this when the puppy sits up, shaking its head so that its little ears flap noisily. When it stops Sophia apologises on its behalf. "Oh my God, I didn't know they did that."

"You're not familiar with puppies?" Papadakis asks her.

"Sophia's always wanted a dog," Maria cuts in. "But we've never had one. My husband was allergic."

He's thoughtful a moment, then nods. "I was very sorry to hear about your husband passing away," he says next, and Maria looks surprised, but smiles quietly.

"Thank you."

Then Papadakis turns back to her question. "It was a high-profile crime. Rumours were inevitable."

"But there were problems? With the murder-suicide explanation?"

"Such as?"

"I'm not sure," – she looks down at the ground – "perhaps that it's unusual for a man to kill his girlfriend, then himself, but to leave a baby alive?"

"It's not usual – thankfully – that a man kills his girlfriend at all."

"But it does happen?" Maria presses. "Even in a quiet place such as Alythos?"

"Infrequently."

"And when it does, is it normal to leave the baby alive?"

"I think I would agree that it's less typical, but not unknown."

"Was there anything else about the crime that struck you as unusual?" Maria asks now. "I know there was a note, but it wasn't handwritten? It was written on a computer, and then printed out – which anyone could have done?"

"Now you're really going back." He seems to think again, but finally replies. "Yes, I seem to remember that was the case."

"Did that strike you as unusual at the time?"

Papadakis doesn't answer this, instead he makes himself more comfortable in his chair and draws in a deep breath.

"Maria, you didn't quite explain why it is you're asking these questions?"

She looks at him, her brown eyes unblinking.

"OK."

Then she leans forward. "I've already explained to Sophia and Ava here. I was the one who found the bodies – I know you'll remember. But perhaps you never knew that I *knew* Jason Wright. Not that well, but I knew him. And it always seemed rather convenient how quickly it was declared that he murdered poor Mandy and then killed himself. He was a capable, bright man. He'd only been here for a few years, but he'd learned the language. He seemed to be looking to start a life here. I even spoke to him, after the baby was born, and he was excited. Tired? Yes, and under pressure, because it was a big responsibility running that place. But suddenly he does this terrible thing? I never quite understood it. Perhaps I never quite believed it."

Papadakis strokes his chin, watching her.

"I remember you were delivering vegetables to the resort. When you found them."

"Yes."

"Are you still working, by the way?"

"I am."

"You haven't thought of retirement?"

"I've thought of it. But what would I do?"

"Perhaps you could open a detective agency?" He smiles at his own joke, then glances at Sophia. "Certainly not breed puppies I would hope." He nods now, tapping a finger against his lips.

"It is true, what you say. There was little to say for certain that it *was* a murder-suicide and not something else. But the important counterpoint is this: there was also nothing to suggest any *other* explanation. We searched into Jason's background, and no one seemed to wish him harm."

"What about the drugs?"

"What about them? Jason may have used them, but infrequently, a way to wind down. He was certainly not a dealer. There's no obvious connection."

Maria frowns at this, like she can't beat the logic.

"You didn't find anything else?"

He opens his hands, palm up. "I don't recall."

"What about Andreas Kyriakos?"

Papadakis's easy smile seems to waver at the name. I've no idea who he is.

"What about him?"

"Kyriakos is the Mayor of Alythos," Maria explains to me. "Or was – the current mayor is his son." She turns back to Papadakis. "The rumour is that the family are doing very nicely out of the decision to rebuild the site of the hotel?"

"I don't doubt that for a moment, Maria, but what's your point? Surely you're not suggesting Mayor Kyriakos murdered Jason Wright and Mandy Paul in order for his son to receive a backhander over twenty years later?"

"No, I'm asking how well you were able to investigate? Whether Kyriakos put pressure on you to close the investigation quickly, or if you were allowed to do your job properly?"

Papadakis takes a very long time to reply to this. He looks at each of us, Sophia still stroking the puppy on her lap.

"The answer I can give to that is very much off the record." He waits until Maria nods in agreement at this, and then goes on.

"There was some of that, it's true. Alythos was then, and still is, dependent upon the flow of tourists. And there was concern at the time that visitors would be alarmed by the idea of a murderer running around. It was helpful that the case seemed to have solved itself, the perpetrator already dealt with."

"So if you'd had more time," – Maria leans closer – "if you hadn't been leaned on, you might have discovered something else?"

He shakes his head at once.

"No. That's not what I said." He takes a moment, making a steeple of his fingers.

"Perhaps without that pressure we would have taken a little longer over things. But I'm comfortable that the investigation would have reached the same conclusion."

He sits back again. His demeanour has changed – less welcoming, more distant.

"Now, I really think it's fair that you tell me the reason for these questions?"

Maria frowns, I see the frustration on her face, but she nods too. She opens her mouth to speak again, but I stop her with a touch to the knee.

"This is my problem. I'll say it."

FIFTY-FOUR

"I was born on Alythos. Around the time of the killings," I begin. I'm still not sure how to phrase this. The words seem strange in my head, even more so spoken out loud.

"I came here to try and find my father, but I discovered I was adopted. Probably adopted." I pause, still not wanting to say it. "I think I might be the child that was left alive. Mandy Paul's baby."

His face remains unchanged. For a while he says nothing. Then, "Yes."

"*Yes*, I am or—"

"Yes I can see that you think that."

I blink in surprise. "OK. Well, can you tell me anything about it? What happened to the child, after the murders were discovered?"

He seems to think for a long while.

"That's difficult."

"Why?"

"For one thing, it was a long time ago. My main priority would have been to the investigation – to secure the crime scene, to understand what had happened. But then..." He stops, frowning slightly now.

"But what happened to the child? Where did it go?"

He gives himself a moment to remember.

"As I remember there was some... confusion over what to do with the child. The mother had not properly completed the paperwork to register a birth. It was somewhat messy, but – fortunately for me, not my mess. The child fell under the jurisdiction of EKKA."

"What's EKKA?" I ask.

"It's a... I don't know what you would call it in English." He turns to Maria and they exchange a few words in Greek. Then he turns to me again.

"It's a government department. I think you would call it *social services*?"

"Were you able to contact any relatives in England? Of the parents? Jason, or Mandy?" Maria asks now. He turns to her, thinking again.

"I seem to remember efforts were made..." His brow furrows from the effort of it. "But there were none, or no one willing to intervene. But there's a second problem with what happened to the child, it wouldn't be something I could divulge. It was always the case that the records would be sealed."

"And why was that?" Sophia asks, looking up from the puppy. Papadakis looks at her, considering.

"The intention would have been to protect the child from knowing about the tragedy that befell its parents."

"But that doesn't really work, not if the child now knows who their parents are, but isn't able to prove it?" Sophia asks him, her big eyes looking unblinking into his. He looks away first.

"No." He's silent for a moment, then turns to me. "Do you know for certain that you are this child?"

I shake my head. "No."

He's still a second, then turns back to Sophia. "Then you must appreciate it from the other perspective. If Ava here is *not* the child, what right would she have to expose the true parents of this young woman, potentially ruining her life, wherever she is now?"

"But what if it is her?"

"It may not be."

"We'd know for sure if we could open the file."

"No doubt. But no system is perfect."

"But this is ridiculous," Sophia goes on. "Ava has to wonder about this for the rest of her life, because you won't tell her?"

"It isn't that I won't tell her. I can't. For one thing, I am retired, but if I were still working I would have no more right than anyone else to read the file. If it has been sealed by a court, only a court can open it again."

"And how easy would that be?" Maria cuts in.

For a moment there's silence, then Papadakis turns to me.

"Is this not something you can understand from the other end, so to speak. How were you brought up? Is there no one who can tell you where it was you came from?"

I think of Karen – my mother – and what she would say if she could see me here. The distance I've come unmoors me from the moment. She'd be so mad that I'm doing this.

"No. Not easily, no."

He touches a finger to his lip, disappointed.

"There must be something you can tell us?" Sophia asks now, the puppy forgotten. Papadakis looks at her, and thinks a while.

"Some details were widely known," he says in the end. "It seems harmless for me to share what could be learned by a simple visit to the newspaper archives." He gives a thin-lipped smile.

I wait, feeling the hope rise in me.

"I do remember the child was eventually moved to an orphanage on the mainland. I don't know which one. I don't know what happened after that. And beyond that I cannot say."

"Because the records were sealed?"

"Because the records were sealed, and because I do not know."

"And that's it? That's all you can say?" Sophia presses, and he lifts his palms again.

"I am sorry, I recognise the difficult position you are in, and I have some sympathy. But I don't see there is anything else I can do to help."

He puts his cup and saucer back on the table with an air of finality. That's it. Sympathy is all I'm going to get, but it's not enough. I feel this whole chapter ending, and without any resolution. And there's one thing above all that's hurting me about that.

"Do you know her name?" I hear myself suddenly blurting out. "Everything I've heard about her, everything I've found out. It's always 'her' or even 'it'. No one ever says her name. No one even seems to know it. If I really was that child, it would mean something to know what my mother called me."

He looks at me a long while, his eyes not blinking. Then he turns to Maria.

"Do you remember?" he asks. She looks at me, shaking her head.

"I'm sorry Ava. I don't remember."

I try to smile at her, that it's not her fault, that I'm grateful for what she's trying to do, but Papadakis' voice cuts in again.

"There is perhaps one more thing I can say. Before she went to the orphanage, I believe the child was placed with a carer, here on Alythos. It would be quite wrong for me to reveal the identity of that carer. And yet, it's a small island. Maria here might make an educated guess? A widow, I would imagine, with no children of her own. It's possible she would live in a white house on the way out of Mallios? Before the road bends towards the old monastery?" His eyebrows go up, and I look at Maria, her eyes wide and round.

FIFTY-FIVE

Fifteen minutes later when we're back in Maria's car, she's driving this time, with Sophia in the back, sitting forward between the two front seats.

"You actually know this woman who had the child?" Sophia asks.

"Not well, but yes." Maria glances at me now. "Ava, I think you know already I am not Sophia's biological mother, she is adopted?"

The question surprises me, but I nod. "Yes. She told me."

"I thought so. She doesn't tell this to so many people."

I wait as Maria turns back to the road. "When my husband and I were working through the adoption process, we became familiar with many of the people involved in such things. On Alythos and the mainland."

She slows the car now. Up ahead is a group of three white houses, around them olive trees and a small vineyard. We stop outside the first house. In the distance, where the olives finish, is a large, low building within high walls.

"The old monastery," Maria says, nodding towards it. "Just wait for a moment, I'm not sure which house we need."

I don't say anything as she gets out and goes to the front door of the first house. She knocks, and there's a long delay until it's opened by a young woman in an apron. We're too far away to hear anything that's said, but moments later the door shuts again, and Maria moves to the third of the three houses. She knocks again, and this time when it's opened it's an older woman. Again there's a conversation, and at one point Maria points to the car. I feel the lady's eyes on me. They speak some more, and then disappear into the house.

"So, do you know that woman?" I ask Sophia, more to break the silence than anything.

"No. But it looks like Mum does."

We wait, rolling down the windows as the heat in the little car rises. About fifteen minutes later the door opens, and Maria emerges again. Without hesitating she moves over to the car and then speaks quickly with Sophia in Greek. Then she turns to me.

"Would you mind coming inside? She would like to see you."

So then we climb out of the car, walk towards the front door, and the whole experience feels super freaky. Did I once stay here, after my mother was killed by my father? I can't say, I have no memory of it. It doesn't look familiar, but maybe it feels it? I can't say.

Maria leads us into a small and bare living room. The blinds are closed, not completely but enough to keep the room dark and cool. The woman I saw answering the door gets to her feet. She's maybe seventy with very dark skin, her hair covered with a scarf. She stares at me, her eyes unblinking.

"Ava, this is Eleni Kouris. She took in the baby, in the weeks after the murder. Unfortunately she doesn't speak English." Maria says something then in Greek, but I catch my name. Eleni moves towards me, her eyes not leaving my face. She takes both of my hands and holds them in hers.

"I have asked her if she knows what happened to the child after she was taken to the orphanage," Maria goes on. "But she was not told. She says she tried to find out, but it was not allowed..." Maria's explanation is interrupted by a long stream of Greek from Eleni. At first she directs it at me, but then seems to realise I have no idea what she's saying, so instead she turns to Maria. A few moments later Maria translates.

"She says she tried to find out. That the orphanage where the baby was taken was a very bad place. That it was widely known children there were abused. She has articles about it, from a national newspaper. But they would not allow her to care for the child. They would not tell her what became of her."

Eleni is still holding both of my hands, and she goes back to staring at me, her unchanging smile showing yellowed teeth. I take in more about her, the black shawl that she's wearing, the TV in the corner of the room, an old-style boxy design, the plain white walls, stained in places. Was this how I nearly grew up? Was I taken from this place, or saved from living this life? Or was I never here? It's suffocating, the not knowing, the being here. And still the woman has both my hands in hers. I look down, at her bony fingers. There's more Greek. I wait for Maria to translate it, but she hesitates.

"She says that obviously you turned out OK." Sophia does it for her.

"Um, what does that mean?"

Sophia gives a dry laugh. "She's just saying she remembers you," Sophia tells me, watching me carefully. "She says you have her eyes."

There's a silence.

"She wouldn't actually be able to remember though, would she?" Sophia goes on, in English. "I mean, if the baby was only a few weeks old when this woman had her, she's not going to know for sure?"

"No," Maria agrees. "Probably this is just—" She breaks off

to translate something and then finishes the sentence, looking at me with a concerned smile. "Probably this is just an emotional time for her, remembering."

"Does she know the name? Can you ask her the name?" I say, and Maria nods.

"Yes, that's why we brought you in. Eleni wanted to tell you herself." Then there's more rapid Greek, back and forth, between Maria and the old lady. I look to Sophia for help, but she doesn't translate.

"What's she saying?" I ask in the end.

"She has something for you," Sophia says at last. And now the woman finally releases my hands, and – nodding at me the whole time – she leaves the room.

"What's going on? Where's she going?"

"She said—" Maria stops, she looks perturbed. So it's Sophia that translates again.

"She said she has fostered many children, over many years, and all were special. But of all the children she cared for, it was..." She glances at Maria, like she's not sure she ought to continue. But Maria nods, and Sophia turns back to face me. "It was you that meant the most, because you needed her the most." She shrugs. "I'm sorry Ava, this must be so difficult."

Eleni comes back into the room now, and instantly her eyes lock onto me. Then her hand does too, onto mine, only it's just the one hand this time, the fingers tight against mine. In her other hand she's holding something. I don't see what it is at first. There's more Greek. This time Sophia translates it for me.

"She's saying that for every child she looks after, she likes to keep a... memento, like something to remember them by," – Sophia sends me a look – "a bit like a serial killer I guess." She laughs at her own silly joke, and I see she's doing it only to stop herself from crying, then she keeps translating as Eleni hasn't stopped speaking. "OK... In the case of the baby from the murder, she already had one... It seems when the child was born, the mother made a... I don't know how you say that, a *lefkoma gennisis*?" But then she finds the phrase herself.

"I guess you'd call it a *birth memory book* – something like that. Like it has an image from the mother's pregnancy scan, a handprint of the newborn, that kind of thing..." Eleni holds it up to me now. It's light pink, and on the front it has a name, but I can only make out the first letter, a C. But I hear Eleni say it now. Callie. *Callie*.

"Callie?"

"Callista," Maria says. "In Greek it means beautiful..."

I know it. I've always known it. Of course I have.

It's my middle name.

FIFTY-SIX

I look into Eleni's strange dark eyes, and I know that I've seen her before. I know it has to be me.

"Callie? That's my name?"

"The name of the baby," Maria reminds me, but her voice seems to be coming from far away. "We don't know for sure who the baby—"

"Um, guys, you might want to look at this." Sophia interrupts us both, her voice suddenly very serious. "Oh my God. This is kind of big."

I look at her, with no idea what she's saying.

"What is it?"

Eleni is still talking, opening the book now and showing us the contents. On one page a tiny envelope has been stuck down, the same light pink colour.

"What? *Sophia?* What's she saying?"

"OK. I don't know if this is going to be helpful, but I think it might. Apparently when Mandy Paul made this book, when the baby was born, she cut a lock of hair, it's still here."

Eleni pushes the envelope into my hands. I catch the name on the front, the girlish script, the name, *Callie Paul*, but I'm pushed to open it, the flap is not stuck down. Inside is a tiny cutting of hair, bound together with a rubber band and folded inside a thin strip of muslin. I stare at it in wonder. A fragment of the past. So real I can finally touch it. My past.

"Um, so I think you're getting this without the translation?" Sophia goes on. "When Eleni took custody of the child, she got all this along with all the baby's other things. Only when she had to give the child away she kept it, to remember her. And like, not an expert in forensics and everything, but with this you can prove it, no? Like do a DNA test?" I turn back to look at Eleni, smiling her yellow-toothed smile at me, and now she breaks into a few words of English, stabbing a bony finger towards me.

"Remember you." She turns the finger back towards herself. "*Me. Remember you.*"

We go for lunch in a cafe overlooking Kastria's main square. While we eat Sophia takes the lead, trying to work out the practicalities. Quickly we find that commercial DNA testing is available to ordinary members of the public like us, but it's expensive and would take six to eight weeks to get an answer. Maria shakes her head at this, and puts in a call to Papadakis again. They speak in Greek and I don't understand anything of what's said, except for the look of surprise on Sophia's face as she listens in. When Maria finally hangs up her face is heavy.

"What?"

"He says he will help. He still has a contact at the testing laboratory the police use. He believes they can get an answer in just a few days. If this is what you want?"

It takes me a moment to realise this is a real question. Is this what I want? But I know the answer. I never imagined it could happen like this, but after all these years, I'm finally going to know.

"Yes. I want to know."

After lunch we drive back to Papadakis' house, and wait in the kitchen while he rummages in a drawer for an old Covid testing kit. He explains that the same swab used to check for the Covid virus can be used to take a sample of my DNA, to compare against the hair from the baby.

"Here." He finds what he's looking for and hands me the test. For a second it's weird. There was that time when all these things were so familiar. Now I'd almost forgotten they exist, it's like a reminder that time moves on, our realities with it. But it only lasts a second.

"May I see the hair sample?"

I give him the envelope and he opens it carefully, then takes it out and inspects it.

"There may be a problem."

"What?" It's Maria who answers. He turns to her.

"The hair sample does not contain any remains of the root. Hair fibres only contain mitochondrial DNA, not the nuclear DNA we would usually use to perform a DNA test."

I feel a wobble of worry. Don't do this, not now.

"Does that mean we can't run the test?" I ask.

"No," – he shakes his head seriously – "not exactly. Mitochondrial DNA can tell us if you and the baby come from the same mother – in this case the murdered girl, Mandy Paul. We cannot say anything about the paternal line. We cannot test if you and this baby share a father, the information will not be there."

It takes me some time to understand this, because it seems so simple. If the baby is simply me, wouldn't the test be really easy, to show this? But Sophia gets there quicker.

"But that doesn't really matter? If Ava is this baby, then obviously they're both going to show the same mum? And that's what she wants to know?"

"Yes," Papadakis nods. He takes the hair sample and slips it into a plastic bag taken from the testing kit. Then he watches while I rub the swab around the inside of my cheek. When I'm done I slide it into the plastic tube and fit the stopper. I hand it over. Papadakis seals the bag with practised ease, and I watch as my name is written neatly across the label.

"When will we know?" Sophia asks.

Papadakis keeps writing as he answers. "A few days," he says. "I'll let Maria know."

He puts the tube down, with the words Ava Whitaker written down the side.

My name. Ava Whitaker. Except, if this test comes back positive, it won't be my name anymore.

FIFTY-SEVEN

I wake late the next morning, and manage to make it to the bathroom before the anxiety catches me up. The thought of what I'm about to discover is like a shadow that's following me wherever I go. It carries relief with it, but also a darkness that lurks ever-present in my mind.

When I get to the kitchen there's a message from Sophia on my phone.

> How are you?

I text back, trying not to make too much of it, but saying something about how it's hard to stop worrying about things. She responds at once.

> Meet me at the dive centre. 11.

I look around my little apartment. I don't have anything else to do.

It's a beautiful day as I walk down through the town. Every

day is beautiful, it seems, here in Alythos. Though it's not that every day is identical, it's just that every variation of the weather the island seems to provide is beautiful, in different ways. Some days there's a fresh breeze, never enough to make it cold, but which lends the air a supercharged freshness, where the tones of salt and thyme seem to fill you with a sort of fizz. And then there's days like today, when there isn't a breath of wind, which have a magical quality, as if the whole universe has reached a state of calm. When I get to the seafront and see the bay is so still it could be a giant mirror, reflecting the sky without a ripple to disrupt the perfection. It's so gorgeous I have to take my shoes off and walk through the shallows down the beach to the centre. The water's warmed by the sun, and I see shoals of tiny fish flit away in front of me.

The centre has a relaxed feel. Two of the boats have already gone out, and I can tell they must have been filled with diving clients and their instructors because their shoes and belongings are stacked neatly in the changing area. But Kostas is still there, this time with two children, both boys, maybe seven and ten years old. They're running around as if they own the place, and I quickly learn they sort of do, since they're his sons Theo and Alex. When Kostas sees me though he tenses up – or maybe I just sense that. He sends the boys out to the beach to play then retreats to his office.

"Don't mind him, he's just old and they tire him out." Sophia grins as the boys disappear and the centre quietens down. "But I thought you might need a little distracting this morning?"

I think about joking *"from what?"* but she doesn't give me the chance.

"And when we're not busy here, I get to use any of the toys that aren't needed for the clients. Isn't that right boss?" She calls the last part into Kostas' still-open office door. He looks up, says nothing and goes back to his work. Sophia turns back to me.

"So how about you learn to foil board?"

I blink at her.

"Um, I've no idea what that is?"

"That's OK." She looks delighted. "Kostas doesn't either, even though I keep telling him to learn. I've got this plan to give foil-boarding lessons here. It's perfect for days like this, and the clients love it."

She looks at him again, and I think I hear a grunt. Otherwise he studiously ignores her.

"Kostas only likes things under the water, he doesn't understand how you can have fun on it as well."

"I'm sorry, what exactly is foil boarding?"

I glance again at Kostas, who's shaking his head a little.

"It's this." Sophia pulls me to the noticeboard and points to one of the many photos pinned up on the noticeboard. It's her, and she's doing something like waterskiing, but not quite. Instead of standing on – well, water-skis – she's on a surfboard thing, that seems to be flying a metre above the water.

"It's like a wakeboard, but it has a hydrofoil under the water, so it's a bit more like flying as well. And you can ride the wake like you're surfing." She grins.

"And you want me to do that?"

"It's going to distract you, I promise."

The last few moments are pretty much the only time this morning when I haven't been thinking about DNA results. So maybe she has a point.

"But I don't know how to do it."

"That's alright. I'm going to teach you. Here." She strides over to a rack of wetsuits and flicks past several until she finds one she likes the look of. "Put this on. Have you ever done snowboarding or surfing?"

"No."

"Wakeboarding?"

"No."

"Skateboarding?"

"No. I mean, I've tried it once, for like five seconds."

"Wow. What exactly have you done with your life?"

"Um? Studying? My mum wanted me to be a doctor..." I stop, realising what I've said. I meet her eyes. "What I mean is, the woman who brought me up, who isn't my mother wanted me to be a..." I stop again, feeling my head descend back into this. If my mother isn't my mother, how did I get to live with her? Why do I think she is?

"Stop it. Don't worry about that for now. Focus on this. It's easy. Sort of. Once you get the hang of it."

I ask why I need the wetsuit as I fight to pull the grippy neoprene suit over my ankles, and I don't really like the answer. It's not so much for the cold apparently, as the protection it gives you from crashes. But even that's not enough, because when I finally zip it up she adds a padded buoyancy aid and a helmet. Then she walks me down the beach to where another instructor, an American named Leo, is getting the equipment ready. She shows me the board, which has a giant "mast" attached beneath it, and connected to that something that looks like the wing of an aeroplane.

"It's exactly like flying," she explains. "We'll tow you, very slowly at first, so you can get to your feet. And then a little faster, which will give you enough lift to get up on the foil. Then you lean back to fly higher. Forward to land. Lean left to go left, right to go right."

Before we go out we do lots of drills on the beach, but eventually it's time, and I clamber into the rib while Leo walks into the water with the board, turning it over and sinking the foil. Seconds later we're cruising out into the bay, not as fast as when Kostas took me, but Leo is literally flying behind us. He doesn't even need the tow rope. After he's got the board up in the air it seems to stay up by magic, and he surfs up and down the wake while Sophia drives, occasionally looking back to check he's still up. Finally though he tries to turn too fast and falls off. At once Sophia slows, then circles the boat around to pick him up.

"Jump in," she tells me. "Your turn."

FIFTY-EIGHT

My first attempt lasts less than a second. The moment the boat starts to pull me, the board rears up under my feet like it's being pushed up from below, and I let go of the rope and scream. At least Sophia is right about the water, it's not cold. My second go I manage a few seconds before the board does the same thing, and I'm in again.

Third time lucky doesn't seem to apply either, and after that disaster Sophia circles the boat closer again, for some more shouted instructions. I try to focus on what she says – to keep my weight a bit forward, and not to panic. But it's easier to say than do.

My fourth attempt I last what feels like a long time, but I suspect is less than ten seconds. But in that time something clicks, and when the board rises up beneath me, I bend my legs to absorb it, and for a moment I'm actually balanced, flying in the air. Then I'm flying *through* the air, and crashing headfirst into the water. I come up puffing from the effort, and swim back to the board.

On my tenth attempt I get it. We're only going slowly, but that's all it seems to need. I don't understand how it actually works – but it does work. And it's not even that unstable once it gets up and balanced. And then it's – fantastic, like nothing I've ever experienced before. I'm literally balanced on this board, a metre above the sea, which is flashing by beneath me. And I can almost think myself into little movements left and right. If I put my weight backwards I go higher into the air, but I have to be careful because too high and the foil itself leaves the water and then it all comes crashing back down. I think I only manage thirty seconds, but it feels much longer. When I surface Sophia has the boat beside me, laughing but clapping too.

"That's it, you were doing it!"

I want to do more, but it's Leo's turn. Apparently it's his day off, and for the next twenty minutes I have a rest, sat at the back of the boat, while Leo flies behind us, crossing from one side of the wake to the other, and even pulling little jumps. I watch him, trying to pick up clues as to how he makes it look so easy. Finally he falls again and swims back to the boat. I turn to Sophia, asking if she's going to have a go, but she shakes her head and tells me to go again.

"This is to distract you, right."

I look at her. I'd actually forgotten this time.

It is tiring though. I only manage a few more runs before I'm so exhausted I can't do any more, but I'm pretty thrilled to see where we've got to. My last run I must have done a half kilometre or more actually flying in the air above the water. Leo drives us back to the beach, and Sophia finally has a go. Her technique is different to Leo's. She doesn't try the jumps but her style is much smoother, carving up and down the wake almost like she's dancing above it.

I struggle out of the wetsuit while Sophia and Leo put the boat away, then I walk down, hoping to help, but it seems there's nothing left to do.

"That was amazing, thank you."

"There's a client meal tonight," Sophia says, then she goes

on quickly, "Once a week we all go out to eat with them in the fish restaurant in the harbour. I wondered if you wanted to come?" She looks at me hopefully. "You know, a bit more distraction?"

"OK, yeah," I say after a moment, though I'm not quite sure what she means. Am I a client, or is this something else?

"That would be cool."

FIFTY-NINE

I rest for a while, then walk down to the harbour as the light is falling in the sky. There's just the slightest breeze now, enough to move the boats gently on the still, clear water. The gaps between the boats sparkle and shimmer in the reflected light from the lamps set up by the restaurants that hug the waterfront. Our table – three or four tables pushed together – has been set up right beside the water, impossible to miss, and inviting, despite my nerves.

I meet the group from the dive centre as they're arriving, a big happy gaggle laughing and joking freely. Kostas' boys are here too, which surprises me, but they seem completely at home out this late and with a group of adults. His wife's here too, but I don't get to speak with her. I feel a little shy and out of place at first, but Sophia grabs my arm when we go to sit, and steers me so we can sit together at the opposite end to her boss. She sits with her back to the water, the pretty strings of lanterns around the water's edge illuminating the green streaks in her dark hair. Behind her the boats and the heavy, protective harbour wall loom in the darkness.

The clients from the dive centre are an eclectic mix –

they're fun and they don't give me a chance to think about my problems. Sitting next to Sophia is a guy in his thirties who works in finance. I ask him about it and he begins to explain, but then waves it away and says it doesn't matter, not out here. He tells me instead about the dive they did earlier, to a World War Two wreck that's sunk a mile or so out in the bay. I've never done diving, and to be honest it sounds scary. But cool as well. Next to me is another guy. He doesn't say anything at first, he just listens to the banker, but when I turn to him he surprises me with his pure cockney accent, so strong I think he's putting it on at first.

He tells me he only came to Alythos on a whim, and mostly to make up for a terrible mistake he made with a tattoo. Again I think he's joking, but then he shows me the Manchester City Football Club logo on his upper arm, only apparently the colours are wrong.

"It's Arsenal colours, see?" he says. "I was off me fuckin' head. Me so-called mates thought it would be a laff."

I tell him I think the colours are nice, and he calls me uncivilisable – which I'm not even sure is a word. But that's the feel of the night. A space in time where people from all walks of life can come together and our shared humanity outweighs the differences.

And the food... wow. I thought I'd eaten well already here on Alythos, but this is something else. We don't order from menus, instead Kostas speaks with the owner of the restaurant, and I suppose they must have it all worked out from coming here every week, but soon the waiters begin weaving between the tables, setting down dish after dish.

First it's just bread, but warm and fresh from the oven. It's served alongside small dishes of golden-green olive oil, thick with crushed garlic and oregano. Next to it, bowls of plump, glossy olives, black and green, marinated in citrus and herbs.

Then come the mezze plates – *tzatziki*, thick and creamy.

There's something called *melitzanosalata*, which is smoky and tangy from aubergines. Plates of *saganaki* arrive, wedges of golden, pan-fried cheese, still sizzling. The scent of lemon and honey rises up as the tattoo guy squeezes a wedge over the top, rubbing his hands.

"Wow, let's get stuck into that."

The waiters come next with grilled octopus, tender and charred at the edges, and crispy rings of calamari, served with a wedge of lemon and a sprinkle of sea salt.

The meat dishes follow – plates of *souvlaki*, skewers of charred chicken and pork, the smoky scent mixing with the salty breeze from the harbour. A whole grilled sea bass, its skin crisp and glistening, is placed in the centre of the table, alongside a dish of roasted vegetables, more aubergine, courgette and peppers, caramelised and sweet. There's carafes of red wine, and chilled bottles of white.

"Oh my God," I say to Sophia, when I see the waiters coming out with yet more food. "I can't eat any more." But I do, and it's even more delicious.

"This is amazing," I tell her. "I think I've fallen in love with this place."

"Yeah," she replies, with a strange look in her eyes.

By this time quite a lot of wine has been sunk, and the talk turns again to water sports. It is the one common denominator, at least for most of the people at the table. A woman – I think she's the girlfriend of the banker – tells me she was watching my foiling attempts, and she was impressed. She says she wants to try it, and then the banker agrees. Sophia calls out to Kostas, telling him to make a note.

There's dessert, and afterwards Kostas' wife leaves, taking the two children who finally seem exhausted after spending most of the night running around the restaurant and harbourside with other children from the town. The rest of us are brought tiny cups of Greek coffee, thick and strong. The rich, earthy bitterness cuts through the sweetness perfectly, and I'm done. I can't eat or drink anything more. And then, as the waiters clear the last few plates, I start to worry about the bill. I see the guests begin pulling wallets from their pockets, and I want to contribute too, but Kostas puts a stop to all of it.

"Don't worry," Sophia tells me quietly. "It's all covered by the dive centre. The guests pay, but they get a reduced rate. The instructors get fed free. And tonight, you're one of us."

Her words warm me. I like the thought of being one of them.

Then there's a split. Some of the younger guests want to head on to a bar the other side of the harbour, where there's a dancefloor. Sophia looks at me questioningly, and I'm tempted, but I don't think I can actually move after my crashes and all the food. She laughs when I tell her, and very naturally takes my hand.

"Don't worry then, I'll walk you home."

So then we bid goodnight to the rest of the group and moments later we're alone, walking back up through the town, Sophia still holding my hand.

For just a moment it's awkward, and I'm not sure what exactly is happening, but there's an ease to her that relaxes me. And she knows everything. Every building we pass, she tells me who lives there, and she seems to have a story about everyone. On our right is the home of the man her father fished with. There's a big house on the left, set back from the road, with a lush garden which is where the former owner of the ADR lived, when he was out here and not in England. She shows me Kostas' house too, more modest, its little front yard almost completely taken up with a RIB in for repair.

We fall quiet as we near the back of town where my apartment is. We're still holding hands, and though I definitely want to, I'm not sure what this is, or where it's going. For the first time I sense uncertainty in Sophia too. I glance at her, hoping that she won't notice, and take in the dark strands of her hair falling across her face. She's very pretty – beautiful – and it's not like I hadn't noticed before. Her skin, her bare shoulders, are smooth and look so soft to the touch. Her hand is tanned and delicate in mine. I think suddenly of Kevin, my last boyfriend. He wasn't one for holding hands, but when he did they were like plates of meat. *Boyfriend.* That word stops me in my tracks. Is there something romantic about this?

Suddenly, Sophia stops.

"What?"

Her mood has changed.

"Nothing," – she looks perturbed – "I just thought I saw someone up ahead."

I look, but I don't see anything.

"Where?"

"Up there, they're gone now. If there was anyone."

Somehow this pierces the atmosphere, deflates it quietly. She's already dropped my hand and doesn't re-take it. Sophia seems to read the shift in mood just as I do, but I don't know if she shares my confusion about what *was* happening. We stop outside my door and she points to a passageway between the buildings opposite I hadn't noticed before.

"That's a shortcut to my house," she says, with a kind of goofy smile on her lips. I stare at her face a few moments, unsure how to reply.

"Do you want to come in for a while?" I say in the end. "I don't have much, but I did buy a bottle of Metaxa on my last visit to the supermarket. I wanted to see what my mum saw in it." The word "mum" comes easier to me now, using it almost like a joke. Or perhaps not, I may be about to confirm that she's not my biological mother, but that doesn't mean she's not "Mum". I'm beginning to understand that now.

"OK."

I unlock the outer door and we step inside, cross the dim

hallway to the entrance to my apartment. But at once I see there's something odd. At my front door there's something hanging from the handle. I get closer and see it's a plastic shopping bag.

"What's that?" Sophia asks, but I don't answer. I take it off and look inside. I think I know before I even look, just from the feel of it. But I'm still baffled.

"What is it?" Sofia asks again, confusion in her voice.

"It's my laptop," I say, pulling the shattered glass, plastic and metal parts from inside the bag. The totally smashed-up remains of my laptop. "Someone's brought it back."

SIXTY

Neither of us says anything about it, but I feel that whatever might have been about to happen now isn't. I take the bag, open the door and carry it inside, emptying it carefully onto the kitchen table. It's clear enough what it is, my laptop had butterfly stickers on the lid because *everyone* at university had a MacBook Air. I can still see them, but the lid itself has been ripped off, the screen smashed into black shards of plastic-backed glass.

"What the hell is going on?" Sophia asks, but I can't answer. I have no idea. "Is it yours?"

I nod. I didn't tell her, so I do now. "It was stolen from me, a week ago."

"*What?* How?"

I tell her about the break-in, how I'd been stupid and left it in view on the kitchen table, and how the apartments here all seem to have the same key, so maybe that's how they got in. This time we do check, going back outside and trying the key that fits my front door into the two other apartments on my floor. It doesn't work in either.

We give up and go back into my apartment. I notice the

bottle of Metaxa I was going to offer her. I pick it up with a half-hearted shrug, and she laughs lightly.

"Not sure I'm in the mood now."

"Me neither." Our eyes fall back to the broken laptop on the table.

"I can understand stealing it, but why smash it up?" Sophia asks.

I try to make my brain focus on the question, but I'm tired now, tired and a little drunk still.

"It wasn't a very good laptop. Maybe whoever took it realised that – that it wasn't worth selling, and they were angry?"

It doesn't sound convincing to me, and it seems Sophia agrees.

"Do you believe that?"

I shrug. "I don't know what else to believe."

"Did you have a password?" she asks a moment later. "You'd have to... and your fingerprint for unlocking it?"

"Yeah."

"So they wouldn't have got into it, whoever stole it. Macs are secure," she continues. "So maybe that's what made them angry? They were looking for something, and they couldn't find it? So maybe it's a message?"

That unsettles me even more.

"What kind of message?"

"I don't know, stop digging? What you're doing, looking into your past, it's opening up questions about the ADR? And if Mum's right, and it wasn't Jason Wright who killed Mandy Paul, but both of them were murdered, then maybe whoever did it doesn't want those questions asked?"

"Well who do you think did it?"

"I don't know. I don't have a clue."

I think of everyone I've met from that time. There's one face that sticks in my mind, one presence.

"What about Kostas?"

"*What?*"

"There's something about him, I keep seeing him watching me, it freaks me out..."

"Don't be stupid."

I pause. Something about the way she says the word "stupid" opens an immediate and gaping void between us.

"Why's it stupid? He was there at the time, he lied when I first spoke to him and—"

"Because he's my *boss*." She glares at me now. It's crazy, I really thought something might happen between the two of us tonight. But this isn't what I had in mind.

"Just because you work for the guy doesn't mean you know what he was doing twenty years ago."

She gives me an angry look, but I think she isn't going to argue with the logic.

"What about Gregory Duncan? He's a weirdo," she says instead. My mind goes right back to the meeting I had with him, in his house. He seemed scared of something, could it have been me that worried him, and what I might find out?

"There's loads of people it could have been," I reply. "If it was anyone. The simplest answer is that Jason Wright did it. My dad."

"Yeah," she shrugs. The gap closes, a sort of truce between us.

We're both quiet a moment, and I think of something else, something I meant to ask her before.

"The other day I was walking past the old Aegean Dream Resort, and I thought I saw something there – *someone* there. Maybe watching me?" As I say it I remember how freaked out I was by the sound of breathing inside the ruined room. I should have told her before. But I didn't really know her then.

"Who?"

"I don't know." I hesitate. "I don't even know for certain if it was someone. I mean it could have been an animal. But I wondered, is it a place teenagers make out? That kind of thing?"

She thinks before answering.

"I don't know. I never made out there." She flashes a mirthless smile. "But when I was younger we used to hang out there sometimes. Me and some friends. We used to play a game of hide and seek, a sort-of daring version because we all knew why it was closed. So maybe it was that?" She doesn't look convinced.

Sophia doesn't stay much longer. I say she can stay if she likes and offer her the bed, saying I'll sleep on the little sofa, but she gives me a strange look and says it's only a ten-minute walk to her house. Then I suggest walking her home, just to make sure she's safe, but she points out the obvious – that if I walk her home, she'll then have to walk me home, and we'll be stuck in an ever-repeating loop, where each of us walks the other one home. I see her point. I still don't like it though, but when she does leave I realise it's not just her that I'm worried about. Left alone in my apartment with my ruined laptop I worry again about who took it, who smashed it up, and why they left it hanging on my door for me to find. The one person who couldn't have done that was Jason Wright. But then my thoughts are interrupted by a text: *Still alive...* Then two emoticons: a house and a smiley face. So, finally, I take myself off to bed.

I have to work the next two days. Sophia too, so I can't even see her in the mornings. And Bar Sunset is busy enough that I don't get much time to think, which is probably good. Then on the third day, while I'm doing my laundry, I get a message from Sophia. Papadakis has dropped the results of my DNA test at her house. I can come round whenever I want to get them.

I can't leave right away, I have a washing machine filled with clothes, but suddenly the weight of everything seems to hit me. These last few days I've been operating with a lightness of thinking I already know who my real mother is, but suddenly I'm about to discover for real. And my father too – a man who might or might not have murdered my mother, ripping away the life I should have had, and replacing it with what I know instead. How do I feel about all that? It's a lot. It's really hard to know what to feel.

I both want the stupid washing machine to finish already, and for it to never stop. I want to end the agony, and extend this limbo forever. I seriously consider not going to Sophia's house at all. Because once I do know this, I can't unknow it. And once I know, the next stage has to be speaking to Mum – Karen. And I've no idea how I'm going to do that, how she'll react. But I do know it's going to change everything about me.

When the machine does finally stop, I dump everything into the dryer. It has a glass door so I stare into it, letting the rhythmic swirl of my clothes lull me into a near hypnotic state. My life going around and around and around.

"Hey," Sophia says quietly, when I knock on her door a half-hour later.

"Hey." I nod. She's wearing her TEAM T-shirt. "Are you supposed to be working?"

"I told Kostas I had something to do." Her eyes bore into my face. "I wanted to be here for you." Her lips curl into a smile that doesn't quite work. I nod.

She leads me into the garden with its flowers and the lemon tree. But my eye goes straight to the table, empty except for a slim envelope with my name on it.

"Do you know what it says? Have you looked?"

Sophia shakes her head. "No. Papadakis dropped it off early this morning. If he looked he didn't say."

I don't pick it up. I don't even want to touch it.

"I already know what it's going to tell me." I try to smile at Sophia, but I can feel how crooked it comes out. She nods at me.

"Yeah. It'll be good to have it confirmed though. Like, to know for sure."

I know she's right, but it also feels like she's wrong. My stomach hurts. Once I had really bad food poisoning, and it's like that – when you've been throwing up so much and there's nothing left to get out, but so just breathing hurts. I force my hand towards the envelope, but it's like I'm pushing against some invisible force. I pull it back.

"Can we find them?" I ask suddenly.

"What?"

"Like, a picture? Of Mandy and Jason. Can you get your computer? Try and find a picture of them online?"

Sophia pauses a moment, then silently nods and disappears. She's back a moment later, and she sits down at the table. I take the seat next to her and watch her work. It takes only a few seconds, and she's on the website of some Greek newspaper. It's probably best that I can't read what the headline says. But underneath it are two photographs. One is a pretty woman, in her late twenties I'd guess. She has blonde hair, mid-length and cut into a bob. Her eyes are blue and wide, and there's an – innocence, I suppose you'd call it – about her. Perhaps it accords with the way my mother – Karen, I mean – and Simon described her, as not too bright. I drop my eyes to the table a moment, contemplating what I may have inherited there. Then when I'm ready I look at Jason. *Dad.*

He's probably a little older than she is. He looks... quite English, I suppose. He doesn't have the dark hair and skin of the Greek people. But there's nothing in his appearance to suggest he could be a killer. I wonder what happened, what it was that drove him to do what he did? Or was it not him at all? It's impossible to say from a photograph.

"Are you OK?" Sophia asks.

I take a long time to answer. But then I nod, chewing a little on the corner of my lower lip. "Yeah. I'm good. I think I'm going to open it now."

I pick up the envelope. It's light, just as if this has no consequence. No more meaning than a circular letter or a piece of junk mail. Inside is a folded sheet of paper, and I slip it out. I hesitate though, once more, before unfolding it. If the result of this test is positive, my life will never be the same again.

I unfold the envelope and start to read. For a few moments it's unclear – I don't understand the technical language I'm reading. But then there's a bit underlined and written in bold. And that's as clear as can be.

Test Result: No Maternal Match Found.

My stomach turns cold. No maternal match?
What does that mean? That Mandy Paul *isn't* my mother?
Then who the hell is?

SIXTY-ONE

Sophia takes her time, reading the whole paper carefully before setting it down and looking at me.

"Wow. So the sample you gave *doesn't* match? That kid wasn't you?"

"No." I feel utterly baffled. More than that, crushed. I want the last few seconds to not have happened, to open the envelope again and it go the other way.

"Could it be a mistake?" Sophia asks. She reads the paper again.

"I don't think so. Isn't the chance that these things are wrong something like one in ten billion?"

"Oh. That's a big number."

"Yeah. I guess I'm more likely to be..." – I pause, reaching for an example – "Elon Musk's daughter than Mandy Paul's."

"Yeah. I guess." She doesn't know how to react. "Does Elon Musk even have a daughter?"

"Not sure. But I'm probably not her either."

We both fall silent then.

"What now?" Sophia asks, after a long while.

"I don't know." But she looks at her watch.

"Oh shit, I have to get to work." She pauses, looking concerned. "Are you gonna be OK?"

I nod, before I even consider the question.

"We'll talk tonight. OK? I'll cook something. I get off at seven, come round then?"

I nod.

"Yeah. Alright."

I'm in a daze the rest of the afternoon. I walk again, up the beach towards the old Aegean Dream Resort. There's a couple of guys here now, putting a new fence around it, I suppose because they're going to knock it down at last. Only they're working in typical Greek style, incredibly slowly. And there's still nothing to stop anyone walking into the site where they haven't yet put the fence. But I don't go in. It doesn't matter to me now. It doesn't affect me. Whether Jason Wright did or didn't kill his girlfriend, I don't really care, because the baby left behind wasn't me after all.

Yet everything I've learned won't quite leave me alone. My mind goes back to the crazy story Simon Denzil-Walker told me. About how they lost – or nearly lost – Mandy's baby, the day before she died.

There's another thing. The seed of an idea I don't want to examine at first, but which I can almost feel take root in my mind. Sophia told me that we share the same birthday, or at least nearly. She also told me that she's adopted. And it's not hard to put two and two together, or at least begin to. What if *I'm* not the adopted baby, but somehow Sophia is? I just can't get my head around any of this, but perhaps that makes some sense? I'm not sure.

I didn't want Sophia to go to work, but now she has, I find I almost prefer to be alone. I don't know why exactly, but I sense it has something to do with how we nearly argued about Kostas. I sit for a while, and just try to empty my mind. Instead I pick up handfuls of the soft pale sand and let them run out through my fingers. And then I find that I'm on my feet and walking inland, away from the men building the fence and up towards the mountain that sits behind the resort.

For a few minutes I can kid myself that I don't know where I'm going, but of course I do. Maria told me how she found the bodies, and she also told me where, and I can see the building up ahead of me. There's no fence, there's no one around. There's nothing stopping me from taking a look.

When I get there, I wish I hadn't. There's a sadness to the place. It's not just that it's been used to house animals – I can see that by the goat droppings littered around – there's something deeper, but I suppose that's just in my mind because of what I know happened here. I'm not that far away from the main resort, but it's far enough that no one would really have heard Mandy if she'd screamed when she was attacked. Did she scream? Did she try and protect the baby? Did she actually succeed? Is that how it somehow stayed alive?

The door is still there but barely hanging on its hinges. I push it open, and step into the cool, dark interior. I don't know what I'm looking for, it's not as if I'm going to find any clues, it's not as if this has anything to do with me anymore, but I still try and imagine the scene. It's obvious where the bed would have been – though there isn't one here now. Maria said Jason's body was by the door, Mandy's further inside. There are dark stains on the wall, could it still be blood, all these years later?

Suddenly I hear a noise. Footsteps outside. There's a second when I think it might be just in my mind, but then I'm sure, and I don't know what to do. If I go back out there, whoever it is will see me, so I figure the best thing to do is stay here and wait until they go by. But then the footsteps get louder and there's a shout, urgent and angry. It sounds like they're coming right up to the building. I look around for another exit, but all I see is a little bathroom. I try it, and there's a smashed-up toilet and a very broken shower tray. So I come out again, just in time to see the building's main entrance – the only entrance – blocked by the silhouette of a large man.

He sees me the same time I see him, and for a second or two we just stare at each other. But then he starts yelling again. It's all in Greek, except then I make out a few words: *private*, and another word: *dangerous*

And then I understand. He's one of the men fixing the fence. He must have seen me come up here and followed, to tell me that people aren't allowed here anymore, because of how the resort has been sold. How it's going to be knocked down.

I have to push right past him to get out and get away. As I do I feel my cheeks flush, a little bit with fear, but with embarrassment too. Because what am I doing here? I should just leave it well alone.

These people have nothing to do with me. And it's not like I don't still have my own mystery to solve.

SIXTY-TWO

When Sophia says she'll cook, it turns out to mean that Maria will cook. But I'm certainly not complaining. Before I even got in the door I could smell it: herby, garlicky, rich. Sophia pours me some wine, and I sit at their table, and Maria brings an oven tray filled with tomatoes and peppers, stuffed with minced lamb, rice and herbs. There's a simple salad too, with fresh oregano and cubes of Greek cheese. We eat while Sophia tells us about her day, taking the tattoo guy out, who is finding diving harder than he anticipated. When we're done I help clear the plates, and then Maria tells us she's feeling tired and disappears upstairs, I guess to give us space. Sophia tops up our wine glasses and leads me around a corner, to a part of the house I haven't seen before. Here there's a large swinging chair, a double seater, hanging from the balcony above.

"Sit," Sophia tells me. "Let's talk."

So, we do. I tell her how I spent my day, and how confused and frustrated I am, that nothing makes any sense. The one thing I don't tell her though is my slight suspicion that – even if I'm not Mandy Paul's baby – then perhaps she is. I think I feel it sitting between us though, this unsaid thing. I wonder if she wonders too. I wonder if she knows that I'm thinking it.

We're both drinking steadily, not fast, but at one point Sophia upends the bottle over my glass, giving me the last few drops of wine.

"Do you want any more? We've got more bottles."

I shake my head. The wine's delicious, but I don't like the way it's dulling my senses. I feel this problem is hard enough. Sophia looks a little disappointed though, with the tiny amount in her glass, and I think of saying I don't mind if she carries on. But I don't say anything. She can work that out for herself.

"So, what are you going to do now?" she says instead.

I pull in a deep breath of the warm, scented air. I close my eyes, trying to feel whether the idea I have is a good one. It seems as though all my ideas have got me precisely nowhere. I'm more confused now about my identity than when I arrived here. But maybe that's the reason that I need to turn my thoughts back to England.

"There is something I'm thinking about," I say.

Sophia turns to me, a little surprised.

"OK, what?"

But I don't answer at once. I look instead at the roses growing up the wall. I wonder how much they've contributed to this thought. I sense Sophia's impatience, and turn to face her, trying to find the right way to explain this. It's not easy.

"There's one person I haven't talked to." I pause, considering. "One person apart from my mother, I mean – and I can't speak to her, not until I know something for sure." I lift a hand in acknowledgement that I'm not explaining this well. "There's one other person who might be able to help."

Sophia waits, then when I don't go on, she prompts.

"Alright, who?"

"Imogen Grant."

I glance across and see her frowning, so I go on. "She was

there at the time, and she was close to my mum, and they're still in touch now. So if anyone's going to know something, it's probably her."

Sophia nods now. "OK. That's a good idea."

But I bite my lip. "Yeah. Except, it's difficult."

"Why?"

I take my time answering. "Imogen's been in my life for years, but she's still a stranger. She's one of those adults who's always been 'around', but never quite *in* it. Do you know what I mean?"

Sophia thinks for a moment, then shakes her head. "No."

"OK, what I mean is, they're friends, but not really friends. It's like Imogen relies on Mum for support, and she knows she's going to get it, because they've been friends so long. But instead of a real friendship now, it's like Imogen only comes to see Mum when she's really struggling, and needs help."

"Struggling with what?"

"I don't know, her health – her mental health?"

Sophia draws in a breath, like this is troubling her but she's not sure why. She shrugs. "OK. How does your mum support her?"

"I don't know really. Imogen would come around to our house, but Mum would try and keep me away from her. It was like Imogen being there was a sort of crisis somehow. Like she was close to a breakdown and that's why Mum wanted to keep me away. But at the same time, Imogen herself would always try and be friendly to me, like everything was normal. She'd try too hard – like she was rehearsing some idea of what being an aunt should look like?"

"Alright."

"And then," I carry on, quicker now, "when she left, Mum would always warn me about her, saying I had to make sure I didn't mess my life up like Imogen did, that I had to be strong, not weak." I pause now, but Sophia's face is screwed up.

"I don't understand."

I puff out my cheeks. "OK, so I think basically Imogen's on a lot of drugs, and has been for a long time. Like, depression drugs – Prozac, Valium? That sort of thing. I think that's what Mum meant. There's this state they taught us about in medical school, it's called benzo-haze – people who are properly addicted to these types of drugs, and they're slow, they're kind of out of it the whole time. That's what Imogen's like. She's not quite there, because of all the medications she'd been on for so long."

"OK. Why's she so depressed?"

I shake my head. "It's not like that. Depression doesn't need a reason. Some people just are depressed."

Sophia cocks her head on one side, thinking this over. "And Imogen's one of those people?"

"I guess so. I am *only* guessing," I clarify. Then add, "I've maybe seen her a dozen times in my whole life, and talked to her maybe half of that. But those times, they're hard to forget, and Mum talks about her a lot, warning me not to end up like her."

Sophia studies me, and I don't know what she's thinking.

"So can you talk to her now? Or is she too far gone?"

I consider this before answering.

"I think so. She's... *functioning*, in that sense. It's more that it's awkward, since she's Mum's friend, and I don't really know her at all."

This time Sophia considers for a moment. But she doesn't seem to consider "awkward" much of a problem.

"So what will you ask her?"

I draw in a deep breath now. In a way it's the hardest question of all.

"I guess I could ask if she remembers Karen being pregnant. Like at any time after they left the ADR. And if not, if she knows anything about how I turned up, and when. I just need to know something?" I make it a question, and Sophia thinks for a while then nods.

"Yeah. It has to be worth a shot. Do you have a number for her?"

"No." I look at the roses again. "But I know she works in a florist. In London – Clapham High Street."

SIXTY-THREE

It takes Sophia less than five minutes to find her. There are three florists on the high street in Clapham, and when I saw them I even remembered the name of hers, because she must have told me once. But anyway, it has a website, and it helpfully lists "our people" with a photo and a picture of all the staff. Here's what it says about Imogen:

Imogen Grant – Senior Florist

Imogen has been with us for over 15 years and brings a wealth of experience in floral design. She has a particular passion for wildflowers and delicate, seasonal arrangements. Whether you're looking for a wedding bouquet or just something to brighten your day, she's always happy to help!

In the picture she looks like the smile is an effort, you can see the camera-shyness in her eyes.

"I think I see the benzo-haze," Sophia says, as she clicks around the site. She stops at the Contact Us page, which also has the opening hours.

"What's the time difference between Greece and England?"

It takes me a few moments to remember. "Two hours, I think. Why?"

"It says it closes at seven. It's only just past nine now here, so she might still be there. If she's working today. You could call and find out?"

Both of our eyes go towards my phone, resting on the cushion beside us. I see Imogen in my mind, as if she were already coming to answer my call. She has a way of moving that's more drifting than walking, her legs hidden under long flowing dresses. I let the picture in my mind run on, seeing her reaction when I tell her it's me.

"I can't."

"Why not?"

I feel my heart rate kicking up. It's hard to explain.

"If you don't do it now, are you actually gonna do it?"

I look at her, not sure where she's going with that.

"If you don't do it right away, you'll lose your nerve," she explains. "Or you'll do it eventually, but it'll take you ages, and you'll beat yourself up for not doing it." She picks up my phone and holds it out to me. "So you might as well just try now."

I try to go back to the image in my mind, but now Imogen's just floating there, surrounded by millions of flowers.

"What am I going to say?"

"What you just told me. Tell her the truth. You're on Alythos, you're trying to find out how you came to be born here because nothing makes any sense. You found your mum's diary and she doesn't seem to be your mum." Sophia shrugs again, matter of fact. "Ask her what she knows? What's the worst that can happen?"

I almost laugh. The way Sophia puts it sounds so simple. And I realise it *is* simple. I'm only asking a question. And she's right too, about the other thing. If I don't do this now, I probably will lose my nerve.

"She's probably not there anyway," Sophia's realism interjects. "But you might as well try." She holds the phone closer to me.

I'm in a sort of dream state as I take the phone and tap in the number from the laptop screen, like I'm doing this and not doing it at the same time. But I'm jerked back to reality when a woman's voice answers:

"Lavender and Vine, can I help you?"

"Oh! Um..." There's nothing to do now but try. "I'm looking for... I was wondering if... Imogen was there? Imogen Grant? I'm a friend of hers."

The voice changes, instantly less professional and more casual.

"Sure she's... actually she's just walking out the door. Hold on and I'll see if I can catch her."

I hear noises in the background, a few bangs, voices I can't make out. Then the same woman is back.

"Yep, she's still here, just on her way." Then the line goes quiet again. Then there's another voice.

"Hello?"

I know it. "Imogen?"

"Yes? Who is this?"

"It's Ava." I pause. "Karen's daughter."

There's a silence. Then, just as I start to speak again to give my surname she says my name.

"Ava."

"Yeah. Um, I don't know if you remember me..."

"Of course I remember."

I stop, and this time the pause stretches so long it's her that speaks next.

"What do you want?"

Oh God. I'm making a mess of this. It's easier, maybe, to get straight to the point.

"Yeah, so I know this is going to sound weird, but I wanted to ask you some questions, about me." There's another silence, but this time I can hear her breathing.

"What kind of questions?"

"Like, about Greece. Alythos. And maybe about Mum too." Calling Karen that still comes so easily to my mind, but my doubts now make it catch somehow every single time. I realise I've fallen silent again, leaving her waiting.

"I'm here now, in Greece. I left med school, I was... I don't know if you even know I was there..."

"In Sunderland. Yes, I knew."

"Oh. OK. Well, I... actually I didn't leave, they kicked me out. Because my grades were shocking, and... I don't think I was cut out to be a doctor." *Shit, I'm rambling.* I catch Sophia's eye and understand her look. I need to get to the point.

"What I mean is. I came to Alythos. I'm here now."

I stop, but there's just more silence.

"Imogen? Are you still there?"

"Yes. I'm listening. Do you mean Alythos in Greece?"

I didn't know there was another one.

"Yeah."

"Oh." A pause, then: "Why are you there?"

"That's what I wanted to speak with you about. I came to... I don't know exactly why I came. But I wanted to find out more about how I came to be born here. Mum's never spoken to me about it." I stop. "I thought maybe I'd be able to find out who my dad was." I shake my head at how ridiculous this sounds.

"You're really on Alythos?"

"Yeah."

"And you're there now?"

"Yes," I tell her again.

"Oh." I have the phone close enough to Sophia that she can hear what's being said, and she mouths to me now.

Tell her about the diary.

I nod when I understand her, and then there's still silence on the line, so I do what she says.

"I found my mum's diary. From when she was working here. It says she was sharing a room with you. And there's this really weird thing, it shows that she wasn't pregnant, with me, when she was supposed to be. So I don't understand it, and I wondered if you knew something, like maybe she was pregnant later, after the murders and the resort closed down?"

"The murders?" Imogen cuts in suddenly.

"Yeah, the manager of the Aegean Dream Resort. He killed his girlfriend?" I'm confused. She must know this.

She's silent again, and I give her space. Or maybe, I just don't know what more to say. After a very long time she speaks again.

"And you're on Alythos? In Greece?"

"Yes."

Another pause. A little shorter this time, but her voice is strange now, I hear an edge to it.

"Is Karen with you?"

"No."

"Does she know you're there?"

"Yes. Of course, she's my..." I don't finish the sentence.

"Are you going to be there for long?"

I don't know how to answer this. I think about telling her I have a job and I planned to stay for the summer, but that's not quite it.

"I was going to stay until I found out the truth," I say in the end, and it sounds corny. It's made worse because she doesn't reply at once, so my words just hang there, in the space between us.

"The truth," she repeats at last. And then she's silent again.

"Yeah, so I wondered if it was OK to ask you about it?" I mean, I already have, but she just keeps repeating the questions back to me. But then she surprises me. Big time.

"I can come out there. I can get a flight from Heathrow. Will you let me? Will you wait for me there?"

The idea takes me so much by surprise that I'm unable to answer.

"Will you wait for me?" she asks again. "I'll look at flights right away, or as soon as I get home. I'll buy the first one I find. I can take time off here, that won't be a problem." I hear her calling out to someone in the room with her. I don't catch the words exactly but she's confirming she's due holiday time. Then she's back, speaking to me.

"I'll find a hotel. In Skalio – is that where you are? Are you in Skalio, it's so pretty there, is it still that pretty?"

"Um, yeah. I'm in Skalio. And yeah, it's still..." I look around at Sophia and Maria's little garden, the darkness drawing in close around it. They have a trail of pretty white lanterns that hug the line of the wall, Sophia switched them on when we came out here.

"It's beautiful."

"Stay there. Promise me you'll stay there. I don't know how long it will take me. There might even be a flight tomorrow. Give me your number, so I can reach you. I'll tell you what flight I'm on. We can meet. And I'll tell you."

"Um, OK." I feel how wide my eyes are as I glance at Sophia, who's covering her mouth with her hand.

"Is this your number, on the screen?" Imogen reads my phone number back to me.

"Yeah."

"I have it. I've written it down. Now wait there. And I'll tell you."

"Tell me what?"

There's a pause.

"You said you wanted the truth. It's awful, but I have it. And you deserve to have it too. You always did. But it can't be on the phone. I have to look into your eyes. I have to be there with you. *For* you. Wait for me there and I'll tell you. I'll tell you everything."

"Um. OK."

"You'll wait for me?"

"Yeah, I guess..."

"Good. Great. That's... I..." She doesn't finish either sentence.

And then, just before she hangs up she goes on, her voice almost too soft to hear. "Oh, Ava. You have no idea. No idea at all."

The line goes dead.

I lower the phone slowly.

"Oh my God," Sophia says beside me.

SIXTY-FOUR

There's a moment, after that, when I'm not sure if Sophia wants me to stay the night, or thinks I might want to. But it's not awkward, somehow. We don't actually say anything about it, either of us, but I feel there's an understanding. That, whatever we might want now, there's no way anything can happen between us, at least until I know who I am. Or maybe I just imagine the whole thing. Either way, I leave soon after.

By the time I get back to my apartment that night, I already have three messages from Imogen. The first two just tell me which airlines fly from the UK to Greece, and to which airports. The third says she wants to fly direct if she can, because of how difficult the bus journey is from Athens. I don't know if I'm supposed to text back, to tell her it's not that hard, but I reply in the end, just thanking her and saying I'm looking forward to speaking, but she replies almost at once with links to different hotels. I figure she must be on some app on her phone and just sending me the links as she comes across them. The texts keep coming, it seems she can't find any rooms at such late notice, at least not at a price she can afford. It's late here, and I wonder about replying, reminding her that Greece is two hours ahead –

and that this is super-weird behaviour and freaking me out – but instead I just put my phone onto "do not disturb" and try and get some sleep.

In the morning there's another six messages. At first it seems positive. She's found a room, in a hotel that's not that far from Skalio, and she's actually booked it. But then it seems there was a problem with the flight. She filled in all the details but didn't hit "book now" until she had the hotel taken care of, and then by the time she'd done that the flight had gone, and there weren't any more seats until two days later. It's all a lot more than I need to know, and it's hard to untangle what she's actually managed to book, from all the details she's given me. But in the end I figure it out. She's booked into the Aegean View Hotel a few miles east of Skalio, and she's flying into the regional airport in Panachoria, the day after tomorrow. Then I get a message to follow her on Instagram, which I do, even though I haven't posted anything on my channels for ages. And I see she's put the details on there, with a link to the hotel. It's a kind of spa resort. It looks nice. But her words are weird. She says:

> Heading back to Alythos. I always knew this day would come.

I speak with Hans next. I'm working the next three afternoons, but if I can move those times I could meet her at the airport – I sense she'd like that – but he says no. The island is getting busier now. But when I text Imogen to say I can't meet her she says not to worry, she never expected me to. In the end we arrange to meet the day after she arrives, when I don't have to work – she says it might be better that way anyhow, to give her a chance to settle herself. Whatever that means.

But the next two days drag. It's just hard to be in the same space as people who are happy and enjoying their holidays, when I'm not here for that. And when I'm also not part of the group of people who are working hard and playing hard. I'm here on my own, private mission, and it's kind of lonely. Even if I am about to finally learn the truth. Whatever it might be.

Sophia is the only person who seems to understand. In fairness, she's the only person I've shared all of this with. Or at least, almost all of it. I still haven't told her about my suspicion that she might actually be Mandy Paul and Jason Wright's baby. But I do wonder if this is part of the secret that Imogen is going to share. And that's kind of a heavy thought too.

On the afternoon of her arrival, I can't help but look up in the sky. I'm clearing glasses at the time, in Bar Sunset. From there you can see the planes circling above Skalios Bay as they come in to land at Panachoria. I don't know if it's actually her plane of course. But I see one, the orange livery of EasyJet clearly visible in the vivid blue sky. I stop what I'm doing to watch. From here, Panachoria is hidden behind the mountains that make up the spine of Alythos, so from my angle it looks as if the plane is flying *into* the mountain. And when it disappears it's easy to convince yourself that actually it's crashed, and everything she knows, everything she's going to tell me, has just blown up in a fiery ball of flame. But, of course, it hasn't. I check on my phone the airport's arrivals page, which updates a couple of minutes later to say the London flight has landed. And then I get another text from Imogen.

> Landed! Now I need a taxi. And a ferry! We'll arrange a place to meet when I've settled in!

SIXTY-FIVE

> Do you know the Trikremnos Coves?

This is the only message I wake up to the day we're due to meet. I don't – know it, I mean – but I look it up and see there's a little trio of beaches between Skalio and Kastria, near to where Imogen is staying. I text back saying I've seen it, and a few minutes later I get a long reply:

> I remember it from when I worked here. It's very beautiful. Three tiny perfect coves. It's not as quiet as I remember it, because now there's a cafe on the first beach, but if you keep going it's quieter, and there's a wonderful flat rock in the final beach. It's lovely in the sun. I think it's a good place to talk. Can you be there at eleven?

My fingers toy with the phone for a few moments before I reply. I guess it sounds like a good idea, but I sort of hoped that Sophia could come with me. Except she can't, because she has to work this morning. And if I try to push it later, then I have to be at the Bar Sunset. I puff out my cheeks, but tap out a reply:

> OK. See you there.

Then I text Sophia, asking if she minds me borrowing her moped again. Then I have a shower, not really caring when the hot water runs out and I just stand there in the not-quite-cold of the water from the pipes.

At ten I walk down to the dive centre. I'm not able to speak properly with Sophia, she's busy handing out wetsuits to a group of Germans. But she tosses me the moped key and tells me good luck. And then when I'm back outside strapping on the helmet she comes out and makes me promise to tell her everything, unless it's too horrible and I don't want to. She leans in and gives me a hug, and I can smell the peach-perfume of the shampoo she uses. I don't want to let her go.

It's only ten minutes on the moped, which seems easier to drive this time, I guess I'm practised now. Soon I reach a rough parking area, with steps that lead down through some scrubland. At the bottom I can see the yellow of the sand and a sliver of water – vivid turquoise and inviting. I take off the helmet and check my watch. Ten fifty. I try to calm my nerves. I don't really understand *why* I'm so nervous. I've known this woman for years, she's not at all scary, not really. She's just really odd. But maybe what she's going to tell me will be frightening.

I hesitate about whether to leave Sophia's helmet dangling from the handlebars or carry it with me. It's quite isolated here, and I don't want someone to steal it. So in the end I carry it as I set off down the steps.

They're uneven, stones cut roughly into the earth, worn smooth by years of use. Dry grass and thyme brush against my ankles as I descend, and the scent of sun-baked herbs fills the air.

From the bottom, the cove is truly stunning – a perfect crescent of golden sand, the sea curling gently at its edge. There's a handful of people, a couple lying on towels, a man standing in the shallows in bright red speedos. A little wooden cafe sits off to the side, its terrace shaded by a straw awning.

Her message said she'd wait in the third cove by the flat rock, so I keep walking.

The cliffs here extend like fingers, cutting the beach into three. The rock is tall but narrow, almost like a curtain that conceals the next little bay beyond, but there's plenty of beach extending beyond it to step around into the next bay. And here there's only two people, lying on towels under a sun umbrella and lazily kissing each other. They stop when they see me, glaring as if they want me to turn back. I don't, crossing in front of them around the next finger of cliff into the final bay.

And straight away I sense something's not right.

The first clue is the towel, floral patterned and scrunched into the sand at the bottom of this big flat rock that comes out of nowhere in the middle of the beach. It looks like someone's stood on the towel, twisting it, driving it deep into the sand. There's a bag too, but upside down, the contents spilling out.

I hesitate, then step closer, looking around, but there's nothing else here. And then my heart stops. There's *is* something else. Protruding from the other side of the rock, on the beach beyond it. It's a foot. A bare human foot.

For a second, my mind refuses to process what I'm seeing.

Stupidly I call out her name, but obviously she doesn't move. I can see that the angle of the foot is all wrong. But still, I have to force myself forward, feeling the blood pumping through my head. Every step I take reveals more of her – pale calves, a white flowery dress, wet in places – I don't know what with, but sand has stuck to it. Her arm is draped across her belly.

I feel my throat tighten.

No, no, no.

I drop Sophia's helmet onto the sand with a thud and stumble forward, my knees hitting the ground beside her.

"Imogen?"

My voice wobbles as I reach out, my hands hovering over her shoulder, over her arm, not quite daring to touch her. Her hair is tangled, dark strands plastered to her cheek, her neck. But it's her head that's the most horrible of all. A wound on the back, seeping fresh blood into her hair and onto the ground, where it sinks at once. Like the very essence of her is disappearing into the sand around her.

SIXTY-SIX

I've seen dead bodies before. In medical school we were given a cadaver to learn anatomy. There weren't enough to go around, so me and two friends had to share one, a man in his sixties we called Doug – because he'd been dug up – though of course he hadn't really. I've seen people die too, in my hospital placements. But that was different, there were qualified people there who took over, who knew what to do. Here I'm alone. But after a few moments, something from those experiences kicks in: the first thing is to establish if the person really is dead.

Check for signs of life.

"Imogen?" It's stupid, calling out to her, but I still feel that squeamish sense I had with Doug. I don't want to touch her, I don't want to get near. I look at her chest. Is it moving? I can't see. *The carotid artery*, it's on the neck. It's the surest place to find a pulse. I hold my breath and press two fingers to the side of her neck. She's still warm to the touch, hot even -- I register that – but I can't *feel* anything. And then I can. It's faint, but there's something there. And then maybe my fingers slip, because I don't feel it anymore. Maybe I only imagined it the first time? I look around, but there's still no one here. No one to help. In a panic I check her eyes. They're closed but I gently lift one lid. If she's dead the pupil will be fixed and dilated – wide and unresponsive to light – but at once I see it contract from the bright sunlight. She's alive. I rock back on my heels, still shocked and stunned, and I have no idea what to do next.

Help, I need help.

I look around. There's no one else in this tiny cove, but I saw people in the one before. I run back, a few steps away, already panicking that I'm doing the wrong thing in leaving her, but I push on, around the corner, where the couple I saw before are now laid one on top of the other. They might even be having sex, but I don't care.

"Help! Help me please!" I run halfway towards them, and the man jumps off the woman like they're hit with a bolt of electricity. He rolls over, he still has his shorts on, thank God.

"Help! Please, help me." Slowly the man climbs to his feet, looking at me, half-scared, half-angry.

"What?" His accent is heavily Greek, but he speaks in English. I didn't even consider he might not be able to.

"There's a woman. She's been attacked, in the next bay. I need you to phone an ambulance." I breathe out. "Please, hurry."

He stares at me – does he understand? *Can* he speak English? I start to repeat myself. But he cuts me off, speaking quickly in Greek to the woman. She doesn't move, and he speaks again, faster, more urgent.

"Please, you must phone an ambulance," I begin, and he cuts me off again.

"Yes, she is doing. Where is this woman?"

Slowly – too slowly – the woman takes her phone and, her eyes on the man, she begins to dial. It's strange, I see the keys she presses. In Greece the number is 112. Finally, I know.

I realise the man is still waiting for me. "It's this way." I start back towards the narrow headland and to where I left Imogen.

It only takes a few moments, but I wonder in that time if I've imagined it, if I'm going to find Imogen there perfectly healthy, or if she's not there at all. But nothing has changed. Except maybe she looks worse somehow, the wound on her head still seeping blood that's running through her hair, over her face and torso – and now I realise all over my hands as well. The wetness on her dress. I smell it now, it's urine.

"What happened?" the man asks, his eyes are wide open, his pupils flared.

"I don't know. I just found her like this."

He nods, but he doesn't seem to know what to do. I hear a woman's voice and realise the girl has followed us, she must be on the phone to the emergency services.

"Tell them it's a head wound," I spin to her. "Possible brain injury. They have to come more quickly for that." I have no idea if this is true in Greece, but I remember being told this back home. The woman doesn't react though, I realise maybe she doesn't understand me. So I say it again, turning to the man this time.

"It's a head wound. Brain injury, they need to come quickly."

He translates it, then nods at me when his girlfriend has relayed the message. His face is sickly white now and I hope he's not going to throw up. Somehow this helps me though, and I start looking around for something to help control the bleeding. There isn't anything except a scarf where Imogen's bag has been emptied. I grab and fold it, shaking off the sand, before pressing it gently against the wound, just enough to stem the flow of blood, but not to press against her brain, some of which – I now see – is visible through the mess of her hair. This is horrible. Awful.

"They are coming," the man tells me. "The doctors are coming. They say they will come by boat, because is difficult to get here by car."

I nod, thinking. What else should I do? Now I'm so close to her, I can see the rise and fall of her chest, hear the air flowing in and out. I need to keep the airways open. Talk to her, try to get a response.

"Imogen? Can you hear me?"

Nothing.

I have no idea how much time passes. I can't remember how long the man told me the ambulance would be, or even whether he did. I feel like I've been here for ever, holding the scarf against Imogen's head, just enough to stop the flow of blood, feeling my hands pressing against her actual brain. There are more people around us now. I suppose it's the people from the first bay, where the cafe was. Some people are asking questions, but most are just watching. Then another man squats down, he's middle aged, he tells me he's a doctor, gently he takes over from me. His hands move across her body with more confidence.

"What's your name?" he asks me, and I tell him.

"You've done well, Ava, you've done really well. Take a step back now."

So I do, and a space opens out in the little crowd around me, as if no one wants to stand too close to the English girl with blood all over her hands and top. I glance at my watch, it's eleven fifty-five. I've been here nearly an hour. Time flies when you're having fun, even more when you're terrified. I look at my hands, my blouse, stained red with Imogen's blood. Still I'm not really thinking, I'm just *being*, reacting. Here in this impossible space on this beach, with the world spinning out of control around me.

A boat arrives, causing a buzz among the watchers on the beach. It's similar to Kostas' dive boats – I almost think at first that it is one of his, but I remember there were dozens of similar boats moored in the harbour in Kastria. There's two men sitting at the front in red uniforms, another man is driving. They nudge the bow onto the shore, and the men in red step out and jog up the beach. One's carrying a medical bag. They kneel beside the doctor, and between the three of them I lose sight of Imogen's body. And then the magnitude of it all hits me. I feel suddenly sick, like I might actually throw up, and I find myself moving towards the sea, to wash the blood from my hands. I wade in, still with my shoes on, and scrub my hands, splashing water over my face and top. Then I stagger back onto the sand and fall to my knees.

Another boat arrives. This one is obviously some sort of police boat. It's bigger, with actual blue lights and a siren. Perhaps it ought to sharpen my mind, but it doesn't. I just watch it arrive, two officers jumping clear into the shallow water, even though they have boots on, which get wet before they wade up the shore. They have radios and speak into them almost constantly while they assess the scene. I'm apart from everything now, away from where Imogen is being transferred onto a type of sled thing. I'm late in realising I can't just sit here, watching from afar – they're going to want to speak to me. And then they do. I watch as the man I first called for help points me out. Then one of the police officers strides over to me.

SIXTY-SEVEN

"You are English, yes?"

I nod.

"You were the first person to find the body, yes?"

The body? I glance across, but I can't see her. *Has she died?*

"Yes."

"What is your full name?" He pulls out a notepad, opens it and flicks a few pages forward, then he waits, a pen ready.

"Um, Ava Whitaker."

"Are you a tourist? Where are you staying?"

I tell him that I work here, at the Bar Sunset, and give him as much of my address as I can remember.

"Do you know the woman who was attacked?"

I open my mouth to answer, and then freeze. It occurs to me – and I don't know if it's crazy – but if I say "yes", am I going to be a suspect? But if I say no, then I'll be lying to the police. I just freeze, my mouth open. But then I have to say *something*, the police officer is staring at me, his face darkening the longer I hesitate.

"Um, yes." I don't make any decision that this is the best answer, the word just comes out.

"She is a friend of yours?" he confirms, apparently this doesn't surprise him. "You will give me her name?"

"Imogen Grant. She's not really a friend, she's a friend of my mother."

"OK." It takes him an age to get the spelling of her name right. In the background I see they're moving the sled that Imogen is now on, carrying it down the beach towards the medic boat.

"Is she still alive?"

"We will need a statement." The officer acts as if he didn't hear me. "At the police station. For now, can you tell me what you saw? Did you see who attacked the woman?"

I shake my head and try to focus. I recount what happened when I came around the headland into the third bay. But I'm starting to think now, behind the words that fall from my mouth. How much can I say to the police? How much should I say? I don't know the answers, and I need space to think, but luckily I get it.

"Please wait here. We will speak with you more." The officer goes off, speaking to the other people still standing around the little cove.

I watch as the medical team finish their work. They have Imogen in the boat now, and they're strapping her in securely. It takes me a moment, but I realise the way they're dealing with her, she must still be alive. She has to be, because now more than ever I need to hear what she has to say. I find my feet taking me forward, down towards the boat.

"Is she OK? Can I go with her? To the hospital?" I call out. The doctor is there too, the man who took over from me. But no one answers me.

"Please? Is she OK?"

"She is unconscious," the doctor answers me at last. "She must be taken to the hospital as quickly as possible."

I nod, thanking him.

The policeman who spoke to me before turns around now. "You will come with us. You can wait in the boat." I don't know what he means, but then he takes my arm and leads me along the beach to where the police boat is moored, a rope coming off its bow leading to an anchor dug into the sand.

"Please, wait here. You must give a statement."

I want to protest, but he helps me up into the boat, and I take a seat on one side.

I stare at the boat. It's so strange. It looks so real, yet all of this is so unreal. A statement. What am I going to say?

More elements of my predicament bombard into me. I was the first person to find Imogen, she's clearly been attacked, so might the police think *I* attacked her? Should I have just run off when I saw Imogen lying in the sand? But of course not. Trying to help someone can't make you look guilty. But should I tell them I was meeting her? Does that make me a suspect? It's like being in a dream, where you suddenly find yourself in a trap that you didn't notice at first, where you don't quite know where the walls are, but there doesn't seem to be any way to escape.

Maybe I should just tell them everything? But it's so confusing. I don't *know* anything. The whole point of coming to Alythos, the whole point of Imogen coming out here, was so that I could find out the truth...

Suddenly I freeze, the obvious reality of this hits me. How did I not see this before? Imogen was going to tell me everything, and suddenly she's been attacked. That's not a coincidence. That cannot be a coincidence. Someone hit her, *someone tried to kill her*, to stop her from talking to me.

I cannot get this thought out of my head, even as the policemen finish up what they're doing and start preparing to leave. There are more police now, I think they must have come from the land, and then I'm being told that we're going back on the boat, that I should hold on tightly when we start moving. I nod dumbly, still reeling.

Somebody tried to kill Imogen, to stop her talking to me.

Who? Who could it possibly have been? My mind goes first to Gregory Duncan, he lied to me about knowing her. I suspected it at the time, but now I'm sure of it. But why would he try to kill her? How about Kostas? He knew her, and he'd have the strength to do this. Easily. But how did he know she's here? Maybe Sophia inadvertently said something? What about Simon Walker Denzil, or the men who work for him on that crazy superyacht? I've no doubt some of them are the violent type. Or could it be someone else? I have literally no idea who might have done this, or why.

We're pushed out backwards into the bay, the anchor passed across the bow where one of the police officers stores it away. Then the powerful engine whines as it tugs us backwards slowly out into deeper water. Then it growls as the prop bites and spins us around, pointing towards the open sea. Moments later we're flying along, turning – to my surprise – left. Away from Skalio and along the rocky, cliffy coast.

The journey only takes fifteen minutes, flat out the whole way, until we slow down as we enter the rock arms of the harbour in Kastria. It's much bigger than Skalio, and we tie up alongside a pontoon. I'm helped ashore, and then led up a ramp onto the harbourside, where a police car is waiting for me. It takes me on a short drive to a whitewashed building with the words *Hellenic Police* on the outside in English – along with plenty in Greek I can't read. I'm led inside and finally into an interview room, where I'm left alone with a bottle of water. It's fifteen minutes later when the door opens again, and the policeman who spoke to me on the beach sits down in the chair opposite.

I've decided now, I'm going to tell the truth – as much as I can – without confusing the investigation they're going to lead. I sit forward in my chair, preparing to tell the policeman everything.

SIXTY-EIGHT

"Thank you for waiting Miss..." – he flips open his notebook – "Whit-a-ker, this shouldn't take long." He gives me a solemn smile.

I nod, readying myself.

"When you found the body, did you see or hear anybody else in the bay?"

"No."

"Did you see anybody when you approached the area? Anybody acting suspiciously?"

I think about this, retracing my path in my mind.

"No. I don't think so."

He reads through something in his notebook. I can't see what, but he flips the pages several times. Suddenly he looks up.

"What time was it that you found... Ms Grant?"

"Um, I think it was... We were meeting at eleven. I think it was about five to. Ten fifty-five."

The officer nods.

"OK." He looks up, meets my eye for a moment, then repeats himself. "OK." He flips the notebook shut.

I'm confused. "Is that it? Is that all you need to know?"

"For the moment yes, if I need to ask anything more I know where to find you."

"But I was meeting her," I protest. "Doesn't that make me... a suspect?"

He smiles, but doesn't quite laugh at this, except he nearly does. Then he seems to gain control of himself. "Do you think you *should* be suspect?"

"No. Of course not. I didn't do anything, but—"

"Calm yourself, Miss Whitaker. It is very clear what has happened here, I am sorry to say."

"What?"

He looks thoughtful a moment, as if this isn't something he should say, but then tells me anyway.

"Your friend Imogen arrived yesterday and checked into the Aegean View Hotel – you probably know this. It seems as she was arriving – into the airport, and taking taxi, into the hotel – she was paying with cash, from a purse with many banknotes. Too many. This was noted at the hotel, but perhaps noticed also at the airport, who can say...?"

"Noticed by who?"

He pauses, makes a face, but then decides to be understanding of my ignorance. "Unfortunately there are gangs of Albanians who target tourists on the island. Not just here on Alythos, but across Greece. It is a wide problem."

I stare at him, not understanding.

"Our neighbours to the north." He sighs, like he's talking about a troublesome family member. "It is a difficult place to live, and many cross the border – illegally of course – to target the tourists here."

"But I was *meeting* her. She was going to speak with me, to explain something. What if she was attacked for that instead?"

"I think this is unlikely, we did not find the purse, nor Ms Grant's telephone, most probably it was stolen."

"*No*, no. The thing she was going to explain is important, it might be dangerous."

He seems taken aback by this. But at least he seems interested.

"What was she going to explain?"

I pause, trying to think clearly. "I don't know, that's the point. She didn't get the chance to tell me, but couldn't that *be* the motive? Someone attacked her to stop her talking?"

He frowns at me now, like he doesn't understand suddenly. "What was it..." – he stops, searching for the word – "*referring to*, do you know this?"

I take a breath before replying, but nod at the same time. "She was going to tell me what happened, here on Alythos, when I was born. Something about my mother." I try to make my explanation sound heavy and important, but as I finish I realise just how weak it really sounds. "What I mean is, there was something she had to tell me, about what happened when I was a baby." I want to tell him about the other baby, the one involved in the murders, but I can't because that's not me. He gives me an awkward smile and glances to the door, like he wants to get away.

"OK, well I think this is not something to kill over, yes?" He gives me a final smile, dismissive. I sit back. One of his words hits me hard.

Kill? I know she's been attacked. Did someone really try and *kill* her? New questions come to my mind quickly.

"How is Imogen?" I ask. "Where is she now, is there a hospital here on the island?"

The policeman nods now, happier to be on familiar ground again. "Yes. Your friend is alive, but it is serious. This is all I know for the moment."

"Can I see her?"

"This you will need to check at the hospital."

"What hospital, where do I need to go?"

He looks uncomfortable for a moment, but answers anyway.

"She was taken first to the medical centre here in Kastria, but I believe now she has been transferred to the hospital in Panachoria. It is larger, with more facilities." He stands, and this time it's clear the interview is over.

SIXTY-NINE

I phone Sophia in the reception area of the police station, then wait outside until her and Maria arrive. Right away they agree to take me to see Imogen, and we drive the few minutes down to the ferry terminal. We have to wait here, and I explain everything that happened at the beach. On the ferry Maria hands me a coffee, and I sit drinking it, staring at the churning white water pushed out behind as we chug away from the island.

The world is slightly different on the mainland. Even though we're still a half-hour from the city of Panachoria, it already feels busier, less cut-off, and as we get closer to Panachoria there's that city feel, dual-carriageway roads full of cars, a train running by the side and planes moving overhead. The hospital is on the outskirts, a big building with multiple car parks and different departments, most of the signs in Greek. We go inside, into the Emergency Department, and from there we're told it's Neurology we need. Finally we find it, and Maria and Sophia explain at the reception desk who we are and that we're looking for Imogen Grant, the woman who was attacked on the beach. At least I assume that's what they're saying, they speak mostly in Greek, switching only to English when it's clear the person they're talking to understands it. I find myself drifting away, first mentally then physically, stepping past the desk where they're speaking and looking into the ward beyond. I did a placement on a Neurology Intensive Care Unit when I was studying. And I'd begun to think that maybe this was where I might like to specialise. If I hadn't been kicked out. It's strange to be back now. The ward here is made up of private rooms, the door of the first room is half open and when I just move a few steps to see the patient, to my amazement it's her – Imogen – in the bed. I look back, but Maria and Sophia are still talking with the woman at the desk, not looking at me. So I just go inside.

She's hooked up to a ventilator that hisses slowly as it fills and empties. Two IV lines run into her left wrist, and there's a plastic endotracheal tube taped into her mouth. Her eyes are closed, and she's either asleep or unconscious, I'm not sure which. I'm sort of familiar with the machines around her, I learned about them. There's an ICP – an intercranial pressure monitor – which will be tracking swelling inside her skull. She has a catheter, I see the output bag hanging under the bed. A pulse oximeter is clipped to her finger. I move closer, checking the readings. Her heart rate is stable, oxygen saturation high. That's good.

I'm startled by a voice behind me in clipped Greek and I spin to see a doctor, a woman, frowning at me from the doorway. Before she can speak again, Maria cuts in, presumably explaining who I am. The doctor listens, then nods and when she speaks again it's in English. She comes into the room and picks up the notes from the foot of the bed.

"You are the next of kin?" she asks me. Maria gives me a look that I should say yes.

"Um, yeah."

"Ava...?"

"Whitaker. Ava Whitaker."

"OK. Hello Ava. I understand you want to know how she is?"

"That's right."

The doctor nods. "I must warn you, it is early to say anything. The lady has suffered a severe traumatic brain injury. The blow to her head caused a skull fracture, with haemorrhages. There is also cerebral oedema – this is a swelling of the brain tissue inside the skull. Too much swelling can cause pressure and this can be very dangerous, it can lead to—"

"I know. I worked in an ICU."

The doctor pauses, surprised by my interruption. "You are a doctor?"

"Not exactly. Sort of." I give an apologetic smile, then quickly go on. "Is she in a coma?"

"Yes."

"Induced?"

"Yes. When she arrived, she was unconscious. Her Glasgow coma score was very low. To protect her brain she was put into an induced coma. This will allow the brain to rest and heal without more stress."

I nod. I don't exactly understand, but I've listened to explanations like this before. I've had to give them too, with my tutors watching me.

"We also did a CT scan. There is no large haematoma. That's good, but there are contusions – bruising on the brain. This will take time to heal."

"But will she wake up?" It's Sophia who asks this question. "There's something she needs to explain, something really important she needs to say." Both the doctor and I turn to look at Sophia, but the doctor answers.

"Likely yes. But I cannot say for sure."

"How long?"

"I would say she will stay in the coma for... perhaps three

days. We hope that will be enough to allow the swelling to reduce."

"And then she'll wake up?" Sophia looks at me as she speaks. "Then she'll be able to speak?"

The doctor is about to answer when the pager clipped to her waist buzzes. She glances at it, grimaces slightly and drops it back down. She turns to Sophia.

"I'm sorry, I have to go. But yes, we hope."

SEVENTY

We're left alone in the room with Imogen, the machines monitoring her softly beeping. For a while no one says anything. I take a step closer and look into her face, her eyes closed, her expression peaceful. *What is it you were going to tell me?* I want to ask her. *What is it you know?* I think back to all the times I've seen this woman, the time she appeared at my birthday party completely unannounced and even more out of place. How old was I then, eight or nine? She's always been this strange presence in my life. Turning up as if she were Mum's best friend, when Mum never seemed to like her much. Why has Mum used her over the years as an example of a weak person, an example of how not to live my life?

I believed it too. There was always a softness, a weakness if you like, in Imogen that frightened me a little. Not because I thought I really would turn out like her, but of the terrible implications if I did. That my life would pass by while I lived inside a dream. Then I feel a hand on my shoulder and turn to see Maria smiling softly at me. There's a nurse now, standing in the doorway.

"We should go," Maria tells me, and she guides me away.

. . .

We don't talk as we wind our way through the hospital corridors back to the outside, but we stop as we reach the car. Maria zaps the button to unlock it but doesn't pull open her door.

"What will you do now?" she asks instead.

"I don't know." I wait too, my fingers touching the handle but not pulling it.

"Perhaps it is time that you spoke with your mother?"

I look at her. I look down at the door handle, and suddenly the world in front of me melts behind watery tears. They come on so quickly and so strongly that when I blink, two fat drops of water fall onto my hand, only to be replaced at once by more liquid welling up in my eyes. I try to wipe them away, choking back more tears. I feel Sophia beside me, her arm around my shoulder, pulling me into her. Maria comes too, and both of them hug me for a long while, stroking my head, my hair, my shoulders. A long time later I'm able to speak again.

"But she's not my mother, is she?" I turn to Maria, feeling the heat on my face, wiping away more tears. "I know that. I don't know who she is, but I know she's not my mother."

"Whether she's your biological mother or not," Maria speaks quietly, "you know she's the person who's brought you up, who's made you who you are. And nothing will change that."

She takes a deep breath and looks around while I slump more onto Sophia.

"And what you said about your birthday," she says now. "About how your mother said it might not be your actual birthday. Maybe she *is* your real mum, and all this is just some confusion about dates?"

I know she's only saying this. To make it easier, to make me less scared about what I know I need to do now.

None of us have got in the car yet, and Maria sighs again

and looks around. Very much unlike any British hospital I've ever seen, there's a strip of cafes across the road which look both welcoming and pleasant.

"Maybe we should get something to eat?" Maria says, and I nod. I don't feel hungry, but somehow the thought of getting into the car and returning to Alythos, away from Imogen, seems wrong. The problem is I don't know what would feel right.

"OK," I say, and a moment later I hear the car blip and see the locking lights flash. Sophia leads me through the car park and across a busy road to the cafes. They all have tables on the pavement, but Maria leads us inside, where it's cooler and there's less noise from the road. We sit, and they order coffee and pastries.

"I think you should call her, let her know what's happened," Maria tells me when the food has arrived. Only Sophia has touched it at all. I don't answer.

"Where is she?" Maria asks me.

I shrug. "At home."

"You say Imogen is a friend of hers. At least you ought to tell her that she's been hurt."

I let her words wash through me, not really hearing them. But it's as if they snag on something, they spark a reaction.

"But she wasn't hurt, someone attacked her. Someone wanted to stop her talking to me." I look at Maria, my eyes pleading with her to explain this to me. For a long time her eyes rest on mine, then she sighs.

"It could just be a coincidence. There are gangs of Albanians, I've read about—"

"Oh, come on, Mum," Sophia cuts in, angry. "You know it's not true." She turns to me. "Everything here gets blamed on Albanians." She shakes her head.

"I agree, Sophia, but what's the alternative? Do you really believe that someone attacked this poor woman just so that she couldn't tell Ava who her real mother is? Why would that happen?"

"I don't know. But you don't know either."

I see the frustration on Sophia's face, a moment later she speaks again. "Ava had her room broken into as well. Stole her laptop. Do you think that was Albanians?"

Maria stays silent.

"And then whoever did it smashed the laptop up and hung a bag with the bits in on her front door. Like they were sending a message."

"What message?"

"I don't know I don't have a clue. But something."

I thought it would all make sense if I turned out to be Mandy Paul's baby. But if I'm not, then I don't understand anything.

There's a silence. Then Maria tries again.

"Maybe she'll be able to explain this to you, your mother? Now you can show her you know you weren't born when she said you were. Or weren't born to her?"

I don't answer.

"Either way, you're going to have to face this. Sooner or later. And with Imogen..." – her eyes slide to the hospital over the road – "it would be better sooner."

For a long time I stay quiet. Then I quickly pull out my phone. They both watch me as I stare at the screen. It's weird to think that with this device I can speak with this woman, thousands of miles away. This woman who has brought me up, who has been my mother my entire life, but who clearly isn't. This woman who's lied to me about who I am. Idly I press a button and the phone comes to life. My lockscreen image. A smile comes to my lips. It's me and Kevin, arm-in-arm, with the cold North Sea behind us.

"I keep meaning to change that," I say, my eyes finding Sophia's. She doesn't look away.

Mum's listed in my phone as "Mum" – what else would I put? What will I have to change it to after this conversation? I have no idea.

"Do you want some privacy, honey?" Maria asks, and I'm almost surprised, because I've retreated so far into myself that I'd almost zoned them out. I bite my lip, then shake my head.

"I'll go outside."

I stand, walking the few steps to the doorway of the cafe with my thumb resting over the "call" button. I find a quiet corner in the shade, close my eyes, and press.

After six rings it goes to voicemail. Mum's voice, cool and brusque, leave a message, she'll get back to me. Obviously I don't. Instead I hang up, then stare at my hands, which are shaking wildly. I literally have to use my other hand to steady the one holding the mobile. Then my focus shifts, wider than my hand, the street in front of me, the hospital behind it. The thousand-mile gulf that's opened up between me and Karen – whoever she is to me. Or the gulf that was always there.

I go back inside, both Maria and Sophia trying to read my face. I shake my head.

"No answer. I think I need a drink."

At once Sophia gets up and goes to the bar. I watch her back as she speaks with the barman, and moments later she comes back with a tall glass of cloudy white liquid.

"Raki," she says, putting it down in front of me. "It'll help."

I take a sip, it's strong aniseed and frankly horrible, but I take a large mouthful and force myself to swallow it. Something about the burning sensation in my throat does help a little.

"Is there another number you could try?" Maria asks. "A work number perhaps?"

I blink at her, then half-nod, half-shrug. "There's the pharmacy." I check my watch, trying to work out what time it would be in the UK now, but give up because my brain isn't working properly. "I could try there." I look at her and see she's nodding, that I should. That I ought to try. I nod back, but take another large drink from the raki first.

"OK."

I stand again and walk back outside. Mum's work number is listed on my phone as "Mum Pharmacy". I blink at it a few times and press dial.

This time it goes straight to voicemail. The office hours are eight to five thirty, and the store is now closed. I don't let it finish, I don't let it tell me the location of the out-of-hours service, because I've heard it thousands of times before. Instead, I hang up and screw my eyes shut. Fuck, why does *this* part have to be so difficult? Isn't the whole thing hard enough? Why is it so hard now just to reach her? Without really thinking I try her mobile again, not really expecting anything other than her voicemail a second time, but this time she surprises me.

"Ava?" Her voice is sharp, surprised.

"*Mum?*"

"What is it? What's going on?"

SEVENTY-ONE

I pause, frozen. Captured in a moment speaking to her, with nothing to say.

"What's going on, Ava?"

"Nothing, nothing's going on."

Silence. "OK. Well, it's taken you long enough to get around to calling me. Did you run out of money?"

"No. *No.* That's not why I'm calling."

"OK. That's something at least. Well, I'd love to hear an update."

"Where are you?"

There's a pause. "I'm at home. I'm watching television. Where are you?"

I look around. "I'm in Panachoria, in Greece." I wait, wondering if she'll remember the name. It seems she does.

"Have you been to Alythos yet?"

"Yes. I've been there the last three weeks."

"What have you found out?"

"That's a weird question. What do you think I might have found out?"

There's a sound down the phone. I can almost see her on

the sofa in our front room, wine glass on the table beside her, as she balances the remote on her knee.

"I don't think you'll have found anything out. There's nothing to find out. But I know you went looking for something."

"I met a man called Kostas Aetos," I hear myself saying. Blurting out really. It silences Mum, at least for a few moments.

"Who?"

"Kostas. You might remember him better as the gardener of the Aegean Dream Resort? Or Imogen's boyfriend, does that help?"

There's another pause.

"You met Kostas? He's still there?"

"Yes, he's still here. He runs a dive centre now. In Skalio."

There's a long silence. "I see. And what did Kostas have to say?"

This time it's me that's quiet. I've unleashed this conversation, but I haven't planned it. Maybe that's for the best, but maybe it isn't.

"He didn't have much to say. At first at least. He told me he didn't remember you."

She's not quick to answer, but when she does I'm certain I hear relief in her voice.

"OK. That's not a surprise, it was a long time ago—"

"But then he changed his mind," I cut in. "He said he did remember you. Except you weren't..." My mouth stops working. I can't produce the last word.

"Weren't what, Ava?"

Pregnant. Pregnant. *Pregnant!* My mind screams down to my mouth, but my voice won't produce the word.

"What did he '*say I wasn't*'? Ava?"

I close my eyes, see only my mother, curled up on our sofa. I shake my head to release the image.

"He had your diary, Mum. He found it in your room."

This time it's incredulity I hear. This stuns her.

"My *diary*?"

"Yes."

And now calculation. A long pause of calculation.

"I see. Did he tell you what was in it?"

"He did more than that. He *gave* it to me. I read the whole thing."

She's silent. So am I, for a few moments, then my words come in a rush.

"You weren't pregnant, Mum. *Mum. You weren't fucking pregnant.* I read it, thinking I was going to find out who my dad was and it told me I don't have a mother! You didn't have a *baby*, Mum, not when I was supposed to be born—"

"No. *Stop.*" Her voice is biting, slicing into me. Cutting me dead. "You don't know anything. You *do* have a mother, but you don't understand."

"What don't I understand? *What?* Tell me, please. I don't understand anything, that's the whole fucking problem."

"Who else have you spoken to? Out there, have you talked with anyone else?"

I try to think, my mind has gone temporarily blank. "Simon Walker-Denzil."

"Simon? Oh my God."

I try to work out whether I should tell her about the baby. The baby she nearly killed, the baby I thought was me, but now I know can't be. In the end I don't get the chance, because she moves on quicker than I do.

"Simon doesn't know anything. Is there anyone else you've spoken with?"

The question makes my mind spin through everyone I've talked to here, but I don't say anything. At least not about that.

"There's a reason I called." I screw my eyes shut, trying to focus.

"Well obviously, I had no idea you were digging all of this nonsense up—"

"I spoke to Imogen. A few days ago." I cut her off the same way she did to me. "I told her some of the things I found out—"

"You haven't *found* anything, Ava. There's nothing to find out—"

"Even so," I cut back in, "I spoke to her."

Silence.

"And what did *Imogen* say?" She layers something onto the name. A familiar note of contempt.

I take a deep breath, "She told me she was going to come out. I lere to Alythos. And she was going to tell me everything."

"Oh my God, now *Imogen's* going to Alythos? Oh, this is fantastic. Bravo Ava, this just gets better and better. Listen to me Ava, you cannot listen to what that woman says. She's been on Seroquel for *years*. Twelve hundred milligrams a day. You know what that's for, don't you? It's an anti-psychotic drug. One that doesn't always work too well. I've always told you, Imogen is a weak, weak person. You can't trust her."

"She's already here." I can't listen to my mother anymore. The rant flowing out of her. "But she didn't get the chance to say anything. Someone attacked her. Someone tried to kill her."

Finally, *finally* my mother shuts up.

"What?"

I tell her again.

"I was going to meet her. When I got there she'd been attacked, someone hit her on the head. She was nearly dead."

A silence. "Oh my goodness." I hear her breaths. "Where are you now?"

"I told you. In Panachoria, outside the hospital."

"She's in *hospital*? Imogen's in hospital?"

"I just told you Mum, someone attacked her. To stop her talking to me, someone smashed her head in, and I don't know who, or what they're trying to hide—"

"What hospital?"

I shake my head. "Panachoria. It's the town on the mainland near—"

"I know where it is. Is she OK? Is she going to be OK? Is she *speaking*? Does she know who attacked her?"

"No. The hospital put her in an induced coma. The police say it was probably Albanians. Apparently they have a problem with them here."

"Oh my goodness, Ava. A coma? Is she going to be alright? Have you spoken to anyone who knows?"

"I've spoken with the doctor. She says they'll know more in a few days. She might have brain damage, or she might be OK. They won't know until she wakes up."

"Oh my gosh. This is horrible news. Horrible, Ava."

"I think she was attacked to stop her talking to me." I say it again, but she ignores me.

"OK. Ava, you need to stay there. Wherever you are, just wait there. I'll come out. I'll get the first flight I can, and I'll meet you wherever you're staying – are you in a hotel?"

"No..."

"Never mind. Just stay there. Keep your phone switched on. I'll be on the next flight. We'll get through this, we'll make this right." Then she sighs down the phone at me. "For God's sake, Ava. I did tell you not to go out there. Why couldn't you just listen to me?"

SEVENTY-TWO

The way Mum books her flight is very different. I get one text message, telling me she'll be in the Alythos Hotel in Kastria in two days. That's it, nothing more. And then I have to wait. I visit the hospital on one day because I don't have to work and I need something to occupy my mind. Imogen is still unconscious, and it takes me forever to find a doctor who will tell me anything about her situation. When I do it seems that little has changed. Then I do one shift at the bar, and then I find myself on the bus from Skalio into Kastria, finally ready to have the conversation with my mother that's been brewing for so many years.

I ask at the front desk for Mum's room number, but the girl points me towards the bar. So I walk in and there she is. Sat at a table by the window, a bottle of wine in front of her. She beckons me over, then snaps her fingers at the barman to bring a second glass.

"You made it," I say, as the barman comes over. I pay no attention to his appreciative glances, not just at me but Mum too. But her eyes flick over to his.

"How was your flight?"

"Fine." She pours me some wine, not a full glass though. I don't care. I don't want any, but it pisses me off nonetheless. I'm not fifteen anymore.

"I've hired a car. I'm going to see Imogen later on," she tells me. I nod. "Would you like to come with me?"

"I think that depends on how this conversation goes," I reply. I force myself to look her in the eyes, not lower my gaze, and I'm dimly aware this is how I've lived for as long as I can remember. Not quite looking her in the eye, not quite telling her what I feel. Or maybe there's nothing unusual in this. Maybe this is just how any child treats their parent, until the moment they finally grow up and take their independence.

"Fair enough. A fair point." She looks pointedly at my untouched glass, but picks hers up and takes a small sip. Then a second. She swallows.

"I didn't want you to come here, because I didn't want you digging into all this. But I didn't know how to stop you," she begins. Then she stops. I wait a moment then press.

"Why would you stop me?"

"I think you know that."

"I don't know anything, that's the problem, I don't know—"

"Lower your voice, Ava." Her words are like knives, stabbing into me. She stops, then offers an apologetic half-smile. "Please, Ava. Lower your voice."

I don't say a word, just stare at her.

"I hadn't even remembered that I kept a diary. I don't remember anything about what I wrote in it, but I can imagine it wasn't exactly a work of literature," she starts again, and I watch her face, I feel how sullen my eyes are.

"It definitely wasn't."

"It certainly never occurred to me, when you announced you were coming here, that anyone could be so... I don't know, reckless – to hand it to you. It's an outrageous breach of my privacy. But there we are."

"It shows you weren't pregnant, you didn't…" Somehow my argument feels weak, the proof that she's been lying to me should trump whatever rights she has, but I barely convince myself. "You didn't *have a baby* when I was supposed to be born?"

"Of course I didn't," she snaps back. "Can you imagine being pregnant while working at the Aegean Dream Resort? Ridiculous." She shakes her head, as if I'm being unbelievably stupid for even imagining it. "Had any of the staff got pregnant they'd have been on the first flight home." She stops again and sighs. "Except for Mandy,"

"So?" I open my hands in despair. "So, who the hell am I?"

She takes another sip of wine, brushes an eyelash or a piece of dust from her eye, sits up taller in her chair.

"To be quite honest, I don't exactly know."

Then she sits back and watches me.

"What the hell? What does that mean?" I say. I feel like I need to pinch myself, to wake up from this conversation.

"This isn't the way I ever imagined this going, Ava. But I have imagined it, many times. I've always thought that one day we'll need to have this talk."

"What talk?"

"*This* one. Ava, you're quite right, I wasn't pregnant with you. There's only one conclusion from that." She stops again, and for a moment she covers her face with her hands.

"Ava, I'm sorry to tell you like this, but you were adopted. When you were very young. I never told you because I wanted you to have as normal a life as I could give you, and I thought it was for the best this way."

Her words are like being sideswiped by an iceberg. A wall of cold that freezes my brain. I already knew – of course I knew – what other solution could there be? But at the same time it still feels as if the ground shifts. I wanted to believe it wasn't true.

"Who are my real parents?"

"I have no idea."

I shake my head. I can't form the words.

"What do you mean?"

"You're Greek, or at least you came from Greece, that much is true – like I always told you. But the way the adoption system here works, the records are sealed. Not even the adopting parents are told about the child's history."

I blink at her, my mother, except she's actually not my mother. And I never knew. I never even suspected it. Not for a moment.

"Well, they'll tell *me*. Surely they'll let me know?"

"No, they won't. That's not how it works here. It's one reason I decided not to tell you. The system here is that not even the child is allowed to know. Not once the records have been sealed. If I'd have told you, it would just pose you a question that couldn't be answered."

My mouth drops open to protest, but I already know that this part is true. This part at least.

"Am I from Alythos?"

"No."

I shake my head, my mouth open, speechless.

"I'm *not* from Alythos?"

"It's highly unlikely. When I took custody, I was told you would be given a Greek passport. I couldn't prevent that, though I wanted to. I was allowed to allocate a place of birth. Because I'd worked here, on Alythos, I chose the island."

I blink at her.

"What about my date of birth?"

"I'm not sure. It's possible the adoption agency didn't even know your exact date of birth. We decided upon May 20. It seemed as good a day as any."

I'm silent, processing this.

"I actually told you once. I don't know if you remember, you were ten or eleven—"

"Yes. I remember."

Now Mum's quiet, watching me with cautious eyes.

"But May 20 is also the date that Mandy Paul had her baby," I begin, because I'm still stuck on this, even though I'm not *that* child. I regret it at once.

"Mandy Paul has nothing to do with it." She shakes her head, takes another sip of wine.

"But she had a child, on the same day. And she was murdered, when the Aegean Dream Resort shut down. It was left alive. I thought that might be me…"

"Oh, Ava." Mum shakes her head now, then offers the first smile that looks even vaguely genuine. "Oh goodness. That has nothing to do with this. Nothing at all."

"I took a DNA test," I hear myself blurting out. "Mandy Paul kept a lock of the child's hair. I had my DNA tested against it."

"You did *what?*" She looks aghast. "Oh good heavens." She tips her head to one side, curious suddenly. "What did it say?"

"It was negative. Of course it was negative," I tell her. "That's not me." I see the look on Mum's face – like it obviously had to be negative and she's almost laughing at herself for asking, but that's just the kind of conversation this is, intense for both of us.

Mum even smiles now as I go on. "But I *thought* I was. For a while. Because you didn't tell me. You didn't tell me the truth."

This seems to change her mood. The smile settles, becomes almost genuine. Finally she nods.

"I'm sorry, Ava. I only ever meant the best for you. And I promise you this isn't how I wanted you to find out. I hope you'll believe me on that."

I still feel like the base upon which my life was built has been entirely washed away. Like I'm untethered, like my connection to reality is now so fragile that just one wrong word, one errant thought and I'll be swept away from it, never able to return. But I can't just sit here. I can't stay in this place, I have to move forward.

"Why did you adopt me?"

She takes a long time answering this, sipping again from her glass before she speaks. Maybe because she wants to tell me very carefully, because she understands how devastating all this is for me. Or maybe because she's trying out different versions in her head.

"I was with Shawn at the time, your..." She pauses, and I know it's because she was about to call him my father – because that's what she always used to call him, but she leaves it. "He wanted a child – we both did, and I wasn't able... And..." Her eyes flick to mine. "The truth is I was very taken by my time in Greece, and I was very affected by what happened, to poor Mandy and to her baby. It seemed like a way to put right some of that horror."

We're both quiet a while. Me trying to process this, and Mum – I don't know what.

"Simon Walker-Denzil. I told you I spoke to him."

Her smile quivers a little, she seems alert. "Yes?"

I draw in a deep breath. "He told me a story. About how you and he lost Mandy's baby, overboard on his yacht." I watch her, challenging her to deny this or explain it away. She begins by reaching for her wine glass again.

"Simon," she says instead. "I heard he's working for some rich Russian."

"Is it true? Did that happen?"

"I told you. I warned you when you came here that I wasn't proud of my behaviour."

"Oh God."

"We were lucky, we were incredibly lucky—"

"You lost a baby. You were in the boat taking drugs, having sex, and you left it to be washed overboard."

"*Ava!*" My voice has risen again and she glances around the bar once I'm silenced. A dark look crosses her face, warning me again to watch myself.

"No harm was done," she hisses back. "We were lucky, very lucky and horribly, unforgivably stupid. Not to mention lazy and arrogant, and..." Suddenly she screws up her face and covers it with her hands. When she removes them her eyes are tightly shut.

"I cannot begin to tell you how terrified I felt, how awful I knew I was for what we had done. But when we went below it was as calm as a mirror. It didn't cross my mind that the weather could change so suddenly. I told you, I've been deeply ashamed of what happened every single day since. *But no harm was done.* We found the baby, it was fine. It was just a coincidence that Jason snapped that night."

The tension between us is interrupted by the mundane alert as a message hits my mobile. I don't react at first, but eventually I pull it out and check the screen. It's from Sophia, three words:

Call me. Now.

I look at my mother. The woman who I now know for sure isn't my actual mother, but perhaps who still remains the person who brought me up, the person who's done the best for me that she could, however weird the circumstances. I just don't know.

"I have to take this," I say and stand up to go.

SEVENTY-THREE

"Hi," I say when Sophia answers. I'm in the corner of the hotel bar now, where my mother can't hear me.

"How's it going?"

"I'm not sure. She says I am adopted. But not from Alythos. Somewhere else in Greece, she doesn't even know where."

"Wow. OK. How do you feel?"

"I don't know. I need time to process."

"OK. That makes sense." Sophia hesitates.

"What is it?"

"Well... it's good news. You know Mum asked the nurse to keep us informed if anything changed with Imogen? She's just called."

"And?" I hold my breath.

"I told you. It's good news. She's awake. She's out of the coma. They don't want anyone to visit her now because she's really weak, but you can visit her tomorrow. You can hear her side of the story. Whatever it is."

I don't reply, instead I look over at Mum, who's sitting up straight, adjusting her hair like she's about to take a selfie for Instagram. Mum who said Imogen has nothing to tell me, just drug-fuelled paranoia. Except, why would she come all the way out here if she had nothing to say? And why would someone attack her on the beach?

"Ava, you still there?"

"Yeah. Thanks."

"Are you gonna go, do you want me to come with you? I can get the day off."

"Um..."

"I don't have to come in there with you. I'll wait outside. Whatever it is she has to say, you don't have to tell me, or anyone else. Not if you don't want to."

I feel myself smiling, I feel the relief in my jaw.

"Thanks, Sophia. That would be good."

SEVENTY-FOUR

Mum offers to drop me back in Skalio with the car she's rented, but I refuse. I don't know why exactly. Maybe I just want to be alone. Maybe it's that I don't want her to see the horrible little apartment I've been living in. But the bus takes ages to arrive so I just end up walking, and then I'm committed, and I have to walk the whole five miles from Kastria to Skalio. It's good for thinking. Or maybe for not thinking. Maybe that's what I'm doing. Finding ways to let time pass by without having to examine this – wound – that I've opened up in my life.

Maybe Mum was right. Maybe I shouldn't have come here and dug into this? What has it actually achieved? So, I know I was adopted, what does that get me? But the more I do actually start thinking, the more my mind drags me towards Imogen. Why did *she* come here? Even if she is taking anti-psychotic drugs because she's crazy. What is it she *thinks* she can tell me?

I wonder if maybe it's just the baby thing. Perhaps she knows about what happened with Mum and Simon, and she wanted to confess to that. If so, it would make sense that maybe Simon had his men attack her – maybe he regretted telling me the story? But at the same time, what does that have to do with *me*, really? And as bad as it was, it was a lucky escape. It didn't harm the child, so why try and kill over it? Unless… unless it somehow contributed to what happened that night? It seems an impossible coincidence that it happened and then that night they both died. But what happened to link those events?

And if it wasn't Simon who attacked Imogen, then who was it? Kostas? Duncan? Or are the police right, and it was just bad luck? She was careless with her money, and a gang of thieves saw her? It's hard to accept. But then, the police are the police. And they're going to know far more about this kind of thing than me.

I have to stop off at a little shop that's on the way, and I buy a bottle of water and a bag of peaches. I eat two of them quickly, sucking the sweet juice as I bite. I think for a moment without really thinking, just that the fruit here is totally different to what I'm used to at home. But then I realise what I'd just said in my mind. This *is* my home. I'm twice as Greek as I thought I was. I believed I had an English mother and a Greek father, probably a waiter. But now I know that's not true, both my parents were Greek. It's just that I'll probably never know a thing about them.

The one thing I do know is that Alythos isn't my home after all. I've nothing to do with this island, no connection at all. Everything that happened here might be part of Karen Whitaker's history, but it's not part of mine. There's no reason for me to even be here.

Sophia calls me half an hour later. She's finished work at the dive centre, and she offers to borrow Maria's car and come and pick me up. But I tell her not to bother, I've almost walked the whole way back to Skalio now and I'm shattered. I just want to get back to my apartment and crawl into bed.

SEVENTY-FIVE

I'm in the shower the next morning when I hear a banging on my door. I grab my towel and wrap it around me, then when I walk out of the bathroom I can see it's Sophia through the frosted glass. Here to pick me up for the trip to the hospital. I open the door and beckon her in.

"I'll just be a few minutes," I say, turning around at once. "Do you want to make coffee, or shall we get some on the way?"

There's something wrong though. I turn back round. The look on her face is weird. She's been crying.

"What is it?"

She doesn't answer. But after a moment she reaches out and rests a hand against the door frame, like she needs it to keep herself up.

"Sophia? What's happened?"

Her eyes meet mine, then flicker away again, her mouth opens but no words come out. Until they do.

"I'm really sorry, Ava."

"What for? What's happened?"

Now she shakes her head. It seems like she forces her eyes to rest on mine.

"It's Imogen."

Something shifts inside me. Like I know what she's going to say before she says it.

"She died. In the night. The nurse phoned Mum this morning. She passed away."

Now my mouth opens. Ready to speak, but there are no words. I cover it with my hand, then turn away. I find myself staring at my tiny, shitty kitchen. How is that real? How is any of this real?

"What happened?"

"I don't know. The nurse said she woke up yesterday and seemed OK, she could talk at least. And then in the night she just died. The nurse said this happens sometimes with patients like this."

"Like what?"

Sophia frowns a little. "Like with a head injury." She stops, her lips quiver. "I don't know."

She's still standing there in the doorway. I open the door wider and she comes inside. I don't expect her to but she comes right up to me and wraps her arms around me. But it's not for my benefit, it's for hers.

"*Christé mou!*" Sophia says, when she finally pulls away, pushing the towel back up onto my shoulder where she'd pushed it down. I don't know what the words mean. But at the same time, I know exactly.

I suppose I must have got dressed. I don't remember. At some point Maria turns up, and then later on I get a call from Mum. I hear in her voice, right away, that she knows – so I don't have to tell her. And I must have given her my address too, because sometime after she turns up, and it's crazy weird to have all of them here – Maria, Sophia and my mother – all in the same tiny, crappy apartment. No one knows how to talk to one another nor what to say.

I don't know what Sophia's said to her mum about what my

mum said to me – I literally can't keep up with it all, but somehow we get some more details. It seems that Imogen suffered a cardiac arrest in the night, at around one o'clock. They say that this can happen with traumatic brain injury, you can see a patient initially improve, but there are complications, like brain swelling, blood clots or autonomic dysfunction, that can cause rapid deterioration. I feel like I'm back in one of my lectures, not in the wreck of my own life.

The police turn up later on, I don't really know why. They speak mostly in Greek and mostly to Maria, but at one point Sophia asks them in English if Imogen said anything about who attacked her when she woke up yesterday afternoon. The officer – the same one who interrogated me, if that's the right word – he starts to answer in Greek, but she interrupts him.

"In English, please." She shifts her gaze onto me.

"Yes. Of course." The man shifts his weight. "Unfortunately we were unable to get a chance to ask her directly, but she didn't say anything at all to any of the nurses or doctors. So we assume she didn't."

No one speaks – especially me, I'm too far gone with all of this. And he goes on.

"Even if she had, the members of these gangs, they are hard to tell apart."

I can't listen to any more.

The police go, and eventually most of the day is gone too. My mother is in the kitchen talking on her phone. Maria is telling Sophia she has to get back to the store.

"Will you be OK on your own?" Sophia asks me, and I try to nod but it comes out as a shrug.

"That was my hotel," my mother cuts in. "I've reserved a room for you there. You're not staying here tonight, it's out of the question."

And it's like I'm twelve years old again. I just nod at my mother and do as she says.

SEVENTY-SIX

I spend most of the next day in my room. It's nice in some ways to be here. The bathroom is big and light, and the bed is three times the size of the one in my cell of an apartment bedroom. Mum comes in every now and then. Her room is next door to mine, and there's a door that links the two. Mostly she wants to check up on me, and she gives me some pills too, they're only mild sedatives but they help me relax a little. I can see she's also sorting things out. It turns out that Imogen really didn't have many other friends, at least not the sort who can organise the repatriation of a body out of Greece. Mum has to decide whether Imogen would want her funeral in England, or America where she's originally from, and in the end she decides that probably the UK is more appropriate, because that's where she's lived for the last twenty years. Mum's good at this stuff – she always has been.

"Are you hungry, darling?" She surprises me now as I'm sat by the window, looking out on the pool. I shake my head.

"You should eat. You have to eat."

I think about protesting that I ate some salad at lunch, but I'm tired.

"The funeral is set for Monday. Clapham crematorium. I fear there won't be many people there."

I glance at her, the words make it seem real. I picture a giant hall, with a coffin at the front and dozens of empty pews. It's so sad.

"So I'd like us to attend. I think she'd like that."

The image in my head persists a moment, then dissolves as I try to place myself there.

"In London?"

"Mmmm."

I can still see the hotel's swimming pool out of the window, aquamarine under a deep blue sky.

"But how will we get there?"

"I've reserved some flights. Tomorrow evening."

I get a jolt of something at this. Finality? Something like that.

"Poor Imogen is travelling on a different flight, this evening." Whatever I was thinking is pushed away by this new thought. Imogen – this woman I've sort-of-known my whole life, this woman who wanted to talk to me. This woman whose life I tried to save. She's gone. She's in a box, somewhere on the island – presumably – and she's going to be loaded into the hold of a plane. She'll just be lying there, a few feet under where the alive passengers are sitting, completely unaware there's a dead body underneath them. It's such a strange thought. Reality is so strange, when you suddenly see it from a different angle.

"Do you have your passport?"

I give a little shake, refocusing on the question she's just asked. "What?"

"Your passport? I need it to finish the flight booking. And we'll need to collect the rest of your things from that apartment you were renting."

Her words wash over me. I hear them, but they don't

connect. There's something else though, something trying to push into my consciousness. "Did they do a post mortem?"

"What?"

"A post mortem, did the hospital do one?"

Mum's voice is cool. "No. There was no need."

"Why not?"

She looks at me strangely, and I try to hold on to wherever this thought came from. It seems important, even though I can't exactly say why.

"Because she died of a heart attack." She softens her face. "Following complications of her brain injury. It was expected."

I nod. "Mmmm," thinking, and then making the connection "But she was attacked. On the beach someone tried to kill her. Shouldn't they look into it, at least?"

It looks as if Mum's going to answer, but then she just shrugs her shoulders.

"I don't know, darling. They've decided they don't need one, and I think we should trust them to know what's best. It means we can spare Imogen from the extended trauma of it. And we should be grateful for that. We can close this horrible chapter as soon as possible."

"But... it's not a trauma though, is it? A post mortem, I mean. She won't know about it. And wouldn't *she* want to be sure? That it was Albanians who killed her, and not someone else?"

Mum smiles at me soothingly. "Who else could it be, darling?" I try to think again, getting my mind to show me the suspects I still have. But I can't get any of them to focus.

"What were those tablets you gave me?" I say instead.

She looks startled, almost irritated. "Ativan. I told you. It's just a little something to help with the shock."

"They're making me drowsy."

"They're meant to. So you can sleep." She looks at me, her head on one side. "Perhaps it would help if you got out of the room? You could have a swim – the pool's lovely, and you could borrow my bikini." She smiles brightly at the idea, and I look away. She's proud that her bikini fits me. I know it, and I sense she's going to mention it now, make some joke perhaps about how Imogen's wouldn't because it would be too big. The joke repulses me, even though she doesn't even say it. Of course she doesn't. I'm the repulsive one for even thinking of it.

"I don't want to swim," I say.

"Well that's fine. I was only offering."

"What's *Ativan*?" I ask.

The irritation's back. "It's a very mild sedative."

I don't answer her, but I remember now, I remember from my classes. It's a benzodiazepine. Did they say it was mild? I don't remember.

"I might just have a sleep."

Mum softens again. "OK, well that's a good idea. But just for a couple of hours. I do need you to go and clear out your things from that apartment. At least collect your passport, we can always replace the rest of your things when we're home."

I blink at her. The attraction of the big, comfortable bed is almost magnetic, pulling me towards its soft pillow. I nod.

"OK, have a sleep, darling. I'll wake you in a while."

SEVENTY-SEVEN

Mum wakes me in time for dinner, and we eat together in the hotel's restaurant. Neither of us speaks much, but I feel her watching me, making sure I eat something substantial this time, and not just a few leaves of lettuce. It's dark outside now, the night warm and inviting. I can still see the pool, the water illuminated from below. I don't know why, but I get a flash in my mind of Mum, working in her pool bar in the old Aegean Dream Resort. It's the same colour – the pool here and the one I've constructed in my mind. The way I've somehow mentally emptied the garbage and the dirt from the old, broken ADR pool, and filled it with clear cool water. I'm about to ask her about it. Whether it was as pretty as this, but she speaks before I get the chance.

"I've got a message from the airport," she sighs. "I thought we had everything covered, but it turns out I need to go and sign a different release form before they'll load her onto the plane." She gives me a look of apologetic frustration.

"Imogen?"

"Yes Imogen, who else?" She frowns, just for a moment, then goes right on. "So I'm afraid you're going to have to do the apartment on your own. But I've booked you a taxi, and I've spoken to the man on the front desk and told him to tell the taxi driver that he's to stay outside until you're done, and then bring you right back. Are you going to be OK with that?" She glances at her watch, and sighs again. "I'm afraid you'll have to be."

I think for a moment, working out how this works. Then I nod. "Yeah."

"It's just your passport you need. Do you have your key?"

I nod again.

"OK, well let's go. This is all charged to the room." We get up from the table, and she leads me through the restaurant, towards the reception and the front of the hotel. I still have this weird feeling, like I'm slightly floating or I'm not quite me, which is kind of funny, because I'm not sure who I am anymore.

There's a taxi waiting outside the hotel, the lights on, engine running. Mum speaks again to the receptionist, and he comes out and opens the door for me. I smile my thanks and climb into the back seat. It smells of leather, or that fake vinyl leather, or maybe it's the air freshener dangling from the mirror. Something anyway. Mum leans down to speak to me.

"Just make sure you get the passport, the rest isn't important. And don't worry at all about the rent and deposit, we can sort all of that out from England."

I nod. She closes the door and is about to remind the driver of my address but he cuts her off, he already knows, maybe the receptionist told him.

As we drive away I look back and see her watching the taxi leave, and then turning and walking to her hire car parked up outside the hotel. Then I lose her as we turn the corner.

"Excuse me," I say to the driver. Trying to speak feels like stirring thick honey.

"Yes?"

"Before we go to the apartment, can we make a stop somewhere else?" I don't know Maria's address exactly, but I describe where it is and the driver nods rapidly.

"OK. No problem."

The truth is I'm glad Mum can't come with me to do this. I don't want to leave without saying thank you to Maria, for everything she's done. And goodbye to Sophia.

SEVENTY-EIGHT

The taxi stops outside the gate to Maria and Sophia's house, but I can see right away they're not home. The little house is in darkness, but even so I get out and go up to the door and check. But there's no answer. I shake my head to try and clear it, why didn't I message Sophia? What am I thinking, why *aren't* I thinking? I pull out my phone and send her a quick text, saying I'm going to be at my apartment for an hour or so if she's around. Then I turn and walk back to the taxi. I'm about to open the door and climb in when I change my mind. It's a lovely warm evening, the air soft and infused with the scents of the flowers in Maria's garden. Except here by the car it's overpowered by the smell of the exhaust fumes and the cloying chemical from the air freshener. I think of how Sophia insisted she was fine to walk back from my apartment. It seems a lifetime ago, but still I trust that she was right. My hand hesitates on the door handle.

"Actually, I think I'm going to walk," I say to the driver through his open window. "Can you still pick me up though, in an hour?"

He shrugs, but looks happy enough – which helps me not

second-guess my idea. It doesn't even occur to him to be concerned about a female walking alone at night. I step back to let him turn the car around, then watch the rear lights disappear back down Maria's little lane.

There are street lights – not the harsh type we have in England, but soft and pretty – that illuminate the route from Sophia's house to my apartment. And quite a few of them are softened further by the blooms of bougainvillea and other flowers that have been planted in this part of the town. And even though the walk is only short it does me good, and I start to think how I'm going to pack my things. It's not even that big a job. But when I step around the final corner – so that the front door of my apartment is over the road, opposite – something stops me. There's a car, parked just in front of me, and I can clearly see there's a man in it. He has his back to me – he's sitting in the driver's seat, as if he's watching the front door. *Of my apartment block.* I don't move for a moment, and at first I'm just confused. Is he waiting for someone? But then I realise I'm being stupid. There's loads of people he could be waiting for, any of the other residents of the building. Maybe they're going out and he's just picking them up.

But then I have another thought – I guess it's triggered by my wondering earlier whether it's safe to walk here at night. Someone attacked Imogen – in broad daylight – and I don't know who they are. And they didn't get caught.

Either way, there's no way I can get to my apartment without walking past this car. So I take a deep breath, and drop my head and just power past. But then the moment I draw level with the driver's window, I sense more than see – because I'm keeping my eyes forward – the man duck down into his seat. Like he's trying to hide.

I keep going, pretending I didn't see, but I can't not notice. And then another thought fires in my mind. Before the man dropped down, I recognised him. I stop, my thigh level with the front of the car, and I turn around. And then very slowly – carefully – the man pulls himself back up, like he's expecting I've gone past now and I won't see him. But I do. I look right into his face. And I don't understand at all.

"Gregory Duncan?"

SEVENTY-NINE

I'm close enough to see his hand snatching for the key in the ignition, but something stops him from turning it. I can see what. The way he's parked he's backed the car right up close to the one behind him, so the only way out is forwards. And where I'm standing, I'm already one step in front of the car. He'd have to run me over to get away. For a wild second I think he might do it anyway, start the car and surge forward before I could even get out the way. But he doesn't, and I do something else. I step more in front of him so that he can't leave. We stay there a few moments, staring at each other through the windscreen. Then I see him swallow, and buzz down the window.

"What are you doing?" I ask.

He doesn't answer. He doesn't seem to have any idea what to say.

"You're Gregory Duncan. I remember you. Why are you outside my apartment?" As I speak I remember my break-in, how my laptop was stolen and the weird way it was returned to me, smashed up.

"Are you gonna say anything?" I demand. I take a half step back, so I could get out of the way if he did decide to start the car. I can't see his hand now from where I am. It might still be on the ignition.

"Do you know?" he asks.

I wait, expecting something more, but it doesn't come.

"Do I know what?"

"About Imogen?"

I stare at him, not understanding. "Do I know she's dead? Yes, how do you..." Then I remember the portrait he had on his wall, the pencil sketch of Imogen when she was younger. He was in love with her, that's what Kostas told me.

"No, not that she's dead. Do you know the other thing?"

I feel my forehead pinching into a frown. "What other thing? What are you doing here? Are you spying on me? On my apartment?" I want to ask if it was him who broke in, did he smash my laptop?

"I'm not spying, I'm... observing." He's silent. So am I, for a few seconds.

"Observing what?"

Gregory doesn't answer. But then he surprises me by suddenly pushing open the door. He unfolds himself from the seat. I'd forgotten how tall he is. When he stands straight he looks down on me, and I see his Adam's apple roll up and down as he swallows.

"Do you *know*?" he says again. There's a desperation to his tone, like he can't bear not knowing my answer. But I still don't understand the question.

There's no need to stand in front of his car anymore, but there might be a need to run. So I take a step back, away from him.

"Do I know *what*?" I say again, trying to sound tougher than I feel right now. He just observes me.

"You don't know," he says now. He shakes his head a little, like this development is almost too much for him to bear. "You actually don't know."

"Are you going to tell me? What it is I don't know?"

He doesn't. Instead he moves suddenly and I think he's about to grab me, but instead he simply rests his lanky frame against the car and drops his head onto the roof. He even hits his head against it a couple of times, like he wants to hurt himself. I don't know what to do. I don't know what the hell is going on. But then I hear a familiar sound – the buzzy whine from the motor on Sophia's scooter. A few seconds later I see the headlight, and then she pulls up over the road from us. She takes off the helmet, pulls the bike onto its stand and moves for the door, but then senses us. She turns around.

"Ava? Hey..." Her eyes move from me to Duncan, and her eyebrows go an inch up her forehead. "Mr Duncan?"

None of us speak.

"Ava, are you OK?" She comes across to me now, moving quickly. But already I'm not feeling threatened by Duncan. Whatever this is, it's something else.

"What is it?" I demand from him again. "That I don't know?"

I feel Sophia staring, but my eyes don't leave Gregory. He looks at me, then Sophia, then at the open car door as if he wants to drive away now. And then something weird happens. He lets out a sound, but not human, more like a wild animal, a kind of mix of a roar and a sob. In the dim glow from the streetlights I catch the flash of wetness on his cheek, he's crying, sobbing wildly. After nearly a minute he finally falls silent, then he turns back to me, grunting to himself like he's trying to pull himself together.

"We need to talk."

EIGHTY

We go inside my apartment, it just seems like a natural thing to do. And Gregory seems to completely expect that Sophia will come with us. And I sense the reason why. He's been watching me, he knows how close we've become.

"I don't have anything to drink." I say it almost as a joke, I feel a need to try and lighten the mood, but Gregory doesn't answer, let alone laugh. He just looks around. There's only really one place to sit, around my tiny kitchen table.

"Can I sit down?"

I hold out my hand, watching as he finds a way to fit all his angles into the small chair. After a while I take the only other chair, opposite him. Sophia jumps up and sits directly on the worktop, facing us both.

"What is it I don't know?" I ask again.

It takes him a long time to begin, but when he does his first word is Imogen. Then he stops again.

"What about her?"

He pants, but finally it seems he's found the words.

"She's dead. I know that now."

"So do I. The hospital told me. She died of a heart attack."

"No." He shakes his head, but offers no explanation. Instead he draws in a deep breath. "She's dead, and I've failed her. I thought you might be able to help. That's why I was here. Why I was observing you."

I glance at Sophia, but she seems as confused as I am.

"Help Imogen? How?"

"If this happened, she asked me to help. To do something."

"If what happened..." I begin, but then answer him myself. "If she *died?*"

He just nods. I don't know what to do next.

"Was it you that broke into my apartment?" I ask. The question seems to surprise him for a moment, but then he nods again.

"Yes. I once wrote a character who was a locksmith. I practised with picks so I could write him authentically. You never know when it'll come in handy."

"And it was you who was spying on me from the ADR right after I came to see you."

He gives a chuckle. "Yes, I suppose I was clumsy at first. I got better though, I don't believe you saw me after that?"

I try and make sense of this.

"So it was you who smashed my laptop?"

"You had a password on it. I couldn't get into it."

"I know I had a..." I stop myself. "Why did you want to see my laptop?" I literally can't think of a single thing on it that had any value.

"I thought she might have sent it to you too. I *hoped* she did."

This means nothing to me. It doesn't help at all, and I guess Sophia must think the same.

"Maybe you should start at the beginning, because I don't think Ava is understanding much of this?"

His eyes move to her. He seems a little confused by her presence suddenly. As he turns I notice the stubble on his jowls.

He looked better the other time I saw him, like a man who liked to be well turned out, now he looks a mess. He nods in agreement, but then does nothing.

"What do you think Imogen would have sent me?" I ask again. "Because I assure you she didn't."

This seems to hurt him a little, like it's the final confirmation of something he already knows, but isn't quite ready to accept.

"The file." He looks away from both of us now, then covers his mouth. A few moments later he looks back at me. "I'm sorry, this is very difficult. Very difficult indeed." Something makes me wait. As I do I remember I was supposed to be here packing up my apartment. Getting my passport. I don't know where that fits suddenly – into how things are unfolding. But I'm interrupted as he begins to speak again.

"Imogen and I were... not close exactly, when she worked here, but we were friends." Duncan nods to himself at the idea of this. "We understood each other, is what I'm trying to say."

"OK."

"She was seeing Kostas – the man from the dive centre – at the time. He was a gardener back then." He stops, glances at Sophia with a snatched smile. "Of course, you work for him now, you'll know all that."

"Yeah. I do. But keep going."

He settles again, seems to miss the bitter sarcasm in her voice, maybe even appreciates the prompt.

"When she left, I tried to stay in touch with her, and eventually I tracked her down. Obviously her time on the island ended with the terrible tragedy, the murders in the Aegean Dream Resort, so I reached out to her. I asked if I could support her in any way." He looks away, his head shivers a little. "She turned me down. Rejected me, you might say. But occasionally we talked. Very occasionally." He clears his throat.

"Eventually we became friends. She supported my writing... and then one day something happened."

"What?"

"She sent me a file."

"What file?" Sophia asks, from her perch on the work surface. I sense the impatience in her voice, but I don't share it. I'm not sure I want to hear this.

"A video file. She sent me a video file, and she gave me a set of instructions." He pushes on, not letting himself stop. "The instructions were that I wasn't to watch it, under any circumstances. She absolutely forbade it. She told me that if I loved her – which I suppose I did," – he pauses, as if he's surprised himself by saying this part out loud – "then I must keep it, but *never watch it*."

"Well then, what's the point of it?" Sophia asks now.

"The point was," – he takes a breath – "were she ever to die, of anything other than old age – I should send the file to the police investigating her death, or if she died in a way that didn't arouse enough suspicion for the police to be involved, then I should send it to the newspapers. Or I should publish it on my blog. That generally I should do whatever it took to make this video file public." I see him sitting up straighter in his chair as he says this, as if this were all some noble quest.

"And now she *is* dead," – Sophia speaks slowly, carefully, trying to follow – "you're going to do that?"

It's almost imperceptible, but he shakes his head.

"No."

"Why not?" I ask.

He swallows. "Because I don't have it. I deleted it."

"You deleted it, without watching it?"

Again the shake of the head.

"No. I deleted it *because* I watched it. I broke her trust. I betrayed her. I watched the video file, and what I saw on it was so dreadful, so horribly awful that I knew I could never hurt her by making it public. So I deleted it and I erased it from my computer, so that I could never recover it. But now that she has... been killed. Now finally I understand what she was doing. She was so clever, so brilliant. Now I understand. It wasn't about her, but about justice. About doing the right thing, the only possible way she could." He stops, his narrow chest rising and falling fast from the effort of his words.

"That's why I hoped Ava might have been sent the same file." He lifts a hand to smooth down an eyebrow. "Why I wanted to check her computer. I had to know."

"So we have a video file," – Sophia speaks slowly, summing up, "that might finally explain what the hell is going on here." She pauses, thinking. "But we don't know what's on it, and now we never will because you deleted it."

"No." He turns to her, and then slowly his gaze returns to me. "I know exactly what's on it. And I can tell you."

EIGHTY-ONE

"Did you say you had a drink?" Gregory asks me a moment later.

"No. I didn't," I reply. I'm not sure he hears, but Sophia jumps down from the worktop, fills a glass with water and bangs it down on the table in front of him.

"What did the file say?" she asks.

Gregory stares at the water, as if it's somehow fascinating to watch the liquid settle. Finally he starts speaking again.

"This really is not an easy thing to say. Especially to Ava here." His eyes glance up at mine, just for a second.

"I still need to hear it," I reply.

He gives a single nod.

"The file was a... confession. I suppose you would call it that?"

"Go on." Sophia and I wait.

"It was June when the Aegean Dream Resort closed. June 26, the day that the murders were discovered. The season was just getting going. A few weeks later and perhaps it wouldn't have happened – because we didn't get days off in midsummer."

He blinks, not seeing us. Then seems to reconsider what he's just said. "Although of course *something* would have happened." I feel him glancing up at me again, then resetting his mind. Why is this so hard? What the hell am I about to hear?

"Your mother – the woman you believe is your mother – Karen Whitaker. She was Imogen's roommate, I suppose you already know this?" I nod. There's not a moment when it occurs to me to correct him about Mum. He takes a breath.

"She was close with a man named Simon. He looked after the resort's fleet of small yachts. He was... uncouth, not a man I liked."

"OK."

"He used drugs. I knew that then, but Imogen confirmed this to me in her confession." His tongue flicks out, wetting his lips in a way that makes me think he's not so unfamiliar with them himself. "Cocaine, I believe."

"OK, but so what?" Sophia says.

"It was Simon's day off. Karen's too. Simon had access to the yachts – he was allowed to use them on his day off, which was unwise in my view – but they made some plan to go sailing. What they really wanted to do was go afloat to take drugs. And probably to..." He stops, and I get the sense he wants to use the word *fornicate*. But he doesn't.

"Fuck, I suppose. It doesn't matter."

I know this, I know about the baby, but I let him tell me again.

"There was a problem. Jason and Mandy – the manager and deputy manager of the resort – they'd had a child. Very recently. It was maybe four weeks old, I don't remember exactly. But Mandy was a strange girl. Some of us thought she was rather simple even. When she had the baby she became deeply untrusting, except for the second-seasoners, the people she'd known the longest. She asked Karen to look after the baby that day, while Mandy went to Athens for some paperwork. We all had to do it from time to time."

"And?" Sophia says. I hear in her voice that she's letting him give his side of the story too.

"And Karen went straight to Imogen asking her to look after the infant, so that she – Karen – could go out with Simon and have sex and take cocaine." His eyebrows, flecked with white, furrow into his brow.

"But Imogen couldn't. She was feeling unwell." He pauses, his tongue slipping out again, this time licking away a piece of spittle from his lips. "Karen was unwilling to do the right thing and cancel her sex party, and she took the child onto the yacht. She says she strapped it into a car seat, and the car seat into the cockpit, but that last part is a lie."

I wait, and Sophia does the same.

"There was a change in the weather. What had been a mirror-calm day was interrupted by a sudden squall. But it was nothing that any decent sailor wouldn't have seen coming, but Simon was anything but, he was down below filling his nostrils and *fornicating*, and the yacht was put on its side. The baby was swept away." He stares at me now, his eyes wide. "The baby was lost, into the sea."

I stare back at him. But I know all this. I hear myself responding.

"Simon told me. I went to see him. He told me this. But she found the baby. On the shore. She found the baby. It wasn't harmed."

His eyes widen even more as he learns I've seen Simon. I see how much it shocks him.

"Simon told me everything," I say. But then Duncan shakes his head.

"No."

"I wish that were the truth, but no. Simon doesn't know what really happened. That was only the beginning of it."

EIGHTY-TWO

"Karen and Simon planned to escape from justice, in the yacht." Gregory Duncan resumes his story, looking at me out of the tops of his eyes. "Karen returned to her room to gather her things. I doubt she even remembered how she had left poor Imogen there feeling poorly that morning."

I wait, but he doesn't go on.

"What happened next?" My mouth is dry.

"It is not a common thing, but there are instances..." Gregory pauses, glancing at Sophia as if he wonders whether she should hear this. "When a woman who has conceived is unaware of the fact, right up until very late."

He stops, then shoots a glance at me, like he wants to know my reaction before he goes on. I don't see the relevance, don't understand what he's talking about suddenly.

"It's known as a cryptic pregnancy. One in four hundred and seventy-five women do not realise they are pregnant until after twenty weeks." He pauses. "One in two thousand women don't realise it until labour begins..." He stops, moves his face like he's biting his cheeks from the inside. "Imogen was such a woman."

"What?" I ask, because it's all I can think to say.

"When Karen returned to her room that day, she walked in to find Imogen deep in labour. She was having a baby. A baby she had no idea she was pregnant with."

"What? That's impossible?"

Duncan shakes his head. "No. It is rare, but I assure you it happens. Some babies grow backwards towards the spine rather than pushed outward. And Imogen wasn't fat, not by any means, but she had a rounder figure. Generous."

"What the fuck are you talking about?" I hear Sophia ask, but I talk over her.

"I still don't understand."

He sighs, rubs the side of his head like he's developed a headache.

"When Karen returned from the yacht, having just committed the manslaughter of a baby, she found her roommate Imogen in the midst of labour, literally giving birth to a child that neither of them had any idea existed. A complete and overwhelming surprise. And not a good one."

He breaks off and finishes the water in front of him. Then he turns and holds the glass out to Sophia. She stares at him in bewilderment, but finally slips down again and fills it up. This time she gets a second glass and gives it to me.

"Thank you," Duncan says to her.

"What happened then?" I hear myself ask. My head is ringing like a bell.

He drinks half the glass, then sets it down again. "On this point at least, Karen's role is due some merit. She had – I believe – some medical training before she arrived in Greece, and she didn't panic. She understood what was happening, although I don't suppose that was terribly difficult to diagnose, with a baby's head emerging from between poor Imogen's thighs..." He stops, re-centres himself again, then carries on.

"But she helped. She leapt into action and she delivered the baby. Imogen was adamant that she saved both the baby's life and her own." He stops again.

"Then what?" Sophia asks.

"Then..." He hesitates, he takes another pair of huffing, deeper breaths. "Then I'm afraid, things took a much darker turn."

EIGHTY-THREE

I already know. I don't want to know, but I do. And I can see that Duncan knows I know. He can see it in my eyes. But he doesn't spare me.

"Both women were left in an almost impossible position. Imogen's family situation was difficult, her parents – I'm not sure if you're aware, but they were from the Mormon faith. They hadn't approved of her prolonged stay in Greece, but the idea of her returning with a baby? Unthinkable. Impossible. She would have been disowned, cut off. And as for Karen, she'd just murdered Mandy and Jason's baby. She was facing years in jail."

I don't know if Sophia doesn't see it yet, or if she's just braver than me.

"What did they do?" she asks, her face white.

He eyes her a moment, then he fixes his gaze on me. "I suppose there was a certain elegance to the idea," he scoffs suddenly. "Perhaps in fiction at least." At once he's serious again.

"I told you that Mandy was simple. What I didn't say was

that Jason was so busy, he had barely had time to spend five minutes with their child." He pauses. "Either way, it was Karen's idea."

"What was the idea?"

"They wanted to swap the babies," I say.

Surprised by the interruption, Duncan nods at me.

"Yes. Exactly."

"But that would never have worked?" I see the objections at once. "There's no way a woman wouldn't recognise her own child? Would accept a newborn child instead of a four-week-old, that's insane..."

"Obviously. But you have to appreciate the stress both women were under. Karen, presumably still with a significant amount of drugs running through her veins. Imogen who had just given birth, quite unexpectedly, and without any kind of pain medication I should add. The sense of pressure, the disorientation of it all..." He shakes his head. "It would have been immense."

I don't answer.

"So what happened?"

"As I understand it, Karen was the one who tried to return the baby. She waited until Mandy had returned to her room, and then she attempted to 'return' Mandy's baby, but really gave her Imogen's child."

"Oh my God. What happened?"

"It went badly. As you foresaw, Mandy realised at once that the child wasn't hers, and she became hysterical. You can perhaps understand her reasoning. And this panicked Karen. There was only one thing she could do at this point. There was a lamp in the room, heavy, it was made from the local rock..."

I shake my head, not believing that he's including this detail, but knowing now exactly where this is going.

"She took the lamp, and she hit Mandy over the head with

it. I accept she only meant to render her unconscious, but as I say, it was a heavy lamp. She killed her. Karen struck Mandy too hard and killed her outright."

EIGHTY-FOUR

"We'd all heard the rumour." Duncan sniffs as he continues. "That Jason had a gun. I don't know where he got it from – the man who was selling the drugs, I suppose."

It's as if he's forgotten that Sophia and I are here. His words are painting a story so horrible, so obvious now, that it's all we can do to sit dumbstruck and let him finish this.

"If you'd asked me then, I probably wouldn't have believed it. He was alright, Jason was. He was tough, that part is true, but if you worked hard, if you turned up on time, he didn't mind if you had a drink every now or then..." He shakes his head.

"They said he kept it under his bed. I guess it must have been true."

I feel myself swallowing. I'm not able to say anything. I feel my eyelids blinking at the unreal world that's just replaced the one I thought I knew.

"Imogen didn't say, in her video file," Duncan explains. Suddenly he seems to remember where he is. "But they must have found it somewhere in his room."

"What exactly happened next?" Sophia manages to ask.

She sounds totally shaken, I've never seen her like this. Duncan puffs out his cheeks.

"I don't know the details exactly. Now that she's..." – he shakes his head again – "Now she's dead, we'll maybe never know. But Karen returned to her and Imogen's room. They weren't that far apart, both up towards the mountain, behind where the guests stayed."

"And?"

"Well, she told Imogen what had happened."

"And then what?"

He puffs his cheeks a second time. "Imogen says it was Karen's idea. After that. And I believe her, I do."

I wait.

"They went back to Mandy and Jason's room. Obviously Mandy was still there, dead on the floor, and they had the gun...

"We had these walkie-talkies. Around the hotel. Jason was never without his, always on duty. And there was one in reception, of course. This is before people had mobile phones you understand."

"Yes, I understand."

"Karen told Imogen to get the walkie-talkie from reception, and they used it to put a call out for Jason, asking him to come to his room, his and Mandy's room. That was normal, no one would have thought it strange, not even the next day when they found them both dead. I don't think anyone would have even remembered it."

"What did they do then?" I swallow.

"They dragged Mandy's body so he wouldn't see it when he walked in the room, and they called him, and they waited behind the door. And when he came in they jumped out at him. Apparently Karen had the presence of mind to put the gun up under his chin before she fired it, they wanted to make it look like a suicide. They blew the top of his head off."

There's a silence in the kitchen. A very long silence.

"Imogen used the reception computer to print out a suicide note. They made him confess to hitting Mandy, then say he couldn't live with himself. I've thought about the gunshot, over the years, wondered how come nobody ever heard it, but it's easily explained. They used to go hunting in the hills behind the resort. You still hear them today." He shrugs. "It would have been late for hunting, but no one would have suspected what it really was."

Somehow, there are elements of the story that I can't connect with, that won't process. But then I see it.

"What about the baby?"

Duncan looks at me sharply. "Which one?"

"The... Imogen's baby. What happened to it?"

He frowns, like the question is irrelevant. "They left it there. I guess they couldn't bring themselves to kill it. Or maybe they didn't think it would survive the night. I don't know. It hardly matters. Either way, when the bodies were found the next morning, everything went crazy. We had over a hundred guests that week. The resort manager and his girlfriend both dead. Total disaster."

Gregory looks at me suddenly and shrugs, like the whole thing was just a really bad day at work.

EIGHTY-FIVE

I've never known a moment like this. I thought I had – I thought it was something to discover that the only parent you've ever known isn't your real mother. I thought that was enough. I thought it was going to be something that hits me, again and again, over the course of my life. No matter how long I'll live. But now I know it's nothing. It's *this* moment. Sitting here, in this shitty little kitchen, this is the moment that will echo forever through the rest of my life.

I don't know what to say. There isn't a single thing I can say. Nothing anyone can say.

"You didn't have anything to drink?" Duncan asks. "I sort of need something. Like I said, it's a bit heavy." I suddenly remember the stupid bottle of Metaxa I bought, and get up, find it in a cupboard and pour some in his empty glass.

"That can't be true," Sophia says from somewhere. I don't understand how she has the presence of mind to say anything.

"Oh I'm quite sure it is. I mean, why would Imogen confess to it if it wasn't true?" He doesn't thank me, but takes a large sip from the glass. "And you should have seen her, the way she explained it on the video. It was quite clear how much this weighed on her mind." The weird, matter-of-fact Duncan that told the final details of the story seems to have gone now. He seems to have recovered a little now that the story is told, the job done. He's back to the man he was before, fretting, self-loathing.

"And now she's gone. Imogen's gone, and the one thing she asked me to do, the one time she trusted me, I let her down." He drinks again. More this time.

This shakes something loose in my mind, I've lost the thread on this.

"Tell me again. What was it she wanted you to do?"

He frowns at me. "Isn't it obvious?" He shakes his head again. "She was worried about Karen *killing* her. Silencing her. Karen – I suppose – was also worried, about Imogen confessing to what they'd done. And Karen had good reason to be concerned. After all, Imogen sent me the video file. But also she told me, in the video, how often she'd begged Karen to go with her to the police, to confess what they'd done. But Karen refused of course, because she thought they'd got away with it. And they did, after a fashion." He closes his eyes, like all this is giving him a hell of a migraine.

"It was an insurance policy," he tries again. "Imogen's video file was an insurance policy. She sent it to me, in case Karen ever did her harm, so that the truth could finally come out. And now Karen's killed her, but I've deleted the file, so I can't prove a thing."

Sophia gets down again and takes the bottle of Metaxa. She pours herself a glass, then another for me. She leaves the bottle out of Duncan's reach as he glances at it hungrily.

"Why not just go to the police anyway, tell them what you've just told us?"

He shakes his head. "The only piece of evidence that proves Karen did anything wrong is gone. Evidentially, everything I could tell the police would count as hearsay. It's inadmissible in a Greek court. And for a crime where the case was closed over twenty years ago... they wouldn't even listen to me. Believe me, I researched this thoroughly for a book I—"

"Wait, hold on, what are you saying?" I try to filter his words.

"What am I saying? That I failed her. I loved that woman, I would have done anything for her, and what do I *actually* do? I let her down. I meant to protect her but I did the exact opposite. The one thing she asks me to do—"

"No. You said Karen... you think my mum..." I stop, trying to order my thoughts. "Are you saying it was *Karen* who attacked Imogen on the beach?"

"Of course. I thought you realised that?"

I blink at him.

"But she wasn't even *here*. I called her *after* Imogen was attacked. She was at home. In England."

Gregory shakes his head with a chuckle. "No she was not. I was watching you, remember? And I wasn't the only one. I was pretty shaken up the first time I saw her, when I was waiting outside your apartment. I didn't even believe it was her at first, but she doesn't look so different."

"But she was at home. When I called!"

He looks at me steadily. "How do you know that, Ava? For sure?"

I try to think. "She told me." As the words leave my mouth I can see how easy it would have been.

Gregory shrugs. "Presumably you called her mobile? Or if not she could have redirected calls to a mobile if you called a landline..."

I don't believe this, but of course it makes sense. She told me she was at home. I press my eyes closed, trying to remember. She told me she was watching television. So my imagination furnished me with an image of her at home, sitting in our lounge with her wine glass.

"Oh my God."

"Exactly. And this was why I hoped you might have the file," Gregory goes on. "So we'd have some proof to finally stop her. But you don't, so we have nothing... there's nothing we can do to stop her, nothing..."

"I don't have it," I barely hear him. "I don't have the file."

Finally he seems to understand that I'm in shock, and that's why I'm finding it so hard to keep up with him. He pauses a moment, then nods his head.

"That's the problem, Ava. That's why she's going to get away with murder. Again."

A thought attaches itself to those words, like a piece of cloth caught on the bare branches of a winter tree. Red cloth. Blood-red.

"Mum pushed for the body to be repatriated without having a post mortem," I say, not really following through with what I'm saying. "What if she didn't attack Imogen once, but two times? The second time in the hospital?"

"That's what I've been—" Duncan begins, but Sophia speaks over him.

"Could she have done that? Can you make something look like a heart attack?"

I don't reply at first, but the answer is screaming at me inside my head. We had to be so careful when we treated actual patients.

"Imogen was on an IV. If Karen had got into her room she could have injected air into it. It would have given her an air embolism. It wouldn't have acted immediately, it would have given Karen time to escape, but soon after, Imogen's heart would have stopped. It would look just like a heart attack."

"This is exactly what I'm saying," Duncan replied. "And there's not a thing we can do about it, she's beaten us. Beaten me..."

"Is there anything we can do?" Sophia turns to me. "If we asked for a post mortem now, would they find it? Would they open a proper investigation?" Her mouth stays open when she finishes speaking. But I don't know the answer, I just look at her, and open my hands into a shrug. In response she pulls out her phone and starts quickly tapping away at it. A moment later she speaks.

"What airport did you say Imogen's body was being flown out of?"

"Panachoria, the local one," I tell her.

"Shit."

"What is it?"

"I'm just checking the flight departures. The only one for London left half an hour ago. She's already gone."

I don't say anything, then there's a car horn coming from outside. Sophia goes to the window to look.

"It's a taxi."

"Oh shit."

"It's for you?"

Sophia's question reconnects me to the world I was living just an hour before. I almost laugh.

"I'm supposed to go back there. Karen sent a taxi to take me back to the hotel. Then tomorrow she and I are flying back to England."

Sophia's quiet for a moment.

"Well, I'm not sure that's such a good idea," she says at last.

EIGHTY-SIX

Sophia goes outside and tells the taxi we don't need it after all. She asks the driver to say that it was just me here, in case Mum asks, and then I text her. I tell her it took me longer than expected to sort out the apartment, and it's easier to sleep here tonight. I'm just playing for time really. She comes back to me right away, and I sense the suspicion under her words. She tells me she's finished at the airport now, and she can come pick me up herself. It's obvious now, she just wants to keep an eye on me. I text back again, telling her it's fine, that I'm just really tired and I'm already in bed. This seems to work, since she doesn't reply.

Then Gregory leaves. We exchange numbers first so we can contact each other, and I promise to tell him what I'm going to do once I've figured it out. If I ever figure it out. And then Sophia and I sit and talk.

The first thing is this: It's obvious that Gregory was telling the truth. But maybe it's not so obvious that Imogen was. There's not a lot of me that believes this, but it is possible that Imogen really was just full-on crazy, maybe from her medication or maybe just because she was nuts underneath it, and she imagined this whole thing. But it's only a small part of me that's holding onto this, and maybe I really don't believe it at all.

That leads to the second thing. Assuming all this is true, assuming that I really was brought up by a killer, a woman who could do these horrible things, then where does that leave me? Why did she adopt me, and how? Was she actually telling me the truth when she said she didn't know who my real parents were? And why did she adopt me at all, since it's never really felt like she loved me?

There's still so many questions, so many answers that I don't have. And the time is ticking away. My flight tomorrow leaves at six in the evening and I'll need to check in before that. *We'll* need to check in before that – if I'm going back to England with Mum, that is. Or whatever I now have to call this woman. And if I'm not going back to England with her, then I'm going to have to explain to her why not. And she's going to know that I know.

We discuss going to the police. But Duncan's right. With no proof at all, of any of this, all we have is his word that Imogen said all this. We even phone Duncan again, asking if he will go to the police if that's an option, but he refuses point blank. He says that if we tell the police what he's told us he'll deny everything, because all it will do is set Karen against him, and he's scared of what she might do. So that route's out of the question.

Midnight comes and goes, then I notice the clock on my mobile says it's past two in the morning and I still have no idea what I'm going to do. But by three o'clock we do have something that you might call a plan. Or maybe it's not, maybe it's just a desperate idea because we have to do something, and we're running out of time. We stay up past four in the end, going over the idea again and again, trying to think through everything we're going to need, assess whether it has any chance of working. And then, with the light of dawn already showing through the windows outside, I go to sleep for a couple of hours.

Because I'm going to need to be ready for this.

EIGHTY-SEVEN

I wake up at seven thirty because Mum's an early riser, she always has been. Sophia runs down to Maria's supermarket to grab a few things we need, and I send Mum another text. This one takes a bit longer to craft:

> Hi Mum. I need to speak to you, it's important. I suggest we meet in the old Aegean Dream Resort. I think that's a good place to have this out.

I know this is going to make her suspicious as hell, there's no avoiding that. But what I want to do is stop her steamrolling me into leaving the island. She's so good at that, making me do what I don't want to do. It's what she's done to me my whole life. This time it takes her a long time to reply, even though I can see from the message receipt that she's read it. Eventually a message comes in:

> Ava, what is this? Why would we go there? It isn't safe, the resort's in ruins. If there's something you need to say, I'll come to you. Wait there.

I can see she's already typing a second part to the message, so I fire back before she can send it:

> I'll meet you there at 11. By the old pool bar.

Then immediately I switch off my phone so she'll see I won't receive anything she writes after that. She's got no choice then, she'll have to come, and she'll absolutely hate that. Then I leave to meet Sophia in a cafe – just in case Mum jumps straight in her car to catch me at the apartment.

I try to eat something, but mostly I just sip at strong black coffee, drinking one straight after the other. We go through the plan a final time. It still seems basically crazy and doomed to fail, perhaps even more so now that we're out of the late-night, unreal setting of my apartment and back in the bright sunshine of the real world. But it feels a pretty damn bleak world right now, and neither of us can come up with anything better.

"It's ten o'clock," Sophia says to me, touching my shoulder with her hand. "Time to go." She tries to force a confident smile, but it looks twisted on her face. "You got this."

I nod, hoping I don't look as wretched as I feel. I get up and look down to the sea, then I start walking. Down the beach, towards the faded glory of the Aegean Dream Resort.

EIGHTY-EIGHT

The fence going up around the old resort is half-complete now, so that from some directions it might appear hard to break in. But from others you can still just walk right in. The men who were putting the fence up are nowhere to be seen, but that's not a surprise: Sophia told me last night that there'd been a dispute over payment that will take weeks to sort out. So the place is abandoned again. It's just me.

The sun is already hot on my back as I leave the footpath and follow the fence line, until it abruptly stops where a fence post stands entombed in its concrete footing. Up close there's a menacing aspect to the old buildings, and it occurs to me that however well I think I know it, Karen's going to know it far better. Am I giving her an advantage coming here, one I didn't see last night? If so it's too late now. I step over weeds and shards of broken glass as I make my way to the heart of the old resort, the swimming pool with its smashed blue tiles and years of dust and junk accumulated at the bottom. Next to it is the bar, the roof broken and collapsed at one end but still in place at the other. I walk behind the bar, looking out. It's a good place, a natural vantage point from where you can see almost everywhere in the resort. I check my watch. Ten thirty already, I wanted to get here early because I have a hunch that Mum will try to do the same...

"Hello, Ava."

Her voice shocks me, makes me physically jump. She's sitting calmly on an old broken chair under the shelter of the half-fallen portion of the roof. My hand goes to my chest.

"I didn't..." I try to strip the panic from my voice. "I didn't see you there."

She doesn't answer, but stares at me intently, and I take a few steps back so that I'm not behind the old concrete bar with her. That's where I wanted to be so that there would be a physical barrier between us, but she got here first. I move around the other side of the bar, where there are still a few tiled concrete posts that once served as fixed stools. To try and calm myself – and give an illusion of calm – I sit on one, looking at my mother, who now stands, leaning her arms on the bar between us.

"So, what's this about then?"

She's like a vixen, tasting the air carefully with every word she utters. Alert to how dangerous I can be if she doesn't handle me *just right*.

"Why are we here, Ava?"

There's no point with preamble, pretending this is anything other than it is. From my pocket I pull a pen drive, purchased this morning from Maria's little store, quite possibly it's the only one she's sold in years.

"What's that?"

"It's a USB stick."

"I can see it's a USB stick. I'm wondering why you're waving it in my face?"

Till now I haven't been looking her in the eyes. I maybe don't even mean today, maybe I never have. But now I do.

They're bright, bright blue, like the sky above. Not like mine, which are dark chestnut brown.

"Imogen sent it to me."

Her expression cracks. The calm, confident shell. It doesn't collapse – far from it, but it slips a little. My words concern her.

"Imogen? What did she put on it? More drug-fuelled hallucinations?"

"She told me everything." I ignore the excuse she's trying to make, before I've even said anything. "She told me the truth."

"I've told you, Ava, that woman – that poor woman – has said all kinds of things over the years, but very rarely the truth. That's why I've tried to stick with her. To support her. It's why I flew out here when I heard she'd been attacked. To help her."

Except you were already here, I think to myself, but I don't say that. *Except you were the one who attacked her.* There'll be time for that.

"She's told me everything, Mum. It arrived by courier yesterday evening, when I was cleaning out my apartment."

"OK. I'll bite." She gives me a sharp smile. "What exactly does Imogen say?"

She'll dismiss everything, I know it. But even a psychopath must flinch when they're hit with the truth?

"She told me how you lost Mandy's baby overboard from Simon's yacht, the day before the murders. I know that's true."

Her eyebrows go up, but she says nothing.

"And then she tells me how you came back to the room you shared, and found her giving birth. To a baby she didn't even know she was having. A cryptic pregnancy."

I let her absorb the words. I'm close enough to see her pupils expand, the surprise dissipating backwards into her brain. But apart from that, the only physical reaction is a slight smile that creeps onto her lips.

"I see."

"Then she told me how you helped her deliver the baby, she

says you probably saved her life. But then the two of you were stuck. You'd lost Mandy's baby, you knew how much trouble you were in for that, and she's suddenly found herself with a child that no one expected. That she couldn't possible keep. And you found a solution, to both problems."

"Oh yes? This is an interesting one. She's told me some stories over the years, but I haven't heard this one. What was this 'solution'?"

"You thought you could swap the babies. Take Imogen's newborn, and trick Mandy into believing it was her child, that you never killed her baby." I try to put real force into my words, to make them sound convincing. But Mum's smiling warmly now.

"Really. *Really*, Ava?" She shakes her head. "Well, tell me, how sensible does that sound? Do you think it's an idea that anyone would think would work? Or is it the deluded fantasy of a deeply broken woman, addicted to a wide range of medication—"

"But that plan didn't go so well, did it, Mum?" I force my voice over hers, then don't give her space to come back at me. "Because Mandy wasn't as stupid as you thought she was. You're right, no one could be, except that you were, because it was your idea." I smile for a moment, then go on.

"Don't beat yourself up, Mum. In your defence you were off your head on coke, and stressed up to your eyeballs. Everyone makes mistakes, even you." I twist my own lips into a sarcastic smile now, and I see how much she hates it.

"Mandy saw at once that you'd given her the wrong baby, and I can imagine what happened next. She freaked out, didn't she? She would have done, anyone would have done. And then you panicked and what, picked up the closest heavy object and smashed her over the head with it? What was it Mum, a lamp? I can't remember what Imogen said, can you remind me?"

I stare at her again, my own words causing me to evaluate

her anew. Reassess the person I've known longer than any other on this earth. This is what evil looks like. Before she speaks again, her tongue appears for just a moment. I'm surprised it's not forked.

"And then what happened, in Imogen's little fairy tale?"

I pause, before going on. If I'd hoped that being confronted with this would cause her to collapse and confess, begging for my forgiveness, I was wrong. But I didn't really think that was how it would go.

"You tell me. You did it."

She scoffs at the idea, then brushes a strand of her blonde hair from her forehead. "OK, I'll play. Since I know that Jason Wright tragically murdered Mandy Paul and then shot himself, I imagine Imogen's story would proceed along those lines. Unless she really goes off the rails at that point?" She lifts her shoulders, making it a question.

I just wait.

"So I imagine she says I waited for Jason, and then, somehow already knowing he had a gun hidden in his room – which of course I couldn't know – I shot him with it, and made the whole think look like a murder-suicide?"

"You did know he had a gun. You wrote about it in your diary."

This unsettles her, not much, but a bit. The expression that passes across her face is self-questioning, checking, dark and scary, but it's gone as fast as it arrives.

"If I did it's only because it was a rumour flying around the hotel. I certainly didn't know where it would have been hidden."

"Your diary says the cleaners discovered it hidden under the mattress. They put it back there. So you knew exactly where to look."

"Oh, come on, Ava. I can't remember what I wrote…" She stops, realising that not remembering now doesn't help her if it proves she knew back then. "It's a fantasy, Ava. A delusional fantasy. Entertaining, but not a reason to drag me all the way out here."

"I've sent Imogen's confession to the police. They're on their way here. Right now."

Mum turns back to me, her eyes level, intense, probing. She stays like that a long while.

"I very much doubt that, Ava."

Her certainty shakes me. "Why not?"

"Because they won't believe it. Because the case was closed and shelved a long time ago. But most of all, because it's not true."

"Imogen's just been murdered. Even if it wasn't you at the hospital, someone attacked her on the beach. That case is open."

Her lips twitch as she acknowledges this. "Even so."

"I'm your daughter. If I tell them I believe Imogen, that will count for something."

She smiles now, beatific. "A little, perhaps. They might want to speak to me. But I'll be able to convince them. Of the *truth*. After all, you've had a shock, you've discovered you're adopted. And maybe I'll even be able to convince *you* in the end, when we get home, away from this place, which I will admit does invoke a certain ghostly atmosphere."

I shake my head. "I'm not coming home with you. You're a killer."

"Are you recording this, Ava?" she answers at once. "Is this how this is supposed to work? You tell me all this, in the hope I'll say something incriminating, and then you can take it to the police, because as we both know, the testimony of a known drug addict like Imogen Grant is utterly worthless. And that's if there even is anything on that pen drive." She stops, her eyes probing into mine again, trying to drag my secrets from me. I don't say anything, but I can't help but swallow.

"Show me your phone," she asks.

I don't move.

"Ava, your phone? You must have it, I've never seen you without it."

Slowly I reach into the pocket of my shorts. The truth is, she surprised me by being here so early, I didn't even have time to start the recording. I hold it up, showing her the screen.

"Why don't you hand it over?"

I try to resist, to defy her, but I feel my hand disobeying me. I lay the phone on the counter top and slide it over towards her. She picks it up, inspects it at once. It's not recording, but she doesn't seem satisfied by that. She presses the power button until the option comes up to switch it off completely. She's silent until the screen goes black, the buttons unresponsive. She looks at me, gives a sad little laugh.

"Imogen was a drug addict, Ava. A junkie. I know because I was the one supplying her." My eyes flick up from my phone, like I'm willing it to magically still be on and recording. "*Legally*, I should add, from the pharmacy. But I have the records, Ava." She pauses, her eyes going back to the pen drive that I'm still gripping tightly. "Whatever you have on there, it's not what you believe it is, and the police won't fall for it. Not for long. Not when I show them the dosage she was on."

I'm silent again.

"I don't suppose there's any point asking you for it? I expect you'll have made copies?"

I nod.

She purses her lips, thinking.

"Why are we here, Ava? What is *this* about?" She waves a hand around, indicating that "this" means here.

"I wanted to give you the opportunity to explain. I want to know where I fit into all this."

She's quiet a moment, thinking, and I go on.

"Imogen really did have a baby, didn't she?" I say, then watch her carefully, lowering my voice.

"I kept the clothes I was wearing when Imogen was attacked on the beach. They were soaked with her blood. I've sent a sample off for DNA testing. If I'm her daughter, I'll know. In two days the results come back, and I'll know." I fix my eyes on her, willing myself not to look away, for her to see my fury. And I see it, this time a flicker of real panic. A major shifting inside her mind this time. She wasn't expecting this. Not at all. She gives herself a moment, but not more than a few seconds. Then a smile.

"Yes. Damnit." She shakes her head again, runs a hand through her hair. "Do you know I never suspected a thing. I worked with her, I slept in the same room as that stupid girl, who obviously was too stupid to even operate a condom. Oh, I realised there was *something*, she complained a little more than usual, maybe she'd filled out a bit, but nothing that I really noticed – and believe me I was a hawk about her weight. The way she looked in a swimsuit actually reflected on me..."

"Oh, I believe you. On that I believe you."

She pauses, then smiles sarcastically. But then she softens it.

"But I never thought for a second she might be pregnant. I didn't even know she was having sex."

We're both silent for a while, then she begins again. "You know, I've noticed over the years since, how you see stories about this from time to time. Girls who find themselves with a baby without ever knowing they were pregnant. It's surprising how often it happens. And it rarely ends well."

"And that was me? I was Imogen's child?"

Her tongue comes out again to wet her lip, but her mouth must be dry. She holds up a finger to tell me to wait and reaches into her shoulder bag, pulling out a bottle of water. Carefully she breaks the seal and takes a sip, then a longer swig. When she's done she offers the bottle to me.

"No. Thank you."

She puts the bottle down on the bar between us, next to

where she put my phone. She glances at it now, the screen black. Then she taps the home button again, checking it's definitely switched off.

"OK, Ava. I suppose I owe you the truth."

EIGHTY-NINE

"I think you owe me more than that," I say. And Mum nods, thinking.

"Some of it's true," she says in the end. I wait, but she doesn't go on.

"What parts?"

"The police, are they really coming?" she asks, but I don't reply. "How long have I got?"

"Long enough for the truth."

She swallows now. Her face is changed, the almost sneering confidence she projected earlier is gone, she's trying for something else.

"We did lose the baby overboard." She looks down as she says the words, then glances up at me, testing how they land. I don't reply at once. I've heard this story several times now, but I never quite believed it. But coming from her like this, I know it's real.

"Oh my God, Mum..." For a second I'm a girl again, this is my mother telling me this.

"It wasn't our fault! It wasn't my fault..." Her eyes narrow, flick left and right. "With any boat or ship, the person in charge is responsible. But Simon was... irresponsible. I had no idea about the weather, he told me it would be fine to leave the baby where she was, it was too hot down below, we put a sunshade on her..."

"But you were responsible for the baby?"

"I was twenty-four years old, Ava. I have no idea why Mandy thought I was a suitable person to look after her child."

Her words shock me. Even amongst this, that she can still speak like this shocks me.

"So what really happened?"

"You've heard the story..." – she shrugs meekly – "It was an accident, a complete freak accident that could have happened to anyone. We were just unlucky."

"Not as unlucky as the baby."

These words seem to wound her, she tries a smile to acknowledge this truth, but it doesn't come out.

"It was more Simon's fault than mine. He said so, at the time. I should have gone to the police, I know I should, but he begged me not to. He..." Her voice quietens, as if this part cannot be said out loud. "He had drugs on him. In our panic when the boat capsized they went everywhere. Powder down the seats. It would have been impossible to clean it up had they checked the boat with dogs. The police would have taken this into account, and he'd have been put in prison for life. And Greek prisons..." She leaves the sentence unfinished.

"So it was all Simon's fault?" I ask.

She opens her mouth to reply, then lifts a hand, as if acknowledging how this must sound.

"What could I do, Ava? I was in shock, I was terrified, and I thought I loved him. I didn't know what else to do."

I listen to her words, and for the first time I actually hear them. What it must have been like to make a mistake like that. Because whatever happened next, that part at least *was* a mistake. And I've made plenty of my own.

"What happened after that? What really happened?"

Karen looks away from me, pursing her lips like she's reliving it. "We took the yacht back into the harbour in town, and I came back here. I don't know if we were serious – we weren't thinking straight, that's for sure – but I came for my passport." She shakes her head, as if accepting how crazy an idea it was to try and run. "And then, when I got to my room..."

"You found Imogen, in labour?"

She nods.

"You can't imagine, Ava. You simply can't imagine what that was like."

She's right. I can't.

"She'd lost a lot of blood. The baby was... twisted inside her. I suppose that's why it hadn't shown. I had to make sense of what was going on. I wanted to get help, but Imogen begged me not to. She told me she'd kill herself if I left her, even for a moment. So I did the only thing I could, I helped her deliver the baby."

We both fall silent, me imagining, her remembering, I suppose.

"It was Imogen's idea. To swap them."

I glance back, surprised. I wasn't ready to move on.

"I told her my story and she couldn't believe it, but she was always a bit hippy. She said it was the universe 'finding a way'." She shakes her head, then shrugs. "An hour after the baby was born, she wrapped it in a blanket and went to Mandy's room – she was back by then from her trip to Athens. She tried to give it back to her, but of course Mandy knew at once. So Imogen panicked. She picked up a lamp, the base was made of rock. She hit her with it, beating her over and over to stop her from yelling out. Then she left the baby there and came running back to get me.

"I was stunned. I had no idea what to do. I wanted to call the police, I wanted to do the right thing, but I couldn't. Simon would go to prison, and now Imogen as well – the two people I loved most in the world. Their lives would be over."

"And Jason?"

Karen's eyes, which are downcast and staring at the battered, sun-weathered old bar top, lift and meet mine for a moment.

"That was Imogen too. She said we could use the gun and make it look like a murder-suicide. I was in no state, after everything that had happened. It was Imogen who called him on the radio. Her who waited behind the door with the gun, her who leapt on him the moment he walked in. And then she shot him. She did it all, Ava."

I take a long moment, considering this. I can feel my heart racing in my chest, the blood pounding in my head.

"And me? I really am Imogen's baby?"

She hesitates. Then nods. "I wanted to give you a happier ending than the orphanage you ended up in, I felt we owed you that much."

I screw my eyes shut. Somehow, despite everything, I still want to believe this. Maybe I even *should* believe her? I can feel her staring at me, willing me to, and when I open my eyes, hers are fixed on mine, pleading with me to understand. I can feel the empathy radiating off her body.

"Ava, I'm sorry. So dreadfully, awfully sorry. You can see why I could never tell you this?"

I can. *I can.* That's the problem. Of course I can see. It all makes perfect sense.

Except for one thing.

One tiny flaw.

"So you're saying it was Imogen that did all this?" I tell her, feeling the tears welling up in my eyes. "That's what you're telling me?"

"Yes." Her voice is soft now. Caring. "I'm so sorry, Ava."

I open my mouth, momentarily I can't find the words I need to do this. But then they're here. I'm ready.

"So it was Imogen who was the mastermind behind this crime? Imogen Grant. But how is that possible? When you've told me my whole life what a failure she is? How you're the one who built a business, while she couldn't? How she's a drug addict, who doesn't have the strength of character to succeed in life? How I mustn't turn out like she did?"

Karen opens her mouth to argue, but now she doesn't have the words.

"After all, you were the one who was capable enough to adopt me."

I see it in her eyes. As clear as the decrepit bar around me. She *knows* I know. I might not be able to convince the police, let alone a jury, but she knows there's no way back with me. We're *over*. And what's more, she can't help herself. The smile comes back to her thin lips, turns into a twisted sneer.

"You're right. Imogen wouldn't ever have been strong enough in a crisis like that. And she wasn't either. She was a mess. A blubbering, pathetic mess. Just like she's been ever since. Of course it was my idea to switch the babies, and it might have worked too, except Mandy freaked out. I was just trying to calm her down, I couldn't let her scream the way she was. Nobody could have done."

My heart rate, already flashing blood past my brain like a jackhammer, speeds up even more. I swallow.

"And Jason?"

The sneer deepens. "All me. Obviously. Somebody had to take control, or we'd have been finished. So I did. I knew where the gun was, and I took it and radioed for him to come to the room, and shot him the moment he walked in. It was easy."

I don't say a word, just let her go on.

"Imogen didn't have the guts to pull it off. She didn't have the character. She's never had the character. But I did. So I killed them. And so what if I did? I had no choice. And I did it for the right reasons. I did it for you, Ava."

I screw my eyes shut, trying to replay what I've just heard, what she's just said. But I can't go on. I can't make myself hear any more of this. I reach into the other pocket of my shorts, and I pull out Sophia's phone, the one I set recording as I stepped past the fence. I check it now, and see the timer still running, a thirty-four-minute audio file, capturing everything Karen's just said and automatically uploading it to the cloud server that Sophia set up. I hold it up to her. Out of her reach.

"I had two phones, Mum," I say. "Two phones."

There's a long silence. Karen stares at the phone in shock. Fear. Disgust. A vicious anger. I shake the phone at her.

"I don't really have a confession from Imogen, but now I do have one from you."

She moves much faster than I anticipate. Stepping towards me, so that we're still a metre apart, but the old bar is no longer between us.

"Well, well. Aren't you the clever one?" She strokes her lips, thinking hard. Then she reaches for something inside her bag, hiding it from me until she's changed her stance. And then dropping the bag away. Now I see what it is – a silver long-bladed knife.

"You're not the only one who came prepared this morning, Ava. I didn't know what this was about, but just in case I made a small detour into the hotel kitchen."

"What are you doing?"

"I've killed before. You really think I won't do it again?"

"You wouldn't," I hear myself say. "I'm your daughter. I'm your fucking daughter..."

But of course I'm not. I watch in slow motion as she moves again, tossing the knife into her stronger hand and holding it out in front of her like a dagger. I'm stunned, and far too slow to move. I only have Sophia's phone to hold up, like a useless shield.

But we planned for this too. Moving so stealthily that I don't even see her move, Sophia steps out from behind the old pool storage area, a favourite place from her childhood games of hide-and-seek. In her hands she's got a speargun from the dive centre, the vicious pointed spear ready to spring forward, propelled by the taut rubber arms. One twitch of her fingers and the trigger will release.

"Back the fuck off bitch," she says, aiming it towards Mum's stomach. "Drop the knife, and back the *fuck off*."

NINETY

The knife falls to the ground. Sophia steps closer and kicks it away.

"Ava, in my bag."

Dumbly I obey, slipping my hand into the bag hanging from her shoulder, without obstructing her grip on the weapon. I pull out the zip ties, again bought that morning from Maria's little supermarket. My hands are shaking in fear as I wrap them around Mum's wrist, pulling them as tight as I physically can, not caring if they hurt her. Sticking out of the damaged concrete is a rusting loop of iron, and I thread another through there and then quickly use one more to secure Mum to it. Then I take two or three fast steps away and drop to the ground, the tears coming now. A moment later I feel Sophia's hand on my shoulder. I think she's just supporting me but I'm wrong.

"My phone. I need to check it's uploaded. And call Duncan."

I don't hear all of what she does next, but when I look around she's speaking on the phone, her eyes and the speargun both trained on Mum.

"We've got her. Get the police here now."

She ends the call, moves a step forward and checks the zip ties securing Mum to the remains of her old bar.

"Now the police *are* on their way. You sick bitch."

NINETY-ONE

One Week Later

I'm still on the island. I moved back into my apartment, but I haven't slept there alone, since Sophia's been with me the whole time. I think after what we've both endured she needs me as much as I need her. I won't stay here long though, Sophia knows of much better places, kept for the locals and not usually available to the foreign workers who fill up Alythos each summer. I tell Hans I'm not going to work in the bar anymore. At least not for a while. Not until I work out what I'm going to do next.

At first Mum refused to speak to the police. I'm still calling her that. Whatever else has happened here, she's still the person who looked after me, who brought me up from just before I was three years old. I know more about that now, and I'll get to it, as soon as I can. But first Mum.

For two whole days, the police tried to ask her questions, and she would either refuse to answer, or she would tell them one lie after another – that it wasn't true that she and Imogen killed

Mandy and Jason, or that they did do it, but it was all Imogen, and Karen only helped with the cover-up. But the police had the recording I made, and once Gregory Duncan knew that, he was more than happy to back it up with what he saw on Imogen's confession video. Plus they went to speak with Simon Walker-Denzil, and he confirmed the story about the missing baby. And slowly the police understood, and that's when I think Mum saw there was just no way to maintain the lies anymore. She got a lawyer too, who told her she'd face less time in prison if she finally admitted what had happened. And so finally she began to tell the truth. The version she gave them was pretty much what Imogen said, and it's the version that makes the most sense to me.

Mum admitted to attacking Imogen on the beach too. She followed her there and crushed her skull in with a rock, because she couldn't let her speak to me. And then, when she learned that Imogen hadn't died, and had woken up in hospital, she went there too and injected air into the IV port when Imogen was sleeping. They found CCTV footage of Mum entering the hospital, wearing dark sunglasses and a baseball cap. They also sent Imogen's body back from the UK to Greece for a post mortem, and the pathologist found air bubbles in her heart, which is consistent with an air embolism. The detective who's leading the case has good English. He told me it was a cold, clean way to kill somebody.

As for her sentencing – I don't know yet what will happen. They've only charged her with two murders – Jason Wright and Imogen Grant. Apparently because of the way Mandy Paul reacted when she saw Karen trying to give her back the wrong baby, it only counts as manslaughter, and there's a statute of limitations in Greek law which means they can't prosecute a manslaughter case that's more than twenty years old. Tragically that also means they can't do anything about the baby – Callie – who was washed overboard from Mum and Simon's yacht. Poor

Callie Paul. I think that's the saddest thing of all, she doesn't get any justice.

We do know what happened to her though, at least where she ended up. One of the detectives working the case – there's lots now – she remembered reading, a long time ago, about a baby who was found dead, strapped to a car seat, by fishermen off the coast of Turkey. The case was never solved, but it stuck with her because of how awful it was. And it was never linked to Alythos, because it was a long way away and there are hundreds of islands out here. The Turkish police kept samples of the baby's DNA, and they're now being matched to the DNA from baby Callie's birth memory book. We don't have the results yet, but it's pretty clear that they're the same child. She drifted nearly two hundred miles.

I don't have to do any more DNA tests though, to find out who I am. My adoption case has now been unsealed, which gives one half of the story, and Mum has agreed to talk about it too, which gives the other. I'm grateful to her for that.

I am Imogen Grant's child. Fathered by Kostas Aetos and born on Alythos, but not in the little medical clinic in Kastria where Mandy Paul had her baby. I was the result of a cryptic pregnancy, and appeared almost out of the blue, in the room on the end of the staff dorm of the old Aegean Dream Resort. I was delivered by Karen Whitaker, out of her head on cocaine and fear.

And then I was swapped, presented to Mandy as her child, Callie. And when Mandy saw at once that I was a different baby, Karen killed Mandy, and later Jason. But I was left alive.

When the bodies were found I was put into temporary foster care, with Eleni Kouris, the woman who lives in the white house on the road out to the monastery. Who knows if she really did remember me, probably not, but she *was* right about it. And the reason the DNA test didn't confirm it was because I arrived there with the birth book that Mandy Paul made for *her* child, Callie. Who wasn't me.

As for the adoption, that's more complicated. Mum said that, a couple of years after the murders, Imogen was really struggling with what they'd done. Plus she'd learned that the baby they'd swapped – her baby, me – had been placed into an orphanage and wasn't doing well. Imogen became obsessed with the idea that she could adopt me back, and that this would somehow assuage the terrible guilt she felt. But she couldn't do it on her own.

Mum says that Imogen begged Karen for months to help her with this, and Karen kept refusing – telling her the idea was ridiculous. But eventually Imogen threatened to go to the police and tell them what really happened if Karen didn't do something. Mum was trapped, she had no choice.

But she also knew the authorities would never give a child to someone like Imogen – someone who was clearly a mess. But they might to a person who by then was in a relationship, and running a successful business. Someone like Mum. And Karen says she felt guilt too, for all that had happened. So the whole idea of doing something good, taking me in and giving me a better life, it appealed to her as well.

As for the how, she'd just come into some money. Her parents – I've always thought of them as my grandparents, though I never got to meet them – had just passed away, leaving her a significant inheritance, and she was able to use this to hire a lawyer who understood the Greek adoption system. Apparently it's not unusual for foreigners to adopt from Greece, with a big-enough sweetener. Bribes were paid, the rules were bent, and I was transferred out of the orphanage and given to Karen. It was just about enough to keep Imogen happy, as long as Karen let her see me every now and then. Which was a convenient moment for Karen to slip Imogen a few packets of sedatives to keep her calm. Karen did try to get me British paperwork, a passport and birth certificate, deleting all records linking me to my birth in Greece, but that proved impossible, even for her dodgy lawyer. So I kept my Greek birth certificate, and the Alythos listing on my passport. Meanwhile my records here in Greece were sealed, the false secret that I was Mandy and Jason's baby put under official lock and key.

Karen said she'd hoped one day Imogen would go back to America and forget all that had happened, but she never did. Instead she kept turning up at our house, trying to get to speak to me. And she'd watch me. She just watched me, as I grew.

I don't know how I feel about all this. Not yet. To be honest, I'm not sure if I'll ever know.

It's funny though, how the world keeps turning, even when for me it's been tipped upside down. The tourists keep turning up – Sophia has to go to work to teach them diving. Maria has to open the supermarket, and after a week or so, I don't even hear from the detectives working the case anymore. The big questions are answered, it's just up to me now to work out what comes next.

And here the sun keeps rising. Like today, it's one of those beautiful Alythos days, where there isn't a breath of wind over the bay. The sun is already high, and the sky a deep, deep blue. I don't know how I feel. Maybe in the years to come I'll find a way to forgive Mum, maybe I won't. There's time for that though. For now, I want to find a way to keep living.

EPILOGUE

I leave the apartment and make my way through the town towards the seafront. The sun is still warm on my face, even though it's late in the day. I'm glad I took my sunglasses and a hat. I pause as I pass Maria's supermarket, but it's not her waiting at the till this afternoon, it's another woman instead who I still only know by sight. I step inside. By the door there's a fridge with a few bottles of soft drinks and a few of white wine. I pick one out, feeling the cool, heavy weight of it, and take it to the till, where the woman wraps it in a sheet of paper as I pay the few euros. She gives me a friendly, sympathetic smile and I guess she knows my story now. It's a small place, Alythos.

I keep going, passing the harbour, with the fishing boats and the few small yachts resting perfectly still on the mirror-like water. Each one sits on its own reflection, and you could take a photograph with the sun going down behind and turn it into a postcard, just like the ones that sit in the racks in the restaurants and shops here, for the tourists to remember the beauty of this place when they go home. Most of the restaurants are already open, getting ready for the evening rush. But I don't stop. I walk on, towards the dive centre.

Two of the boats are just coming back from wherever they've been this afternoon. Even from here I can make out the TEAM lettering on the backs of the staff's T-shirts. And as the first boat comes nearer, I see that it's Kostas driving, with his son Theo standing up in the front of the boat. They slow as they come into the shallow water near the jetty. Here Theo leaps off expertly, ducking down to secure the boat before running back to start unloading the equipment. They haven't been told yet – Theo and Alex – that I'm their half-sister. But I met with Kostas and his wife Alexa the other night and they're understanding. Or at least as understanding as I have any right to expect. Kostas had no idea of Imogen's pregnancy, and it all happened five years before he even met Alexa, so it's not like he's done anything wrong. And he needn't have anything to do with me, but he said he wants to acknowledge the responsibility that he has for me, and Alexa did too, which was kind. I'm not sure what any of that means though, but it feels like a promising start. To something.

I sit down on the soft, warm sand. Now the equipment has been unloaded I watch Theo push the boat out. He looks excited because Kostas is going to let him take it along the bay to the harbour where the boats are stored overnight. Barefoot he leaps aboard and seats himself on the centre console, his back straight and proud. Alex jumps aboard too. Then Theo very carefully lowers the propellor into the water and backs the RIB out into the bay. I see Kostas watching them, his face wearing that dark expression that first scared me, but I now see is nothing more than a reflection of his belief that things should be done the right way. Kostas doesn't take his eyes off his boys until they slowly and carefully drive the powerful boat around the harbour wall. And then my new brothers move out of sight.

Sophia is driving the other boat. She had to wait for Theo to clear the jetty before she could get in, but now her and Kostas and the other TEAM members unload the half-dozen oxygen tanks onto the pontoon, and begin to carry them back up to the centre. I get up now too, and jog down to lend a hand. Sophia greets me with a hi, a touch of my shoulder.

And then there's a surprise. There's a yip, squeaky and excited, and suddenly the puppy is among us, still on the long lead, with Maria on the other end and apologising for the chaos the dog is causing. But no one minds. Sophia bends down and picks it up, nuzzling her nose against its wet black button, while its pink tongue covers her face with kisses. It's the puppy from Nikos Papadakis, the runt of the litter. I'm not sure what's going on with Maria and Nikos – Sophia isn't either – but they've been spending a bit of time together, and now Maria has the dog. She's called her Callie. It seemed fitting.

Twenty minutes pass and the centre is packed up for the night, and Maria's taken Callie away too. There's another client-instructor meal tonight, but I've already said I'm not going this evening, and when I did, Kostas gave Sophia the night off too. So that soon all the dive-centre staff and clients have left and it's just Sophia and me left. The sun is now almost touching the water in front of us. We sit, with our backs against the warm wooden side of the centre, and I pull the bottle of wine from my bag, while Sophia holds out two plastic wine glasses with a dramatic flourish.

"Ta da."

"I really shouldn't, you know. I'm technically a Mormon."

She pushes me aside in disgust. "Bet you didn't remember an opener?"

I confess I didn't, and she climbs back to her feet. She disappears inside for a moment, then reappears holding a corkscrew.

"OK, so I can't think of everything. Only most things."

She hands me the corkscrew and I open the bottle, then slosh a serving of wine into each glass.

It's still cool, sweet and refreshing.

"You know, there's one thing I still haven't told you," I say, without looking at her. When I do, she has one eyebrow raised.

"Go on."

I suppress a smile. "When the DNA test said I wasn't Mandy and Jason's baby..." I hesitate, but not for long. "I thought that you might be. I didn't want to tell you."

"Me?" She breaks into a look of surprise. "Why would I be that baby?"

I shrug. "I don't know. We nearly have the same birthday. You're Greek. It just seemed to make sense."

She thinks about this for a few moments, then settles herself more comfortably on the sand. "That's funny. You should have said something. I always knew exactly who my mother was." She shakes her head. "I mean, my mother is Maria as far as I'm concerned, but she never hid from me that I was adopted, and who my birth parents were. I'll tell you about it sometime. But not now."

She holds up her glass to mine, and we touch them together. "You're an idiot, Ava."

"Thanks."

"No problem. *Yamas!*" Sophia says. *Cheers.*

"*Yamas,*" I reply. She looks thoughtful at my pronunciation.

"We're going to have to teach you some better Greek, if you're staying," she says. And I'm quiet, sipping on the wine. "*Are* you staying?" She raises an eyebrow to me.

I still don't speak, but after a few moments I reach out and touch her face. Softly at first, but then pulling her gently around to face me, and then I lean forward and kiss her.

A moment later I pull back. And think. *Am I staying?* Right now I'm pretty happy here. Sophia wants to talk with Kostas, to convince him that it makes good business sense to expand the dive centre to include the other water sports she wants to teach, and that sounds like a fun thing to be involved in. But eventually I think I want to go back to medicine. To finish my degree.

Maybe not in Sunderland – *definitely* not in Sunderland – maybe not even in England. And like my old tutor said, maybe only when I've grown up a bit. I take another sip of wine. The sun is half gone now, a perfect half-circle, still too bright to quite see as it slips away.

"I don't know." Finally I answer Sophia's question. "But maybe I don't need to know right now?"

And finally that thought doesn't scare me. Because, for the first time in my whole life, I know where I come from.

Finally, I know who I am.

A LETTER FROM THE AUTHOR

Dear reader,

Hello – and thank you for reading *Deep Blue Lies*, I hope you enjoyed reading it as much as I enjoyed writing it. The book was quick to write – I came up with the idea while walking on the beach one January and had a first draft by March. But there's a much longer backstory too, and I'll do my best to explain that below.

First, if you want to join other readers in hearing all about my new releases and bonus content, you can sign up here:

www.stormpublishing.co/gregg-dunnett

And if you enjoyed this book and could spare a few moments to leave a review that would be hugely appreciated. Even a short review can make all the difference in encouraging a reader to discover my books for the first time. Thank you so much!

The secrets behind Deep Blue Lies...

In my twenties I spent a summer working in Greece, a naïve boy from East Anglia who'd been lucky enough to learn how to sail as a kid. It wasn't quite Alythos, but the centre where I worked wasn't so different to the Aegean Dream Resort. Like

Karen it was my first taste of freedom. Like Karen I probably leaned in a little too hard.

I still remember the feeling of flying out there, my first time alone on a plane. There were other young people who looked like they might be going to work in the same place, but I was far too shy to ask them. Until the bus ride to the resort, where I could no longer avoid it. There was one guy who stood out. He was incredibly self-confident, ridiculously good-looking, loud and intimidating. I prayed I wouldn't get put in a room with him, but obviously that's exactly what happened. The idea of Imogen having to sleep in a hammock outside her room comes from my roommate, and his need for privacy while he worked his way through the centre's female staff.

My main job was to look after strangers' children. I remember the parents dropping them off, trusting me – and others like me – barely old enough to look after ourselves, and often still drunk from the night before. But we knew how to have fun. We'd take the kids out on sailing trips around the bay, or run treasure hunts in the gardens. We'd tire them out, fill them with pizza and hand them back to their parents, ready to start another evening's drinking and do it all again the next day. But it was the time off I treasured the most. We would cram five or six into a tiny hire car and explore the island, seeking out secret bays and caves. Once we broke into an abandoned castle and spent the night around a camp fire. Another time we planned to climb a mountain, packing a fridge with bottles of water the night before in preparation for a scorching-hot day. Only we forgot to bring them, and tried to hike up anyway, a thousand metres in forty degrees with only Metaxa to quench our thirst.

That's the background – but what about the story? Every novel – at least every novel I write – is a blend of ideas, taken from different places and woven together. I first read about a cryptic pregnancy when it happened to a girl at university. I didn't really know her, but I'd probably seen her around. A foreign student, far from home, who just felt ill one morning. She took herself to the bathroom, and there – alone in a stall – gave birth, with no idea that she'd even been pregnant. I don't know why it stuck with me so much but it did, probably the suddenness of the change. One moment carefree, the next with this ultimate responsibility, and no possible chance of being ready for it. I'm not sure what happened next, but I read about it in the paper after she'd been arrested. So I don't think it went that well.

I didn't just sleep in the hammock when my roommate was having sex. We had a few of them strung up, made from old yacht sails, and this was before the time of social media and smart phones. We would teach ourselves to splice rope, drink long into the hot nights, and we'd talk. First the loud people, broadcasting their story to whoever would listen, but eventually the quieter people too, you could coax their stories out of them.

Once a week the staff were obliged to have dinner with the guests. It felt like a chore at the time: the guests were older, their lives unimaginably different to ours, and mostly I squandered the opportunity. But I remember one guy who explained to me how he'd started a clothing company I'd actually heard of, and sold it for twenty million. I don't remember anything more than that – except the way he looked at me. That one day I'd understand, and now finally I think I'm beginning to. I'd underestimated him, but everyone has their story. *Everyone.* You just have to listen.

The centre manager wasn't called Jason, and to my knowledge nobody shot him. But in many ways he was like Jason. Overworked and overstressed, a huge amount of responsibility resting on young shoulders. Just about fair, but certainly firm. The first-plane-home threat was real. I saw it happen many times. More stories there.

Some nights we ran a baby-listening service – putting our ears against the guests' doors while they were in the restaurant – to check all was OK with their kids. We took silence to mean there was nothing to worry about, but it could also have meant the exact opposite. We all know the story of poor Madeleine McCann, whose abduction in Portugal some years later stopped that practice.

The longer I stayed in Greece the more I understood how the resort worked, the systems behind the façade. I saw the locals who cleaned the rooms, the drivers who delivered fresh bread to the restaurant. They spoke no English and seemed to come from a closed-off world. But the man who cheerfully pumped seawater from the rental yachts every morning had learned English to compensate for our failure with Greek. He said the boats were so full of holes they'd sink if he didn't pump them out. A hundred and fifty different guests every week, all holidaying on a wing and a prayer.

The deadliest air crash in history occurred on the island of Tenerife. The story of what went wrong is often used to illustrate how disasters most often occur not because one big thing goes wrong, but when a chain of smaller events compound upon each other. In that case the problems were an inexperienced air traffic controller, a long fog delay that had grounded several aircraft and an impatient pilot. He was waiting to take off, on a runway with a hump in it, hiding the far end from his view. When he asked the tower for permission to take off he didn't fully hear the response, but pushed the four throttles forward anyway. He sent his 747 thundering towards another plane that hadn't quite cleared the runway. The 747 got off the ground, but its wheels clipped the second plane, dragging it back down to earth. There were two huge explosions, and 583 people died. Not because of one thing, but because of many. A chain of mini-mistakes – each small enough on its own to seem harmless, until they twist together into what we call life.

It's an idea I try to put into my books. On its own Imogen's cryptic pregnancy wouldn't have been enough to lead to Jason and Mandy's deaths. But put together with Karen and Simon's immature recklessness losing Mandy's baby – which itself could only have come about from the two of them growing tired and frustrated with the culture of the island and the resort – it just might.

My own Greek adventure only lasted one summer. There was only so much I could take of the heat and the drinking, and the ever-changing cast of characters. I didn't kill anyone, but I maybe buried a few secrets – enough that I sometimes wonder who might read this book and remember them.

But it gave me a lot. I probably remember more from that summer than any other. Yet there's no way I could have written this story when I flew home to England back then. It took twenty years to let it settle into the past, into half-forgotten history. But looking back now, I can see how much of that summer is woven into this book. And not just the details. Greece was where I began to understand that each and every one of us is brimming with secrets, and that behind every secret is a story. You just have to listen, store them away, and one day string them all together. If there is a backstory to *Deep Blue Lies* it's that.

That – and how in Greece I learned that every person and every paradise shows its best face – and hides its shadows.

Thank you so much for reading *Deep Blue Lies*. It's amazing to have people reading my books, and I'm so grateful to all the readers out there. If you'd like to hear more of the stories behind the stories – the secrets I didn't share here – I'd also love you to join my newsletter for free, at www.greggdunnett.co.uk. There's also a couple of free books waiting for you there. Or just scan the QR code below.

Thanks for being a reader!

Gregg Dunnett, May 2025

www.greggdunnett.co.uk

instagram.com/greggdunnettauthor
facebook.com/greggwriter

ACKNOWLEDGEMENTS

First and foremost, thank you to everyone who has picked up *Deep Blue Lies*. This book is for you, and I'm so grateful for every reader who gives my stories a chance. Secondly to Maria, my partner and now wife, who was with me when I first started thinking about this story and has been there every step of the way since. I couldn't do it without you, and I wouldn't want to either. Thank you!

Then to my editor Kathryn, who found a polite way to tell me the first draft wasn't quite a thriller, and then came up with a pretty comprehensive plan to make it one. Thank you for your help. And then to everyone else at Storm Publishing, for everything, but especially the brownies you send every time we publish a book. It's a very good way to ensure there'll be many, many more.